Croaker spoke to the assembled Company:

"In olden times the outfit consisted entirely of black soldiers. Thus the name. Its slow drift northward has seen not only its diminution but a shift in its makeup. One-Eye is the only black man with us today.

"We are the last of the Twelve True Companies. We have out-endured the others by more than a century, but I fear we're into our twilight days. I fear this may be the Company's final commission. A page of history is about to turn. Once it does, the great warrior brotherhoods will be gone and forgotten."

But Croaker was wrong. . . .

The first volume of
THE BLACK COMPANY trilogy.

Also by Glen Cook
Published by Tor Books

An Ill Fate Marshalling
Reap the East Wind
Shadow Games
The Silver Spike
Tower of Fear

THE BLACK COMPANY

BY GLEN COOK

TOR
fantasy

A TOM DOHERTY ASSOCIATES BOOK
NEW YORK

THE BLACK COMPANY

A TOR Book

Published by:

Tom Doherty Associates, Inc.
49 West 24 St.
New York, New York 10010

First printing, May 1984

ISBN: 0-812-50389-9   Can. ISBN: 0-812-50390-2

Printed in the United States of America

0 9 8 7 6 5 4 3 2

DEDICATION

This one is for the people of the St. Louis Science Fiction Society. Love you all.

Chapter One: LEGATE

There were prodigies and portents enough, One-Eye says. We must blame ourselves for misinterpreting them. One-Eye's handicap in no way impairs his marvelous hindsight.

Lightning from a clear sky smote the Necropolitan Hill. One bolt struck the bronze plaque sealing the tomb of the forvalaka, obliterating half the spell of confinement. It rained stones. Statues bled. Priests at several temples reported sacrificial victims without hearts or livers. One victim escaped after its bowels were opened and was not recaptured. At the Fork Barracks, where the Urban Cohorts were billeted, the image of Teux turned completely around. For nine evenings running, ten black vultures circled the Bastion. Then one evicted the eagle which lived atop the Paper Tower.

Astrologers refused readings, fearing for their lives. A mad soothsayer wandered the streets proclaiming the imminent end of the world. At the Bastion, the eagle not only departed, the ivy on the outer ramparts withered and gave way to a creeper which appeared black in all but the most intense sunlight.

But that happens every year. Fools can make an omen of anything in retrospect.

We *should* have been better prepared. We did have four modestly accomplished wizards to stand sentinel against predatory tomorrows—though never by any means as sophisticated as divining through sheeps' entrails.

Still, the best augurs are those who divine from the portents of the past. They compile phenomenal records.

Beryl totters perpetually, ready to stumble over a precipice into chaos. The Queen of the Jewel Cities was old and decadent and mad, filled with the stench of degeneracy and moral dryrot. Only a fool would be surprised by anything found creeping its night streets.

I had every shutter thrown wide, praying for a breath off the harbor, rotting fish and all. There wasn't enough breeze to stir a cobweb. I mopped my face and grimaced at my first patient. "Crabs again, Curly?"

He grinned feebly. His face was pale. "It's my stomach, Croaker." His pate looks like a polished ostrich egg. Thus the name. I checked the watch schedule and duty roster. Nothing there he would want to avoid. "It's bad, Croaker. Really."

"Uhm." I assumed my professional demeanor, sure what it was. His skin was clammy, despite the heat. "Eaten outside the commissary lately, Curly?" A fly landed on his head, strutted like a conqueror. He didn't notice.

"Yeah. Three, four times."

"Uhm." I mixed a nasty, milky concoction. "Drink this. All of it."

His whole face puckered at the first taste. "Look, Croaker, I. . . ."

The *smell* of the stuff revolted me. "Drink, friend. Two

men died before I came up with that. Then Pokey took it and lived.'' Word was out about that.

He drank.

"You mean it's poison? The damned Blues slipped me something?"

"Take it easy. You'll be okay. Yeah. It looks that way.'' I'd had to open up Walleye and Wild Bruce to learn the truth. It was a subtle poison. "Get over there on the cot where the breeze will hit you—if the son of a bitch ever comes up. And lie still. Let the stuff work.'' I settled him down.

"Tell me what you ate outside.'' I collected a pen and a chart tacked onto a board. I had done the same with Pokey, and with Wild Bruce before he died, and had had Walleye's platoon sergeant backtrack his movements. I was sure the poison had come from one of several nearby dives frequented by the Bastion garrison.

Curly produced one across-the-board match. "Bingo! We've got the bastards now.''

"Who?" He was ready to go settle up himself.

"You rest. I'll see the Captain.'' I patted his shoulder, checked the next room. Curly was it for morning sick call.

I took the long route, along Trejan's Wall, which overlooks Beryl's harbor. Halfway over I paused, stared north, past the mole and lighthouse and Fortress Island, at the Sea of Torments. Particolored sails speckled the dingy grey-brown water as coastal dhows scooted out along the spiderweb of routes linking the Jewel Cities. The upper air was still and heavy and hazy. The horizon could not be discerned. But down on the water the air was in motion. There was always a breeze out around the Island, though it avoided the shore as if fearing leprosy. Closer at hand, the wheeling gulls were as surly and lackadaisical as the day promised to make most men.

Another summer in service to the Syndic of Beryl,

sweating and grimy, thanklessly shielding him from political rivals and his undisciplined native troops. Another summer busting our butts for Curly's reward. The pay was good, but not in coin of the soul. Our forebrethren would be embarrassed to see us so diminished.

Beryl is misery curdled, but also ancient and intriguing. Its history is a bottomless well filled with murky water. I amuse myself plumbing its shadowy depths, trying to isolate fact from fiction, legend, and myth. No easy task, for the city's earlier historians wrote with an eye to pleasing the powers of their day.

The most interesting period, for me, is the ancient kingdom, which is the least satisfactorily chronicled. It was then, in the reign of Niam, that the forvalaka came, were overcome after a decade of terror, and were confined in their dark tomb atop the Necropolitan Hill. Echoes of that terror persist in folklore and matronly admonitions to unruly children. No one recalls what the forvalaka were, now.

I resumed walking, despairing of beating the heat. The sentries, in their shaded kiosks, wore towels draped around their necks.

A breeze startled me. I faced the harbor. A ship was rounding the Island, a great lumbering beast that dwarfed the dhows and feluccas. A silver skull bulged in the center of its full-bellied black sail. That skull's red eyes glowed. Fires flickered behind its broken teeth. A glittering silver band encircled the skull.

"What the hell is that?" a sentry asked.

"I don't know, Whitey." The ship's size impressed me more than did its flashy sail. The four minor wizards we had with the Company could match that showmanship. But I'd never seen a galley sporting five banks of oars.

I recalled my mission.

I knocked on the Captain's door. He did not respond. I

invited myself inside, found him snoring in his big wooden chair. "Yo!" I hollered. "Fire! Riots in the Groan! Dancing at the Gate of Dawn!" Dancing was an old time general who nearly destroyed Beryl. People still shudder at his name.

The Captain was cool. He didn't crack an eyelid or smile. "You're presumptuous, Croaker. When are you going to learn to go through channels?" Channels meant bug the Lieutenant first. Don't interrupt his nap unless the Blues were storming the Bastion.

I explained about Curly and my chart.

He swung his feet off the desk. "Sounds like work for Mercy." His voice had a hard edge. The Black Company does not suffer malicious attacks upon its men.

Mercy was our nastiest platoon leader. He thought a dozen men would suffice, but let Silent and me tag along. I could patch the wounded. Silent would be useful if the Blues played rough. Silent held us up half a day while he made a quick trip to the woods.

"What the hell you up to?" I asked when he got back, lugging a ratty-looking sack.

He just grinned. Silent he is and silent he stays.

The place was called Mole Tavern. It was a comfortable hangout. I had passed many an evening there. Mercy assigned three men to the back door, and a pair each to the two windows. He sent another two to the roof. Every building in Beryl has a roof hatch. People sleep up top during the summer.

He led the rest of us through the Mole's front door.

Mercy was a smallish, cocky fellow, fond of the dramatic gesture. His entry should have been preceded by fanfares.

The crowd froze, stared at our shields and bared blades, at snatches of grim faces barely visible through gaps in our face guards. "Verus!" Mercy shouted. "Get your butt out here!"

The grandfather of the managing family appeared. He sidled toward us like a mutt expecting a kick. The customers began buzzing. "Silence!" Mercy thundered. He could get a big roar out of his small body.

"How may we help you, honored sirs?" the old man asked.

"You can get your sons and grandsons out here, Blue."

Chairs squeaked. A soldier slammed his blade into a tabletop.

"Sit still," Mercy said. "You're just having lunch, fine. You'll be loose in an hour."

The old man began shaking. "I don't understand, sir. What have we done?"

Mercy grinned evilly. "He plays the innocent well. It's murder, Verus. Two charges of murder by poisoning. Two of attempted murder by poisoning. The magistrates decreed the punishment of slaves." He was having fun.

Mercy wasn't one of my favorite people. He never stopped being the boy who pulled wings off flies.

The punishment of slaves meant being left up for scavenger birds after public crucifixion. In Beryl only criminals are buried uncremated, or not buried at all.

An uproar rose in the kitchen. Somebody was trying to get out the back door. Our men were objecting.

The public room exploded. A wave of dagger-brandishing humanity hit us.

They forced us back to the door. Those who were not guilty obviously feared they would be condemned with those who were. Beryl's justice is fast, crude, and harsh, and seldom gives a defendant opportunity to clear himself.

A dagger slipped past a shield. One of our men went down. I am not much as a fighter, but I stepped into his place. Mercy said something snide that I did not catch.

"That's your chance at heaven wasted," I countered. "You're out of the Annals forever."

"Crap. You don't leave out anything."

A dozen citizens went down. Blood pooled in low places on the floor. Spectators gathered outside. Soon some adventurer would hit us from behind.

A dagger nicked Mercy. He lost patience. "Silent!"

Silent was on the job already, but he was Silent. That meant no sound, and very little flash or fury.

Mole patrons began slapping their faces and pawing the air, forsaking us. They hopped and danced, grabbed their backs and behinds, squealed and howled piteously. Several collapsed.

"What the hell did you do?" I asked.

Silent grinned, exposing sharp teeth. He passed a dusky paw across my eyes. I saw the Mole from a slightly altered perspective.

The bag he had lugged in from out of town proved to be one of those hornets' nests you can, if you're unlucky, run into in the woods south of Beryl. Its tenants were the bumblebee-looking monsters peasants call bald-faced hornets. They have a foul temper unrivalled anywhere in Nature. They cowed the Mole crowd fast, without bothering our lads.

"Fine work, Silent," Mercy said, after having vented his fury on several hapless patrons. He herded the survivors into the street.

I examined our injured brother while the unharmed soldier finished the wounded. Saving the Syndic the cost of a trial and a hangman, Mercy called that. Silent looked on, still grinning. He's not nice either, though he seldom participates directly.

We took more prisoners than expected. "Was a bunch of them." Mercy's eyes twinkled. "Thanks, Silent." The line stretched a block.

Fate is a fickle bitch. She'd led us to Mole Tavern at a critical moment. Poking around, our witch man had unearthed a prize, a crowd concealed in a hideout beneath the wine cellar. Among them were some of the best known Blues.

Mercy chattered, wondering aloud how large a reward our informant deserved. No such informant existed. The yammer was meant to save our tame wizards from becoming prime targets. Our enemies would scurry around looking for phantom spies.

"Move them out," Mercy ordered. Still grinning, he eyed the sullen crowd. "Think they'll try something?" They did not. His supreme confidence cowed anyone who had ideas.

We wound through mazelike streets half as old as the world, our prisoners shuffling listlessly. I gawked. My comrades are indifferent to the past, but I cannot help being awed—and occasionally intimidated—by how time-deep Beryl's history runs.

Mercy called an unexpected halt. We had come to the Avenue of the Syndics, which winds from the Customs House uptown to the Bastion's main gate. There was a procession on the Avenue. Though we reached the intersection first, Mercy yielded the right-of-way.

The procession consisted of a hundred armed men. They looked tougher than anyone in Beryl but us. At their head rode a dark figure on the biggest black stallion I've ever seen. The rider was small, effeminately slim, and clad in worn black leather. He wore a black morion which concealed his head entirely. Black gloves concealed his hands. He seemed to be unarmed.

"Damn me," Mercy whispered.

I was disturbed. That rider chilled me. Something primitive deep inside me wanted to run. But curiosity plagued

me more. Who was he? Had he come off that strange ship
in the harbor? Why was he here?

The eyeless gaze of the rider swept across us indifferently,
as though passing over a flock of sheep. Then it jerked
back, fixing on Silent.

Silent met stare for stare, and showed no fear. And still
he seemed somehow diminished.

The column passed on, hardened, disciplined. Shaken,
Mercy got our mob moving again. We entered the Bastion
only yards behind the strangers.

We had arrested most of the more conservative Blue
leadership. When word of the raid spread, the volatile
types decided to flex their muscles. They sparked something monstrous.

The perpetually abrasive weather does things to men's
reason. The Beryl mob is savage. Riots occur almost
without provocation. When things go bad the dead number
in the thousands. This was one of the worst times.

The army is half the problem. A parade of weak, short-
term Syndics let discipline lapse. The troops are beyond
control now. Generally, though, they will act against rioters.
They see riot suppression as license to loot.

The worst happened. Several cohorts from the Fork
Barracks demanded a special donative before they would
respond to a directive to restore order. The Syndic refused
to pay.

The cohorts mutinied.

Mercy's platoon hastily established a strongpoint near
the Rubbish Gate and held off all three cohorts. Most of
our men were killed, but none ran. Mercy himself lost an
eye, a finger, was wounded in shoulder and hip, and had
more than a hundred holes in his shield when help arrived.
He came to me more dead than alive.

In the end, the mutineers scattered rather than face the rest of the Black Company.

The riots were the worst in memory. We lost almost a hundred brethren trying to suppress them. We could ill afford the loss of one. In the Groan the streets were carpetted with corpses. The rats grew fat. Clouds of vultures and ravens migrated from the countryside.

The Captain ordered the Company into the Bastion. "Let it run its course," he said. "We've done enough." His disposition had gone beyond sour, disgusted. "Our commission doesn't require us to commit suicide."

Somebody made a crack about us falling on our swords.

"Seems to be what the Syndic expects."

Beryl had ground our spirits down, but had left none so disillusioned as the Captain. He blamed himself for our losses. He did, in fact, try to resign.

The mob had fallen into a sullen, grudging, desultory effort to sustain chaos, interfering with any attempt to fight fires or prevent looting, but otherwise just roamed. The mutinous cohorts, fattened by deserters from other units, were systematizing the murder and plunder.

The third night I stood a watch on Trejan's Wall, beneath the carping stars, a fool of a volunteer sentinel. The city was strangely quiet. I might have been more anxious had I not been so tired. It was all I could do to stay awake.

Tom-Tom came by. "What are you doing out here, Croaker?"

"Filling in."

"You look like death on a stick. Get some rest."

"You don't look good yourself, runt."

He shrugged. "How's Mercy?"

"Not out of the woods yet." I had little hope for him, really. I pointed. "You know anything about that out there?" An isolated scream echoed in the distance. It had a quality which set it aside from other recent screams. Those had been filled with pain, rage, and fear. This one was redolent of something darker.

He hemmed and hawed in that way he and his brother One-Eye have. If you don't know, they figure it's a secret worth keeping. Wizards! "There's a rumor that the mutineers broke the seals on the tomb of the forvalaka while they were plundering the Necropolitan Hill."

"Uh? Those things are loose?"

"The Syndic thinks so. The Captain don't take it seriously."

I didn't either, though Tom-Tom looked concerned. "They looked tough. The ones who were here the other day."

"Ought to have recruited them," he said, with an undertone of sadness. He and One-Eye have been with the Company a long time. They have seen much of its decline.

"Why were they here?"

He shrugged. "Get some rest, Croaker. Don't kill yourself. Won't make a bit of difference in the end." He ambled away, lost in the wilderness of his thoughts.

I lifted an eyebrow. He was *way* down. I turned back to the fires and lights and disturbing absence of racket. My eyes kept crossing, my vision clouding. Tom-Tom was right. I needed sleep.

From the darkness came another of those strange, hopeless cries. This one was closer.

"Up, Croaker." The Lieutenant was not gentle. "Captain wants you in the officers' mess."

I groaned. I cursed. I threatened mayhem in the first degree. He grinned, pinched the nerve in my elbow, rolled me onto the floor. "I'm up already," I grumbled, feeling around for my boots. "What's it about?"

He was gone.

"Will Mercy pull through, Croaker?" the Captain asked.

"I don't think so, but I've seen bigger miracles."

The officers and sergeants were all there. "You want to know what's happening," the Captain said. "The visitor the other day was an envoy from overseas. He offered an alliance. The north's military resources in exchange for the support of Beryl's fleets. Sounded reasonable to me. But the Syndic is being stubborn. He's still upset about the conquest of Opal. I suggested he be more flexible. If these northerners are villains then the alliance option could be the least of several evils. Better an ally than a tributary. Our problem is, where do we stand if the legate presses?"

Candy said, "We should refuse if he tells us to fight these northerners?"

"Maybe. Fighting a sorcerer could mean our destruction."

Wham! The mess door slammed open. A small, dusky, wiry man, preceded by a great humped beak of a nose, blew inside. The Captain bounced up and clicked his heels. "Syndic."

Our visitor slammed both fists down on the tabletop. "You ordered your men withdrawn into the Bastion. I'm not paying you to hide like whipped dogs."

"You're not paying us to become martyrs, either," the Captain replied in his reasoning-with-fools voice. "We're a bodyguard, not police. Maintaining order is the task of the Urban Cohorts."

The Syndic was tired, distraught, frightened, on his last emotional legs. Like everyone else.

"Be reasonable," the Captain suggested. "Beryl has passed a point of no return. Chaos rules the streets. Any attempt to restore order is doomed. The cure now is the disease."

I liked that. I had begun to hate Beryl.

The Syndic shrank into himself. "There's still the

forvalaka. And that vulture from the north, waiting off the Island.''

Tom-Tom started out of a half-sleep. ''Off the Island, you say?''

''Waiting for me to beg.''

''Interesting.'' The little wizard lapsed into semi-slumber.

The Captain and Syndic bickered about the terms of our commission. I produced our copy of the agreement. The Syndic tried to stretch clauses with, ''Yeah, but.'' Clearly, he wanted to fight if the legate started throwing his weight around.

Elmo started snoring. The Captain dismissed us, resumed arguing with our employer.

I suppose seven hours passes as a night's sleep. I didn't strangle Tom-Tom when he wakened me. But I did grouse and crab till he threatened to turn me into a jackass braying at the Gate of Dawn. Only then, after I had dressed and we had joined a dozen others, did I realize that I didn't have a notion what was happening.

''We're going to look at a tomb,'' Tom-Tom said.

''Huh?'' I am none too bright some mornings.

''We're going to the Necropolitan Hill to eyeball that forvalaka tomb.''

''Now wait a minute. . . .''

''Chicken? I always thought you were, Croaker.''

''What're you talking about?''

''Don't worry. You'll have three top wizards along, with nothing to do but babysit your ass. One-Eye would go too, but the Captain wants him to hang around.''

''Why is what I want to know.''

''To find out if vampires are real. They could be a put-up from yon spook ship.''

''Neat trick. Maybe we should have thought of it.'' The

forvalaka threat had done what no force of arms could: stilled the riots.

Tom-Tom nodded. He dragged fingers across the little drum that gave him his name. I filed the thought. He's worse than his brother when it comes to admitting shortcomings.

The city was as still as an old battlefield. Like a battlefield, it was filled with stench, flies, scavengers, and the dead. The only sound was the tread of our boots and, once, the mournful cry of a sad dog standing sentinel over its fallen master. "The price of order," I muttered. I tried to run the dog off. It wouldn't budge.

"The cost of chaos," Tom-Tom countered. *Thump* on his drum. "Not quite the same thing, Croaker."

The Necropolitan Hill is taller than the heighth on which the Bastion stands. From the Upper Enclosure, where the mausoleums of the wealthy stand, I could see the northern ship.

"Just lying out there waiting," Tom-Tom said. "Like the Syndic said."

"Why don't they just move in? Who could stop them?"

Tom-Tom shrugged. Nobody else offered an opinion.

We reached the storied tomb. It looked the part it played in rumor and legend. It was very, very old, definitely lightning-blasted, and scarred with tool marks. One thick oak door had burst asunder. Toothpicks and fragments lay scattered for a dozen yards around.

Goblin, Tom-Tom, and Silent put their heads together. Somebody made a crack about that way they might have a brain between them. Goblin and Silent then took stations flanking the door, a few steps back. Tom-Tom faced it head on. He shuffled around like a bull about to charge, found his spot, dropped into a crouch with his arms flung up oddly, like a parody of a martial arts master.

"How about you fools open the door?" he growled.

"Idiots. I had to bring idiots." *Wham-wham* on the drum. "Stand around with their fingers in their noses."

A couple of us grabbed the ruined door and heaved. It was too warped to give much. Tom-Tom rapped his drum, let out a villainous scream, and jumped inside. Goblin bounced to the portal behind him. Silent moved up in a fast glide.

Inside, Tom-Tom let out a rat squeak and started sneezing. He stumbled out, eyes watering, grinding his nose with the heels of his hands. He sounded like he had a bad cold when he said, "Wasn't a trick." His ebony skin had gone grey.

"What do you mean?" I demanded.

He jerked a thumb toward the tomb. Goblin and Silent were inside now. They started sneezing.

I sidled to the doorway, peeked. I couldn't see squat. Just dust thick in the sunlight close to me. Then I stepped inside. My eyes adjusted.

There were bones everywhere. Bones in heaps, bones in stacks, bones sorted neatly by something insane. Strange bones they were, similar to those of men, but of weird proportion to my physician's eye. There must have been fifty bodies originally. They'd really packed them in, back when. Forvalaka for sure, then, because Beryl buries its villains uncremated.

There were fresh corpses too. I counted seven dead soldiers before the sneezing started. They wore the colors of a mutinous cohort.

I dragged a body outside, let go, stumbled a few steps, was noisily sick. When I regained control, I turned back to examine my booty.

The others stood around looking green. "No phantom did that," Goblin said. Tom-Tom bobbed his head. He was more shaken than anyone. More shaken than the sight demanded, I thought.

Silent got on with business, somehow conjuring a brisk, small maid of a breeze that scurried in through the mausoleum door and bustled out again, skirts laden with dust and the smell of death.

"You all right?" I asked Tom-Tom.

He eyed my medical kit and waved me off. "I'll be okay. I was just remembering."

I gave him a minute, then prodded, "Remembering?"

"We were boys, One-Eye and me. They'd just sold us to N'Gamo, to become his apprentices. A messenger came from a village back in the hills." He knelt beside the dead soldier. "The wounds are identical."

I was rattled. Nothing human killed that way, yet the damage seemed deliberate, calculated, the work of a malign intelligence. That made it more horrible.

I swallowed, knelt, began my examination. Silent and Goblin eased into the tomb. Goblin had a little amber ball of light rolling around his cupped hands. "No bleeding," I observed.

"It takes the blood," Tom-Tom said. Silent dragged another corpse out. "And the organs when it has time." The second body had been split from groin to gullet. Heart and liver were missing.

Silent went back inside. Goblin came out. He settled on a broken grave marker and shook his head. "Well?" Tom-Tom demanded.

"Definitely the real thing. No prank by our friend." He pointed. The northerner continued its patrol amidst a swarm of fishermen and coasters. "There were fifty-four of them sealed up here. They ate each other. This was the last one left."

Tom-Tom jumped as if slapped.

"What's the matter?" I asked.

"That means the thing was the nastiest, cunningest, cruelest, and craziest of the lot."

"Vampires," I muttered. "In this day."

Tom-Tom said, "Not strictly a vampire. This is the wereleopard, the man-leopard who walks on two legs by day and on four by night."

I'd heard of werewolves and werebears. The peasants around my home city tell such tales. I'd never heard of a wereleopard. I told Tom-Tom as much.

"The man-leopard is from the far south. The jungle." He stared out to sea. "They have to be buried alive."

Silent deposited another corpse.

Blood-drinking, liver-eating wereleopards. Ancient, darkness-wise, filled with a millenium of hatred and hunger. The stuff of nightmare all right. "Can you handle it?"

"N'Gamo couldn't. I'll never be his match, and he lost an arm and a foot trying to destroy a young male. What we have here is an old female. Bitter, cruel, and clever. The four of us might hold her off. Conquer her, no."

"But if you and One-Eye know this thing. . . ."

"No." He had the shakes. He gripped his drum so tight it creaked. "We can't."

Chaos died. Beryl's streets remained as starkly silent as those of a city overthrown. Even the mutineers concealed themselves till hunger drove them to the city granaries.

The Syndic tried to tighten the screws on the Captain. The Captain ignored him. Silent, Goblin, and One-Eye tracked the monster. The thing functioned on a purely animal level, feeding the hunger of an age. The factions besieged the Syndic with demands for protection.

The Lieutenant again summoned us to the officers' mess. The Captain wasted no time. "Men, our situation is grim." He paced. "Beryl is demanding a new Syndic. Every faction has asked the Black Company to stand aside."

The moral dilemma escalated with the stakes.

"We aren't heroes," the Captain continued. "We're

tough. We're stubborn. We try to honor our commitments. But we don't die for lost causes.''

I protested, the voice of tradition questioning his unspoken proposition.

"The question on the table is the survival of the Company, Croaker.''

"We have taken the gold, Captain. Honor is the question on the table. For four centuries the Black Company has met the letter of its commissions. Consider the Book of Set, recorded by Annalist Coral while the Company was in service to the Archon of Bone, during the Revolt of the Chiliarchs.''

"You consider it, Croaker.''

I was irritated. "I stand on my right as a free soldier.''

"He has the right to speak,'' the Lieutenant agreed. He is more a traditionalist than I.

"Okay. Let him talk. We don't have to listen.''

I reiterated that darkest hour in the Company's history . . . till I realized I was arguing with myself. Half of me wanted to sell out.

"Croaker? Are you finished?''

I swallowed. "Find a legitimate loophole and I'll go along.''

Tom-Tom gave me a mocking drumroll. One-Eye chuckled. "That's a job for Goblin, Croaker. He was a lawyer before he worked his way up to pimping.''

Goblin took the bait. "*I* was a lawyer? Your mother was a lawyer's. . . .''

"Enough!'' The Captain slapped the tabletop. "We've got Croaker's okay. Go with it. Find an out.''

The others looked relieved. Even the Lieutenant. My opinion, as Annalist, carried more weight than I liked.

"The obvious out is the termination of the man holding our bond,'' I observed. That hung in the air like an old, foul smell. Like the stench in the tomb of the forvalaka.

"In our battered state, who could blame us if an assassin slipped past?"

"You have a disgusting turn of mind, Croaker," Tom-Tom said. He gave me another drumroll.

"Pots calling kettles? We'd retain the appearance of honor. We *do* fail. As often as not."

"I like it," the Captain said. "Let's break this up before the Syndic comes asking what's up. You stay, Tom-Tom. I've got a job for you."

It was a night for screamers. A broiling, sticky night of the sort that abrades that last thin barrier between the civilized man and the monster crouched in his soul. The screams came from homes where fear, heat, and over-crowding had put too much strain on the monster's chains.

A cool wind roared in off the gulf, pursued by massive storm clouds with lightning prancing in their hair. The wind swept away the stench of Beryl. The downpour scoured its streets. By morning's light Beryl seemed a different city, still and cool and clean.

The streets were speckled with puddles as we walked to the waterfront. Runoff still chuckled in the gutters. By noon the air would be leaden again, and more humid than ever.

Tom-Tom awaited us on a boat he had hired. I said, "How much did you pocket on this deal? This scow looks like it'd sink before it cleared the Island."

"Not a copper, Croaker." He sounded disappointed. He and his brother are great pilferers and black-marketeers. "Not a copper. This here is a slicker job than it looks. Her master is a smuggler."

"I'll take your word. You'd probably know." Nevertheless, I stepped gingerly as I boarded. He scowled. We were supposed to pretend that the avarice of Tom-Tom and One-Eye did not exist.

We were off to sea to make an arrangement. Tom-Tom had the Captain's carte blanche. The Lieutenant and I were along to give him a swift kick if he got carried away. Silent and a half dozen soldiers accompanied us for show.

A customs launch hailed us off the Island. We were gone before she could get underway. I squatted, peered under the boom. The black ship loomed bigger and bigger. "That damned thing is a floating island."

"Too big," the Lieutenant growled. "Ship that size couldn't hold together in a heavy sea."

"Why not? How do you know?" Even boggled I remained curious about my brethren.

"Sailed as a cabin boy when I was young. I learned ships." His tone discouraged further interrogation. Most of the men want their antecedants kept private. As you might expect in a company of villains held together by its now and its us-against-the-world gone befores.

"Not too big if you have the thaumaturgic craft to bind it," Tom-Tom countered. He was shaky, tapping his drum in random, nervous rhythms. He and One-Eye both hated water.

So. A mysterious northern enchanter. A ship as black as the floors of hell. My nerves began to fray.

Her crew dropped an accomodation ladder. The Lieutenant scampered up. He seemed impressed.

I'm no sailor, but the ship did look squared away and disciplined.

A junior officer sorted out Tom-Tom, Silent, and myself and asked us to accompany him. He led us down stairs and through passageways, aft, without speaking.

The northern emissary sat crosslegs amidst rich cushions, backed by the ship's open sternlights, in a cabin worthy of an eastern potentate. I gaped. Tom-Tom smouldered with avarice. The emissary laughed.

The laughter was a shock. A high-pitched near giggle

more appropriate to some fifteen year old madonna of the tavern night than to a man more powerful than any king. "Excuse me," he said, placing a hand daintily where his mouth would have been had he not been wearing that black morion. Then, "Be seated."

My eyes widened against my will. Each remark came in a distinctly different voice. Was there a committee inside that helmet?

Tom-Tom gulped air. Silent, being Silent, simply sat. I followed his example, and tried not to become too offensive with my frightened, curious stare.

Tom-Tom wasn't the best diplomat that day. He blurted, "The Syndic won't last much longer. We want to make an arrangement. . . ."

Silent dug a toe into his thigh.

I muttered, "This is our daring prince of thieves? Our man of iron nerve?"

The legate chuckled. "You're the physician? Croaker? Pardon him. He knows me."

A cold, cold fear enfolded me in its dark wings. Sweat moistened my temples. It had nothing to do with heat. A cool sea breeze flowed through the sternlights, a breeze for which men in Beryl would kill.

"There is no cause to fear me. I was sent to offer an alliance meant to benefit Beryl as much as my people. I remain convinced that agreement can be forged—though not with the current autocrat. You face a problem requiring the same solution as mine, but your commission puts you in a narrow place."

"He knows it all. No point talking," Tom-Tom croaked. He thumped his drum, but his fetish did him no good. He was choking up.

The legate observed, "The Syndic is not invulnerable. Even guarded by you." A great big cat had Tom-Tom's tongue. The envoy looked at me. I shrugged. "Suppose the Syndic expired while your company was defending the Bastion against the mob?''

"Ideal," I said. "But it ignores the question of our subsequent safety."

"You drive the mob off, then discover the death. You're no longer employed, so you leave Beryl."

"And go where? And outrun our enemies how? The Urban Cohorts would pursue us."

"Tell your Captain that, on discovery of the Syndic's demise, if I receive a written request to mediate the succession, my forces will relieve you at the Bastion. You should leave Beryl and camp on the Pillar of Anguish."

The Pillar of Anguish is an arrowhead of a chalk headland wormholed with countless little caverns. It thrusts out to sea a day's march east of Beryl. A lighthouse/watchtower stands there. The name comes from the moaning the wind makes passing through the caverns.

"That's a goddamned deathtrap. Those bugger-masters would just besiege us and giggle till we ate each other."

"A simple matter to slip boats in and take you off."

Ding-ding. An alarm bell banged away four inches behind my eyes. This sumbitch was running a game on us. "Why the hell would you do that?"

"Your company would be unemployed. I would be willing to assume the commission. There is a need for good soldiers in the north."

Ding-ding. That old bell kept singing. He wanted to take us on? What for?

Something told me that was not the moment to ask. I shifted my ground. "What about the forvalaka?" Zig when they expect you to zag.

"The thing out of the crypt?" The envoy's voice was that of the woman of your dreams, purring "come on." "I may have work for it too."

"You'll get it under control?"

"Once it serves its purpose."

I thought of the lightning bolt that had obliterated a spell of confinement on a plaque that had resisted tampering for a millenium. I kept my suspicions off my face, I'm sure. But the emissary chuckled. "Maybe, physician. Maybe not. An interesting puzzle, no? Go back to your captain. Make up your minds. Quickly. Your enemies are ready to move." He made a gesture that dismissed us.

"Just deliver the case!" the Captain snarled at Candy. "Then get your butt back here."

Candy took the courier case and went.

"Anybody else want to argue? You bastards had your chance to get rid of me. You blew it."

Tempers were hot. The Captain had made the legate a counter-proposal, been offered his patronage should the Syndic perish. Candy was running the Captain's reply to the envoy.

Tom-Tom muttered, "You don't know what you're doing. You don't know who you're signing with."

"Illuminate me. No? Croaker. What's it like out there?" I had been sent to scout the city.

"It's plague all right. Not like any I've seen before, though. The forvalaka must be the vector."

The Captain gave me the squinty eye.

"Doctor talk. A vector is a carrier. The plague comes in pockets around its kills."

The Captain growled, "Tom-Tom? You know this beast."

"Never heard of one spreading disease. And all of us who went into the tomb are still healthy."

I chimed in, "The carrier doesn't matter. The plague does. It'll get worse if people don't start burning bodies."

"It hasn't penetrated the Bastion," the Captain observed. "And it's had a positive effect. The regular garrison have stopped deserting."

"I encountered a lot of antagonism in the Groan. They're on the edge of another explosion."

"How soon?"

"Two days? Three at the outside."

The Captain chewed his lip. The tight place was getting tighter. "We've got to. . . ."

A tribune of the garrison shoved through the door. "There's a mob at the gate. They have a ram."

"Let's go," the Captain said.

It took only minutes to disperse them. A few missiles and a few pots of hot water. They fled, pelting us with curses and insults.

Night fell. I stayed on the wall, watching distant torches roam the city. The mob was evolving, developing a nervous system. If it developed a brain we would find ourselves caught in a revolution.

The movement of torches eventually diminished. The explosion would not come tonight. Maybe tomorrow, if the heat and humidity became too oppressive.

Later I heard scratching to my right. Then clackings. Scrapings. Softly, softly, but there. Approaching. Terror filled me. I became as motionless as the gargoyles perched over the gate. The breeze became an arctic wind.

Something came over the battlements. Red eyes. Four legs. Dark as the night. Black leopard. It moved as fluidly as water running downhill. It padded down the stair into the courtyard, vanished.

The monkey in my backbrain wanted to scamper up a tall tree, screeching, to hurl excrement and rotted fruit. I fled toward the nearest door, took a protected route to the Captain's quarters, let myself in without knocking.

I found him on his cot, hands behind his head, staring at the ceiling. His room was illuminated by a single feeble candle. "The forvalaka is in the Bastion. I saw it come over the wall." My voice squeaked like Goblin's.

He grunted.

"You hear me?"

"I heard, Croaker. Go away. Leave me alone."

"Yes sir." So. It was eating him up. I backed toward the door. . . .

The scream was loud and long and hopeless, and ended abruptly. It came from the Syndic's quarters. I drew my sword, charged through the door—smack into Candy. Candy went down. I stood over him, numbly wondering why he was back so soon.

"Get in here, Croaker," the Captain ordered. "Want to get yourself killed?" There were more cries from the Syndic's quarters. Death was not being selective.

I yanked Candy inside. We bolted and barred the door. I stood with my back against it, eyes closed, panting. Chances are it was imagination, but I thought I heard something growl as it padded past.

"Now what?" Candy asked. His face was colorless. His hands were shaking.

The Captain finished scribbling a letter. He handed it over. "Now you go back."

Someone hammered on the door. "What?" the Captain snapped.

A voice muted by thick wood responded. I said, "It's One-Eye."

"Open up."

I opened. One-Eye, Tom-Tom, Goblin, Silent, and a dozen others pushed inside. The room got hot and tight. Tom-Tom said, "The man-leopard is in the Bastion, Captain." He forgot to punctuate with his drum. It seemed to droop at his hip.

Another scream from the Syndic's quarters. My imagination *had* tricked me.

"What're we going to do?" One-Eye asked. He was a

wrinkled little black man no bigger than his brother, usually possessed by a bizarre sense of humor. He was a year older than Tom-Tom, but at their age no one was counting. Both were over a hundred, if the Annals could be believed. He was terrified. Tom-Tom was on the edge of hysteria. Goblin and Silent, too, were rocky. "It can take us off one by one."

"Can it be killed?"

"They're almost invincible, Captain."

"Can they be killed?" The Captain put a hard edge on his voice. He was frightened too.

"Yes," One-Eye confessed. He seemed a whisker less scared than Tom-Tom. "Nothing is invulnerable. Not even that thing on the black ship. But this is strong, fast, and smart. Weapons are of little avail. Sorcery is better, but even that isn't much use." Never before had I heard him admit limitations.

"We've talked enough," the Captain growled. "Now we act." He was difficult to know, our commander, but was transparent now. Rage and frustration at an impossible situation had fixed on the forvalaka.

Tom-Tom and One-Eye protested vehemently.

"You've been thinking about this since you found out that thing was loose," the Captain said. "You decided what you'd do if you had to. Let's do it."

Another scream. "The Paper Tower must be an abattoir," I muttered. "The thing is hunting down everybody up there."

For a moment I thought even Silent would protest.

The Captain strapped on his weapons. "Match, assemble the men. Seal all the entrances to the Paper Tower. Elmo, pick some good halberdiers and crossbowmen. Quarrels to be poisoned."

Twenty minutes fled. I lost count of the cries. I lost track of everything but a growing trepidation and the question, *why* had the forvalaka invaded the Bastion? Why did it persist in its hunt? More than hunger drove it.

That legate had hinted at having a use for it. What? This? What were we doing working with someone who could do that?

All four wizards collaborated on the spell that preceded us, crackling. The air itself threw blue sparks. Halberdiers followed. Crossbowmen backed them. Behind them another dozen of us entered the Syndic's quarters.

Anticlimax. The antechamber to the Paper Tower looked perfectly normal. "It's upstairs," One-Eye told us.

The Captain faced the passageway behind us. "Match, bring your men inside." He planned to advance room by room, sealing all exits but one for retreat. One-Eye and Tom-Tom did not approve. They said the thing would be more dangerous cornered. Ominous silence surrounded us. There had been no cries for several minutes.

We found the first victim at the base of the stair leading into the Tower proper. "One of ours," I grumbled. The Syndic always surrounded himself with a squad from the Company. "Sleeping quarters upstairs?" I'd never been inside the Paper Tower.

The Captain nodded. "Kitchen level, stores level, servants' quarters on two levels, then family, then the Syndic himself. Library and offices at the top. Wants to make it hard to get to him."

I examined the body. "Not quite like the ones at the tomb. Tom-Tom. It didn't take the blood or organs. How come?"

He had no answer. Neither did One-Eye.

The Captain peered into the shadows above. "Now it gets tricky. Halberdiers, one step at a time. Keep your points low. Crossbows, stay four or five steps behind. Shoot anything that moves. Swords out, everybody. One-Eye, run your spell ahead."

Crackle. Step, step, quietly. Stench of fear. *Quang!* A man discharged his crossbow accidentally. The Captain spit and grumbled like a volcano in bad temper.

There wasn't a damned thing to see.

Servants' quarters. Blood splashed the walls. Bodies and pieces of bodies lay everywhere amidst furniture invariably shredded and wrecked. There are hard men in the Company, but even the hardest was moved. Even I, who as physician see the worst the battlefield offers.

The Lieutenant said, "Captain, I'm getting the rest of the Company. This thing isn't getting away." His tone brooked no contradiction. The Captain merely nodded.

The carnage had that effect. Fear faded somewhat. Most of us decided the thing had to be destroyed.

A scream sounded above. It was like a taunt hurled our way, daring us to come on. Hard-eyed men started up the stair. The air crackled as the spell preceded them. Tom-Tom and One-Eye bore down on their terror. The death hunt began in earnest.

A vulture had evicted the eagle nesting atop the Paper Tower, a fell omen indeed. I had no hope for our employer.

We climbed past five levels. It was gorily obvious the forvalaka had visited each. . . .

Tom-Tom whipped up a hand, pointed. The forvalaka was nearby. The halberdiers knelt behind their weapons. The crossbowmen aimed at shadows. Tom-Tom waited half a minute. He, One-Eye, Silent, and Goblin posed intently, listening to something the rest of the world could only imagine. Then, "It's waiting. Be careful. Don't give it an opening."

I asked a dumb question, altogether too late for its answer to have bearing. "Shouldn't we use silver weapons? Quarrel heads and blades?"

Tom-Tom looked baffled.

"Where I come from the peasants say you have to kill werewolves with silver."

"Crap. You kill them same as you kill anything else. Only you move faster and hit harder 'cause you only get one shot."

The more he revealed the less terrible the creature seemed. This was like hunting a rogue lion. Why all the fuss?

I recalled the servant's quarters.

"Everybody just stand still," Tom-Tom said. "And be quiet. We'll try a sending." He and his cohorts put their heads together. After a while he indicated we should resume our advance.

We eased onto a landing, packed tightly, a human hedgehog with quills of steel. The wizards sped their enchantment. An angry roar came from the shadows ahead, followed by the scrape of claws. Something moved. Crossbows twanged. Another roar, almost mocking. The wizards put their heads together again. Downstairs the Lieutenant was ordering men into positions the forvalaka would have to pass to escape.

We eased into the darkness, tension mounting. Bodies and blood made the footing treacherous. Men hastened to seal doors. Slowly, we penetrated a suite of offices. Twice movement drew fire from the crossbows.

The forvalaka yowled not twenty feet away. Tom-Tom released a sigh that was half groan. "Caught it," he said, meaning they had reached it with their spell.

Twenty feet away. Right there with us. I could see nothing. . . . Something moved. Quarrels flew. A man cried out. . . . "Damn!" the Captain swore. "Somebody was still alive up here."

Something as black as the heart of night, as quick as unexpected death, arced over the halberds. I had one thought, *Fast!*, before it was among us. Men flew around, yelled, got into one another's way. The monster roared and growled, threw claws and fangs too fast for the eye to follow. Once I thought I slashed a flank of darkness, before a blow hurled me a dozen feet.

I scrambled up, got my back to a pillar. I was sure I was going to die, sure the thing would kill us all. Pure hubris, us thinking we could handle it. Only seconds had passed. Half a dozen men were dead. More were injured. The forvalaka didn't seem slowed, let alone harmed. Neither weapons nor spells hampered it.

Our wizards stood in a little knot, trying to produce another enchantment. The Captain cored a second clump. The rest of the men were scattered. The monster flashed around, picking them off.

Grey fire ripped through the room, for an instant exposing its entirety, branding the carnage on the backs of my eyeballs. The forvalaka screamed, this time with genuine pain. Point for the wizards.

It streaked toward me. I hacked in panic as it whipped past. I missed. It whirled, took a running start, leapt at the wizards. They met it with another flashy spell. The forvalaka howled. A man shrieked. The beast thrashed on the floor like a dying snake. Men stabbed it with pikes and swords. It regained its feet and streaked out the exit we had kept open for ourselves.

"It's coming!" the Captain bellowed to the Lieutenant.

I sagged, knowing nothing but relief. It was gone. . . . Before my butt hit the floor One-Eye was dragging me up. "Come on, Croaker. It hit Tom-Tom. You got to help."

I staggered over, suddenly aware of a shallow gash down one leg. "Better clean it good," I muttered. "Those claws are bound to be filthy."

Tom-Tom was a twist of human wreckage. His throat had been torn out, his belly opened. His arms and chest had been ripped to the bone. Amazingly, he was still alive, but there was nothing I could do. Nothing any physician could have done. Not even a master sorcerer, specializing in healing, could have salvaged the little black man. But One-Eye insisted I try, and try I did till the Captain dragged me off to attend men less certain of dying. One-Eye was bellowing at him as I left.

"Get some lights in here!" I ordered. At the same time the Captain began assembling the uninjured at the open doorway, telling them to hold it.

As the light grew stronger the extent of the debacle became more evident. We had been decimated. Moreover, a dozen brothers who had not been with us lay scattered around the chamber. They had been on duty. Among them were as many more of the Syndic's secretaries and advisers.

"Anybody see the Syndic?" the Captain demanded. "He must have been here." He and Match and Elmo started searching. I did not have much chance to follow that. I patched and sewed like a madman, comandeering all the help I could. The forvalaka left deep claw wounds which required careful and skillful suturing.

Somehow, Goblin and Silent managed to calm One-Eye enough so he could help. Maybe they did something to him. He worked in a daze barely this side of unconsciousness.

I took another look at Tom-Tom when I got a chance. He was *still* alive, clutching his little drum. Damn! That much stubbornness deserved reward. But how? My expertise simply was not adequate.

"Yo!" Match shouted. "Captain!" I glanced over. He was tapping a chest with his sword.

The chest was of stone. It was a strongbox of a type favored by Beryl's wealthy. I guess this one weighed five hundred pounds. Its exterior had been fancifully carved. Most of the decoration had been demolished. By the tearing of claws?

Elmo smashed the lock and pried the lid open. I glimpsed

a man lying atop gold and jewels, arms around his head, shaking. Elmo and the Captain exchanged grim looks.

I was distracted by the Lieutenant's arrival. He had held on downstairs till he got worried about nothing having happened. The forvalaka had not gone down.

"Search the tower," the Captain told him. "Maybe it went up." There were a couple levels above us.

When next I glanced at the chest it was closed again. Our employer was nowhere in evidence. Match was seated atop it, cleaning his nails with a dagger. I eyed the Captain and Elmo. There was something the slightest bit odd about them.

They would not have finished the forvalaka's task for her, would they? No. The Captain couldn't betray Company ideals that way. Could he?

I did not ask.

The search of the tower revealed nothing but a trail of blood leading to the tower top, where the forvalaka had lain gathering strength. It had been badly hurt, but it had escaped by descending the outer face of the tower.

Someone suggested we track it. To that the Captain replied, "We're leaving Beryl. We're no longer employed. We have to get out before the city turns on us." He sent Match and Elmo to keep an eye on the native garrison. The rest evacuated the wounded from the Paper Tower.

For several minutes I remained unchaperoned. I eyed the big stone chest. Temptation arose, but I resisted. I did not want to know.

Candy got back after all the excitement. He told us the legate was at the pier offloading his troops.

The men were packing and loading, some muttering about events in the Paper Tower, others bitching about having to leave. You stop moving and immediately put down roots. You accumulate things. You find a woman.

Then the inevitable happens and you have to leave it all. There was a lot of pain floating around our barracks.

I was at the gate when the northerners came. I helped turn the capstan that raised the portcullus. I felt none too proud. Without my approval the Syndic might never have been betrayed.

The legate occupied the Bastion. The Company began its evacuation. It was then about the third hour after midnight and the streets were deserted.

Two-thirds of the way to the Gate of Dawn the Captain ordered a halt. The sergeants assembled everyone able to fight. The rest continued with the wagons.

The Captain took us north on the Avenue of the Older Empire, where Beryl's emperors had memorialized themselves and their triumphs. Many of the monuments are bizarre, and celebrate such minutia as favorite horses, gladiators, or lovers of either sex.

I had a bad feeling even before we reached the Rubbish Gate. Uneasiness grew into suspicion, and suspicion blossomed into grim certainty as we entered the martial fields. There is nothing near the Rubbish Gate but the Fork Barracks.

The Captain made no specific declaration. When we reached the Fork compound every man knew what was afoot.

The Urban Cohorts were as sloppy as ever. The compound gate was open and the lone watchman was asleep. We trooped inside unresisted. The Captain began assigning tasks.

Between five and six thousand men remained there. Their officers had restored some discipline, having enticed them into restoring their weapons to the armories. Traditionally, Beryl's captains trust their men with weapons only on the eve of battle.

Three platoons moved directly into the barracks, killing

men in their beds. The remaining platoon established a
blocking position at the far end of the compound.

The sun was up before the Captain was satisfied. We
withdrew and hurried after our baggage train. There wasn't
a man among us who hadn't had his fill.

We were not pursued, of course. No one came besieging
the camp we established on the Pillar of Anguish. Which
was what it was all about. That and the release of several
years of pent-up anger.

Elmo and I stood at the tip of the headland, watching
the afternoon sun play around the edges of a storm far out
to sea. It had danced in and swamped our encampment
with its cool deluge, then had rolled off across the water
again. It was beautiful, though not especially colorful.

Elmo had not had much to say recently. "Something
eating you, Elmo?" The storm moved in front of the light,
giving the sea the look of rusted iron. I wondered if the
cool had reached Beryl.

"Reckon you can guess, Croaker."

"Reckon I can." The Paper Tower. The Fork Barracks.
Our ignoble treatment of our commission. "What do you
think it will be like, north of the sea?"

"Think the black witch will come, eh?"

"He'll come, Elmo. He's just having trouble getting his
puppets to jig to his tune." As who did not, trying to tame
that insane city?

"Uhm." And, "Look there."

A pod of whales plunged past rocks lying off the headland.
I tried to appear unimpressed, and failed. The beasts were
magnificent, dancing in the iron sea.

We sat down with our backs toward the lighthouse. It
seemed we looked at a world never defiled by Man.
Sometimes I suspect it would be better for our absence.

"Ship out there," Elmo said.

I didn't see it till its sail caught the fire of the afternoon sun, becoming an orange triangle edged with gold, rocking and bobbing with the rise and fall of the sea. "Coaster. Maybe a twenty tonner."

"That big?"

"For a coaster. Deep water ships sometimes run eighty tons."

Time pranced along, fickle and faggoty. We watched ship and whales. I began to daydream. For the hundredth time I tried to imagine the new land, building upon traders' tales heard secondhand. We would likely cross to Opal. Opal was a reflection of Beryl, they said, though a younger city. . . .

"That fool is going to pile onto the rocks."

I woke up. The coaster was perilously near said danger. She shifted course a point and eluded disaster by a hundred yards, resumed her original course.

"That put some excitement into our day," I observed.

"One of these first days you're going to say something without getting sarcastic and I'll curl up and die, Croaker."

"Keeps me sane, friend."

"That's debatable, Croaker. Debatable."

I went back to staring tomorrow in the face. Better than looking backward. But tomorrow refused to shed its mask.

"She's coming around," Elmo said.

"What? Oh." The coaster wallowed in the swell, barely making way, while her bows swung toward the strand below our camp.

"Want to tell the Captain?"

"I expect he knows. The men in the lighthouse."

"Yeah."

"Keep an eye out in case anything else turns up."

The storm was sliding to the west now, obscuring that horizon and blanketing the sea with its shadow. The cold grey sea. Suddenly, I was terrified of the crossing.

*   *   *

That coaster brought news from smuggler friends of
Tom-Tom and One-Eye. One-Eye became even more dour
and surly after he received them, and he had reached all
time lows already. He even eschewed squabbling with
Goblin, which he made a second career. Tom-Tom's death
had hit him hard, and would not turn loose. He would not
tell us what his friends had to say.

The Captain was little better. His temper was an
abomination. I think he both longed for and dreaded the
new land. The commission meant potential rebirth for the
Company, with our sins left behind, yet he had an intima-
tion of the service we were entering. He suspected the
Syndic had been right about the northern empire.

The day following the smuggler's visit brought cool
northern breezes. Fog nuzzled the skirts of the headland
early in the evening. Shortly after nightfall, coming out of
that fog, a boat grounded on the beach. The legate had
come.

We gathered our things and began taking leave of camp
followers who had trickled out from the city. Our animals
and equipment would be their reward for faith and friendship.
I spent a sad, gentle hour with a woman to whom I meant
more than I suspected. We shed no tears and told one
another no lies. I left her with memories and most of my
pathetic fortune. She left me with a lump in my throat and
a sense of loss not wholly fathomable.

"Come on, Croaker," I muttered as I clambered down
to the beach. "You've been through this before. You'll
forget her before you get to Opal."

A half dozen boats were drawn up on the strand. As
each filled northern sailors shoved it into the surf. Oarsmen drove it into the waves, and in seconds it vanished
into the fog. Empty boats came bobbing in. Every other
boat carried equipment and possessions.

A sailor who spoke the language of Beryl told me there was plenty of room aboard the black ship. The legate had left his troops in Beryl as guards for the new puppet Syndic, who was another Red distantly related to the man we had served.

"Hope they have less trouble than we did," I said, and went away to brood.

The legate was trading his men for us. I suspected we were going to be used, that we were headed into something grimmer than we could imagine.

Several times during the wait I heard a distant howl. At first I thought it the song of the Pillar. But the air was not moving. When it came again I lost all doubt. My skin crawled.

The quartermaster, the Captain, the Lieutenant, Silent, Goblin, One-Eye, and I waited till the last boat. "I'm not going," One-Eye announced as a boatswain beckoned us to board.

"Get in," the Captain told him. His voice was gentle. That is when he is dangerous.

"I'm resigning. Going to head south. Been gone long enough, they should've forgotten me."

The Captain jabbed a finger at the Lieutenant, Silent, Goblin, and me, jerked his thumb at the boat. One-Eye bellowed. "I'll turn the lot of you into ostriches. . . ." Silent's hand sealed his mouth. We ran him to the boat. He wriggled like a snake in a firepit.

"You stay with the family," the Captain said softly.

"On three," Goblin squealed merrily, then quick-counted. The little black man arced into the boat, twisting in flight. He bobbed over the gunwale cursing, spraying us with saliva. We laughed to see him showing some spirit. Goblin led the charge that nailed him to a thwart.

Sailors pushed us off. The moment the oars bit water

One-Eye subsided. He had the look of a man headed for the gallows.

The galley took form, a looming, indeterminate shape slightly darker than the surrounding darkness. I heard the fog-hollowed voices of seamen, timbers creaking, tackle working, long before I was sure of my eyes. Our boat nosed in to the foot of an accomodation ladder. The howl came again.

One-Eye tried to dive overboard. We restrained him. The Captain applied a bootheel to his butt. "You had your chance to talk us out of this. You wouldn't. Live with it."

One-Eye slouched as he followed the Lieutenant up the ladder, a man without hope. A man who had left a brother dead and now was being forced to approach that brother's killer, upon which he was powerless to take revenge.

We found the Company on the maindeck, snuggled amongst mounds of gear. The sergeants threaded the mess toward us.

The legate appeared. I stared. This was the first I had seen him afoot, standing. He was *short*. For a moment I wondered if he were male at all. His voices were often otherwise.

He surveyed us with an intensity that suggested he was reading our souls. One of his officers asked the Captain to fall the men in the best he could on the crowded deck. The ship's crew were taking up the center flats decking over the open well that ran from the bow almost to the stern, and from deck level down to the lower oar bank. Below, there was muttering, clanking, rattling, as the oarsmen wakened.

The legate reviewed us. He paused before each soldier, pinned a reproduction of the device on his sail over each heart. It was slow going. We were under way before he finished.

The nearer the envoy approached, the more One-Eye

shook. He almost fainted when the legate pinned him. I was baffled. Why so much emotion?

I was nervous when my turn came, but not frightened. I glanced at the badge as delicate gloved fingers attached it to my jerkin. Skull and circle in silver, on jet, elegantly crafted. A valuable if grim piece of jewelry. Had he not been so rattled, I would have thought One-Eye to be considering how best to pawn it.

The device now seemed vaguely familiar. Outside the context of the sail, which I had taken as showmanship and ignored. Hadn't I read or heard about a similar seal somewhere?

The legate said, "Welcome to the service of the Lady, physician." His voice was distracting. It did not fit expectations, ever. This time it was musical, lilting, the voice of a young woman putting something over on wiser heads.

The Lady? Where had I encountered that word used that way, emphasized as though it was the title of a goddess? A dark legend out of olden times. . . .

A howl of outrage, pain, and despair filled the ship. Startled, I broke ranks and went to the lip of the air well.

The forvalaka was in a big iron cage at the foot of the mast. In the shadows it seemed to change subtly as it prowled, testing every bar. One moment it was an athletic woman of about thirty, but seconds later it had assumed the aspect of a black leopard on its hind legs, clawing the imprisoning iron. I recalled the legate saying he might have a use for the monster.

I faced him. And the memory came. A devil's hammer drove spikes of ice into the belly of my soul. I knew why One-Eye did not want to cross the sea. The ancient evil of the north. . . . "I thought you people died three hundred years ago."

The legate laughed. "You don't know your history well

enough. We weren't destroyed. Just chained and buried alive.'' His laughter had an hysterical edge. "Chained, buried, and eventually liberated by a fool named Bomanz, Croaker.''

I dropped to my haunches beside One-Eye, who buried his face in his hands.

The legate, the terror called Soulcatcher in old tales, a devil worse than any dozen forvalaka, laughed madly. His crewmen cringed. A great joke, enlisting the Black Company in the service of evil. A great city taken and little villains suborned. A truly cosmic jest.

The Captain settled beside me. "Tell me, Croaker.''

So I told him about the Domination, and the Dominator and his Lady. Their rule had spanned an empire of evil unrivalled in Hell. I told him about the Ten Who Were Taken (of whom Soulcatcher was one), ten great wizards, near-demigods in their power, who had been overcome by the Dominator and compelled into his service. I told him about the White Rose, the lady general who had brought the Domination down, but whose power had been insufficient to destroy the Dominator, his Lady, and the Ten. She had interred the lot in a charm-bound barrow somewhere north of the sea.

"And now they're restored to life, it seems,'' I said. "They rule the northern empire. Tom-Tom and One-Eye must have suspected. . . . We've enlisted in their service.''

"Taken,'' he murmured. "Rather like the forvalaka.''

The beast screamed and hurled itself against the bars of its cage. Soulcatcher's laughter drifted across the foggy deck. "Taken by the Taken,'' I agreed. "The parallel is uncomfortable.'' I had begun to shake as more and more old tales surfaced in my mind.

The Captain sighed and stared into the fog, toward the new land.

One-Eye stared at the thing in the cage, hating. I tried to

ease him away. He shook me off. "Not yet, Croaker. I have to figure this."

"What?"

"This isn't the one that killed Tom-Tom. It doesn't have the scars we put on it."

I turned slowly, studied the legate. He laughed again, looking our way.

One-Eye never figured it out. And I never told him. We have troubles enough.

Chapter Two: RAVEN

"The crossing from Beryl proves my point," One-Eye growled over a pewter tankard. "The Black Company doesn't belong on water. Wench! More ale!" He waved his tankard. The girl could not understand him otherwise. He refused to learn the languages of the north.

"You're drunk," I observed.

"How perceptive. Will you take note, gentlemen? The Croaker, our esteemed master of the arts cleric and medical, has had the perspicacity to discover that I am drunk." He punctuated his speech with belches and mispronunciations. He surveyed his audience with that look of sublime solemnity only a drunk can muster.

The girl brought another pitcher, and a bottle for Silent. He, too, was ready for more of his particular poison. He was drinking a sour Beryl wine perfectly suited to his personality. Money changed hands.

There were seven of us altogether. We were keeping our heads down. The place was full of sailors. We were outsiders, outlanders, the sort picked for pounding when the brawling started. With the exception of One-Eye, we prefer saving our fight for when we are getting paid.

Pawnbroker stuck his ugly face in through the street doorway. His beady little eyes tightened into a squint. He spotted us.

Pawnbroker. He got that name because he loansharks the Company. He doesn't like it, but says anything is better than the monniker hung on him by his peasant parents: Sugar Beet.

"Hey! It's the Sweet Beet!" One-Eye roared. "Come on over, Sugar Baby. Drinks on One-Eye. He's too drunk to know any better." He was. Sober, One-Eye is tighter than a collar of day-old rawhide.

Pawnbroker winced, looked around furtively. He has that manner. "The Captain wants you guys."

We exchanged glances. One-Eye settled down. We had not seen much of the Captain lately. He was all the time hanging around with bigwigs from the Imperial Army.

Elmo and the Lieutenant got up. I did too, and started toward Pawnbroker.

The barkeeper bellowed. A serving wench darted to the doorway, blocked it. A huge, dull bull of a man lumbered out of a back room. He carried a prodigious gnarly club in each hogshead hand. He looked confused.

One-Eye snarled. The rest of our crowd rose, ready for anything.

The sailors, smelling a riot, started choosing sides. Mostly against us.

"What the hell is going on?" I shouted.

"Please, sir," said the girl at the door. "Your friends haven't paid for their last round." She sped the barkeeper a vicious look.

"The hell they didn't." House policy was payment on delivery. I looked at the Lieutenant. He agreed. I glanced

at the barkeep, sensed his greed. He thought we were
drunk enough to pay twice.

Elmo said, "One-Eye, you picked this thieves' den.
You straighten them out."

No sooner said than done. One-Eye squealed like a hog
meeting the butcher. . . .

A chimp-sized, four-armed bundle of ugly exploded
from beneath our table. It charged the girl at the door, left
fang-marks on her thigh. Then it climbed all over the
club-wielding mountain of muscle. The man was bleeding
in a dozen places before he knew what was happening.

A fruit bowl on a table at the room's center vanished in
a black fog. It reappeared a second later—with venomous
snakes boiling over its rim.

The barkeep's jaw dropped. And scarab beetles poured
out of his mouth.

We made our exit during the excitement. One-Eye howled
and giggled for blocks.

The Captain stared at us. We leaned on one another
before his table. One-Eye still suffered the occasional
spate of giggles. Even the Lieutenant could not keep a
straight face. "They're drunk," the Captain told him.

"We're drunk," One-Eye agreed. "We're palpably,
plausibly, pukingly drunk."

The Lieutenant jabbed him in the kidney.

"Sit down, men. Try to behave while you're here."

Here was a posh garden establishment socially miles
above our last port of call. Here even the whores had
titles. Plantings and tricks of landscaping broke the gardens into areas of semi-seclusion. There were ponds,
gazebos, stone walkways, and an overwhelming perfume
of flowers in the air.

"A little rich for us," I remarked.

"What's the occasion?" the Lieutenant asked. The rest of us jockied for seats.

The Captain had staked out a huge stone table. Twenty people could have sat around it. "We're guests. Act like it." He toyed with the badge over his heart, identifying him as receiving the protection of Soulcatcher. We each possessed one but seldom wore them. The Captain's gesture suggested we correct that deficiency.

"We're guests of the Taken?" I asked. I fought the effects of the ale. This should go into the Annals.

"No. The badges are for the benefit of the house." He gestured. Everyone visible wore a badge declaring an alignment with one or another of the Taken. I recognized a few. The Howler. Nightcrawler. Stormbringer. The Limper.

"Our host wants to enlist in the Company."

"He wants to join the Black Company?" One-Eye asked. "What's wrong with the fool?" It had been years since we had taken a new recruit.

The Captain shrugged, smiled. "Once upon a time a witchdoctor did."

One-Eye grumbled, "He's been sorry ever since."

"Why is he still here?" I asked.

One-Eye did not answer. Nobody leaves the Company, except feet first. The outfit is home.

"What's he like?" the Lieutenant asked.

The Captain closed his eyes. "Unusual. He could be an asset. I like him. But judge for yourselves. He's here." He flicked a finger at a man surveying the gardens.

His clothing was grey, tattered, and patched. He was of modest heighth, lean, dusky. Darkly handsome. I guessed him to be in his late twenties. Unprepossessing. . . .

Not really. On second glance you noted something striking. An intensity, a lack of expression, something in his stance. He was not intimidated by the gardens.

People looked and wrinkled their noses. They did not

see the man, they saw rags. You could feel their revulsion. Bad enough that we had been allowed inside. Now it was ragpickers.

A grandly accoutred attendant went to show him an entrance he'd obviously entered in error.

The man came toward us, passing the attendant as if he did not exist. There was a jerkiness, a stiffness, to his movements which suggested he was recovering from recent wounds. "Captain?"

"Good afternoon. Have a seat."

A ponderous staff general detached himself from a clutch of senior officers and svelte young women. He took a few steps our way, paused. He was tempted to make his prejudices known.

I recognized him. Lord Jalena. As high as you could get without being one of the Ten Who Were Taken. His face was puffed and red. If the Captain noticed him, he pretended otherwise.

"Gentlemen, this is . . . Raven. He wants to join us. Raven isn't his birthname. Doesn't matter. The rest of you lied too. Introduce yourselves and ask questions."

There was something odd about this Raven. We were his guests, apparently. His manner was not that of a street beggar, yet he looked like a lot of bad road.

Lord Jalena arrived. His breath came in wheezes. Pigs like him I would love to put through half what they inflict on their troops.

He scowled at the Captain. "Sir," he said between puffs, "Your connections are such that we can't deny *you*, but. . . . The Gardens are for persons of refinement. They have been for two hundred years. We don't admit. . . ."

The Captain donned a quizzical smile. Mildly, he replied, "I'm a guest, Milord. If you don't like my company, complain to my host." He indicated Raven.

Jalena made a half-right turn. "Sir. . . ." His eyes and mouth went round. "You!"

Raven stared at Jalena. Not one muscle twitched. Not an eyelash flickered. The color fled the fat man's cheeks. He glanced at his own party almost in supplication, looked at Raven again, turned to the Captain. His mouth worked but no words came out.

The Captain reached toward Raven. Raven accepted Soulcatcher's badge. He pinned it over his heart.

Jalena went paler still. He backed away.

"Seems to know you," the Captain observed.

"He thought I was dead."

Jalena rejoined his party. He gabbled and pointed. Pale-faced men looked our way. They argued briefly, then the whole lot fled the garden.

Raven did not explain. Instead, he said, "Shall we get to business?"

"Care to illuminate what just happened?" The Captain's voice had a dangerous softness.

"No."

"Better reconsider. Your presence could endanger the whole Company."

"It won't. It's a personal matter. I won't bring it with me."

The Captain thought about it. He is not one to intrude on a man's past. Not without cause. He decided he had cause. "How can you avoid bringing it? Obviously, you mean something to Lord Jalena."

"Not to Jalena. To friends of his. It's old history. I'll settle it before I join you. Five people have to die to close the book."

This sounded interesting. Ah, the smell of mystery and dark doings, of skulduggery and revenge. The meat of a good tale. "I'm Croaker. Any special reason for not sharing the story?"

Raven faced me, obviously under rigid self-control. "It's private, it's old, and it's shameful. I don't want to talk about it."

One-Eye said, "In that case I can't vote for acceptance."

Two men and a woman came down a flagstone pathway, paused overlooking the place where Lord Jalena's party had been. Latecomers? They were surprised. I watched them talk it over.

Elmo voted with One-Eye. So did the Lieutenant.

"Croaker?" the Captain asked.

I voted aye. I smelled a mystery and did not want it to get away.

The Captain told Raven, "I know part of it. That's why I'm voting with One-Eye. For the Company's sake. I'd like to have you. But. . . . Settle it before we leave."

The latecomers headed our way, noses in the air but determined to learn what had become of their party.

"When are you leaving?" Raven asked. "How long do I have?"

"Tomorrow. Sunrise."

"What?" I demanded.

"Hold on," One-Eye said. "How come already?"

Even the Lieutenant, who never questions anything, said, "We were supposed to get a couple weeks." He had found a lady friend, his first since I had known him.

The Captain shrugged. "They need us up north. The Limper lost the fortress at Deal to a Rebel named Raker."

The latecomers arrived. One of the men demanded, "What became of the party in the Camellia Grotto?" His voice had a whiny, nasal quality. My hackles rose. It reeked of arrogance and contempt. I hadn't heard its like since I joined the Black Company. People in Beryl hadn't used that tone.

They don't know the Black Company in Opal, I told myself. Not yet, they don't.

The voice hit Raven like a sledge whack on the back of the head. He stiffened. For a moment his eyes were pure ice. Then a smile crinkled their corners—as evil a smile as I have ever seen.

The Captain whispered, "I know why Jalena suffered his attack of indigestion."

We sat motionless, frozen by deadly imminence. Raven turned slowly, rising. Those three saw his face.

Whiny-voice choked. His male companion began shaking. The woman opened her mouth. Nothing came out.

Where Raven got the knife I do not know. It went almost too fast to follow. Whiny-voice bled from a cut throat. His friend had steel in his heart. And Raven had the woman's throat in his left hand.

"No. Please," she whispered without force. She expected no mercy.

Raven squeezed, forced her to her knees. Her face purpled, bloated. Her tongue rolled out. She seized his wrist, shuddered. He lifted her, stared into her eyes till they rolled up and she sagged. She shuddered again, died.

Raven jerked his hand away. He stared at that rigid, shaking claw. His face was ghastly. He surrendered to the all-over shakes.

"Croaker!" the Captain snapped. "Don't you claim to be a physician?"

"Yeah." People were reacting. The whole garden was watching. I checked Whiny-voice. Dead as a stone. So was his sidekick. I turned to the woman.

Raven knelt. He held her left hand. There were tears in his eyes. He removed a gold wedding band, pocketed it. That was all he took, though she sported a fortune in jewelry.

I met his gaze over the body. The ice was in his eyes again. It dared me to voice my guess.

"I don't want to sound hysterical," One-Eye growled, "but why don't we get the hell out of here?"

"Good thinking," Elmo said, and started heeling and toeing it.

"Get moving!" the Captain snapped at me. He took Raven's arm. I trailed.

Raven said, "I'll have my affairs settled by dawn."

The Captain glanced back. "Yeah," was all he said.

I thought so too.

But we would leave Opal without him.

The Captain received several nasty messages that night. His only comment was, "Those three must have been part of the in-crowd."

"They wore the Limper's badges," I said. "What's the story on Raven, anyway? Who is he?"

"Somebody who didn't get along with the Limper. Who was done dirty and left for dead."

"Was the woman something he didn't tell you?"

The Captain shrugged. I took that as an affirmative.

"Bet she was his wife. Maybe she betrayed him." That kind of thing is common here. Conspiracies and assassinations and naked power-grabs. All the fun of decadence. The Lady does not discourage anything. Maybe the games amuse her.

As we travelled north we moved ever nearer the heart of the empire. Each day took us into emotionally bleaker country. The locals became ever more dour, grim, and sullen. These were not happy lands, despite the season.

The day came when we had to skirt the very soul of the empire, the Tower at Charm, built by the Lady after her resurrection. Hard-eyed cavalrymen escorted us. We got no closer than three miles. Even so, the Tower's silhouette loomed over the horizon. It is a massive cube of dark stone. It stands at least five hundred feet high.

I studied it all day. What was our mistress like? Would I ever meet her? She intrigued me. That night I wrote an exercise in which I tried to characterize her. It degenerated into a romantic fantasy.

Next afternoon we encountered a pale-faced rider galloping south in search of our Company. His badges proclaimed him a follower of the Limper. Our outriders brought him to the Lieutenant.

"You people are taking your damned sweet time, aren't you? You're wanted in Forsberg. Quit shitting around."

The Lieutenant is a quiet man accustomed to the respect due his rank. He was so startled he said nothing. The courier became more offensive. Then the Lieutenant demanded, "What's your rank?"

"Corporal Courier to the Limper. Buddy, you'd better get hauling. He don't put up with no shit."

The Lieutenant is the Company disciplinarian. It is a load he takes off the Captain. He is a reasonable, just sort of guy.

"Sergeant!" he snapped at Elmo. "I want you." He was angry. Usually only the Captain calls Elmo Sergeant.

Elmo was riding with the Captain at the time. He trotted up the column. The Captain tagged along. "Sir?" Elmo asked.

The Lieutenant halted the Company. "Flog some respect into this peasant."

"Yes sir. Otto. Crispin. Turn a hand here."

"Twenty strokes should do it."

"Twenty strokes it is, sir."

"What the hell do you think you're pulling? No stinking hiresword is going to. . . ."

The Captain said, "Lieutenant, I think that calls for another ten lashes."

"Yes sir. Elmo?"

"Thirty it is, sir." He struck out. The courier flopped

out of his saddle. Otto and Crispin picked him up and ran him to a rail fence, draped him over it. Crispin slit the back of his shirt.

Elmo plied the strokes with the Lieutenant's riding crop. He did not lean into it. There was no rancor in this, just a message to those who thought the Black Company second-class.

I was there with my kit when Elmo finished. "Try to relax, lad. I'm a physician. I'll clean your back and bandage you." I patted his cheek. "You took it pretty good for a northerner."

Elmo gave him a new shirt when I finished. I offered some unsolicited advice on treatment, then suggested, "Report to the Captain as if this hadn't happened." I pointed toward the Captain. . . . "Well."

Friend Raven had rejoined us. He watched from the back of a sweaty, dusty roan.

The messenger took my advice. The Captain said, "Tell the Limper I'm traveling as fast as I can. I won't push so hard I'll be in no shape to fight when I get there."

"Yes sir. I'll tell him, sir." Gingerly, the courier mounted his horse. He concealed his feelings well.

Raven observed, "The Limper will cut your heart out for that."

"The Limper's displeasure doesn't concern me. I thought you were going to join us before we left Opal."

"I was slow closing accounts. One wasn't in the city at all. Lord Jalena warned the other. It took me three days to find him."

"The one out of town?"

"I decided to join you instead."

That was not a satisfactory answer, but the Captain slid around it. "I can't let you join us while you have outside interests."

"I let it go. I repaid the most important debt." He meant the woman. I could taste it.

The Captain eyed him sourly. "All right. Ride with Elmo's platoon."

"Thank you. Sir." That sounded strange. He was not a man accustomed to sirring anyone.

Our northward journey continued, past Elm, into the Salient, past Roses, and northward still, into Forsberg. That one-time kingdom had become a bloody killing-ground.

The city Oar lies in northernmost Forsberg, and in the forests above lies the Barrowland, where the Lady and her lover, the Dominator, were interred four centuries ago. The stubborn necromantic investigations of wizards from Oar had resurrected the Lady and Ten Who Were Taken from their dark, abiding dreams. Now their guilt-ridden descendants battled the Lady.

Southern Forsberg remained deceptively peaceful. The peasantry greeted us without enthusiasm, but willingly took our money.

"That's because seeing the Lady's soldiers pay is such a novelty," Raven claimed. "The Taken just grab whatever strikes their fancy."

The Captain grunted. We would have done so ourselves had we not had instructions to the contrary. Soulcatcher had directed us to be gentlemen. He had given the Captain a plump war chest. The Captain was willing. No point making enemies needlessly.

We had been travelling two months. A thousand miles lay behind us. We were exhausted. The Captain decided to rest us at the edge of the war zone. Maybe he was having second thoughts about serving the Lady.

Anyway, there is no point hunting trouble. Not when not fighting pays the same.

The Captain directed us into a forest. While we pitched camp, he talked with Raven. I watched.

Curious. There was a bond developing there. I could not understand it because I did not know enough about either man. Raven was a new enigma, the Captain an old one.

In all the years I have known the Captain I have learned almost nothing about him. Just a hint here and there, fleshed out by speculation.

He was born in one of the Jewel Cities. He was a professional soldier. Something overturned his personal life. Possibly a woman. He abandoned commission and titles and became a wanderer. Eventually he hooked up with our band of spiritual exiles.

We all have our pasts. I suspect we keep them nebulous not because we are hiding from our yesterdays but because we think we will cut more romantic figures if we roll our eyes and dispense delicate hints about beautiful women forever beyond our reaches. Those men whose stories I have uprooted are running from the law, not a tragic love affair.

The Captain and Raven, though, obviously found one another kindred souls.

The camp was set. The pickets were out. We settled in to rest. Though that was busy country, neither contending force noticed us immediately.

Silent was using his skills to augment the watchfulness of our sentries. He detected spies hidden inside our outer picket line and warned One-Eye. One-Eye reported to the Captain.

The Captain spread a map atop a stump we had turned into a card table, after evicting me, One-Eye, Goblin, and several others. "Where are they?"

"Two here. Two more over there. One here."

"Somebody go tell the pickets to disappear. We'll sneak

out. Goblin. Where's Goblin? Tell Goblin to get with the illusions." The Captain had decided not to start anything. A laudable decision, I thought.

A few minutes later, he asked, "Where's Raven?"

I said, "I think he went after the spies."

"What? Is he an idiot?" His face darkened. "What the hell do you want?"

Goblin squeaked like a stomped rat. He squeaks at the best of times. The Captain's outburst had him sounding like a baby bird. "You called for me."

The Captain stamped in a circle, growling and scowling. Had he the talent of a Goblin or a One-Eye, smoke would have poured from his ears.

I winked at Goblin, who grinned like a big toad. This shambling little war dance was just a warning not to trifle with him. He shuffled maps. He cast dark looks. He wheeled on me. "I don't like it. Did you put him up to it?"

"Hell no." I do not try to create Company history. I just record it.

Then Raven showed up. He dumped a body at the Captain's feet, proffered a string of grisly trophies.

"What the hell?"

"Thumbs. They count coup in these parts."

The Captain turned green around the gills. "What's the body for?"

"Stick his feet in the fire. Leave him. They won't waste time wondering how we knew they were out there."

One-Eye, Goblin, and Silent cast a glamour over the Company. We slipped away, slick as a fish through the fingers of a clumsy fisherman. An enemy battalion, which had been sneaking up, never caught a whiff of us. We headed straight north. The Captain planned to find the Limper.

Late that afternoon One-Eye broke into a marching song. Goblin squawked in protest. One-Eye grinned and sang all the louder.

"He's changing the words!" Goblin squealed.

Men grinned, anticipating. One-Eye and Goblin have been feuding for ages. One-Eye always starts the scraps. Goblin can be as touchy as a fresh burn. Their spats are entertaining.

This time Goblin did not reciprocate. He ignored One-Eye. The little black man got his feelings hurt. He got louder. We expected fireworks. What we got is bored. One-Eye could not get a rise. He started sulking.

A bit later, Goblin told me, "Keep your eyes peeled, Croaker. We're in strange country. Anything could happen." He giggled.

A horsefly landed on the haunch of One-Eye's mount. The animal screamed, reared. Sleepy One-Eye tumbled over its tail. Everybody guffawed. The wizened little wizard came up out of the dust cursing and swatting with his battered old hat. He punched his horse with his free hand, connecting with the beast's forehead. Then he danced around moaning and blowing on his knuckles.

His reward was a shower of catcalls. Goblin smirked.

Soon One-Eye was dozing again. It's a trick you learn after enough weary miles on horseback. A bird settled on his shoulder. He snorted, swatted. . . . The bird left a huge, fetid purple deposit. One-Eye howled. He threw things. He shredded his jerkin getting it off.

Again we laughed. And Goblin looked as innocent as a virgin. One-Eye scowled and growled but did not catch on.

He got a glimmer when we crested a hill and beheld a band of monkey-sized pygmies busily kissing an idol reminiscent of a horse's behind. Every pygmy was a miniature One-Eye.

The little wizard turned a hideous look on Goblin. Goblin responded with an innocent, don't look at me shrug.

"Point to Goblin," I judged.

"Better watch yourself, Croaker," One-Eye growled. "Or you'll be doing the kissing right here." He patted his fanny.

"When pigs fly." He is a more skilled wizard than Goblin or Silent, but not half what he would have us believe. If he could execute half his threats, he would be a peril to the Taken. Silent is more consistent, Goblin more inventive.

One-Eye would lie awake nights thinkings of ways to get even for Goblin's having gotten even. A strange pair. I do not know why they have not killed one another.

Finding the Limper was easier said than done. We trailed him into a forest, where we found abandoned earthworks and a lot of Rebel bodies. Our path tilted downward into a valley of broad meadows parted by a sparkling stream.

"What the hell?" I asked Goblin. "That's strange." Wide, low, black humps pimpled the meadows. There were bodies everywhere.

"That's one reason the Taken are feared. Killing spells. Their heat sucked the ground up."

I stopped to study a hump.

The blackness could have been drawn with a compass. The boundary was as sharp as a penstroke. Charred skeletons lay within the black. Swordblades and spearheads looked like wax imitations left too long in the sun. I caught One-Eye staring. "When you can do this trick you'll scare me."

"If I could do that I'd scare myself."

I checked another circle. It was a twin of the first.

Raven reined in beside me. "The Limper's work. I've seen it before."

I sniffed the wind. Maybe I had him in the right mood. "When was that?"

He ignored me.

He would not come out of his shell. Would not say hello half the time, let alone talk about who or what he was.

He is a cold one. The horrors of that valley did not touch him.

"The Limper lost this one," the Captain decided. "He's on the run."

"Do we keep after him?" the Lieutenant asked.

"This is strange country. We're in more danger operating alone."

We followed a spoor of violence, a swath of destruction. Ruined fields fell behind us. Burned villages. Slaughtered people and butchered livestock. Poisoned wells. The Limper left nothing but death and desolation.

Our brief was to help hold Forsberg. Joining the Limper was not mandatory. I wanted no part of him. I did not want to be in the same province.

As the devastation grew more recent, Raven showed elation, dismay, introspection easing into determination, and ever more of that rigid self-control he so often hid behind.

When I reflect on my companions' inner natures I usually wish I controlled one small talent. I wish I could look inside them and unmask the darks and brights that move them. Then I take a quick look into the jungle of my own soul and thank heaven that I cannot. Any man who barely sustains an armistice with himself has no business poking around in an alien soul.

I decided to keep closer watch on our newest brother.

*   *   *

We did not need Doughbelly coming in from the point to tell us we were close. All the forward horizon sprouted tall, leaning trees of smoke. This part of Forsberg was flat and open and marvelously green, and against the turquoise sky those oily pillars were an abomination.

There was not much breeze. The afternoon promised to be scorching.

Doughbelly swung in beside the Lieutenant. Elmo and I stopped swapping tired old lies and listened. Doughbelly indicated a smoke spire. "Still some of the Limper's men in that village, sir."

"Talk to them?"

"No sir. Longhead didn't think you'd want us to. He's waiting outside town."

"How many of them?"

"Twenty, twenty-five. Drunk and mean. The officer was worse than the men."

The Lieutenant glanced over his shoulder. "Ah. Elmo. It's your lucky day. Take ten men and go with Doughbelly. Scout around."

"Shit," Elmo muttered. He is a good man, but muggy spring days make him lazy. "Okay. Otto. Silent. Peewee. Whitey. Billygoat. Raven. . . ."

I coughed discreetly.

"You're out of your head, Croaker. All right." He did a quick count on his fingers, called three more names. We formed outside the column. Elmo gave us the once-over to make sure we hadn't forgotten our heads. "Let's go."

We hurried forward. Doughbelly directed us into a wood-lot overlooking the stricken town. Longhead and a man called Jolly waited there. Elmo asked, "Any developments?"

Jolly, who is professionally sarcastic, replied, "The fires are burning down."

We looked at the village. I saw nothing that did not turn

my stomach. Slaughtered livestock. Slaughtered cats and dogs. The small, broken forms of dead children.

"Not the kids too," I said, without realizing I was speaking. "Not the babies again."

Elmo looked at me oddly, not because he was unmoved himself but because I was uncharacteristically sympathetic. I have seen a lot of dead men. I did not enlighten him. For me there is a big difference between adults and kids. "Elmo, I have to go in there."

"Don't be stupid, Croaker. What can you do?"

"If I can save one kid. . . ."

Raven said, "I'll go with him." A knife appeared in his hand. He must have learned that trick from a conjurer. He does it when he is nervous or angry.

"Think you can bluff twenty-five men?"

Raven shrugged. "Croaker is right, Elmo. It's got to be done. Some things you don't tolerate."

Elmo surrendered. "We'll all go. Pray they aren't so drunk they can't tell friend from foe."

Raven started riding.

The village was good-sized. There had been more than two hundred homes before the Limper's advent. Half were burned or burning. Bodies littered the streets. Flies clustered round their sightless eyes. "Nobody of military age," I noted.

I dismounted and knelt beside a boy of four or five. His skull had been smashed, but he was breathing. Raven dropped beside me. "Nothing I can do," I said.

"You can end his ordeal." There were tears in Raven's eyes. Tears and anger. "There's no excuse for this." He moved to a corpse lying in shadow.

This one was about seventeen. He wore the jacket of a Rebel Mainforcer. He had died fighting. Raven said, "He must have been on leave. One boy to protect them." He pried a bow from lifeless fingers, bent it. "Good wood. A few thousand of these could rout the Limper.'' He slung the bow and appropriated the boy's arrows.

I examined another two children. They were beyond help. Inside a burned hut I found a grandmother who had died trying to shield an infant. In vain.

Raven exuded disgust. "Creatures like the Limper create two enemies for every one they destroy.''

I became aware of muted weeping, and of cursing and laughter somewhere ahead. "Let's see what that is.''

Beside the hut we found four dead soldiers. The lad had left his mark. "Good shooting,'' Raven observed. "Poor fool.''

"Fool?''

"He should've had the sense to run. Might've gone easier on everyone.'' His intensity startled me. What did he care about a boy from the other side? "Dead heroes don't get a second chance.''

Aha! He was drawing a parallel with an event in his own mysterious past.

The cursing and weeping resolved into a scene fit to disgust anyone tainted with humanity.

There were a dozen soldiers in the circle, laughing at their own crude jokes. I remembered a bitch dog surrounded by males who, contrary to custom, were not fighting for mounting rights but were taking turns. They might have killed her had I not intervened.

Raven and I mounted up, the better to see.

The victim was a child of nine. Welts covered her. She was terrified, yet making no sound. In a moment I understood. She was a mute.

War is a cruel business prosecuted by cruel men. The gods know the Black Company are no cherubim. But there *are* limits.

They were making an old man watch. He was the source of both curses and weeping.

Raven put an arrow into a man about to assault the girl.

"Dammit!" Elmo yelled. "Raven! . . ."

The soldiers turned on us. Weapons appeared. Raven loosed another arrow. It dropped the trooper holding the old man. The Limper's men lost any inclination to fight. Elmo whispered, "Whitey, go tell the old man to haul ass over here."

One of the Limper's men took a like notion. He scampered off. Raven let him run.

The Captain would have his behind on a platter.

He did not seem concerned. "Old timer. Come here. Bring the child. And get some clothes on her."

Part of me could not help but applaud, but another part called Raven a fool.

Elmo did not have to tell us to watch our backs. We were painfully aware that we were in big trouble. Hurry, Whitey, I thought.

Their messenger reached their commander first. He came tottering up the street. Doughbelly was right. He was worse than his men.

The old timer and girl clung to Raven's stirrup. The old man scowled at our badges. Elmo nudged his mount forward, pointed at Raven. I nodded.

The drunken officer stopped in front of Elmo. Dull eyes assayed us. He seemed impressed. We have grown hard in a rough trade, and look it.

"You!" he squealed suddenly, exactly the way Whiny-voice had done in Opal. He stared at Raven. Then he spun, ran.

Raven thundered, "Stand still, Lane! Take it like a man, you gutless thief!" He snatched an arrow from his quiver.

Elmo cut his bowstring.

Lane stopped. His response was not gratitude. He cursed. He enumerated the horrors we could expect at the hand of his patron.

I watched Raven.

He stared at Elmo in cold fury. Elmo faced it without flinching. He was a hard guy himself.

Raven did his knife trick. I tapped his blade with my swordtip. He mouthed one soft curse, glared, relaxed. Elmo said, "You left your old life behind, remember?"

Raven nodded once, sharply. "It's harder than I thought." His shoulders sagged. "Run away, Lane. You're not important enough to kill."

A clatter rose behind us. The Captain was coming.

That little wart of the Limper's puffed up and wriggled like a cat about to pounce. Elmo glared at him down the length of his sword. He got the hint.

Raven muttered, "I should know better anyway. He's only a butt boy."

I asked a leading question. It drew a blank stare.

The Captain rattled up. "What the hell is going on?"

Elmo began one of his terse reports. Raven interrupted. "Yon sot is one of Zouad's jackals. I wanted to kill him. Elmo and Croaker stopped me."

Zouad? Where had I heard that name? Connected with the Limper. Colonel Zouad. The Limper's number one villain. Political liaison, among other euphemisms. His name had occurred in a few overheard conversations between Raven and the Captain. Zouad was Raven's intended fifth victim? Then the Limper himself must have been behind Raven's misfortunes.

Curiouser and curiouser. Also scarier and scarier. The Limper is not anybody to mess with.

The Limper's man shouted, "I want this man arrested." The Captain gave him a look. "He murdered two of my men."

The bodies were there in plain sight. Raven said nothing. Elmo stepped out of character and volunteered, "They were raping the child. Their idea of pacification."

The Captain stared at his opposite number. The man reddened. Even the blackest villain will feel shame if caught unable to justify himself. The Captain snapped, "Croaker?"

"We found one dead Rebel, Captain. Indications were this sort of thing started before he became a factor."

He asked the sot, "These people are subjects of the Lady? Under her protection?" The point might be arguable in other courts, but at the moment it told. By his lack of a defense the man confessed a moral guilt.

"You disgust me." The Captain used his soft, dangerous voice. "Get out of here. Don't cross my path again. I'll leave you to my friend's mercy if you do." The man stumbled away.

The Captain turned to Raven. "You mother-lorn fool. Do you have any idea what you've done?"

Wearily, Raven replied, "Probably better than you do, Captain. But I'd do it again."

"And you wonder why we dragged our feet taking you on?" He shifted subject. "What are you going to do with these people, noble rescuer?"

That question had not occurred to Raven. Whatever the upheaval in his life, it had left him living entirely in the present. He was compelled by the past and oblivious to the future. "They're my responsibility, aren't they?"

The Captain gave up trying to catch the Limper. Operating independently now seemed the lesser evil.

The repercussions began four days later.

We had just fought our first significant battle, having crushed a Rebel force twice our size. It had not been difficult. They were green, and our wizards helped. Not many escaped.

The battlefield was ours. The men were looting the dead. Elmo, myself, the Captain, and a few others were standing around feeling smug. One-Eye and Goblin were celebrating in their unique fashion, taunting one another through the mouths of corpses.

Goblin suddenly stiffened. His eyes rolled up. A whine slipped past his lips, rose in pitch. He crumpled.

One-Eye reached him a step ahead of me, began slapping his cheeks. His habitual hostility had vanished.

"Give me some room!" I growled.

Goblin wakened before I could do more than check his pulse. "Soulcatcher," he murmured. "Making contact."

At that moment I was glad I did not own Goblin's talents. Having one of the Taken inside my mind seemed a worse violation than rape. "Captain," I called. "Soulcatcher." I stayed close.

The Captain ran over. He never runs unless we are in action. "What is it?"

Goblin sighed. His eyes opened. "He's gone now." His skin and hair were soaked with sweat. He was pale. He started shaking.

"Gone?" the Captain demanded. "What the hell?"

We helped Goblin get comfortable. "The Limper went to the Lady instead of coming at us head on. There's bad blood between him and Soulcatcher. He thinks we came out here to undermine him. He tried to turn the tables. But Soulcatcher is in high favor since Beryl, and the Limper isn't because of his failures. The Lady told him to leave us alone. Soulcatcher didn't get the Limper replaced, but he figures he won the round."

Goblin paused. One-Eye handed him a long drink. He drained it in an instant. "He says stay out of the Limper's way. He might try to discredit us somehow, or even steer the Rebel toward us. He says we should recapture the fortress at Deal. That would embarrass the Rebel and the Limper both.''

Elmo muttered, "He wants flashy, why don't he have us round up the Circle of Eighteen?'' The Circle is the Rebel High Command, eighteen wizards who think that between them they have what it takes to challenge the Lady and the Taken. Raker, the Limper's nemesis in Forsberg, belonged to the Circle.

The Captain looked thoughtful. He asked Raven, "You get the feeling there's politics involved?''

"The Company is Soulcatcher's tool. That's common knowledge. The puzzle is what he plans to do with it.''

"I got that feeling in Opal.''

Politics. The Lady's empire purports to be monolithic. The Ten Who Were Taken expend terrible energies keeping it that way. And spend as much more squabbling among themselves like toddlers fighting over toys, or competing for Mother's affection.

"Is that it?'' the Captain grumbled.

"That's it. He says he'll keep in touch.''

So we went and did it. We captured the fortress at Deal, in the dead of night, within howling distance of Oar. They say both Raker and the Limper flew into insane rages. I figure Soulcatcher ate that up.

One-Eye flipped a card into the discard pile. He muttered, "Somebody's sandbagging.''

Goblin snapped the card up, spread four knaves and discarded a queen. He grinned. You knew he was going down next time, holding nothing heavier than a deuce. One-Eye smacked the tabletop, hissed. He hadn't won a hand since sitting down.

"Go low, guys,'' Elmo warned, ignoring Goblin's

discard. He drew, scrunched his cards around just inches from his face, spread three fours and discarded a deuce. He tapped his remaining pair, grinned at Goblin, said, "That better be an ace, Chubby."

Pickles snagged Elmo's deuce, spread four of a kind, discarded a trey. He plied Goblin with an owl-like stare that dared him to go down. It said an ace would not keep him from getting burned.

I wished Raven were there. His presence made One-Eye too nervous to cheat. But Raven was on turnip patrol, which is what we called the weekly mission to Oar to purchase supplies. Pickles had his chair.

Pickles is Company quartermaster. He usually went on turnip patrol. He begged off this one because of stomach troubles.

"Looks like everybody was sandbagging," I said, and glared at a hopeless hand. Pair of sevens, pair of eights, and a nine to go with one of the eights, but no run. Almost everything I could use was in the discard pile. I drew. Sumbitch. Another nine, and it gave me a run. I spread it, dumped the off seven, and prayed. Prayer was all that could help.

One-Eye ignored my seven. He drew. "Damn!" He dumped a six on the bottom of my straight and discarded a six. "The moment of truth, Porkchop," he told Goblin. "You going to try Pickles?" And, "These Forsbergers are crazy. I've never seen anything like them."

We had been in the fortress a month. It was a little big for us, but I liked it. "I could get to like them," I said. "If they could just learn to like me." We had beaten off four counterattacks already. "Shit or get off the pot, Goblin. You know you got me and Elmo licked."

Pickles ticked the corner of his card with his thumbnail, stared at Goblin. He said, "They've got a whole Rebel mythos up here. Prophets and false prophets. Prophetic dreams. Sendings from the gods. Even a prophecy that a child somewhere around here is a reincarnation of the White Rose.''

''If the kid's already here, how come he's not pounding on us?'' Elmo asked.

''They haven't found him yet. Or her. They have a whole tribe of people out looking.''

Goblin chickened. He drew, sputtered, discarded a king. Elmo drew and discarded another king. Pickles looked at Goblin. He smiled a small smile, took a card, did not bother looking at it. He tossed a five onto the six One-Eye had dumped on my run and flipped his draw into the discard pile.

''A five?'' Goblin squeaked. ''You were holding a five? I don't believe it. He had a five.'' He slapped his ace onto the tabletop. ''He had a damned five.''

''Temper, temper,'' Elmo admonished. ''You're the guy who's always telling One-Eye to simmer down, remember?''

''He bluffed me with a damned five?''

Pickles wore that little smile as he stacked his winnings. He was pleased with himself. He had pulled a good bluff. I would have bet he was holding an ace myself.

One-Eye shoved the cards to Goblin. ''Deal.''

''Oh, come on. He was holding a five, and I got to deal too?''

''It's your turn. Shut up and shuffle.''

I asked Pickles, ''Where'd you hear that reincarnation stuff?''

''Flick.'' Flick was the old man Raven had saved. Pickles had overcome the old man's defenses. They were getting thick.

The girl went by the name Darling. She had taken a big shine to Raven. She followed him around, and drove the rest of us crazy sometimes. I was glad Raven had gone to town. We would not see much of Darling till he got back.

Goblin dealt. I checked my cards. The proverbial hand so bad it could not make a foot. Damned near one of Elmo's fabled Pismo straights, or no two cards of the same suit.

Goblin looked his over. His eyes got big. He slapped them down face upward. "Tonk! Goddammed tonk. Fifty!" He had dealt himself five royal cards, an automatic win demanding a double payoff.

"The only way he can win is deal them to himself," One-Eye grumped.

Goblin chortled, "You ain't winning even when you deal, Maggot Lips."

Elmo started shuffling.

The next hand went the distance. Pickles fed us snippets of the reincarnation story between plays.

Darling wandered by, her round, freckled face blank, her eyes empty. I tried imagining her in the White Rose role. I could not. She did not fit.

Pickles dealt. Elmo tried to go down with eighteen. One-Eye burned him. He held seventeen after his draw. I raked the cards in, started shuffling.

"Come on, Croaker," One-Eye taunted. "Let's don't fool around. I'm on a streak. One in a row. Deal me them aces and deuces." Fifteen and under is an automatic win, same as forty-nine and fifty.

"Oh. Sorry. I caught myself taking this Rebel superstition seriously."

Pickles observed, "It's a persuasive sort of nonsense. It hangs together in a certain elegant illusion of hope." I frowned his way. His smile was almost shy. "It's hard to lose when you *know* fate is on your side. The Rebel knows. Anyway, that's what Raven says." Our grand old man was getting close to Raven.

"Then we'll have to change their thinking."

"Can't. Whip them a hundred times and they'll keep on

coming. And because of that they'll fulfill their own prophecy."

Elmo grunted, "Then we have to do more than whip them. We have to humiliate them." *We* meant everybody on the Lady's side.

I flipped an eight into another of the countless discard piles which have become the milemarks of my life. "This is getting old." I was restless. I felt an undirected urge to be doing something. Anything.

Elmo shrugged. "Playing passes the time."

"This is the life, all right," Goblin said. "Sit around and wait. How much of that have we done over the years?"

"I haven't kept track," I grumbled. "More of that than anything else."

"Hark!" Elmo said. "I hear a little voice. It says my flock are bored. Pickles. Break out the archery butts and. . . ." His suggestion died under an avalanche of groans.

Rigorous physical training is Elmo's prescription for ennui. A dash through his diabolical obstacle course kills or cures.

Pickles extended his protest beyond the obligatory groan. "I'm gonna have wagons to unload, Elmo. Those guys should be back any time. You want these clowns to exercise, give them to me."

Elmo and I exchanged glances. Goblin and One-Eye looked alert. Not back yet? They should have been in before noon. I figured they were sleeping it off. Turnip patrol always came back wasted.

"I figured they were in," Elmo said.

Goblin flipped his hand at the discard pile. His cards danced for a moment, suspended by his trickery. He wanted us to know he was letting us off. "I better check this out."

One-Eye's cards slithered across the table, humping like inchworms. "I'll look into it, Chubby."

"I called it first, Toad Breath."

"I got seniority."

"Both of you do it," Elmo suggested. He turned to me. "I'll put a patrol together. You tell the Lieutenant." He tossed his cards in, started calling names. He headed for the stables.

Hooves pounded the dust beneath a continuous, grumbling drumbeat. We rode swiftly but warily. One-Eye watched for trouble, but performing sorceries on horseback is difficult.

Still, he caught a whiff in time. Elmo fluttered hand signals. We split into two groups, ploughed into the tall roadside weeds. The Rebel popped up and found us at his throat. He never had a chance. We were travelling again in minutes.

One-Eye told me, "I hope nobody over there starts wondering why we always know what they're going to try."

"Let them think they're up to their asses in spies."

"How did a spy get the word to Deal so fast? Our luck looks too good to be true. The Captain should get Soulcatcher to pull us out while we still have some value."

He had a point. Once our secret got out, the Rebel would neutralize our wizards with his own. Our luck would take a header.

The walls of Oar hove into view. I started getting the queasy regrets. The Lieutenant hadn't really approved this adventure. The Captain himself would ream me royal. His cussing would scorch the hair off my chin. I would be old before the restrictions ran out. So long madonnas of the streetside!

I was supposed to know better. I was halfway an officer.

The prospect of careers cleaning the Company stables and heads did not intimidate Elmo or his corporals. Forward! they seemed to be thinking. Onward, for the glory of the band. Yech!

They were not stupid, just willing to pay the price of disobedience.

That idiot One-Eye actually started singing as we entered Oar. The song was his own wild, nonsensical composition sung in a voice utterly incapable of carrying a tune.

"Can it, One-Eye," Elmo snarled. "You're attracting attention."

His order was pointless. We were too obviously who we were, and just as obviously were in vile temper. This was no turnip patrol. We were looking for trouble.

One-Eye whooped his way into a new song. "Can the racket!" Elmo thundered. "Get on your goddamned job."

We turned a corner. A black fog formed around our horses' fetlocks as we did. Moist black noses poked up and out and sniffed the fetid evening air. They wrinkled. Maybe they had become as countrified as I. Out came almond eyes glowing like the lamps of Hell. A susurrus of fear swept the pedestrians watching from the streetsides.

Up they sprang, a dozen, a score, five score phantoms born in that snakepit One-Eye calls a mind. They streaked ahead, weasely, toothy, sinuous black things that darted at the people of Oar. Terror outpaced them. In minutes we shared the streets with no one but ghosts.

This was my first visit to Oar. I looked it over like I had just come in on the pumpkin wagon.

"Well, look here," Elmo said as we turned into the street where the turnip patrol usually quartered. "Here's old Cornie." I knew the name, though not the man. Cornie kept the stable where the patrol always stayed.

An old man rose from his seat beside a watering trough.

"Heared you was coming," he said. "Done all what I could, Elmo. Couldn't get them no doctor, though."

"We brought our own." Though Cornie was old and had to hustle to keep pace, Elmo did not slow down.

I sniffed the air. It held a taint of old smoke.

Cornie dashed ahead, around an angle in the street. Weasel things flashed around his legs like surf foaming around a boulder on the shore. We followed, and found the source of the smoke smell.

Someone had fired Cornie's stable, then jumped our guys as they ran out. The villains. Wisps of smoke still rose. The street in front of the stable was filled with casualties. The least injured were standing guard, rerouting traffic.

Candy, who commanded the patrol, limped toward us. "Where do I start?" I asked.

He pointed. "Those are the worst. Better begin with Raven, if he's still alive."

My heart jumped. Raven? He seemed so invulnerable.

One-Eye scattered his pets. No Rebel would sneak up on us now. I followed Candy to where Raven lay. The man was unconscious. His face was paper-white. "He the worst?"

"The only one I thought wouldn't make it."

"You did all right. Did the tourniquets the way I taught you, didn't you?" I looked Candy over. "You should be lying down yourself." Back to Raven. He had close to thirty cuts on his face side, some of them deep. I threaded my needle.

Elmo joined us after a quick look around the perimeter. "Bad?" he asked.

"Can't tell for sure. He's full of holes. Lost a lot of blood. Better have One-Eye make up some of his broth." One-Eye makes an herb and chicken soup that will bring new hope to the dead. He is my only assistant.

Elmo asked, "How did it happen, Candy?"

"They fired the stable and jumped us when we ran out."

"I can see that."

Cornie muttered, "The filthy murderers." I got the feeling he was mourning his stable more than the patrol, though.

Elmo made a face like a man chewing on a green persimmon. "And no dead? Raven is the worst? That's hard to believe."

"One dead," Candy corrected. "The old guy. Raven's sidekick. From that village."

"Flick," Elmo growled. Flick was not supposed to have left the fortress at Deal. The Captain did not trust him. But Elmo overlooked that breach of regulations. "We're going to make somebody sorry they started this," he said. There wasn't a bit of emotion in his voice. He might have been quoting the wholesale price of yams.

I wondered how Pickles would take the news. He was fond of Flick. Darling would be shattered. Flick was her grandfather.

"They were only after Raven," Cornie said. "That's why he got cut so bad."

And Candy, "Flick threw himself in their way." He gestured. "All the rest of this is because we wouldn't stand back."

Elmo asked the question puzzling me. "Why would the Rebel be that hot to get Raven?"

Doughbelly was hanging around waiting for me to get to the gash in his left forearm. He said, "It wasn't Rebels, Elmo. It was that dumbshit captain from where we picked up Flick and Darling."

I swore.

"You stick to your needlepoint, Croaker," Elmo said. "You sure, Doughbelly?"

"Sure I'm sure. Ask Jolly. He seen him too. The rest was just street thugs. We whipped them good once we got going." He pointed. Near the unburned side of the stable were a dozen bodies stacked like cordwood. Flick was the only one I recognized. The others wore ragged local costume.

Candy said, "I saw him too, Elmo. And he wasn't top dog. There was another guy hanging around back in the shadows. He cleared out when we started winning."

Cornie had been hanging around, looking watchful and staying quiet. He volunteered, "I know where they went. Place over to Bleek Street."

I exchanged glances with One-Eye, who was putting his broth together using this and that from a black bag of his own. "Looks like Cornie knows our crowd," I said.

"Know you well enough to know you don't want no-body getting away with nothing like this."

I looked at Elmo. Elmo stared at Cornie. There always was some doubt about the stablekeeper. Cornie got nervous. Elmo, like any veteran sergeant, has a baleful stare. Finally, "One-Eye, take this fellow for a walk. Get his story."

One-Eye had Cornie under hypnosis in seconds. The two of them roamed around chatting like old buddies.

I shifted my attention to Candy. "That man in the shadows. Did he limp?"

"Wasn't the Limper. Too tall."

"Even so, the attack would have had the spook's blessing. Right, Elmo?"

Elmo nodded. "Soulcatcher would get severely pissed if he figured it out. The okay to risk that had to come from the top."

Something like a sigh came out of Raven. I looked down. His eyes were open a crack. He repeated the sound. I put my ear next to his lips. "Zouad . . ." he murmured.

Zouad. The infamous Colonel Zouad. The enemy he

had renounced. The Limper's special villain. Raven's knight-errantry had generated vicious repercussions.

I told Elmo. He did not seem surprised. Maybe the Captain had passed Raven's history on to his platoon leaders.

One-Eye came back. He said, "Friend Cornie works for the other team." He grinned a malific grin, the one he practices so he can scare kids and dogs. "Thought you might want to take that into consideration, Elmo."

"Oh, yes." Elmo seemed delighted.

I went to work on the man next worse off. More sewing to do. I wondered if I would have enough suture. The patrol was in bad shape. "How long till we get some of that broth, One-Eye?"

"Still got to come up with a chicken."

Elmo grumbled, "So have somebody go steal one."

One-Eye said, "The people we want are holed up in a Bleek Street dive. They've got some rough friends."

"What are you going to do, Elmo?" I asked. I was sure he would do something. Raven had put us under obligation by naming Zouad. He thought he was dying. He would not have named the name otherwise. I knew him that well, if I didn't know anything about his past.

"We've got to arrange something for the Colonel."

"You go looking for trouble, you're going to find it. Remember who he works for."

"Bad business, letting somebody get away with hitting the Company, Croaker. Even the Limper."

"That's taking pretty high policy on your own shoulders, isn't it?" I could not disagree, though. A defeat on the battlefield is acceptable. This was not the same. This was empire politics. People should be warned that it could get hairy if they dragged us in. The Limper *and* Soulcatcher had to be shown. I asked Elmo, "What kind of repercussions do you figure on?"

"One hell of a lot of pissing and moaning. But I don't reckon there's much they can *do*. Hell, Croaker, it ain't your no nevermind anyway. You get paid to patch guys up." He stared at Cornie thoughtfully. "I reckon the fewer witnesses left over, the better. The Limper can't scream if he can't prove nothing. One-Eye. You go on talking to your pet Rebel there. I got a nasty little idea shaping up in the back of my head. Maybe he has the key."

One-Eye finished dishing out his soup. The earliest partakers had more color in their cheeks already. Elmo stopped paring his nails. He skewered the stablekeeper with a hard stare. "Cornie, you ever hear of Colonel Zouad?"

Cornie stiffened. He hesitated just a second too long. "Can't say as I have."

"That's odd. Figured you would have. He's the one they call the Limper's left hand. Anyway, I figure the Circle would do most anything to lay hands on him. What do you think?"

"I don't know nothing about the Circle, Elmo." He gazed out over the rooftops. "You telling me this fellow over to Bleek is this Zouad?"

Elmo chuckled. "Didn't say that at all, Cornie. Did I give that impression, Croaker?"

"Hell no. What would Zouad be doing hanging around a crummy whorehouse in Oar? The Limper is up to his butt in trouble over east. He'd want all the help he could get."

"See, Cornie? But look here. Maybe I do know where the Circle could find the Colonel. Now, him and the Company ain't no friends. On the other hand, we ain't friends with the Circle, neither. But that's business. No hard feelings. So I was thinking. Maybe we could trade a favor for a favor. Maybe some big-time Rebel could drop by that place in Bleek Street and tell the owners he don't think they ought to be looking out for those guys. You see what I mean? If it was to go that way, Colonel Zouad just might drop into the Circle's lap.''

Cornie got the look of a man who knows he is trapped. He had been a good spy when we had had no reason to worry about him. He had been just plain old Cornie, friendly stablekeeper, whom we had tipped a little extra and talked around no more nor less than anyone else outside the Company. He had been under no pressure. He hadn't had to be anything but himself.

"You got me all wrong, Elmo. Honest. I don't never get involved in politics. The Lady or the Whites, it's all the same to me. Horses need feeding and stabling no matter who rides them.''

"Reckon you're right there, Cornie. Excuse me for being suspicious.'' Elmo winked at One-Eye.

"That's the Amador where those fellows are staying, Elmo. You better go over there before somebody tells them you're in town. Me, I'd better start getting this place cleaned up.''

"We're in no hurry, Cornie. But you go ahead with whatever you've got to do.''

Cornie eyed us. He went a few steps toward what was left of his stable. He looked us over. Elmo considered him blandly. One-Eye lifted his horse's left foreleg to check its hoof. Cornie ducked into the ruin. "One-Eye?'' Elmo asked.

"Right on out the back. Heeling and toeing.''

Elmo grinned. "Keep your eye on him. Croaker, take notes. I want to know who he tells. And who they tell. We gave him something that ought to spread like the clap.''

"Zouad was a dead man from the minute Raven named his name,'' I told One-Eye. "Maybe from the minute he did whatever it was back when.''

One-Eye grunted, discarded. Candy picked up and spread. One-Eye cursed. "I can't play with these guys, Croaker. They don't play right."

Elmo galloped up the street, dismounted. "They're moving in on that whorehouse. Got something for me, One-Eye?"

The list was disappointing. I gave it to Elmo. He cursed, spat, cursed again. He kicked the planks we were using as a card table. "Pay attention to your damned jobs."

One-Eye controlled his temper. "They're not making mistakes, Elmo. They're covering their asses. Cornie has been around us too long to trust."

Elmo stomped around and breathed fire. "All right. Backup plan number one. We watch Zouad. See where they take him after they grab him. We'll rescue him when he's about ready to croak, wipe out any Rebels around the place, then hunt down anybody who checked in there."

I observed, "You're determined to show a profit, aren't you?"

"Damned straight. How's Raven?"

"Looks like he'll pull through. The infection is under control, and One-Eye says he's started to heal."

"Uhn. One-Eye, I want Rebel names. Lots of names."

"Yes sir, boss, sir." One-Eye produced an exaggerated salute. It became an obscene gesture when Elmo turned away.

"Push those planks together, Doughbelly," I suggested. "Your deal, One-Eye."

He did not respond. He did not bitch or gripe or threaten to turn me into a newt. He just stood there, numb as death, eye barely cracked.

"Elmo!"

Elmo got in front of him and stared from six inches away. He snapped his fingers under One-Eye's nose. One-Eye did not respond. "What do you think, Croaker?"

"Something is happening at that whorehouse."

One-Eye did not move a muscle for ten minutes. Then the eye opened, unglazed, and he relaxed like a wet rag. Elmo demanded, "What the hell happened?"

"Give him a minute, will you?" I snapped.

One-Eye collected himself. "The Rebel got Zouad, but not before he contacted the Limper."

"Uhm?"

"The spook is coming to help him."

Elmo turned a pale shade of grey. "Here? To Oar?"

"Yep."

"Oh, shit."

Indeed. The Limper was the nastiest of the Taken. "Think fast, Elmo. He'll trace our part in it. . . . Cornie is the cutout link."

"One-Eye, you find that old shit. Whitey. Still. Pokey. Got a job for you." He gave instructions. Pokey grinned and stroked his dagger. Bloodthirsty bastard.

I cannot adequately portray the unease One-Eye's news generated. We knew the Limper only through stories, but those stories were always grim. We were scared. Soul-catcher's patronage was no real protection against another of the Taken.

Elmo punched me. "He's doing it again."

Sure enough. One-Eye was stiff. But this time he went beyond rigidity. He toppled, began thrashing and foaming at the mouth.

"Hold him!" I ordered. "Elmo, give me that baton of yours." A half dozen men piled on One-Eye. Small though he was, he gave them a ride.

"What for?" Elmo asked.

"I'll put it in his mouth so he doesn't chew his tongue." One-Eye made the weirdest sounds I've ever heard, and I have heard plenty on battlefields. Wounded men make noises you would swear could not come from a human throat.

The seizure lasted only seconds. After one final, violent surge, One-Eye lapsed into a peaceful slumber.

"Okay, Croaker. What the hell happened?"

"I don't know. The falling sickness?"

"Give him some of his own soup," somebody suggested. "Serve him right." A tin cup appeared. We forced its contents down his throat.

His eye clicked open. "What are you trying to do? Poison me? Feh! What was that? Boiled sewage?"

"Your soup," I told him.

Elmo jumped in. "What happened?"

One-Eye spat. He grabbed a nearby wineskin, sucked a mouthful, gargled, spat again. "Soulcatcher happened, that's what. Whew! I feel for Goblin now."

My heart started skipping every third beat. A nest of hornets swarmed in my gut. First the Limper, now Soulcatcher.

"So what did the spook want?" Elmo demanded. He was nervous too. He is not usually impatient.

"He wanted to know what the hell is going on. He heard the Limper was all excited. He checked with Goblin. All Goblin knew was that we headed here. So he climbed into my head."

"And was amazed at all the wide open space. Now he knows everything you know, eh?"

"Yes." Obviously, One-Eye did not like the idea.

Elmo waited several seconds. "Well?"

"Well what?" One-Eye covered his grin by pulling on the wineskin.

"Dammit, what did he say?"

One-Eye chuckled. "He approves of what we're doing. But he thinks we're showing all the finesse of a bull in rut. So we're getting a little help."

"What kind of help?" Elmo sounded like he knew things were out of control, but could not see where.

"He's sending somebody."

Elmo relaxed. So did I. As long as the spook himself stayed away. "How soon?" I wondered aloud.

"Maybe sooner than we'd like," Elmo muttered. "Lay off the wine, One-Eye. You still got to watch Zouad."

One-Eye grumbled. He went into that semi-trance that means he is looking around somewhere else. He was gone a long time.

"So!" Elmo growled when One-Eye came out of it. He kept looking around like he expected Soulcatcher to pop out of thin air.

"So take it easy. They've got him tucked away in a secret sub-basement about a mile south of here."

Elmo was as restless as a little boy with a desperate need to pee. "What's the matter with you?" I asked.

"A bad feeling. Just a bad, bad feeling, Croaker." His roving gaze came to rest. His eyes got big. "I was right. Oh, damn, I was right."

It looked as tall as a house and half as wide. It wore scarlet bleached by time, moth-eaten, and tattered. It came up the street in a sort of shamble, now fast, now slow. Wild, stringy grey hair tangled around its head. Its bramble patch of a beard was so thick and matted with filth that its face was all but invisible. One pallid, liver-spotted hand clutched a pole of a staff that was a thing of beauty defiled by its bearer's touch. It was an immensely elongated female body, perfect in every detail.

Someone whispered, "They say that was a real woman back during the Domination. They say she cheated on him."

You could not blame the woman. Not if you gave Shifter a good look.

Shapeshifter is Soulcatcher's closest ally among the Ten Who Were Taken. His enmity for the Limper is more virulent than our patron's. The Limper was the third corner in the triangle explaining Shifter's staff.

He stopped a few feet away. His eyes burned with an insane fire that made them impossible to meet. I cannot recall what color they were. Chronologically, he was the first great wizard-king seduced, suborned, and enslaved by the Dominator and his Lady.

Shaking, One-Eye stepped out front. "I'm the wizard," he said.

"Catcher told me." Shifter's voice was resonant and deep and big for even a man of his size. "Developments?"

"I've traced Zouad. Nothing else."

Shifter scanned us again. Some folks were doing a fade. He smiled behind his facial brush.

Down at the bend in the street civilians were gathering to gape. Oar had not yet seen any of the Lady's champions. This was the city's lucky day. Two of the maddest were in town.

Shifter's gaze touched me. For an instant I felt his cold contempt. I was a sour stench in his nostrils.

He found what he was looking for. Raven. He moved forward. We dodged the way small males duck the dominant baboon at the zoo. He stared at Raven for several minutes, then his vast shoulders hunched in a shrug. He placed the toes of his staff on Raven's chest.

I gasped. Raven's color improved dramatically. He stopped sweating. His features relaxed as the pain faded. His wounds formed angry red scar tissue which faded to the white of old scars in minutes. We gathered in a tighter and tighter circle, awed by the show.

Pokey came trotting up the street. "Hey, Elmo. We did it. What's going on?" He got a look at Shifter, squeaked like a caught mouse.

Elmo had himself together again. "Where's Whitey and Still?"

"Getting rid of the body."

"Body?" Shifter asked. Elmo explained. Shifter grunted. "This Cornie will become the basis of our plan. You." He speared One-Eye with a sausage-sized finger. "Where are those men?"

Predictably, One-Eye located them in a tavern. "You." Shifter indicated Pokey. "Tell them to bring the body back here."

Pokey got grey around the edges. You could see the protests piling up inside him. But he nodded, gulped some air, and trotted off. Nobody argues with the Taken.

I checked Raven's pulse. It was strong. He looked perfectly healthy. As diffidently as I could, I asked, "Could you do that for the others? While we're waiting?"

He gave me a look I thought would curdle my blood. But he did it.

"What happened? What are you doing here?" Raven frowned up at me. Then it came back to him. He sat up. "Zouad. . . ." He looked around.

"You've been out for two days. They carved you up like a goose. We didn't think you'd make it."

He felt his wounds. "What's going on, Croaker? I ought to be dead."

"Soulcatcher sent a friend. Shifter. He fixed you up." He had fixed everybody. It was hard to stay terrified of a guy who would do that for your outfit.

Raven surged to his feet, wobbled dizzily. "That damned Cornie. He set it up." A knife appeared in his hand. "Damn. I'm weak as a kitten."

I had wondered how Cornie could know so much about the attackers. "That isn't Cornie there, Raven. Cornie is dead. That's Shifter practicing to be Cornie." He did not need practice. He was Cornie enough to fool Cornie's mother.

Raven settled back beside me. "What's going on?"

I brought him up to date. "Shifter wants to go in using Cornie as credentials. They probably trust him now."

"I'll be right behind him."

"He might not like that."

"I don't care what he likes. Zouad isn't getting out of it this time. The debt is too big." His face softened and saddened. "How's Darling? She hear about Flick yet?"

"I don't think so. Nobody's been back to Deal. Elmo figures he can do whatever he wants here as long as he don't have to face the Captain till it's over."

"Good. I won't have to argue it with him."

"Shifter isn't the only Taken in town," I reminded him. Shifter had said he sensed the Limper. Raven shrugged. The Limper did not matter to him.

The Cornie simulacrum came toward us. We rose. I was shaky, but did note that Raven grew a shade paler. Good. He wasn't a cold stone all the time.

"You will accompany me," he told Raven. He eyed me. "And you. And the sergeant."

"They know Elmo," I protested. And he grinned.

"You will appear to be Rebels. Only one of the Circle would detect the deception. None of them are in Oar. The Rebel here is independently minded. We will take advantage of his failure to summon support." The Rebel is as plagued by personality politics as is our side.

Shifter beckoned One-Eye. "Status of Colonel Zouad?"

"He hasn't cracked."

"He's tough," Raven said, begrudging the compliment.

"You getting any names?" Elmo asked me.

I had a nice list. Elmo was pleased.

"We'd better go," Shifter said. "Before Limper strikes." One-Eye gave us the passwords. Scared, convinced I was not ready for this, more convinced that I did not dare contest Shifter's selections, I trudged along in the Taken's wake.

I don't know when it happened. I just glanced up and found myself walking with strangers. I gobbled at Shifter's back.

Raven laughed. I understood then. Shifter had cast his glamour over us. We now appeared to be captains of the Rebel persuasion. "Who are we?" I asked.

Shifter indicated Raven. "Harden, of the Circle. Raker's brother-in-law. They hate one another the way Catcher and Limper hate one another." Next, Elmo. "Field Major Reef, Harden's chief of staff. You, Harden's nephew, Motrin Hanin, as vicious an assassin as ever lived."

We had heard of none of them, but Shifter assured us their presence would not be questioned. Harden was in and out of Forsberg all the time, making life tough for his wife's brother.

Right, I thought. Fine and dandy. And what about the Limper? What do we do if he shows up?

The people at the place where they were holding Zouad were more embarrassed than curious when Cornie announced Harden. They had not deferred to the Circle. They did not ask questions. Apparently the real Harden possessed a vile, volatile, unpredictable temper.

"Show them the prisoner," Shifter said.

One Rebel gave Shifter a look that said, "Just you wait, Cornie."

The place was packed with Rebels. I could almost hear Elmo thinking out his plan of attack.

They took us down into a basement, through a cleverly concealed doorway, and down deeper still, into a room with earthen walls and ceiling supported by beams and timbers. The decor came straight out of a fiend's imagination.

Torture chambers exist, of course, but the mass of men

never see them, so they never really believe in them. I'd never seen one before.

I surveyed the instruments, looked at Zouad there strapped into a huge, bizarre chair, and wondered why the Lady was considered such a villain. These people said they were the good guys, fighting for the right, liberty, and the dignity of the human spirit, but in method they were no better than the Limper.

Shifter whispered to Raven. Raven nodded. I wondered how we would get our cues. Shifter had not rehearsed us much. These people would expect us to act like Harden and his cutthroats.

We seated ourselves and observed the interrogation. Our presence inspired the questioners. I closed my eyes. Raven and Elmo were less disturbed.

After a few minutes "Harden" ordered "Major Reef" to go handle some piece of business. I do not recall the excuse. I was distracted. Its purpose was to put Elmo back on the street so he could start the roundup.

Shifter was winging it. We were supposed to sit tight till he cued us. I gathered we would make our move when Elmo closed in and panic started seeping down from above. Meantime, we would watch Colonel Zouad's demolition.

The Colonel was not that impressive, but then the torturers had had him a while. I expect anyone would look hollow and shrunken after enduring their mercies.

We sat like three idols. I sent mental hurryups to Elmo. I had been trained to take pleasure in the healing, not the breaking, of human flesh.

Even Raven seemed unhappy. Doubtless he had fantasized torments for Zouad, but when it came to the actuality his basic decency triumphed. His style was to stick a knife in a man and have done.

*   *   *

The earth lurched as if stomped by a huge boot. Soil fell from the walls and overhead. The air filled with dust. "Earthquake!" somebody yelled, and the Rebels all scrambled for the stair. Shifter sat still and smiled.

The earth shuddered again. I fought the instinct of the herd and remained seated. Shifter was not worried. Why should I be?

He pointed at Zouad. Raven nodded, rose, went over. The Colonel was conscious and lucid and frightened by the quaking. He looked grateful when Raven started unbuckling him.

The great foot stamped again. Earth fell. In one corner a supporting upright toppled. A trickle of loose soil began running into the basement. The other beams groaned and shifted. I barely controlled myself.

Sometime during the tremor Raven stopped being Harden. Shifter stopped being Cornie. Zouad looked them over and caught on. His face hardened, went pale. As if he had more to fear from Raven and Shapeshifter than from the Rebel.

"Yeah," Raven said. "It's payoff time."

The earth bucked. Overhead there was a remote rumble of falling masonry. Lamps toppled and went out. The dust made the air almost unbreathable. And Rebels came tumbling back down the stair, looking over their shoulders.

"Limper is here," Shifter said. He did not seem displeased. He rose and faced the stair. He was Cornie again, and Raven was Harden once more.

Rebels piled into the room. I lost track of Raven in the press and poor light. Somebody sealed the door up top. The Rebels got quiet as mice. You could almost hear hearts hammering as they watched the stair and wondered if the secret entrance were well enough hidden.

Despite several yards of intervening earth, I heard something moving through the basement above. Drag-thump.

Drag-thump. The rhythm of a crippled man walking. My gaze, too, locked on the secret door.

The earth shook its most violent yet. The doorway exploded inward. The far end of the sub-basement caved in. Men screamed as the earth swallowed them. The human herd shoved this way and that in search of an escape that did not exist. Only Shifter and I were not caught up in it. We watched from an island of calm.

All the lamps had died. The only light came from the gap at the head of the stair, sliding around a silhouette which, at that moment, seemed vile just in its stance. I had cold, clammy skin and violent shakes. It was not just because I had heard so much about the Limper. He exuded something that made me feel like an arachnophobe might if you dropped a big hairy spider into his lap.

I glanced at Shifter. He was Cornie, just another of the Rebel crew. Did he have some special reason for not wanting to be recognized by the Limper?

He did something with his hands.

A blinding light filled the pit. I could not see. I heard beams creaking and giving way. This time I did not hesitate. I joined the rush to the stair.

I suppose the Limper was more startled than anyone else. He had not expected any serious opposition. Shifter's trick caught him off guard. The rush swept over him before he could protect himself.

Shifter and I were the last up the stair. I skipped over the Limper, a small man in brown who did not look terrible at all as he writhed on the floor. I looked for the stair to the street level. Shifter grabbed my arm. His grip was undeniable. "Help me." He planted a boot against the Limper's ribs, started rolling him through the entrance to the sub-basement.

Down below, men groaned and cried out for help. Sections of floor on our level were sagging, collapsing. More in fear that I would be trapped if we did not hurry than out of any desire to inconvenience the Limper, I helped Shifter dump the Taken into the pit.

Shifter grinned, gave me a thumbs up. He did something with his fingers. The collapse accelerated. He seized my arm and headed for the stairs. We piled into the street amidst the grandest uproar in Oar's recent history.

The foxes were in the henhouse. Men were running hither and yon yelling incoherently. Elmo and the Company were all around them, driving them inward, cutting them down. The Rebels were too confused to defend themselves.

Had it not been for Shifter, I suppose, I would not have survived that. He did something that turned the points of arrows and swords. Cunning beast that I am, I stayed in his shadow till we were safely behind Company lines.

It was a great victory for the Lady. It exceeded Elmo's wildest hopes. Before the dust settled the purge had taken virtually every committed Rebel in Oar. Shifter stayed in the thick of it. He gave us invaluable assistance and had a grand time smashing things up. He was as happy as a child starting fires.

Then he disappeared as utterly as if he had never existed. And we, so exhausted we were crawling around like lizards, assembled outside Cornie's stable. Elmo took the roll.

All accounted for but one. "Where's Raven?" Elmo asked.

I told him, "I think he got buried when that house fell in. Him and Zouad both."

One-Eye observed, "Kind of fitting. Ironic but fitting. Hate to see him go, though. He played a mean game of Tonk."

"The Limper is down there too?" Elmo asked.

I grinned. "I helped bury him."

"And Shifter is gone."

I had begun to sense a disturbing pattern. I wanted to know if it was just my imagination. I brought it up while the men were getting ready to return to Deal. "You know, the only people who saw Shifter were on our side. The Rebel and the Limper saw a lot of us. Especially of you, Elmo. And me and Raven. Cornie will turn up dead. I have a feeling Shifter's finesse didn't have much to do with getting Zouad or wiping out the local Rebel hierarchy. I think we were put on the spot where the Limper is concerned. Very craftily."

Elmo likes to come across as a big, dumb country boy turned soldier, but he is sharp. He not only saw what I meant, he immediately connected it with the broader picture of politicking among the Taken. "We've got to get the hell away from here before the Limper digs his way out. And I don't mean just away from Oar. I mean Forsberg. Soulcatcher has put us on the board as his frontline pawns. We're liable to get caught between a rock and a hard place." He chewed his lip for a second, then started acting like a sergeant, bellowing at anybody not moving fast enough to suit him.

He was in a near panic, but was a soldier to the bone. Our departure was no rout. We went out escorting the provision wagons Candy's patrol had come to collect. He told me, "I'll go crazy after we get back. I'll go out and chew down a tree, or something." And after a few miles, thoughtfully, "Been trying to decide who ought to break the news to Darling. Croaker, you just volunteered. You've got the right touch."

So I had me something to keep my mind occupied during the ride. Damn that Elmo!

The great brouhaha in Oar was not the end of it. Ripples spread. Consequences piled up. Fate shoved its badfinger in.

Raker launched a major offensive while the Limper was digging his way out of the rubble. He did so unaware that his enemy was absent from the field, but the effect was the same. The Limper's army collapsed. Our victory went for naught. Rebel bands whooped through Oar, hunting the Lady's agents.

We, thanks to Soulcatcher's foresight, were moving south when the collapse came, so we avoided becoming involved. We went into garrison at Elm credited with several dramatic victories, and the Limper fled into the Salient with the remnants of his force, branded as an incompetent. He knew who had done him in, but there wasn't anything he could do. His relationship with the Lady was too precarious. He dared do nothing but remain her faithful lapdog. He would have to come up with some outstanding victories before he thought about settling with us or Soulcatcher.

I did not feel that comforted. The worm has a way of turning, given time.

Raker was so enthusiastic over his success that he did not slow down after he conquered Forsberg. He turned southward. Soulcatcher ordered us out of Elm only a week after we had settled in.

Did the Captain get upset about what had happened? Was he displeased because so many of his men had gone off on their own, exceeding or stretching his instructions? Let's just say the extra duty assignments were enough to break the back of an ox. Let's say the madonnas of the night in Elm were severely disappointed in the Black Company. I do not want to think about it. The man is a diabolic genius.

The platoons were on review. The wagons were loaded and ready to roll. The Captain and Lieutenant were conferring with their sergeants. One-Eye and Goblin were playing some sort of game with little shadow creatures making war in the corners of the compound. Most of us were watching and betting this way or that depending on shifts of fortune. The gateman shouted, "Rider coming in."

Nobody paid any attention. Messengers came and went all day.

The gate swung inward. And Darling began clapping her hands. She ran toward the gateway.

Through it, looking as rough as the day we had met him, rode our Raven. He scooped up Darling and gave her a big hug, perched her astride his mount before him, and reported to the Captain. I heard him say that all his debts were paid, and that he no longer had any interests outside the Company.

The Captain stared at him a long time, then nodded and told him to take his place in ranks.

He had used us, and while doing so had found himself a new home. He was welcome to the family.

We rode out, bound for a new garrison in the Salient.

Chapter Three: RAKER

The wind tumbled and bumbled and howled around
Meystrikt. Arctic imps giggled and blew their frigid breath
through chinks in the walls of my quarters. My lamplight
flickered and danced, barely surviving. When my fingers
stiffened, I folded them round the flame and let them toast.

The wind was a hard blow out of the north, gritty with
powdered snow. A foot had fallen during the night. More was
coming. It would bring more misery with it. I pitied Elmo
and his gang. They were out Rebel hunting.

Meystrikt Fortress. Pearl of the Salient defenses. Frozen
in winter. Swampy in spring. An oven in summer. White
Rose prophets and Rebel mainforcers were the least of our
troubles.

The Salient is a long arrowhead of flatland pointing
south, between mountain ranges. Meystrikt lies at its point.
It funnels weather and enemies down onto the stronghold.
Our assignment is to hold this anchor of the Lady's northern defenses.

Why the Black Company?

We are the best. The Rebel infection began seeping through the Salient soon after the fall of Forsberg. The Limper tried to stop it and failed. The Lady set us to clean up the Limper's mess. Her only other option was to abandon another province.

The gate watch sounded a trumpet. Elmo was coming in.

There was no rush to greet him. The rules call for casualness, for a pretense that your guts are not churning with dread. Instead, men peeped from hidden places, wondering about brothers who had gone a-hunting. Anybody lost? Anyone bad hurt? You know them better than kin. You had fought side by side for years. Not all of them were friends, but they were family. The only family you had.

The gateman hammered ice off the windlass. Shrieking its protests, the portcullus rose. As Company historian I could go greet Elmo without violating the unwritten rules. Fool that I am, I went out into the wind and chill.

A sorry lot of shadows loomed through the blowing snow. The ponies were dragging. Their riders slumped over icy manes. Animals and men hunched into themselves, trying to escape the wind's scratching talons. Clouds of breath smoked from mounts and men, and were ripped away. This, in painting form, would have made a snowman shiver.

Of the whole Company only Raven ever saw snow before this winter. Some welcome to service with the Lady.

The riders came closer. They looked more like refugees than brothers of the Black Company. Ice-diamonds twinkled in Elmo's mustache. Rags concealed the rest of his face. The others were so bundled I could not tell who was who. Only Silent rode resolutely tall. He peered straight ahead, disdaining that pitiless wind.

Elmo nodded as he came through the gate. "We'd started to wonder," I said. Wonder means worry. The rules demand a show of indifference.

"Hard travelling."

"How'd it go?"

"Black Company twenty-three, Rebel zip. No work for you, Croaker, except Jo-Jo has a little frostbite."

"You get Raker?"

Raker's dire prophecies, skilled witchcraft, and battle-field cunning had made a fool of the Limper. The Salient had been ready to collapse before the Lady ordered us to take over. The move had sent shock waves throughout the empire. A mercenary captain had been assigned forces and powers usually reserved for one of the Ten!

Salient winter being what it was, only a shot at Raker himself made the Captain field this patrol.

Elmo bared his face and grinned. He was not talking. He would just have to tell it again for the Captain.

I considered Silent. No smile on his long, dreary face. He responded with a slight jerk of his head. So. Another victory that amounted to failure. Raker had escaped again. Maybe he would send us scampering after the Limper, squeaking mice who had grown too bold and challenged the cat.

Still, chopping twenty-three men out of the regional Rebel hierarchy counted for something. Not a bad day's work, in fact. Better than any the Limper turned in.

Men came for the patrol's ponies. Others set out mulled wine and warm food in the main hall. I stuck with Elmo and Silent. Their tale would get told soon enough.

Meystrikt's main hall is only slightly less draughty than its quarters. I treated Jo-Jo. The others attacked their meals. Feast complete, Elmo, Silent, One-Eye, and Knuckles convened around a small table. Cards materialized. One-Eye scowled my way. "Going to stand there with your thumb in your butt, Croaker? We need a mark."

One-Eye is at least a hundred years old. The Annals mention the wizened little black man's volcanic tempers throughout the last century. There is no telling when he joined. Seventy years' worth of Annals were lost when the Company's positions were overrun at the Battle of Urban. One-Eye refuses to illuminate the missing years. He says he does not believe in history.

Elmo dealt. Five cards to each player and a hand to an empty chair. "Croaker!" One-Eye snapped. "You going to squat?"

"Nope. Sooner or later Elmo is going to talk." I tapped my pen against my teeth.

One-Eye was in rare form. Smoke poured out of his ears. A screaming bat popped out of his mouth.

"He seems annoyed," I observed. The others grinned. Baiting One-Eye is a favorite passtime.

One-Eye hates field work. And hates missing out even more. Elmo's grins and Silent's benevolent glances convinced him he had missed something good.

Elmo redistributed his cards, peered at them from inches away. Silent's eyes glittered. No doubt about it. They had a special surprise.

Raven took the seat they had offered me. No one objected. Even One-Eye never objects to anything Raven decides to do.

Raven. Colder than our weather since Oar. A dead soul now, maybe. He can make a man shudder with a glance. He exudes a stench of the grave. And yet, Darling loves him. Pale, frail, etherial, she kept one hand on his shoulder while he ordered his cards. She smiled for him.

Raven is an asset in any game including One-Eye. One-Eye cheats. But never when Raven is playing.

"She stands in the Tower, gazing northward. Her delicate hands are clasped before Her. A breeze steals softly through Her window. It stirs the midnight silk of Her hair. Tear diamonds sparkle on the gentle curve of Her cheek."

"Hoo-wee!"

"Oh, wow!"

"Author! Author!"

"May a sow litter in your bedroll, Willie." Those characters got a howl out of my fantasies about the Lady.

The sketches are a game I play with myself. Hell, for all they know, my inventions might be on the mark. Only the Ten Who Were Taken ever see the Lady. Who knows if she is ugly, beautiful, or what?

"Tear diamonds sparkling, eh?" One-Eye said. "I like that. Figure she's pining for you, Croaker?"

"Knock it off. I don't make fun of your games."

The Lieutenant entered, seated himself, regarded us with a black scowl. Lately his mission in life has been to disapprove.

His advent meant the Captain was on his way. Elmo folded his hand, composed himself.

The place fell silent. Men appeared as if by magic. "Bar the damned door!" One-Eye muttered. "They keep stumbling in like this, I'll freeze my ass off. Play the hand out, Elmo."

The Captain came in, took his usual seat. "Let's hear it, Sergeant."

The Captain is not one of our more colorful characters. Too quiet. Too serious.

Elmo laid his cards down, tapped their edges into alignment, ordered his thoughts. He can become obsessed with brevity and precision.

"Sergeant?"

"Silent spotted a picket line south of the farm, Captain. We circled north. Attacked after sunset. They tried to scatter. Silent distracted Raker while we handled the others. Thirty men. We got twenty-three. We yelled a lot about not letting our spy get hurt. We missed Raker."

Sneaky makes this outfit work. We want the Rebel to believe his ranks are shot with informers. That hamstrings his communications and decision-making, and makes life less chancy for Silent, One-Eye, and Goblin.

The planted rumor. The small frame. The touch of bribery or blackmail. Those are the best weapons. We opt battle only when we have our opponents mousetrapped. At least ideally.

"You returned directly to the fortress?"

"Yes sir. After burning the farmhouse and outbuildings. Raker concealed his trail well."

The Captain considered the smoke-darkened beams overhead. Only One-Eye's snapping of his cards broke the silence. The Captain dropped his gaze. "Then, pray, why are you and Silent grinning like a pair of prize fools?"

One-Eye muttered, "Proud they came home empty-handed."

Elmo grinned some more. "But we didn't."

Silent dug inside his filthy shirt, produced the small leather bag that always hangs on a thong around his neck. His trick bag. It is filled with noxious oddiments like putrified bat's ears or elixer of nightmare. This time he produced a folded piece of paper. He cast dramatic glances at One-Eye and Goblin, opened the packet fold by fold. Even the Captain left his seat, crowded the table.

"Behold!" said Elmo.

"Tain't nothing but hair." Heads shook. Throats grumbled. Somebody questioned Elmo's grasp on reality.

But One-Eye and Goblin had three big coweyes between them. One-Eye chirruped inarticulately. Goblin squeaked a few times, but, then, Goblin always squeaks. "Is it really his?" he managed at last. "Really his?"

Elmo and Silent radiated the smugness of emminently successful conquistadors. "Absodamnlutely," Elmo said. "Right off the top of his bean. We had that old man by the balls and he knew it. He was heeling and toeing it out of there so fast he smacked his noggin on a doorframe. Saw it myself, and so did Silent. Left these on the beam. Whoo, that gaffer can step."

And Goblin, an octave above his usual rusty hinge squall, dancing in his excitement, said, "Gents, we've got him. He's as good as hanging on a meathook right now. The big one." He meowed at One-Eye. "What do you think of that, you sorry little spook?"

A herd of miniscule lightning bugs poured out of One-Eye's nostrils. Good soldiers all, they fell into formation, spelling out the words *Goblin is a Poof*. Their little wings hummed the words for the benefit of the illiterate.

There is no truth to that canard. Goblin is thoroughly heterosexual. One-Eye was trying to start something.

Goblin made a gesture. A great shadow-figure, like Soulcatcher but tall enough to brush the ceiling beams, bent and skewered One-Eye with an accusing finger. A sourceless voice whispered, "It was you that corrupted the lad, sodder."

One-Eye snorted, shook his head, shook his head and snorted. His eye glazed. Goblin giggled, stifled himself, giggled again. He spun away, danced a wild victory jig in front of the fireplace.

Our less intuitive brethern grumbled. A couple of hairs. With those and two bits silver you could get rolled by the village whores.

"Gentlemen!" The Captain understood.

The shadow-show ceased. The Captain considered his wizards. He thought. He paced. He nodded to himself. Finally, he asked, "One-Eye. Are they enough?"

One-Eye chuckled, an astonishingly deep sound for so small a man. "One hair, sir, or one nail paring, is enough. Sir, we have him."

Goblin continued his weird dance. Silent kept grinning. Raving lunatics, the lot of them.

The Captain thought some more. "We can't handle this ourselves." He circled the hall, his pacing portentous. "We'll have to bring in one of the Taken."

One of the Taken. Naturally. Our three sorcerers are our most precious resource. They must be protected. But. . . . Cold stole in and froze us into statues. One of the Lady's shadow disciples. . . . One of those dark lords here? No. . . .

"Not the Limper. He's got a hard-on for us."

"Shifter gives me the creeps."

"Nightcrawler is worse."

"How the hell do you know? You never seen him."

One-Eye said, "We can handle it, Captain."

"And Raker's cousins would be on you like flies on a horseapple."

"Soulcatcher," the Lieutenant suggested. "He *is* our patron, more or less."

The suggestion carried. The Captain said, "Contact him, One-Eye. Be ready to move when he gets here."

One-Eye nodded, grinned. He was in love. Already, tricky, nasty plots were afoot in his twisted mind.

It should have been Silent's game, really. The Captain gave it to One-Eye because he cannot come to grips with Silent's refusal to talk. That scares him for some reason.

Silent did not protest.

*   *   *

Some of our native servants are spies. We know who they are, thanks to One-Eye and Goblin. One, who knew nothing about the hair, was allowed to flee with the news that we were setting up an espionage headquarters in the free city Roses.

When you have the smaller battalions you learn guile.

Every ruler makes enemies. The Lady is no exception. The Sons of the White Rose are everywhere. . . . If one chooses sides on emotion, then the Rebel is the guy to go with. He is fighting for everything men claim to honor: freedom, independence, truth, the right. . . . All the subjective illusions, all the eternal trigger-words. We are minions of the villain of the piece. We confess the illusion and deny the substance.

There are no self-proclaimed villains, only regiments of self-proclaimed saints. Victorious historians rule where good or evil lies.

We abjure labels. We fight for money and an indefinable pride. The politics, the ethics, the moralities, are irrelevant.

One-Eye had contacted Soulcatcher. He was coming. Goblin said the old spook howled with glee. He smelled a chance to raise his stock and scuttle that of the Limper. The Ten squabble and backbite worse than spoiled children.

Winter relaxed its siege briefly. The men and native staff began clearing Meystrikt's courtyards. One of the natives disappeared. In the main hall, One-Eye and Silent looked smug over their cards. The Rebel was being told exactly what they wanted.

"What's happening on the wall?" I asked. Elmo had rigged block and tackle and was working a crennel stone loose. "What're you going to do with that block?"

"A little sculpture, Croaker. I've taken up a new hobby."

"So don't tell me. See if I care."

"Take that attitude if you want. I was going to ask if you could go after Raker with us. So you could put it in the Annals right."

"With a word about One-Eye's genius?"

"Credit where credit is due, Croaker."

"Then Silent is due a chapter, isn't he?"

He sputtered. He grumbled. He cursed. "You want to play a hand?" They had only three players, one of whom was Raven. Tonk is more interesting with four or five.

I won three hands straight.

"Don't you have anything to do? A wart to cut off, or something?"

"You asked him to play," a kibbitzing soldier observed.

"You like flies, Otto?"

"Flies?"

"Going to turn you into a frog if you don't shut your mouth."

Otto was not impressed. "You couldn't turn a tadpole into a frog."

I snickered. "You asked for it, One-Eye. When is Soulcatcher going to show?"

"When he gets here."

I nodded. There is no apparent rhyme or reason to the way the Taken do things. "Regular Cheerful Charlies today, aren't we? How much has he lost, Otto?"

Otto just smirked.

Raven won the next two hands.

One-Eye swore off talking. So much for discovering the nature of his project. Probably for the best. An explanation never made could not be overheard by the Rebel's spies.

Six hairs and a block of limestone. What the hell?

For days Silent, Goblin, and One-Eye took turns working that stone. I visited the stable occasionally. They let me watch, and growl when they would not answer questions.

The Captain, too, sometimes poked his head in, shrugged, and went back to his quarters. He was juggling strategies for a spring campaign which would throw all available Imperial might against the Rebel. His rooms were impenetrable, so thick were the maps and reports.

We meant to hurt the Rebel some once the weather turned.

Cruel it may be, but most of us enjoy what we do—and the Captain more than anyone. This is a favorite game, matching wits with a Raker. He is blind to the dead, to the burning villages, to the starving children. As is the Rebel. Two blind armies, able to see nothing but one another.

Soulcatcher came in the deep hours, amidst a blizzard which beggared the one Elmo endured. The wind wailed and howled. Snow drifted against the northeast corner of the fortress, battlement-high, and spilled over. Wood and hay stores were becoming a concern. Locals said it was the worst blizzard in history.

At its heighth, Soulcatcher came. The boom-boom-boom of his knock awakened all Meystrikt. Horns sounded. Drums rolled. The gatehouse watch screeched against the wind. They could not open the gate.

Soulcatcher came over the wall via the drift. He fell, nearly vanished in the loose snow in the forecourt. Hardly a dignified arrival for one of the Ten.

I hurried to the main hall. One-Eye, Silent, and Goblin were there already, with the fire blazing merrily. The Lieutenant appeared, followed by the Captain. Elmo and Raven came with the Captain. "Send the rest back to bed," the Lieutenant snapped.

Soulcatcher came in, removed a heavy black greatcloak, squatted before the fire. A calculatedly human gesture? I wondered.

Soulcatcher's slight body is always sheathed in black

leather. He wears that head-hiding black morion, and the black gloves and black boots. Only a couple of silver badges break the monotony. The only color about him is the uncut ruby forming the pommel of his dagger. A five-taloned claw clutches the gem to the handle of the weapon.

Small, soft curves interrupt the flatness of Soulcatcher's chest. There is a feminine flair to his hips and legs. Three of the Taken are female, but which are which only the Lady knows. We call them all he. Their sex won't ever mean a thing to us.

Soulcatcher claims to be our friend, our champion. Even so, his presence brought a different chill to the hall. The cold of him has nothing to do with climate. Even One-Eye shivers when he is around.

And Raven? I do not know. Raven seems incapable of feeling anymore, except where Darling is concerned. Someday that great stone face is going to break. I hope I am there to see it.

Soulcatcher turned his back to the fire. "So." High-pitched. "Fine weather for an adventure." Baritone. Strange sounds followed. Laughter. The Taken had made a joke.

Nobody laughed.

We were not supposed to laugh. Soulcatcher turned to One-Eye. "Tell me." This in tenor, slow and soft, with a muffled quality, as if it were coming through a thin wall. Or, as Elmo says, from beyond the grave.

There was no bluster or showman in One-Eye now. "We'll start from the beginning. Captain?"

The Captain said, "One of our informants caught wind of a meeting of the Rebel captains. One-Eye, Goblin, and Silent followed the movements of known Rebels. . . ."

"You let them run around loose?"

"They lead us to their friends."

"Of course. One of the Limper's shortcomings. No

imagination. He kills them where he finds them—along with everyone else in sight." Again that weird laughter. "Less effective, yes?" There was another sentence, but in no language I know.

The Captain nodded. "Elmo?"

Elmo told his part as he had before, word for word. He passed the tale to One-Eye, who sketched a scheme for taking Raker. I did not understand, but Soulcatcher caught it instantly. He laughed a third time.

I gathered we were going to unleash the dark side of human nature.

One-Eye took Soulcatcher to see his mystery stone. We moved closer to the fire. Silent produced a deck. There were no takers.

Sometimes I wonder how the regulars stay sane. They are around the Taken all the time. Soulcatcher is a sweet-heart compared to the others.

One-Eye and Soulcatcher returned, laughing. "Two of a kind," Elmo muttered, in a rare statement of opinion.

Soulcatcher recaptured the fire. "Well done, gentlemen. Very well done. Imaginative. This could break them in the Salient. We start for Roses when the weather breaks. A party of eight, Captain, including two of your witch men." Each sentence was followed by a break. Each was in a different voice. Weird.

I have heard those are the voices of all the people whose souls Soulcatcher has caught.

Bolder than my wont, I volunteered for the expedition. I wanted to see how Raker could be taken with hair and a block of limestone. The Limper had failed with all his furious power.

The Captain thought about it. "Okay, Croaker. One-Eye and Goblin. You, Elmo. And pick two more."

"That's only seven, Captain."

"Raven makes eight."

"Oh. Raven. Of course."

Of course. Quiet, deadly Raven would be the Captain's alter-ego. The bond between those men surpasses understanding. Guess it bothers me because Raven scares the hell out of me lately.

Raven caught the Captain's eye. His right eyebrow rose. The Captain replied with a ghost of a nod. Raven twitched a shoulder. What was the message? I could not guess.

Something unusual was in the wind. Those in the know found it delicious. Though I could not guess what it was, I knew it would be slick and nasty.

The storm broke. Soon the Roses road was open. Soulcatcher fretted. Raker had two weeks start. It would take us a week to reach Roses. One-Eye's planted tales might lose their efficacy before we arrived.

We left before dawn, the limestone block aboard a wagon. The wizards had done little but carve out a modest declivity the size of a large melon. I could not fathom its value. One-Eye and Goblin fussed over it like a groom over a new bride. One-Eye answered my questions with a big grin. Bastard.

The weather held fair. Warm winds blew out of the south. We encountered long stretches of muddy road. And I witnessed an outrageous phenomenon. Soulcatcher got down in the mud and dragged that wagon with the rest of us. That great lord of the Empire.

Roses is the queen city of the Salient, a teeming sprawl, a free city, a republic. The Lady has not seen fit to revoke its traditional autonomy. The world needs places where men of all stripes and stations can step outside the usual strictures.

So. Roses. Owning no master. Filled with agents and spies and those who live on the dark side of the law. In that environment, One-Eye claimed, his scheme had to prosper.

Roses' red walls loomed over us, dark as old blood in the light of the setting sun, when we arrived.

Goblin ambled into the room we had taken. "I found the place," he squeaked at One-Eye.

"Good."

Curious. They had not exchanged a cross word in weeks. Usually an hour without a squabble was a miracle.

Soulcatcher shifted in the shadowed corner where he remained planted like a lean black bush, a crowd softly debating with itself. "Go on."

"It's an old public square. A dozen alleys and streets going in and out. Poorly lighted at night. No reason for any traffic after dark."

"Sounds perfect," One-Eye said.

"It is. I rented a room overlooking it."

"Let's take a look," Elmo said. We all suffered from cabin fever. An exodus started. Only Soulcatcher stayed put. Perhaps he understood our need to get away.

Goblin was right about the square, apparently. "So what?" I asked. One-Eye grinned. I snapped, "Clam-lips! Play games."

"Tonight?" Goblin asked.

One-Eye nodded. "If the old spook says go."

"I'm getting frustrated," I announced. "What's going on? All you clowns do is play cards and watch Raven sharpen his knives." That went on for hours at a time, the movement of whetstone across steel sending chills down my spine. It was an omen. Raven does not do that unless he expects the situation to get nasty.

One-Eye made a sound like a cawling crow.

*   *   *

We rolled the wagon at midnight. The stablekeeper called us madmen. One-Eye gave him one of his famous grins. He drove. The rest of us walked, surrounding the wagon.

There had been changes. Something had been added. Someone had incised the stone with a message. One-Eye, probably, during one of his unexplained forays out of headquarters.

Bulky leather sacks and a stout plank table had joined the stone. The table looked capable of bearing the block. Its legs were of a dark, polished wood. Inlaid in them were symbols in silver and ivory, very complex, hieroglyphical, mystical.

"Where did you get the table?" I asked. Goblin squeaked, laughed. I growled, "Why the hell can't you tell me now?"

"Okay," One-Eye said, chuckling nastily. "We made it."

"What for?"

"To sit our rock on."

"You're not telling me anything."

"Patience, Croaker. All in due time." Bastard.

There was a strangeness about our square. It was foggy. There had been no fog anywhere else.

One-Eye stopped the wagon in the square's center. "Out with that table, boys."

"Out with you," Goblin squawked. "Think you can malinger your way through this?" He wheeled on Elmo. "Damned old cripple's always got an excuse."

"He's got a point, One-Eye." One-Eye protested. Elmo snapped, "Get your butt down off there."

One-Eye glared at Goblin. "Going to get you someday, Chubbo. Curse of impotence. How does that sound?"

Goblin was not impressed. "I'd put a curse of stupidity on you if I could improve on Nature."

"Get the damned table down," Elmo snapped.

"You nervous?" I asked. He never gets riled at their fussing. Treats it as part of the entertainment.

"Yeah. You and Raven get up there and push."

That table was heavier than it looked. It took all of us to get it off the wagon. One-Eye's faked grunts and curses did not help. I asked him how he got it on.

"Built it there, dummy," he said, then fussed at us, wanting it moved a half inch this way, then a half inch that.

"Let it be," Soulcatcher said. "We don't have time for this." His displeasure had a salutory effect. Neither Goblin nor One-Eye said another word.

We slid the stone onto the table. I stepped back, wiped sweat from my face. I was soaked. In the middle of winter. That rock radiated heat.

"The bags," Soulcatcher said. That voice sounded like a woman I would not mind meeting.

I grabbed one, grunted. It was heavy. "Hey. This is money."

One-Eye snickered. I heaved the sack into the pile under the table. A damned fortune there. I had never seen so much in one place, in fact.

"Cut the bags," Soulcatcher ordered. "Hurry it up!"

Raven slashed the sacks. Treasure dribbled onto the cobblestones. We stared, lusting in our hearts.

Soulcatcher caught One-Eye's shoulder, took Goblin's arm. Both wizards seemed to shrink. They faced table and stone. Soulcatcher said, "Move the wagon."

I still had not read the immortal message they had carved on the rock. I darted in for a look.

LET HE WHO WOULD CLAIM THIS WEALTH
SEAT THE HEAD OF THE CREATURE
RAKER
WITHIN THIS THRONE OF STONE

Ah. Aha. Plain-spoken. Straightforward. Simple. Just our style. Ha.

I stepped back, tried to guess the magnitude of Soulcatcher's investment. I spied gold amidst the hill of silver. One bag leaked uncut gems.

"The hair," Soulcatcher demanded. One-Eye produced the strands. Soulcatcher thumbed them into the walls of the head-sized cavity. He stepped back, joined hands with One-Eye and Goblin.

They made magic.

Treasure, table, and stone began to shed a golden glow.

Our archfoe was a dead man. Half the world would try to collect this bounty. It was too big to resist. His own people would turn on him.

I saw one slim chance for him. He could steal the treasure himself. Tough job, though. No Rebel Prophet could out-magic one of the Taken.

They completed their spell-casting. "Somebody test it," One-Eye said.

There was a vicious crackle when Raven's daggertip pricked the plane of the tablelegs. He cursed, scowled at his weapon. Elmo thrust with his sword. *Crackle!* The tip of his blade glowed white.

"Excellent," Soulcatcher said. "Take the wagon away."

Elmo detailed a man. The rest of us fled to the room Goblin had rented.

At first we crowded the window, willing something to happen. That palled fast. Roses did not discover the doom we had set for Raker till sunrise.

Cautious entrepreneurs found a hundred ways to go after that money. Crowds came just to see. One enterprising band started tearing up the street to dig under. Police ran them off.

Soulcatcher took a seat beside the window and never

moved. Once he told me, "Have to modify the spells. I
didn't anticipate this much ingenuity."

Surprised at my own audacity, I asked, "What's the
Lady like?" I had just finished one of my fantasy sketches.

He turned slowly, stared briefly. "Something that will
bite steel." His voice was female and catty. An odd
answer. Then, "Have to keep them from using tools."

So much for getting an eyewitness report. I should have
known better. We mortals are mere objects to the Taken.
Our curiosities are of supreme indifference. I retreated to
my secret kingdom and its spectrum of imaginary Ladies.

Soulcatcher modified the ward sorceries that night. Next
morning there were corpses in the square.

One-Eye wakened me the third night. "Got a customer."

"Hunh?"

"A guy with a head." He was pleased.

I stumbled to the window. Goblin and Raven were there
already. We crowded one side. Nobody wanted to get too
close to Soulcatcher.

A man stole across the square below. A head dangled
from his left hand. He carried it by its hair. I said, "I
wondered how long it would be before this started."

"Silence," Soulcatcher hissed. "He's out there."

"Who?"

He was patient. Remarkably patient. Another of the
Taken would have struck me down. "Raker. Don't give us
away."

I do not know how he knew. Maybe I would not want to
find out. Those things scare me.

"A sneak visit was in the scenario," Goblin whispered,
squeaking. How can he squeak when he whispers? "Raker
has to find out what he's up against. He can't do that from
anywhere else." The fat little man seemed proud.

The Captain calls human nature our sharpest blade.
Curiosity and a will to survive drew Raker into our cauldron.

Maybe he would turn it on us. We have a lot of handles sticking out ourselves.

Weeks passed. Raker came again and again, apparently content to observe. Soulcatcher told us to let him be, no matter how easy a target he made of himself.

Our mentor might be considerate of us, but he has his cruel streak. It seemed he wanted to torment Raker with the uncertainty of his fate.

"This berg is going bounty-crazy," Goblin squealed. He danced one of his jigs. "You ought to get out more, Croaker. They're turning Raker into an industry." He beckoned me into the corner farthest from Soulcatcher, opened a wallet. "Look here," he whispered.

He had a double fistful of coins. Some were gold. I observed, "You're going to be walking tilted to one side."

He grinned. Goblin grinning is a sight to behold. "Made this selling tips on where to find Raker," he whispered. With a glance toward Soulcatcher, "Bogus tips." He put a hand on my shoulder. He had to stretch up to do it. "You can get rich out there."

"I didn't know we were in this to get rich."

He scowled, his round, pale face becoming all wrinkles. "What are you? Some kind of? . . ."

Soulcatcher turned. Goblin croaked, "Just an argument about a bet, sir. Just a bet."

I laughed aloud. "Really convincing, Chubbo. Why not just hang yourself?"

He pouted, but not for long. Goblin is irrepressible. His humor breaks through in the most depressing situations. He whispered, "Shit, Croaker, you should see what One-Eye is doing. Selling amulets. Guaranteed to tell if there's a Rebel close by." A glance toward Soulcatcher. "They really work, too. Sort of."

I shook my head. "At least he'll be able to pay his card

debts." That was One-Eye all over. He had had it rough at Meystrikt, where there was no room for his usual forays into the black market.

"You guys are supposed to be planting rumors. Keeping the pot boiling, not. . . ."

"Sshh!" He glanced at Soulcatcher again. "We are. Every dive in town. Hell, the rumor mill is berserk out there. Come on. I'll show you."

"No." Soulcatcher was talking more and more. I had hopes of inveigling a real conversation.

"Your loss. I know a bookmaker taking bets on when Raker will lose his head. You got inside dope, you know."

"Scoot out of here before you lose yours."

I went to the window. A minute later Goblin scampered across the square below. He passed our trap without glancing its way.

"Let them play their games," Soulcatcher said.

"Sir?" My new approach. Brown-nosing.

"My ears are sharper than your friend realizes."

I searched the face of that black morion, trying to capture some hint of the thoughts behind the metal.

"It's of no consequence." He shifted slightly, stared past me. "The underground is paralyzed by dismay."

"Sir?"

"The mortar in that house is rotting. It'll crumble soon. That would not have happened had we taken Raker immediately. They would have made a martyr of him. The loss would have saddened them, but they would have gone on. The Circle would have replaced Raker in time for the spring campaigns."

I stared into the plaza. Why was Soulcatcher telling me this? And all in one voice. Was it the voice of the real Soulcatcher?

"Because you thought I was being cruel for cruelty's sake."

I jumped. "How did you? . . ."

Soulcatcher made a sound which passed as laughter. "No. I didn't read your mind. I know how minds work. I am the Catcher of Souls, remember?"

Do the Taken get lonely? Do they yearn for simple companionship? Friendship?

"Sometimes." This in one of the female voices. A seductive one.

I half-turned, then faced the square quickly, frightened.

Soulcatcher read that, too. He went back to Raker. "Simple elimination was never my plan. I want the hero of Forsberg to discredit himself."

Soulcatcher knew our enemy better than we suspected. Raker was playing his game. Already he had made two spectacular, vain attempts on our trap. Those failures had ruined his stock with fellow-travellers. To hear tell, Roses seethed with pro-Empire sentiment.

"He'll make a fool of himself, then we'll squash him. Like a noxious beetle."

"Don't underestimate him." What audacity. Giving advice to one of the Taken. "The Limper. . . ."

"That I won't do. I'm not the Limper. He and Raker are two of a kind. In the old times. . . . The Dominator would have made him one of us."

"What was he like?" Get him talking, Croaker. From the Dominator it is only one step to the Lady.

Soulcatcher's right hand rolled palm upward, opened, slowly made a claw. The gesture rattled me. I imagined that claw ripping at my soul. End of conversation.

Later on I told Elmo, "You know, that thing out there didn't have to be real. Anything would have done the job if the mob couldn't get to it."

Soulcatcher said, "Wrong. Raker had to know it was real."

Next morning we heard from the Captain. News, mostly.

A few Rebel partisans were surrendering their weapons in response to an amnesty offer. Some mainforcers who had come south with Raker were pulling out. The confusion had reached the Circle. Raker's failure in Roses worried them.

"Why's that?" I asked. "Nothing has really happened."

Soulcatcher replied, "It's happening on the other side. In peoples' minds." Was there a hint of smugness there? "Raker, and by extension the Circle, looks impotent. He should have yielded the Salient to another commander."

"If I was a bigtime general, I probably wouldn't admit to a screwup either," I said.

"Croaker," Elmo gasped, amazed. I do not speak my mind, usually.

"It's true, Elmo. Can you picture any general—ours or theirs—asking somebody to take over for him?"

That black morion faced me. "Their faith is dying. An army without faith in itself is beaten more surely than an army defeated in battle." When Soulcatcher gets on a subject nothing deflects him.

I had a funny feeling he might be the type to yield command to someone better able to exercise it.

"We tighten the screws now. All of you. Tell it in the taverns. Whisper it in the streets. Burn him. Drive him. Push him so hard he doesn't have time to think. I want him so desperate he tries something stupid."

I thought Soulcatcher had the right idea. This fragment of the Lady's war would not be won on any battlefield. Spring was at hand, yet fighting had not yet begun. The eyes of the Salient were locked on the free city, awaiting the outcome of this duel between Raker and the Lady's champion.

Soulcatcher observed, "It's no longer necessary to kill Raker. His credibility is dead. Now we're destroying the confidence of his movement." He resumed his vigil at the window.

Elmo said, "Captain says the Circle ordered Raker out. He wouldn't go."

"He revolted against his own revolution?"

"He wants to beat this trap."

Another facet of human nature working for our side. Overweening pride.

"Get some cards out. Goblin and One-Eye have been robbing widows and orphans again. Time to clean them out."

Raker was on his own, hunted, haunted, a whipped dog running the alleys of the night. He could trust no one. I felt sorry for him. Almost.

He was a fool. Only a fool keeps betting against the odds. The odds against Raker were getting longer by the hour.

I jerked a thumb at the darkness near the window. "Sounds like a convening of the Brotherhood of Whispers."

Raven glanced over my shoulder, said nothing. We were playing head to head Tonk, a dull time-killer of a game.

A dozen voices murmured over there. "I smell it." "You're wrong." "It's in from the south." "End it now." "Not yet." "It's time." "Needs a while longer." "Pushing our luck. The game could turn." " 'Ware pride." "It's here. The stench of it runs before it like the breath of a jackal."

"Wonder if he ever loses an argument with himself?"

Still Raven said nothing. In my more daring moods I have been trying to draw him out. Without luck. I was doing better with Soulcatcher.

Soulcatcher rose suddenly, an angry noise rising from deep inside him.

"What is it?" I asked. I was tired of Roses. I was

disgusted with Roses. Roses bored and frightened me. It was worth a man's life to go into those streets alone.

One of those spook voices was right. We were approaching a point of diminishing returns. I was developing a grudging admiration for Raker myself. The man refused to surrender or run.

"What is it?" I asked again

"The Limper. He's in Roses."

"Here? Why?"

"He smells a big kill. He wants to steal the credit."

"You mean muscle in on our action?"

"That's his style."

"Wouldn't the Lady? . . ."

"This is Roses. She's a long way off. And she doesn't care who gets him."

Politics among the Lady's viceroys. It is a strange world. I do not understand people outside the Company.

We lead a simple life. No thinking required. The Captain takes care of that. We just follow orders. For most of us the Black Company is a hiding place, a refuge from yesterday, a place to become a new man.

"What do we do?" I asked.

"I'll handle the Limper." He began seeing to his apparel.

Goblin and One-Eye staggered in. They were so drunk they had to prop each other up. "Shit," Goblin squeaked. "Snowing again. Goddamned snow. I thought winter was over."

One-Eye burst into song. Something about the beauties of winter. I could not follow him. His speech was slurred and he had forgotten half the words.

Goblin fell into a chair, forgetting One-Eye. One-Eye collapsed at his feet. He vomited on Goblin's boots, tried to continue his song. Goblin muttered, "Where the hell is everybody?"

"Out carousing around." I exchanged looks with Raven. "Do you believe this? Those two getting drunk together?"

"Where you going, old spook?" Goblin squeaked at Soulcatcher. Soulcatcher went out without answering. "Bastard. Hey. One-Eye, old buddy. That right? Old spook a bastard?"

One-Eye levered himself off the floor, looked around. I don't think he was seeing with the eye he had. "S'right." He scowled at me. "Bassard. All bassard." Something struck him funny. He giggled.

Goblin joined him. When Raven and I did not get the joke, he put on a very dignified face and said, "Not our kind in here, old buddy. Warmer out in the snow." He helped One-Eye stand. They staggered out the door.

"Hope they don't do anything stupid. More stupid. Like show off. They'll kill themselves."

"Tonk," Raven said. He spread his cards. Those two might not have come in for all the response he showed.

Ten or fifty hands later one of the soldiers we had brought burst in. "You seen Elmo?" he demanded.

I glanced at him. Snow was melting in his hair. He was pale, scared. "No. What happened, Hagop?"

"Somebody stabbed Otto. I think it was Raker. I run him off."

"Stabbed? He dead?" I started looking for my kit. Otto would need me more than he would need Elmo.

"No. He's cut bad. Lot of blood."

"Why didn't you bring him?"

"Couldn't carry him."

He was drunk too. The attack on his friend had sobered him some, but that would not last. "You sure it was Raker?" Was the old fool trying to hit back?

"Sure. Hey, Croaker. Come on. He's gonna die."

"I'm coming. I'm coming."

"Wait." Raven was pawing through his gear. "I'm

going." He balanced a pair of finely-honed knives, debating a choice. He shrugged, stuck both inside his belt. "Get yourself a cloak, Croaker. It's cold out there."

While I found one he grilled Hagop about Otto's whereabouts, told him to stay put till Elmo showed. Then, "Let's go, Croaker."

Down the stairs. Into the streets. Raven's walk is deceptive. He never seems hurried, but you have to hustle to stay up.

Snowing was not the half of it. Even where the streets were lighted you could not see twenty feet. It was six inches deep already. Heavy, wet stuff. But the temperature was falling, and a wind was coming up. Another blizzard? Damn! Hadn't we had enough?

We found Otto a quarter block from where he was supposed to be. He had dragged himself under some steps. Raven went right to him. How he knew where to look I will never know. We carried Otto to the nearest light. He could not help himself. He was out.

I snorted. "Dead drunk. Only danger was freezing to death." He had blood all over him but his wound was not bad. Needed some stitches, that is all. We lugged him back to the room. I stripped him and got sewing while he was in no shape to bitch.

Otto's sidekick was asleep. Raven kicked him till he woke up. "I want the truth," Raven said. "How did it happen?"

Hagop told it, insisting, "It was Raker, man. It was Raker."

I doubted that. So did Raven. But when I finished my needlepoint, Raven said, "Get your sword, Croaker." He had the hunter look. I did not want to go out again, but even less did I want to argue with Raven when he was in that mood. I got my swordbelt.

The air was colder. The wind was stronger. The snowflakes were smaller and more biting when they hit my cheek. I stalked along behind Raven, wondering what the hell we were doing.

He found the place where Otto was knifed. New snow had not yet obliterated the marks on the old. Raven squatted, stared. I wondered what he saw. There was not enough light to tell anything, so far as I could see.

"Maybe he wasn't lying," he said at last. He stared into the darkness of the alley whence the attacker had come.

"How do you know?"

He did not tell me. "Come on." He stalked into the alley.

I do not like alleys. I especially do not like them in cities like Roses, where they harbor every evil known to man, and probably a few still undiscovered. But Raven was going in. . . . Raven wanted my help. . . . Raven was my brother in the Black Company. . . . But, damned, a hot fire and warm wine would have been nicer.

I do not think I spent more than three or four hours exploring the city. Raven had gone out less than I had. Yet he seemed to know where he was going. He led me up side streets and down alleys, across thoroughfares and over bridges. Roses is pierced by three rivers, and a web of canals connect them. The bridges are one of Roses' claims to fame.

Bridges did not intrigue me at the moment. I was preoccupied with keeping up and trying to stay warm. My feet were hunks of ice. Snow kept getting into my boots, and Raven was in no mood to stop every time that happened.

On and on. Miles and hours. I never saw so many slums and stews. . . .

"Stop!" Raven flung an arm across my path.

"What?"

"Quiet." He listened. I listened. I did not hear a thing. I had not seen much during our headlong rush, either.

How could Raven be tracking Otto's assailant? I did not doubt that he was, I just could not figure it.

Truth told, nothing Raven did surprised me. Nothing had since the day I watched him strangle his wife.

"We're almost up with him." He peered into the blowing snow. "Go straight ahead, the pace we've been going. You'll catch him in a couple blocks."

"What? Where're you going?" I was carping at a fading shadow. "Damn you." I took a deep breath, cursed again, drew my sword, and started forward. All I could think was, How am I going to explain if we've got the wrong man?

Then I saw him in the light from a tavern door. A tall, lean man shuffling dispiritedly, oblivious to his surroundings. Raker? How would I know? Elmo and Otto were the only ones who had been along on the farm raid. . . .

Came the dawn. Only they could identify Raker for the rest of us. Otto was wounded and Elmo had not been heard from. . . . Where was he? Under a blanket of snow in some alley, cold as this hideous night?

My fright retreated before anger.

I sheathed my sword and drew a dagger. I kept it hidden inside my cloak. The figure ahead did not glance back as I overtook it, drew even.

"Rough night, eh, old-timer?"

He grunted noncommittally. Then he looked at me, eyes narrowing, when I fell into step beside him. He eased away, watched me closely. There was no fear in his eyes. He was sure of himself. Not the sort of old man you found wandering the streets of the slums. They are scared of their own shadows.

"What do you want?" It was a calm, straightforward question.

He did not have to be frightened. I was scared enough for both of us. "You knifed a friend of mine, Raker."

He halted. A glint of something strange showed in his eye. "The Black Company?"

I nodded.

He stared, eyes narrowing thoughtfully. "The physician. You're the physician. The one they call Croaker."

"Glad to meet you." I am sure my voice sounded stronger than I felt.

I thought, what the hell do I do now?

Raker flung his cloak open. A short stabbing sword thrust my way. I slid aside, opened my own cloak, dodged again and tried to draw my sword.

Raker froze. He caught my eye. His eyes seemed to grow larger, larger. . . . I was falling into twin grey pools. . . . A smile tugged at the corners of his mouth. He stepped toward me, blade rising. . . .

And grunted suddenly. A look of total amazement came over his face. I shook his spell, stepped back, came to guard.

Raker turned slowly, faced the darkness. Raven's knife protruded from his back. Raker reached back and withdrew it. A mewl of pain passed his lips. He glared at the knife, then, ever so slowly, began to sing.

"Move, Croaker!"

A spell! Fool! I had forgotten what Raker was. I charged. Raven arrived at the same instant.

I looked at the body. "Now what?"

Raven knelt, produced another knife. It had a serrated edge. "Somebody claims Soulcatcher's bounty."

"He'd have a fit."

"You going to tell him?"

"No. But what will we do with it?" There had been times when the Black Company was prosperous, but never when it was rich. Accumulation of wealth is not our purpose.

"I can use some of it. Old debts. The rest. . . . Divide it up. Send it back to Beryl. Whatever. It's there. Why let the Taken keep it?"

I shrugged. "Up to you. I just hope Soulcatcher don't think we crossed him."

"Only you and me know. I won't tell him." He brushed the snow off the old man's face. Raker was cooling fast.

Raven used his knife.

I am a physician. I have removed limbs. I am a soldier. I have seen some bloody battlefields. Nevertheless, I was queasy. Decapitating a dead man did not seem right.

Raven secured our grisly trophy inside his cloak. It did not bother him. Once, on the way to our part of town, I asked, "Why did we go after him, anyway?"

He did not answer immediately. Then, "The Captain's last letter said to get it over with if I had the chance."

As we neared the square, Raven said, "Go upstairs. See if the spook is there. If he's not, send the soberest man after our wagon. You come back here."

"Right." I sighed, hurried to our quarters. Anything for a little warmth.

The snow was a foot deep now. I was afraid my feet were permanently damaged.

"Where the hell have you been?" Elmo demanded when I stumbled through the doorway. "Where's Raven?"

I looked around. No Soulcatcher. Goblin and One-Eye were back, dead to the world. Otto and Hagop were snoring like giants. "How's Otto?"

"Doing all right. What've you been up to?"

I settled myself beside our fire, prized my boots off. My feet were blue and numb but not frozen. Soon they tingled painfully. My legs ached from all that walking through the snow, too. I told Elmo the whole story.

"You killed him?"

"Raven said the Captain wants done with the project."

"Yeah. I didn't figure Raven would go cut his throat."

"Where's Soulcatcher?"

"Hasn't been back." He grinned. "I'll get the wagon. Don't tell anybody else. Too many big mouths." He flung his cloak about his shoulders, stamped out.

My hands and feet felt halfway human. I scooted over and nabbed Otto's boots. He was about my size, and he did not need them.

Out into the night again. Morning, almost. Dawn was due soon.

If I expected any remonstrance from Raven I was disappointed. He just looked at me. I think he actually shivered. I remember thinking, maybe he is human after all. "Had to change my boots. Elmo is getting the wagon. The rest of them are passed out."

Soulcatcher?"

"Not back yet."

"Let's plant this seed." He strode into the swirling flakes. I hurried after him.

The snow had not collected on our trap. It sat there glowing gold. Water puddled beneath it and trickled away to become ice.

"You think Soulcatcher will know when this thing gets discharged?" I asked.

"It's a good bet. Goblin and One-Eye, too."

"The place could burn down around those two and they wouldn't turn over."

"Nevertheless. . . . Sshh! Somebody out there. Go that way." He moved the other direction, circling.

What am I doing this for? I wondered as I skulked through the snow, weapon in hand. I ran into Raven. "See anything?"

He glared into the darkness. "Somebody was here." He sniffed the air, turned his head slowly right and left. He took a dozen quick steps, pointed down.

He was right. The trail was fresh. The departing half looked hurried. I stared at those marks. "I don't like it, Raven." Our visitor's spoor indicated that he dragged his right foot. "The Limper."

"We don't know for sure."

"Who else? Where's Elmo?"

We returned to the Raker trap, waited impatiently. Raven paced. He muttered. I could not recall ever having seen him this unsettled. Once, he said, "The Limper isn't Soulcatcher."

Really. Soulcatcher is almost human. Limper is the sort that enjoys tormenting babies.

A jangle of traces and squeak of poorly greased wheels entered the plaza. Elmo and the wagon appeared. Elmo pulled up and jumped down.

"Where the hell you been?" Fear and weariness made me cross.

"Takes time to dig out a stableboy and get a team ready. What's the matter? What happened?"

"The Limper was here."

"Oh, shit. What did he do?"

"Nothing. He just. . . ."

"Let's move," Raven snapped. "Before he comes back." He took the head to the stone. The wardspells might not have existed. He fitted our trophy into the waiting declivity. The golden glow winked out. Snowflakes began accumulating on head and stone.

"Let's go," Elmo gasped. "We don't have much time."

I grabbed a sack and heaved it into the wagon. Thoughtful Elmo had laid out a tarp to keep loose coins from dribbling between the floorboards.

Raven told me to rake up the loose stuff under the table. "Elmo, dump some of those sacks out and give them to Croaker."

They heaved bags. I scrambled after loose coins.

"One minute gone," Raven said. Half the bags were in the wagon.

"Too much loose stuff," I complained.

"We'll leave it if we have to."

"What're we going to do with it? How will we hide it?"

"In the hay in the stable," Raven said. "For now. Later we put a false bed in the wagon. Two minutes gone."

"What about wagon tracks?" Elmo asked. "He could follow them to the stable."

"Why should he care in the first place?" I wondered aloud.

Raven ignored me. He asked Elmo, "You didn't conceal them coming here?"

"Didn't think of it."

"Damn!"

All the sacks were aboard. Elmo and Raven helped with the loose stuff.

"Three minutes," Raven said, then, "Quiet!" He listened. "Soulcatcher couldn't be here already, could he? No. The Limper again. Come on. You drive, Elmo. Head for a thoroughfare. Lose us in traffic. I'll follow you. Croaker, go try to cover Elmo's backtrail."

"Where is he?" Elmo asked, staring into the falling snow.

Raven pointed. "We'll have to lose him. Or he'll take it away. Go on, Croaker. Get moving. Elmo."

"Get up!" Elmo snapped his traces. The wagon creaked away.

I ducked under the table and stuffed my pockets, then ran away from where Raven said the Limper was.

I do not know that I had much luck obscuring Elmo's backtrail. I think we were helped more by morning traffic than by anything I did. I did get rid of the stableboy. I gave him a sock full of gold and silver, more than he could make in years of stable work, and asked him if he could lose himself. Away from Roses, preferably. He told me, "I won't even stop to get my things." He dropped his pitchfork and headed out, never to be seen again.

I hied myself back to our room.

Everyone was sleeping but Otto. "Oh, Croaker," he said. " 'Bout time."

"Pain?"

"Yeah."

"Hangover?"

"That too."

"Let's see what we can do. How long you been awake?"

"An hour, I guess."

"Soulcatcher been here?"

"No. What happened to him, anyway?"

"I don't know."

"Hey. Those are my boots. What the hell do you think you're doing, wearing my boots?"

"Take it easy. Drink this."

He drank. "Come on. What're you doing wearing my boots?"

I removed the boots and set them near the fire, which had burned quite low. Otto kept after me while I added coal. "If you don't calm down you're going to rip your stitches."

I will say this for our people. They pay attention when my advice is medical. Angry as he was, he lay back, forced himself to lie still. He did not stop cussing me.

I shed my wet things and donned a nightshirt I found lying around. I do not know where it came from. It was too short. I put on a pot of tea, then turned to Otto. "Let's take a closer look." I dragged my kit over.

I was cleaning around the wound and Otto was cursing

softly when I heard the sound. *Scrape-clump, scrape-clump*. It stopped outside the door.

Otto sensed my fear. "What's the matter?"

"It's. . . ." The door opened behind me. I glanced back. I had guessed right.

The Limper went to the table, dropped into a chair, surveyed the room. His gaze skewered me. I wondered if he recalled what I had done to him in Oar.

Inanely, I said, "I just started tea."

He stared at the wet boots and cloak, then at each man in the room. Then at me again.

The Limper is not big. Meeting him in the street, not knowing what he is, you would not be impressed. Like Soulcatcher, he wears a single color, a dingy brown. He was ragged. His face was concealed by a battered leather mask which drooped. Tangled threads of hair protruded from under his hood and around his mask. It was grey peppered with black.

He did not say a word. Just sat there and stared. Not knowing what else to do, I finished tending Otto, then made the tea. I poured three tin cups, gave one to Otto, set one before the Limper, took the third myself.

What now? No excuse to be busy. Nowhere to sit but at that table. . . . Oh, shit!

The Limper removed his mask. He raised the tin cup. . . .

I could not tear my gaze away.

His was the face of a dead man, of a mummy improperly preserved. His eyes were alive and baleful, yet directly beneath one was a patch of flesh which had rotted. Beneath his nose, at the right corner of his mouth, a square inch of lip was missing, revealing gum and yellowed teeth.

The Limper sipped tea, met my eye, and smiled.

I nearly dribbled down my leg.

I went to the window. There was some light out there

now, and the snowfall was weakening, but I could not see the stone.

The stamp of boots sounded on the stair. Elmo and Raven shoved into the room. Elmo growled, "Hey, Croaker, how the hell did you get rid of that. . ." His words grew smaller as he recognized the Limper.

Raven gave me a questioning look. The Limper turned. I shrugged when his back was to me. Raven moved to one side, began removing his wet things.

Elmo got the idea. He went the other way, stripped beside the fire. "Damn, it's good to get out of those. How's the boy, Otto?"

"There's fresh tea," I said.

Otto replied, "I hurt all over, Elmo."

The Limper peered at each of us, and at One-Eye and Goblin, who had yet to stir. "So. Soulcatcher brings the Black Company's best." His voice was a whisper, yet it filled the room. "Where is he?"

Raven ignored him. He donned dry breeches, sat beside Otto, double-checked my handiwork. "Good job of stitching, Croaker."

"I get plenty of practice with this outfit."

Elmo shrugged in response to the Limper. He drained his cup, poured tea all around, then filled the pot from one of the pitchers. He planted a boot in One-Eye's ribs while the Limper glared at Raven.

"You!" the Limper snapped. "I haven't forgotten what you did in Opal. Nor during the campaign in Forsberg."

Raven settled with his back against the wall. He produced one of his more wicked knives and began cleaning his fingernails. He smiled. At the Limper, he smiled, and there was mockery in his eyes.

Didn't anything scare that man?

"What did you do with the money? That wasn't Soulcatcher's. The Lady gave it to me."

I took courage from Raven's defiance. "Aren't you supposed to be in Elm? The Lady ordered you out of the Salient."

Anger distorted that wretched face. A scar ran down his forehead and left cheek. It stood out. Supposedly it continued down his left breast. The blow had been struck by the White Rose herself.

The Limper rose. And that damned Raven said, "Got the cards, Elmo? The table is free."

The Limper scowled. The tension level was rising fast. He snapped, "I want that money. It's mine. Your choice is to cooperate or not. I don't think you'll enjoy it if you don't."

"You want it, you go get it," Raven said. "Catch Raker. Chop off his head. Take it to the stone. That ought to be easy for the Limper. Raker is only a bandit. What chance would he stand against the Limper?"

I thought the Taken would explode. He did not. For an instant he was baffled.

He was not off balance long. "All right. If you want it the hard way." His smile was wide and cruel.

The tension was near the snapping point.

A shadow moved in the open doorway. A lean, dark figure appeared, stared at the Limper's back. I sighed in relief.

The Limper spun. For a moment the air seemed to crackle between the Taken.

From the corner of one eye I noted that Goblin was sitting up. His fingers were dancing in complex rhythms. One-Eye, facing the wall, was whispering into his bedroll. Raven reversed his knife for a throw. Elmo got a grip on the tea pot, ready to fling hot water.

There was no missile within grabbing distance of me.

What the hell could I contribute? A chronicle of the blowup afterward, if I survived?

Soulcatcher made a tiny gesture, stepped around the Limper, deposited himself in his usual chair. He flung a toe out, hooked one of the chairs away from the table, put his feet up. He stared at the Limper, his fingers steepled before his mouth. "The Lady sent a message. In case I ran into you. She wants to see you." Soulcatcher used only one voice throughout. A hard female voice. "She wants to ask you about the uprising in Elm."

The Limper jerked. One hand, extended over the table, twitched nervously. "Uprising? In Elm?"

"Rebels attacked the palace and barracks."

The Limper's leathery face lost color. The twitching of his hand became more pronounced.

Soulcatcher said, "She wants to know why you weren't there to head them off."

The Limper stayed about three seconds more. In that time his face became grotesque. Seldom have I seen such naked fear. Then he spun and fled.

Raven flipped his knife. It stuck in the doorframe. The Limper did not notice.

Soulcatcher laughed. This was not the laugh of earlier days, but a deep, harsh, solid, vindictive laughter. He rose, turned to the window. "Ah. Someone has claimed our prize? When did that happen?"

Elmo masked his response by going to close the door. Raven said, "Toss me my knife, Elmo." I eased up beside Soulcatcher, looked out. The snowfall had ceased. The stone was visible. Cold, unglowing, with an inch of white on top.

"I don't know." I hoped I sounded sincere. "The snow was heavy all night. Last time I looked—before *he* showed up—I couldn't see a thing. Maybe I'd better go down there."

"Don't bother." He adjusted his chair so he could watch the square. Later, after he had accepted tea from Elmo and finished it—concealing his face by turning away—he mused, "Raker eliminated. His vermin in panic. And, sweeter still, the Limper embarrassed again. Not a bad job."

"Was that true?" I asked. "About Elm?"

"Every word," in a fey, merry voice. "One does wonder how the Rebel knew the Limper was out of town. And how Shapeshifter caught wind of the trouble quickly enough to show up and quash the uprising before it amounted to anything." Another pause. "No doubt the Limper will ponder that while he is recuperating." He laughed again, more softly, more darkly.

Elmo and I busied ourselves preparing breakfast. Otto usually handled the cooking, so we had an excuse for breaking routine. After a time, Soulcatcher observed, "There's no point to you people staying here. Your Captain's prayers have been answered."

"We can go?" Elmo asked.

"No reason to stay, is there?"

One-Eye had reasons. We ignored them.

"Start packing after breakfast," Elmo told us.

"You're going to travel in this weather?" One-Eye demanded.

"Captain wants us back."

I took Soulcatcher a platter of scrambled eggs. I do not know why. He did not eat often, and breakfast almost never. But he accepted it, turned his back.

I looked out the window. The mob had discovered the change. Someone had brushed the snow off Raker's face. His eyes were open, seemed to be watching. Weird.

Men were scrambling around under the table, fighting over the coins we had left behind. The pileup seethed like maggots in a putrid corpse. "Somebody ought to do him honor," I murmured. "He was a hell of an opponent."

"You have your Annals," Soulcatcher told me. And, "Only a conquerer bothers to honor a fallen foe."

I was headed for my own plate by then. I wondered what he meant, but a hot meal was more important at the moment.

They were all down at the stable except me and Otto. They were going to bring the wagon around for the wounded soldier. I had given him something to get him through the rough handling to come.

They were taking their time. Elmo wanted to rig a canopy to shield Otto from the weather. I played solitaire while I waited.

Out of nowhere, Soulcatcher said, "She's *very* beautiful, Croaker. Young-looking. Fresh. Dazzling. With a heart of flint. The Limper is a warm puppy by comparison. Pray you never catch her eye."

Soulcatcher stared out the window. I wanted to ask questions, but none would come at that moment. Damn. I really wasted a chance then.

What color was her hair? Her eyes? How did she smile? It all meant a lot to me when I could not know.

Soulcatcher rose, donned his cloak. "If only for the Limper, it's been worth it," he said. He paused at the door, pierced me with his stare. "You and Elmo and Raven. Drink a toast to me. Hear?"

Then he was gone.

Elmo came in a minute later. We lifted Otto and started back to Meystrikt. My nerves were not worth a damn for a long time.

Chapter Four: WHISPER

The engagement gave us the most gain for least effort of any I can remember. It was pure serendipity that went one hundred percent our way. It was a disaster for the Rebel.

We were in flight from the Salient, where the Lady's defenses had collapsed almost overnight. Running with us were five or six hundred regulars who had lost their units. For speed's sake, the Captain had chosen to cut straight through the Forest of Cloud to Lords, instead of following the longer southern road around.

A Rebel mainforce battalion was a day or two behind us. We could have turned and whipped them, but the Captain wanted to give them the slip instead. I liked his thinking. The fighting around Roses had been grim. Thousands had fallen. With so many extra bodies attaching themselves to the Company, I had been losing men for lack of time to treat them.

Our orders were to report to Nightcrawler at Lords. Soulcatcher thought Lords would be the target of the next

Rebel thrust. Tired as we were, we expected to see more bitter fighting before winter slowed the war's pace.

"Croaker! Lookee here!" Whitey came charging toward where I sat with the Captain and Silent and one or two others. He had a naked woman draped over his shoulder. She might have been attractive had she not been so thoroughly abused.

"Not bad, Whitey. Not bad," I said, and went back to my journal. Behind Whitey the whooping and screaming continued. The men were harvesting the fruits of victory.

"They're barbarians," the Captain observed without rancor.

"Got to let them cut loose sometimes," I reminded him. "Better here than with the people of Lords."

The Captain agreed reluctantly. He just does not have much stomach for plunder and rape, much as they are part of our business. I think he is a secret romantic, at least when females are involved.

I tried to soften his mood. "They asked for it, taking up arms."

Bleakly, he asked me, "How long has this been going on, Croaker? Seems like forever, doesn't it? Can you even remember a time when you weren't a soldier? What's the point? Why are we even here? We keep winning battles, but the Lady is losing the war. Why don't they just call the whole thing off and go home?"

He was partially right. Since Forsberg it has been one retreat after another, though we have done well. The Salient had been secure till Shapeshifter and the Limper got into the act.

Our latest retreat had brought us stumbling into this Rebel base camp. We presumed it was the main training and staging center for the campaign against Nightcrawler. Luckily, we spotted the Rebel before he spotted us. We surrounded the place and roared in before dawn. We were badly outnumbered, but the Rebel did not put up much of a fight. Most were green volunteers. The startling aspect was the presence of an amazon regiment.

We had heard of them, of course. There were several in the east, around Rust, where the fighting is more bitter and sustained than here. This was our first encounter. It left the men disdainful of women warriors, despite their having fought better than their male compatriots.

Smoke began drifting our way. The men were firing the barracks and headquarters buildings. The Captain muttered, "Croaker, go make sure those fools don't fire the forest."

I rose, picked up my bag, ambled down into the din.

There were bodies everywhere. The fools must have felt completely safe. They hadn't put up a stockade or trenched around the encampment. Stupid. That is the first thing you do, even when you *know* there is no enemy within a hundred miles. You put a roof over your head later. Wet is better than dead.

I should be used to this. I have been with the Company a long time. And it does bother me less than it used to. I have hung armor plate over my moral soft spots. But I still try to avoid looking at the worst.

You who come after me, scribbling these Annals, by now realize that I shy off portraying the whole truth about our band of blackguards. You know they are vicious, violent, and ignorant. They are complete barbarians, living out their cruelest fantasies, their behavior tempered only by the presence of a few decent men. I do not often show that side because these men are my brethren, my family, and I was taught young not to speak ill of kin. The old lessons die hardest.

Raven laughs when he reads my accounts. "Sugar and spice," he calls them, and threatens to take the Annals away and write the stories the way he sees them happen.

Hardass Raven. Mocking me. And who was that out there roaming around the camp, breaking it up wherever the men were amusing themselves with a little torture? Who had a ten year old girl trailing him on an old jack mule? Not Croaker, brothers. Not Croaker. Croaker isn't no romantic. That is a passion reserved for the Captain and Raven.

Naturally, Raven has become the Captain's best friend. They sit around together like a couple of rocks, talking about the same things boulders do. They are content just to share one another's company.

Elmo was leading the arsonists. They were older Company men who had sated their less intense hungers for flesh. Those still mauling the ladies were mostly our young regular hangers-on.

They had given the Rebel a good fight at Roses, but he had been too strong. Half the Circle of Eighteen had ranged themselves against us there. We had had only the Limper and Shapeshifter on our side. Those two spent more time trying to sabotage one another than trying to repel the Circle. Result, a debacle. The Lady's most humiliating defeat in a decade.

The Circle pulls together most of the time. They do not spend more energy abusing one another than they spend on their enemies.

"Hey! Croaker!" One-Eye called. "Join the fun." He tossed a burning brand through a barracks doorway. The building promptly exploded. Heavy oaken shutters blew off the windows. A gout of flame enveloped One-Eye. He came charging out, kinky hair smouldering below the band of his weird, floppy hat. I wrestled him down, used that hat to slap his hair. "All right. All right," he growled. "You don't have to enjoy yourself so damned much."

Unable to stifle a grin, I helped him up. "You all right?"

"Singed," he said, assuming that air of phony dignity cats adopt after some particularly inept performance. Something like, "That's what I meant to do all along."

The fire roared. Pieces of thatch soared and bobbed over the building. I observed, "The Captain sent me to make sure you clowns didn't start a forest fire." Just then Goblin ambled around the side of the flaming building. His broad mouth stretched in a smirk.

One-Eye took one look and shrieked. "You maggot brain! You set me up for that." He let out a spine-tingling howl and started dancing. The roar of the flames deepened, became rhythmic. Soon it seemed I could see something prancing among the flames behind the windows.

Goblin saw it too. His smirk vanished. He gulped, went white, began a little dance of his own. He and One-Eye howled and squawked and virtually ignored one another.

A watering trough disgorged its contents, which arced through the air and splashed the flames. The contents of a water barrel followed. The roar of the fire dwindled.

One-Eye pranced over and took a poke at Goblin, trying to break his concentration. Goblin weaved and bobbed and squeaked and kept on dancing. More water hit the fire.

"What a pair."

I turned. Elmo had come over to watch. "A pair indeed," I replied. Fussing, feuding, whining, they could be an allegory of their bigger brethren in the trade. Except their conflict does not run half to the bone, like that between Shifter and the Limper. When you slice through the fog, you find that these two are friends. There are no friends among the Taken.

"Got something to show you," Elmo said. He would not say anything more. I nodded and followed him.

Goblin and One-Eye kept at it. Goblin appeared to be ahead. I stopped worrying about the fire.

*   *   *

"You figured how to read these northern chicken tracks?" Elmo asked. He had led me into what must have been the headquarters for the whole camp. He indicated a mountain of papers his men had piled on the floor, evidently as tinder for another fire.

"I think I can puzzle it out."

"Thought you might find something in this stuff."

I selected a paper at random. It was a copy of an order directing a specific Rebel mainforce battalion to filter into Lords and disappear into the homes of local sympathizers till called to strike at Lords' defenders from within. It was signed *Whisper*. A list of contacts was appended.

"I'll say," I said, suddenly short of breath. That one order betrayed a half-dozen Rebel secrets, and implied several more. "I'll say." I grabbed another. Like the first, it was a directive to a specific unit. Like the first, it was a window into the heart of current Rebel strategy. "Get the Captain," I told Elmo. "Get Goblin and One-Eye and the Lieutenant and anybody else who maybe ought to be. . . ."

I must have looked weird. Elmo wore a strange, nervous expression when he interrupted. "What the hell is it, Croaker?"

"All the orders and plans for the campaign against Lords. The complete order of battle." But that was not the bottom line. That I was going to save for the Captain himself. "And hurry. Minutes might be critical. And stop them from burning anything like this. For Hell's sake, stop them. We've hit paydirt. Don't send it up in smoke."

Elmo slammed through the door. I heard his bellows fade into the distance. A good sergeant, Elmo. He does not waste time asking questions. Grunting, I settled myself on the floor and began scanning documents.

The door creaked. I did not look up. I was in a fever, glancing at documents as fast as I could yank them off the pile, sorting them into smaller stacks. Muddy boots appeared at the edge of my vision. "Can you read these, Raven?" I had recognized his step.

"Can I? Yes."

"Help me see what we've got here."

Raven settled himself opposite me. The pile lay between us, nearly blocking our view of one another. Darling positioned herself behind him, out of his way but well within the shadow of his protection. Her quiet, dull eyes still reflected the horror of that far village.

In some ways Raven is a paradigm for the Company. The difference between him and the rest of us is that he is a little more of everything, a little bigger than life. Maybe, by being the newcomer, the only brother from the north, he is symbolic of our life in the Lady's service. His moral agonies have become our moral agonies. His silent refusal to howl and beat his breast in adversity is ours as well. We prefer to speak with the metallic voice of our arms.

Enough. Why venture into the meaning of it all? Elmo had struck paydirt. Raven and I went sifting for nuggets.

Goblin and One-Eye drifted in. Neither could read the northern script. They started to amuse themselves by sending sourceless shadows chasing one another around the walls. Raven gave them a nasty look. Their ceaseless clowning and bickering can be tiresome when you have something on your mind.

They looked at him, dropped the game, sat down quietly, almost like children admonished. Raven has that knack, that energy, that impact of personality, to make men, more dangerous than he, shudder in his cold dark wind.

The Captain arrived, accompanied by Elmo and Silent. Through the doorway I glimpsed several men hanging around. Funny the way they smell things shaping up.

"What have you got, Croaker?" the Captain asked.

I figured he had milked Elmo dry, so I got straight to the kicker. "These orders." I tapped one of my stacks.

"All these reports." I tapped another. "They're all signed by Whisper. We're kicking up the veggies in Whisper's private garden." My voice was up in the high squeak range.

For a while nobody said anything. Goblin made a few squeaky noises when Candy and the other sergeants rushed in. Finally, the Captain asked Raven, "That right?"

Raven nodded. "Judging by the documents, she's been in and out since early spring."

The Captain folded his hands, began pacing. He looked like a tired old monk on his way to evening prayer.

Whisper is the best known of the Rebel generals. Her stubborn genius has held the eastern front together despite the best efforts of the Ten. She is also the most dangerous of the Circle of Eighteen. She is known for the thoroughness with which she plans campaigns. In a war which, too often, resembles armed chaos on both sides, her forces stand out for their tight organization, discipline, and clarity of purpose.

The Captain mused, "She's supposed to be commanding the Rebel army at Rust. Right?" The struggle for Rust was three years old. Rumor had hundreds of square miles laid waste. During the winter past both sides had been reduced to eating their own dead to survive.

I nodded. The question was rhetorical. He was thinking out loud.

"And Rust has been a killing ground for years. Whisper won't break. The Lady won't back off. But if Whisper is coming here, then the Circle has decided to let Rust fall."

I added, "It means they're shifting from an eastern to a northern strategy." The north remains the Lady's weak flank. The west is prostrate. The Lady's allies rule the sea to the south. The north has been ignored since the Empire's frontiers reached the great forests above Forsberg. It is in the north that the Rebel has managed his most spectacular successes.

The Lieutenant observed, "They have the momentum, with Forsberg taken, the Salient overrun, Roses gone, and Rye besieged. There are Rebel mainforcers headed for Wist and Jane. They'll be stopped, but the Circle must know that. So they're dancing on the other foot and coming at Lords. If Lords goes, they're almost to the edge of the Windy Country. Cross the Windy Country, climb the Stair of Tear, and they're looking down at Charm from a hundred miles away."

I continued scanning and sorting. "Elmo, you might look around and see if you can come up with anything else. She might have something tucked away."

"Use One-Eye, Goblin, and Silent," Raven suggested. "Better chance of finding something."

The Captain okayed the proposal. He told the Lieutenant, "Get that business out there wrapped up. Carp, you and Candy get the men ready to move out. Match, double your perimeter guard."

"Sir?" Candy asked.

"You don't want to be here when Whisper gets back, do you? Goblin, come back here. Get ahold of Soulcatcher. This goes to the top. Now."

Goblin made an awful face, then went into a corner and began murmuring to himself. It was a quiet little sorcery—to start.

The Captain rolled on. "Croaker, you and Raven pack these documents when you're done. We'll want them along."

"I maybe better save the best out for Catcher," I said. "Some will need immediate attention if we're to get any use out of them. I mean, something will have to be done before Whisper can put the word out."

He cut me off. "Right. I'll send you a wagon. Don't

dilly-dally.'' He looked grey around the edges as he stalked outside.

A new strain of terror entered the screaming and shouting outside. I untangled my aching legs and went to the door. They were herding the Rebels together on their drill field. The prisoners sensed the Company's sudden eagerness to cut and run. They thought they were about to die just minutes before salvation arrived.

Shaking my head, I returned to my reading. Raven gave me a look that might have meant he shared my pain. On the other hand, it might have contained contempt for my weakness. With Raven it is hard to tell.

One-Eye shoved through the door, stomped over, dumped an armload of bundles wrapped in oilskin. Moist clods clung to them. ''You were right. We dug these up behind her sleeping quarters.''

Goblin let out a long, shrill screech as chilling as an owl's when you are alone in the woods at midnight. One-Eye charged the sound.

Such moments make me doubt the sincerity of their animosity.

Goblin moaned, ''He's in the Tower. He's with the Lady. I see Her through his eyes . . . his eyes . . . his eyes. . . . The darkness! Oh, God, the darkness! No! Oh, God, no! No!'' His words twisted into a shriek of pure terror. That faded to, ''The Eye. I see the Eye. It's looking right through me.''

Raven and I exchanged frowns and shrugs. We did not know what he was talking about.

Goblin sounded like he was regressing toward childhood. ''Make it stop looking at me. Make it stop. I've been good. Make it go away.''

One-Eye was on his knees beside Goblin. ''It's all right. It's all right. It's not real. It's going to be all right.''

I exchanged glances with Raven. He turned, began gesturing at Darling. "I'm sending her to fetch the Captain."

Darling left reluctantly. Raven took another sheet from the pile and resumed reading. Cool as a stone, that Raven.

Goblin screamed for a while, then got quiet as death. I jerked around. One-Eye lifted a hand to tell me I was not needed. Goblin had finished delivering his message.

Goblin relaxed slowly. The terror left his face. His color improved. I knelt, touched his carotid. His heart was hammering, but its beat was slowing. "Surprised it didn't kill him this time," I said. "It ever been this bad before?"

"No." One-Eye dropped Goblin's hand. "We'd better not put it on him next time."

"Is it progressive?" My trade borders theirs along the shadowed edges, but only in small ways. I did not know.

"No. His confidence will need support for a while. Sounded like he caught Soulcatcher right at the heart of the Tower. I think that would leave anybody rocky."

"While in the presence of the Lady," I breathed. I could not contain my excitement. Goblin had seen the inside of the Tower! He might have seen the Lady! Only the Ten Who Were Taken ever came out of the Tower. Popular imagination invests its interior with a thousand gruesome possibilities. And I had me a live witness!

"You just let him be, Croaker. He'll tell you when he's ready." There was a hard edge to One-Eye's voice.

They laugh at my little fantasies, tell me I have fallen in love with a spook. Maybe they are right. Sometimes my interest scares me. It gets close to becoming an obsession.

For a time I forgot my duty to Goblin. For a moment he stopped being a man, a brother, an old friend. He became a source of information. Then, shamed, I retreated to my papers.

The Captain arrived, puzzled, dragged by a determined

Darling. "Ah. I see. He made contact." He studied Goblin. "Said anything yet? No? Wake him up, One-Eye."

One-Eye started to protest, thought better of it, shook Goblin gently. Goblin took his time awakening. His sleep was almost as deep as a trance.

"Was it rough?" the Captain asked me.

I explained. He grunted, said, "That wagon is on its way. One of you start packing."

I started straightening my piles.

"One of you means Raven, Croaker. You stand by here. Goblin doesn't look too good."

He did not. He had gone pale again. His breath was coming shallower and quicker, getting ragged. "Give him a slap, One-Eye," I said. "He might think he's still out there."

The slap did the job. Goblin opened eyes filled with panic. He recognized One-Eye, shuddered, took a deep breath, and squeaked, "I have to come back to this? After that?" But his voice gave the lie to his protest. The relief there was thick enough to cut.

"He's all right," I said. "He can bitch."

The Captain squatted. He did not say anything. Goblin would talk when he was ready.

He took several minutes to get himself together, then said, "Soulcatcher says to get the hell out of here. Fast. He'll meet us on the way to Lords."

"That's it?"

That is all there ever is, but the Captain keeps hoping for more. The game does not seem worth the candle when you see what Goblin goes through.

I looked at him hard. It was one hell of a temptation. He looked back. "Later, Croaker. Give me time to get it straightened out in my head."

I nodded, said, "A little herb tea will perk you up."

"Oh, no. You're not giving me any of that rat piss of One-Eye's."

"Not his. My own." I measured enough for a strong quart, gave it to One-Eye, closed my kit, returned to the papers as the wagon creaked up outside.

As I carried my first load out, I noticed that the men were at the coup de grace stage on the drill field. The Captain was not fooling around. He wanted to put a lot of distance between himself and the camp before Whisper returned.

Can't say I blame him. Her reputation is thoroughly vile.

I did not get to the oilskin packets till we were travelling again. I sat up beside the driver and started the first, vainly trying to ignore the savage jouncing of the springless vehicle.

I went through the packets twice, growing ever more distressed.

A real dilemma. Should I tell the Captain what I had learned? Should I tell One-Eye or Raven? Each would be interested. Should I save everything for Soulcatcher? No doubt he would prefer that. My question was, did this information fall inside or outside my obligation to the Company? I needed an adviser.

I jumped down from the wagon, let the column drift past till Silent caught up. He had middle guard. One-Eye was on the point and Goblin back in the rear. Each was worth a platoon of outriders.

Silent looked down from the back of the big black he rides when he is in a villainous mood. He scowled. Of our wizards he is the nearest to what you could call evil, though, like so many of us, he is more image than substance.

"I've got a problem," I told him. "A big one. You're

the best sounding board.'' I looked around. ''I don't want anyone else to hear this.''

Silent nodded. He made complicated, fluid gestures too quick to follow. Suddenly, I could not hear anything from more than five feet away. You would be amazed how many sounds you do not notice till they are gone. I told Silent what I had found.

Silent is hard to shock. He has seen and heard it all. But he looked properly astonished this time.

For a moment I thought he was going to say something.

''Should I tell Soulcatcher?''

Vigorous affirmative nod. All right. I hadn't doubted that. The news was too big for the Company. It would eat us up if we kept it to ourselves.

''How about the Captain? One-Eye? Some of the others?''

He was less quick to respond, and less decisive. His advice was negative. With a few questions and the intuition one develops on long exposure, I understood Silent to feel that Soulcatcher would want to spread the word on a need-to-know basis.

''Right, then,'' I said, and, ''Thanks,'' and started trotting up the column. When I was out of sight of Silent, I asked one of the men, ''You seen Raven?''

''Up with the Captain.''

That figured. I resumed trotting.

After a moment of reflection I had decided to buy a little insurance. Raven was the finest policy I could imagine.

''You read any of the old languages?'' I asked him. It was hard talking to him. He and the Captain were mounted and Darling was right behind them. Her mule kept trying to tromp my heels.

''Some. All part of a classical education. Why?''

I scrambled a few steps ahead. ''We're going to be having mule stew if you don't watch it, animal.'' I swear, that beast sneered. I told Raven, "Some of those papers aren't modern. The ones One-Eye dug up."

"Not important then, are they?"

I shrugged and ambled along beside him, picking my words carefully. "You never know. The Lady and the Ten, they go way back." I let out a yelp, spun, ran backward gripping my shoulder where the mule had nipped me. The animal looked innocent, but Darling was grinning impishly.

It was almost worth the pain, just to see her smile. She did so so seldom.

I cut across the column and drifted back till I was walking beside Elmo. He asked, "Is something wrong, Croaker?"

"Uhm? No. Not really."

"You look scared."

I *was* scared. I had tipped the lid off a little box, just to see what was inside, and had found it filled with nastiness. The things I had read could not be unlearned.

When next I saw Raven his face was as grey as mine. Maybe more so. We walked together while he sketched what he had learned from the documents I had not been able to read.

"Some of them belonged to the wizard Bomanz," he told me. "Others date from the Domination. Some are TelleKurre. Only the Ten use that language anymore."

"Bomanz?" I asked.

"Right. The one who wakened the Lady. Whisper got ahold of his secret papers somehow."

"Oh."

"Indeed. Yes. Oh."

We parted, each to be alone with his fears.

Soulcatcher came sneakily. He wore clothing not unlike ours outside his customary leathers. He slipped into the column unremarked. How long he was there I do not know. I became aware of him as we were leaving the forest, after three eighteen hour days of heavy marching. I was putting one foot ahead of the other, aching, and mumbling about getting too old when a soft feminine voice inquired, "How are you today, physician?" It lilted with amusement.

Had I been less exhausted I might have jumped ten feet, screaming. As it was, I just took my next step, cranked my head around, and muttered, "Finally showed up, eh?" Profound apathy was the order of the moment.

A wave of relief would arrive later, but just then my brain was running as sluggishly as my body. After so long on the run it was hard to get the adrenalin pumping. The world held no sudden excitements or terrors.

Soulcatcher marched beside me, matching stride for stride, occasionally glancing my way. I could not see his face, but I sensed his amusement.

The relief came, and was followed by a wave of awe at my own temerity. I had talked back like Catcher was one of the guys. It was thunderbolt time.

"So why don't we look at those documents?" he asked. He seemed positively cheerful. I showed him to the wagon. We scrambled aboard. The driver gave us one wide-eyed look, then stared determinedly forward, shivering and trying to become deaf.

I went straight to the packets that had been buried, started to slip out. "Stay," he said. "They don't need to know yet." He sensed my fear, giggled like a young girl. "You're safe, Croaker. In fact, the Lady sends her personal thanks." He laughed again. "She wanted to know all about you, Croaker. All about you. You've caught her imagination too."

Another hammer blow of fear. Nobody wants to catch the Lady's eye.

Soulcatcher enjoyed my discomfiture. "She might grant you an interview, Croaker. Oh, my. You're so pale. Well, it isn't mandatory. To work, then."

Never have I seen anyone read so fast. He went through the old documents and the new, zip.

Catcher said, "You weren't able to read all of this." He used his businesslike female voice.

"No."

"Neither can I. Some only the Lady will be able to decipher."

Odd, I thought. I expected more enthusiasm. The seizure of the documents represented a coup for him because he had had the foresight to enlist the Black Company.

"How much did you get?"

I talked about the Rebel plan for a thrust through Lords, and about what Whisper's presence implied.

He chuckled. "The old documents, Croaker. Tell me about the old documents."

I was sweating. The softer, the more gentle he became, the more I felt I had to fear. "The old wizard. The one who wakened you all. Some of them were his papers." Damn. I knew I had stuck my foot in my mouth before I finished. Raven was the only man in the Company who could have identified Bomanz's papers as his.

Soulcatcher chuckled, gave me a comradely shoulder slap. "I thought so, Croaker. I wasn't sure, but I thought so. I didn't think you could resist telling Raven."

I did not respond. I wanted to lie, but he *knew*.

"You couldn't have known any other way. You told him about the references to the Limper's true name, so he just had to read everything he could. Right?"

Still I kept my peace. It was true, though my motives had not been wholly brotherly. Raven has his scores to settle, but Limper wants *all* of *us*.

The most jealously guarded secret of any wizard, of

course, is his true name. An enemy armed with that can
stab through any magic or illusion straight to the heart of
the soul.

"You only guessed at the magnitude of what you found,
Croaker. Even I can only guess. But what will come of it
is predictable. The biggest disaster ever for Rebel arms,
and a lot of rattling and shaking among the Ten." He
slapped my shoulder again. "You've made me the second
most powerful person in the Empire. The Lady knows all
our true names. Now I know three of the others, and I've
gotten my own back."

No wonder he was effusive. He had ducked an arrow he
had not known was coming, and had lucked onto a stran-
glehold on the Limper at the same time. He had stumbled
over a rainbow pot of power.

"But Whisper. . . ."

"Whisper will have to go." The voice he used was deep
and chill. It was the voice of an assassin, a voice accustomed to pronouncing death sentences. "Whisper has to
die fast. Otherwise nothing is gained."

"Suppose she told someone else?"

"She didn't. Oh, no. I know Whisper. I fought her at
Rust before the Lady sent me to Beryl. I fought her at
Were. I chased her through the talking menhirs upon the
Plain of Fear. I know Whisper. She's a genius, but she's a
loner. Had she lived during the first era, the Dominator
would have made her one of his own. She serves the
White Rose, but her heart is as black as the night of Hell."

"That sounds like the whole Circle to me."

Catcher laughed. "Yes. Every one a hypocrite. But
there isn't a one like Whisper. This is incredible, Croaker.
How did she unearth so many secrets? How did she get *my*
name? I had it hidden perfectly. I admire her. Truly. Such
genius. Such audacity. A strike through Lords, across the
Windy Country, and up the Stair of Tear. Incredible.

Impossible. And it would have worked but for the accident of the Black Company, and you. You'll be rewarded. I guarantee it. But enough of this. I've got work to do. Nightcrawler needs this information. The Lady has to see these papers.''

"I hope you're right," I grumbled. "Kick ass, then take a break. I'm worn out. We've been humping and fighting for a year."

Dumb remark, Croaker. I felt the chill of the frown inside the black morion. How long had Soulcatcher been humping and fighting? An age. "You go on now," he told me. "I'll talk to you and Raven later." Cold, cold voice. I got the hell out of there.

It was all over in Lords when we got there. Nightcrawler had moved fast and had hit hard. You could not go anywhere without finding Rebels hanging from the trees and lampposts. The Company went into barracks expecting a quiet, boring winter, and a spring spent chasing Rebel leftovers back to the great northern forests.

Ah, it was a sweet illusion while it lasted.

"Tonk!" I said, slapping down five face cards given me on the deal. "Ha! Double, you guys. Double. Pay up."

One-Eye grumbled and growled and shoved coins across the table. Raven chuckled. Even Goblin perked up enough to smile. One-Eye had not won a hand all morning, even when he cheated.

"Thank you, Gentlemen. Thank you. Deal, One-Eye."

"What're you doing, Croaker? Eh? How are you doing it?"

"The hand is quicker than the eye," Elmo suggested.

"Just clean living, One-Eye. Clean living."

The Lieutenant shoved through the door, face drawn into a fierce scowl. "Raven. Croaker. The Captain wants

you. Chop-chop.'' He surveyed the various card games.
''You degenerates.''

One-Eye sniffed, then worked up a wan smile. The
Lieutenant was a worse player than he.

I looked at Raven. The Captain was his buddy. But he
shrugged, tossed his cards in. I filled my pockets with my
winnings and followed him to the Captain's office.

Soulcatcher was there. We had not seen him since that
day at the edge of the forest. I had hoped he had gotten too
busy to get back to us. I looked at the Captain, trying to
divine the future from his face. I saw that he was not
happy.

If the Captain was not happy, I wasn't.

''Sit,'' he said. Two chairs were waiting. He prowled
around, fidgeting. Finally, he said, ''We have movement
orders. Straight from Charm. Us and Nightcrawler's whole
brigade.'' He gestured toward Soulcatcher, passing the
explaining to him.

Catcher seemed lost in thought. Barely audibly, he finally asked, ''How are you with a bow, Raven?''

''Fair. No champion.''

''Better than fair,'' the Captain countered. ''Damned
good.''

''You, Croaker?''

''I used to be good. I haven't drawn one for years.''

''Get some practice.'' Catcher started pacing too. The
office was small. I expected a collision momentarily. After
a minute, Soulcatcher said, ''There have been developments.
We tried to catch Whisper at her camp. We just missed
her. She smelled the trap. She's still out there somewhere,
hiding. The Lady is sending in troops from all sides.''

That explained the Captain's remark. It did not tell me
why I was supposed to hone my archery skills.

''Near as we can tell,'' Soulcatcher continued, ''the
Rebel doesn't know what happened out there. Yet. Whis-

per hasn't found the nerve to pass the word about her failure. She's a proud woman. Looks like she wants to try recouping first.''

''With what?'' Raven asked. ''She couldn't put together a platoon.''

''With memories. Memories of the material you found buried. We don't think she knows we got it. She didn't get close to her headquarters before Limper tipped our hand and she fled into the forest. And just we four, and the Lady, know of the documents.''

Raven and I nodded. Now we understood Catcher's restlessness. Whisper knew his true name. He was on the bull's-eye.

''What do you want with us?'' Raven asked suspiciously. He was afraid Catcher thought we had deciphered that name ourselves. He'd even suggested we kill the Taken before he killed us. The Ten are neither immortal nor invulnerable, but they are damned hard to reach. I did not, ever, want to have a try at one.

''We have a special mission, we three.''

Raven and I exchanged glances. Was he setting us up?

Catcher said, ''Captain, would you mind stepping outside for a minute?''

The Captain shambled through the doorway. His bear act is all for show. I don't suppose he realizes that we have had it figured for years. He keeps on with it, trying for effect.

''I'm not going to take you off where I can kill you quietly,'' Soulcatcher told us. ''No, Raven, I don't think you figured out my true name.''

Spooky. I scrunched my head down against my shoulders. Raven flicked a hand. A knife appeared. He began cleaning already immaculate nails.

''The critical development is this: Whisper suborned the Limper after we made a fool of him in the Raker affair.''

I burst out, "That explains what happened in the Salient. We had it sewed up. It fell apart overnight. And he was a pure shit during the battle at Roses."

Raven agreed. "Roses was his fault. But nobody thought it was treason. After all, he's one of the Ten."

"Yes," Catcher said. "It explains many things. But the Salient and Roses are yesterday. Our interest now is tomorrow. It's getting rid of Whisper before she gifts us with another disaster."

Raven eyed Catcher, eyed me, pursued his needless manicure. I was not taking the Taken at face value either. We lesser mortals are but toys and tools to them. They are the kind of people who dig up the bones of their grandmothers to win points with the Lady.

"This is our edge on Whisper," Soulcatcher said. "We know she has agreed to meet the Limper tomorrow. . . ."

"How?" Raven demanded.

"*I* don't know. The Lady told *me*. Limper doesn't know we know about him, but he does know he can't last much longer. He'll probably try to make a deal so the Circle will protect him. He knows if he doesn't, he's dead. What the Lady wants is them to die together so the Circle will suspect she was selling out to the Limper instead of the other way around."

"It won't wash," Raven grumbled.

"They'll believe it."

"So we're going to knock him off," I said. "Me and Raven. With bows. And how are we supposed to find them?" Catcher would not be there himself, no matter how he talked. Both the Limper and Whisper would sense his presence long before he came within bowshot.

"Limper will be with the forces moving into the forest. Not knowing that he's suspected, he won't hide from the Lady's Eye. He'll expect his movements to be taken as part of the search. The Lady will report his whereabouts to me. I'll put you on his trail. When they meet, you take them out."

"Sure," Raven sneered. "Sure. It'll be a turkey shoot." He threw his knife. It bit deep into a windowsill. He stomped out of the room.

The deal sounded no better to me. I stared at Soulcatcher and debated with myself for about two seconds before I let fear push me in Raven's wake.

My last glimpse of Catcher was of a weary person slumped in unhappiness. I guess it is hard for them to live with their reputations. We all want people to like us.

I was doing one of my little fantasies about the Lady while Raven systematically plunked arrows into a red rag pinned to a straw butt. I had had trouble hitting the butt itself my first round, let alone the rag. It seemed Raven could not miss.

This time I was playing around with her childhood. That is something I like to look at with any villain. What twists and knots went into the thread tying the creature at Charm to the little girl who was? Consider little children. There are not many of them not cute and lovable and precious, sweet as whipped honey and butter. So where do all the wicked people come from? I walk through our barracks and wonder how a giggling, inquisitive toddler could have become a Three Fingers, a Jolly, or a Silent.

Little girls are twice as precious and innocent as little boys. I do not know a culture that does not make them that way.

So where does a Lady come from? Or, for that matter, a Whisper? I was speculating in this latest tale.

Goblin sat down beside me. He read what I had written. "I don't think so," he said. "I think she made a conscious decision in the beginning."

I turned toward him slowly, acutely conscious of

Soulcatcher standing only a few yards behind me, watching the arrows fly. "I didn't really think it was this way, Goblin. It's a. . . . Well, you know. You want to understand, so you put it together some way you can handle."

"We all do that. In everyday life it's called making excuses." True, raw motives are too rough to swallow. By the time most people reach my age, they have glossed their motives so often and so well they fall completely out of touch with them.

I became conscious of a shadow across my lap. I glanced up. Soulcatcher extended a hand, inviting me to take my turn with the bow. Raven had recovered his arrows, and was standing by, waiting for me to step to the mark.

My first three shafts plunked into the rag. "How about that?" I said, and turned to take a bow.

Soulcatcher was reading my little fantasy. He raised his gaze to mine. "Really, Croaker! It wasn't like that at all. Didn't you know that she murdered her twin sister when she was fourteen?"

Rats with icy claws scrambled around on my spine. I turned, let a shaft fly. It ripped wide right of the butt. I sprayed a few more around, and did nothing but irritate the pigeons in the background.

Catcher took the bow. "Your nerves are going, Croaker." In a blur, he snapped three arrows into a circle less than an inch across. "Keep at it. You'll be under more pressure out there." He handed the bow back. "The secret is concentration. Pretend you're doing surgery."

Pretend I'm doing surgery. Right. I have managed some fancy emergency work in the middle of battlefields. Right. But this was different.

The grand old excuse. Yes, but. . . . This is different.

I calmed down enough to hit the butt with the rest of my shafts. After recovering them, I stood aside for Raven.

Goblin handed me my writing materials. Irritably, I crumpled my little fable.

"Need something for your nerves?" Goblin asked.

"Yeah. The iron filings or whatever it is Raven eats." My self-esteem was pretty shaky.

"Try this." Goblin offered me a little six-pointed silver star hanging on a neck chain. At its center was a medusa head in jet.

"An amulet?"

"Yes. We thought you might need it tomorrow."

"Tomorrow?" Nobody was supposed to know what was happening.

"We have eyes, Croaker. This is the Company. Maybe we don't know what, but we can tell when something is going on."

"Yeah. I suppose so. Thanks, Goblin."

"Me and One-Eye and Silent, we all worked on it."

"Thanks. What about Raven?" When somebody makes a gesture like that, I feel more comfortable shifting the subject.

"Raven doesn't need one. Raven is his own amulet. Sit down. Let's talk."

"I can't tell you about it."

"I know. I thought you wanted to know about the Tower." He had not talked about his visit yet. I had given up on him.

"All right. Tell me." I stared at Raven. Arrow after arrow skewered the rag.

"Aren't you going to write it down?"

"Oh. Yeah." I readied pen and paper. The men are tremendously impressed by the fact that I keep these Annals. Their only immortality will be here. "Glad I didn't bet him."

"Bet who?"

"Raven wanted to make a wager on our marksmanship."

Goblin snorted. "You're getting too smart to get hooked by a sucker bet? Get your pen ready." He launched his story.

He did not add much to rumors I had picked up here and there. He described the place he had gone as a big, drafty box of a room, gloomy and dusty. About what I expected of the Tower. Or of any castle.

"What did she look like?" That was the most intriguing part of the puzzle. I had a mental picture of a dark haired, ageless beauty with a sexual presence that hit mere mortals with the impact of a mace. Soulcatcher said she was beautiful, but I had no independent corroboration.

"I don't know. I don't remember."

"What do you mean, you don't remember? How can you not remember?"

"Don't get all excited, Croaker. I can't remember. She was there in front of me, then. . . . Then all I could see was that giant yellow eye that kept getting bigger and bigger and stared right through me, looking at every secret I ever had. That's all I remember. I still have nightmares about that eye."

I sighed, exasperated. "I guess I should've expected that. You know, she could come walking by right now and nobody would know it was her."

"I expect that's the way she wants it, Croaker. If it does all fall apart, the way it looked before you found those papers, she can just walk away. Only the Ten could identify her, and she would make sure of them somehow."

I doubt it would be that simple. People like the Lady have trouble assuming a lesser role. Deposed princes keep acting like princes.

"Thanks for taking the trouble to tell me about it, Goblin."

"No trouble. I didn't have anything to tell. Only reason I put it off was it upset me so much."

Raven finished retrieving his arrows. He came over and told Goblin, "Why don't you go put a bug in One-Eye's bedroll, or something? We've got work to do." He was nervous about my erratic marksmanship.

We had to depend on one another. If either missed, chances were we would die before a second shaft could be sped. I did not want to think about that.

But thinking about it improved my concentration. I got most of my arrows into the rag this time.

It was a pain in the ass damned thing to have to do, night before whatever faced Raven and I, but the Captain refused to part with a tradition three centuries old. He also refused to entertain protests about our having been drafted by Soulcatcher, or demands for the additional knowledge he obviously commanded. I mean, I understood what Catcher wanted done and why, I just could not make sense of why he wanted Raven and I to do it. Having the Captain back him only made it more confusing.

"Why, Croaker?" he finally demanded. "Because I gave you an order, that's why. Now get out there and do your reading."

Once each month, in the evening, the entire Company assembles so the Annalist can read from his predecessors. The readings are supposed to put the men in touch with the outfit's history and traditions, which stretch back centuries and thousands of miles.

I placed my selection on a crude lectern and went with the usual formula. "Good evening, brothers. A reading from the Annals of the Black Company, last of the Free Companies of Khatovar. Tonight I'm reading from the Book of Kette, set down early in the Company's second century by Annalists Lees, Agrip, Holm, and Straw. The Company was in service to the Paingod of Cho'n Delor at that time. That was when the Company really was black.

"The reading is from Annalist Straw. It concerns the Company's role in events surrounding the fall of Cho'n Delor." I began to read, reflecting privately that the Company has served many losing causes.

The Cho'n Delor era bore many resemblances to our own, though then, standing more than six thousand strong, the Company was in a better position to shape its own destiny.

I lost track entirely. Old Straw was hell with a pen. I read for three hours, raving like a mad prophet, and held them spellbound. They gave me an ovation when I finished. I retreated from the lectern feeling as though my life had been fulfilled.

The physical and mental price of my histrionics caught up as I entered my barracks. Being a semi-officer, I rated a small cubicle of my own. I staggered right to it.

Raven was waiting. He sat on my bunk doing something artistic with an arrow. Its shaft had a band of silver around it. He seemed to be engraving something. Had I not been exhausted, I might have been curious.

"You were superb," Raven told me. "Even I felt it."

"Eh?"

"You made me understand what it meant to be a brother of the Black Company back then."

"What it still means to some."

"Yes. And more. You reached them where they lived."

"Yeah. Sure. What're you doing?"

"Fixing an arrow for the Limper. With his true name on it. Catcher gave it to me."

"Oh." Exhaustion kept me from pursuing the matter. "What did you want?"

"You made me feel something for the first time since my wife and her lovers tried to murder me and steal my rights and titles." He rose, closed one eye, looked down the length of his arrow. "Thanks, Croaker. For a while I felt human again." He stalked out.

I collapsed on the bunk and closed my eyes, recalling Raven strangling his wife, taking her wedding ring, and saying not a word. He had revealed more in that one rapid-fire sentence than since the day we had met. Strange.

I fell asleep reflecting that he had evened scores with everyone but the ultimate source of his despair. The Limper had been untouchable because he was one of the Lady's own. But no more.

Raven would be looking forward to tomorrow. I wondered what he would dream tonight. And if he would have much purpose left if the Limper died. A man cannot survive on hatred alone. Would he bother trying to survive what was coming?

Maybe that was what he wanted to say.

I was scared. A man thinking that way could get a little flashy, a little dangerous to those around him.

A hand closed on my shoulder. "Time, Croaker." The Captain himself was doing the wakeup calls.

"Yeah. I'm awake." I had not slept well.

"Catcher is ready to go."

It was still dark out. "Time?"

"Almost four. He wants to be gone before first light."

"Oh."

"Croaker? Be careful out there. I want you back."

"Sure, Captain. You know I don't take chances. Captain? Why me and Raven, anyway?" Maybe he would tell me now.

"He says the Lady calls it a reward."

"No shit? Some reward." I felt around for my boots as he moved to the door. "Captain? Thanks."

"Sure." He knew I meant thanks for caring.

Raven stuck his head in as I was lacing my jerkin. "Ready?"

"One minute. Cold out there?"

"Nippy."

"Take a coat?"

"Wouldn't hurt. Mail shirt?" He touched my chest.

"Yeah." I pulled my coat on, picked up the bow I was taking, bounced it on my palm. For an instant Goblin's amulet lay cool on my breastbone. I hoped it would work.

Raven cracked a smile. "Me too."

I grinned back. "Let's go get them."

Soulcatcher was waiting on the court where we had practiced our archery. He was limned by light from the company mess. The bakers were hard at work already. Catcher stood at a stiff parade rest, a bundle under his left arm. He stared toward the Forest of Cloud. He wore only leathers and morion. Unlike some of the Taken, he seldom carries weapons. He prefers relying on his thaumaturgic skills.

He was talking to himself. Weird stuff. "Want to see him go down. Been waiting four hundred years." "We can't get that close. He'll smell us coming." "Put aside all Power." "Oh! That's too risky!" A whole chorus of voices got into the act. It got really spooky when two of them talked at once.

Raven and I exchanged glances. He shrugged. Catcher did not faze him. But, then, he grew up in the Lady's dominions. He has seen all the Taken. Soulcatcher is supposedly one of the least bizarre.

We listened for a few minutes. It did not get any saner out. Finally, Raven growled, "Lord? We're ready." He sounded a little shaky.

I was beyond speech myself. All I could think of was a bow, an arrow, and a job I was expected to do. I rehearsed the draw, release, and flight of my shaft over and over again. Unconsciously, I rubbed Goblin's gift. I would catch myself doing that often.

Soulcatcher shuddered like a wet dog, drew himself together. Without looking at us, he gestured, said, "Come," and started walking.

Raven turned. He yelled, "Darling, you get back in there like I told you. Go on now."

"How is she supposed to hear you?" I asked, looking back at the child watching from a shadowed doorway.

"She won't. But the Captain will. Go on now." He gestured violently. The Captain appeared momentarily. Darling vanished. We followed Soulcatcher. Raven muttered to himself. He worried about the child.

Soulcatcher set a brisk pace, out of the compound, out of Lords itself, across fields, never looking back. He led us to a large woodlot several bowshots from the wall, to a glade at the lot's heart. There, on the bank of a creek, lay a ragged carpet stretched on a crude wooden frame about a foot high and six feet by eight. Soulcatcher said something. The carpet twitched, wriggled a little, stretched itself taut.

"Raven, you sit here." Catcher indicated the right hand corner nearest us. "Croaker, over here." He indicated the left corner.

Raven placed a foot on the carpet gingerly, seemed surprised that the works did not collapse.

"Sit down." Soulcatcher placed him just so, with his legs crossed and his weapons lying beside him near the carpet's edge. He did the same with me. I was suprised to find the carpet rigid. It was like sitting on a tabletop. "It's imperative that you don't move around," Catcher said, wriggling himself into position ahead of us, centered a foot forward of the carpet's midline. "If we don't stay balanced, we fall off. Understand?"

I did not, but I agreed with Raven when he said yes.

"Ready?"

Raven said yes again. I guess he knew what was happening. I was taken by surprise.

Soulcatcher laid his hands out palms upward beside him, said a few strange words, raised his hands slowly. I gasped, leaned. The ground was receding.

"Sit still!" Raven snarled. "You trying to kill us?"

The ground was only six feet down. Then. I straightened up and went rigid. But I did turn my head enough to check a movement in the brush.

Yes. Darling. With mouth an O of amazement. I faced forward, gripped my bow so tightly I thought I would crush handprints into it. I wished I dared finger my amulet. "Raven, did you make arrangements for Darling? In case, you know. . . ."

"The Captain will look out for her."

"I forgot to fix it with somebody for the Annals."

"Don't be so optimistic," he said sarcastically. I shivered uncontrollably.

Soulcatcher did something. We started gliding over the treetops. Chill air whispered past us. I glanced over the side. We were a good five storeys high and climbing.

The stars twisted overhead as Catcher changed course. The wind rose till we seemed to be flying into the face of a gale. I leaned farther and farther forward, afraid it would push me off. There was nothing behind me but several hundred feet and an abrupt stop. My fingers ached from gripping my bow.

I have learned one thing, I told myself. How Catcher manages to show up so fast when he is always so far from the action when we get in touch.

It was a silent journey. Catcher stayed busy doing whatever it was he did to make his steed fly. Raven closed in on himself. So did I. I was scared silly. My stomach was in revolt. I do not know about Raven.

The stars began to fade. The eastern horizon lightened. The earth materialized below us. I chanced a look. We were over the Forest of Cloud. A little more light. Catcher grunted, considered the east, then the distances ahead. He seemed to listen for a moment, then nodded.

The carpet raised its nose. We climbed. The earth rocked and dwindled till it looked like a map. The air became ever more chill. My stomach remained rebellious.

Way off to our left I glimpsed a black scar on the forest. It was the encampment we had overrun. Then we entered a cloud and Catcher slowed our rush.

"We'll drift a while," he said. "We're thirty miles south of the Limper. He's riding away from us. We're overtaking him fast. When we're almost up to where he might detect me, we'll go down." He used the business-like female voice.

I started to say something. He snapped, "Be quiet, Croaker. Don't distract me."

We stayed in that cloud, unseen and unable to see, for two hours. Then Catcher said, "Time to go down. Grip the frame members and don't let go. It may be a little unsettling."

The bottom fell out. We went down like a stone dropped from a cliff. The carpet began to rotate slowly, so the forest seemed to turn below us. Then it began to slide back and forth like a feather falling. Each time it tilted my way I thought I would tumble over the side.

A good scream might have helped, but you could not do that in front of characters like Raven and Soulcatcher.

The forest kept getting closer. Soon I could distinguish individual trees . . . when I dared to look. We were going to die. I knew we were going to smash right down through the forest canopy fifty feet into the earth.

Catcher said something. I did not catch it. He was talking to his carpet anyway. The rocking and spinning gradually stopped. Our descent slowed. The carpet nosed down slightly and began to glide forward. Eventually Catcher took us below treetop level, into the aisle over a river. We scooted along a dozen feet above the water, with Soulcatcher laughing as birds scattered in panic.

He brought us to earth in a glen beside the river. "Off and stretch," he told us. After we had loosened up, he said, "The Limper is four miles north of us. He's reached the meeting place. You'll go on from here without me. He'll detect me if I get any closer. I want your badges. He can detect those too."

Raven nodded, surrendered his badge, strung his bow, nocked an arrow, pulled back, relaxed. I did the same. It settled my nerves.

I was so grateful to be on the ground I could have kissed it.

"The bole on the big oak." Raven pointed across the river. He let fly. His shaft struck a few inches off center. I took a deep, relaxing breath, followed suite. My shaft struck an inch nearer center. "Should have bet me that time," he remarked. To Catcher, "We're ready."

I added, "We'll need more specific directions."

"Follow the river bank. There are plenty of game trails. The going shouldn't be hard. No need to hurry anyway. Whisper shouldn't be there for hours yet."

"The river heads west," I observed.

"It loops back. Follow it for three miles, then turn a point west of north and go straight through the woods." Catcher crouched and cleared the leaves and twigs off some bare earth, used a stick to sketch a map. "If you reach this bend, you've gone too far."

Then Catcher froze. For a long minute he listened to something only he could hear. Then he resumed, "The Lady says you'll know you're close when you reach a grove of huge evergreens. It was the holy place of a people who died out before the Domination. The Limper is waiting at the center of the grove."

"Good enough," Raven said.

I asked, "You'll wait here?"

"Have no fear, Croaker."

I took another of my relaxing breaths. "Let's go, Raven."

"One second, Croaker," Soulcatcher said. He retrieved something from his bundle. It proved to be an arrow. "Use this."

I eyed it uncertainly, then placed it in my quiver.

Raven insisted on leading. I did not argue. I was a city boy before I joined the Company. I cannot become comfortable with forests. Especially not woods the size of the Forest of Cloud. Too much quiet. Too much solitude. Too easy to get lost. For the first two miles I worried more about finding my way back than I did about the coming encounter. I spent a lot of time memorizing landmarks.

Raven did not speak for an hour. I was busy thinking myself. I did not mind.

He raised a hand. I stopped. "Far enough, I think," he said. "We go that way now."

"Uhm."

"Let's rest." He settled on a huge tree root, his back against a trunk. "Awful quiet today, Croaker."

"Things on my mind."

"Yeah." He smiled. "Like what kind of reward we're set up for?"

"Among other things." I drew out the arrow Catcher had given me. "You see this?"

"A blunt head?" He felt it. "Soft, almost. What the hell?"

"Exactly. Means I'm not supposed to kill her."

There was no question of who would let fly at whom. The Limper was Raven's all the way.

"Maybe. But I'm not going to get killed trying to take her alive."

"Me either. That's what's bothering me. Along with about ten other things, like why the Lady *really* picked you and me, and why she wants Whisper alive. . . . Oh, the hell with it. It'll give me ulcers."

"Ready?"

"I guess."

We left the riverbank. The going became more difficult, but soon we crossed a low ridgeline and reached the edge of the evergreens. Not much grew beneath them. Very little sunlight leaked through their boughs. Raven paused to urinate. "Won't be any chance later," he explained.

He was right. You do not want that sort of problem when you are in ambush a stone's throw from an unfriendly Taken.

I was getting shaky. Raven laid a hand on my shoulder. "We'll be okay," he promised. But he did not believe it himself. His hand was shaky too.

I reached inside my jerkin and touched Goblin's amulet. It helped.

Raven raised an eyebrow. I nodded. We resumed walking. I chewed a strip of jerky, which burned off nervous energy. We did not speak again.

There were ruins among the trees. Raven examined the glyphs incised in the stones. He shrugged. They meant nothing to him.

Then we came to the big trees, the grandfathers of those through which we had been passing. They towered hundreds of feet high and had trunks as thick as the spans of two men's arms. Here and there, the sun thrust swords of light down through the boughs. The air was thick with resin smells. The silence was overwhelming. We moved one step at a time, making sure our footfalls sent no warnings ahead.

My nervousness peaked out, began to fade. It was too late to run, too late to change my mind. My brain cancelled all emotion. Usually that only happened when I was forced to treat casualties while people were killing one another all around me.

Raven signalled a halt. I nodded. I had heard it too. A horse snorting. Raven gestured for me to stay put. He eased to our left, keeping low, and disappeared behind a tree about fifty feet away.

He reappeared in a minute, beckoned. I joined him. He led me to a spot from which I could look into an open area. The Limper and his horse were there.

The clearing was maybe seventy feet long by fifty wide. A tumble of crumbling stone stood at its center. The Limper sat on one fallen rock and leaned against another. He seemed to be sleeping. One corner of the clearing was occupied by the trunk of a fallen giant that had not been down long. It showed very little weathering.

Raven tapped the back of my hand, pointed. He wanted to move on.

I did not like moving now that we had the Limper in sight. Each step meant another chance to alert the Taken to his peril. But Raven was right. The sun was dropping in front of us. The longer we stayed put, the worse the light would become. Eventually, it would be in our eyes.

We moved with exaggerated care. Of course. One mistake and we were dead. When Raven glanced back I saw sweat on his temples.

He stopped, pointed, smiled. I crept up beside him. He pointed again.

Another fallen tree lay ahead. This one was about four feet in diameter. It looked perfect for our purpose. It was big enough to hide us, low enough to let fly over. We found a spot providing a clean aisle of fire to the heart of the clearing.

The light was good, too. Several spears broke through the canopy and illuminated most of the clearing. There was a little haze in the air, pollen perhaps, which made the beams stand out. I studied the clearing for several minutes, imprinting it on my mind. Then I sat behind the log and pretended I was a rock. Raven took the watch.

It seemed weeks passed before anything happened.

Raven tapped my shoulder. I looked up. He made a walking motion with two fingers. The Limper was up and prowling. I rose carefully, watched.

The Limper circled the pile of stones a few times, bad leg dragging, then sat down again. He picked up a twig and broke it into small pieces, tossing each at some target only he could see. When the twig was gone, he scooped up a handful of small cones and threw them lazily. Portrait of a man killing time.

I wondered why he had come on horseback. He could get places fast when he wanted. I supposed because he had been close by. Then I worried that some of his troops might show up.

He got up and walked around again, collecting cones and chucking them at the fallen behemoth across the clearing. Damned, but I wished we could take him then, and have done.

The Limper's mount's head jerked up. The animal whickered. Raven and I sank down, crushed ourselves into the shadows and needles beneath our trunk. A crackling tension radiated from the clearing.

A moment later I heard hooves crunching needles. I held my breath. From the corner of my eye I caught flickers of a white horse moving among the trees. Whisper? Would she see us?

Yes and no. Thank whatever gods there are, yes and no. She passed within fifty feet without noticing us.

The Limper called something. Whisper replied in a melodious voice that did not at all fit the wide, hard, homely woman I had seen pass. She sounded seventeen and gorgeous, looked forty-five and like she had been around the world three times.

Raven prodded me gently.

I rose about as fast as a flower blooms, scared they would hear my sinews crackle. We peeped over the fallen tree. Whisper dismounted and took one of the Limper's hands in both of hers.

The situation could not have been more perfect. We were in shadow, they were fixed in a shaft of sunlight. Golden dust sparkled around them. And they were restricting one another by holding hands.

It had to be now. We both knew it, both bent our bows. We both had additional arrows gripped against our weapons, ready to be snapped to our strings. "Now," Raven said.

My nerves did not bother me till my arrow was in the air. Then I went cold and shaky.

Raven's shaft went in under the Limper's left arm. The Taken made a sound like a rat getting stomped. He arched away from Whisper.

My shaft smashed against Whisper's temple. She was wearing a leather helmet, but I was confident the impact would down her. She spun away from the Limper.

Raven sped a second arrow, I fumbled mine. I dropped my bow and vaulted over the log. Raven's third arrow whistled past me.

Whisper was on her knees when I arrived. I kicked her in the head, whirled to face the Limper. Raven's arrows had struck home, but even Catcher's special shaft had not ended the Taken's story. He was trying to growl out a spell through a throat filled with blood. I kicked him too.

Then Raven was there with me. I spun back to Whisper. That bitch was as tough as her reputation. Whoozy as she was, she was trying to get up, trying to draw her sword, trying to mouth a spell. I scrambled her brains again, got rid of her blade. "I didn't bring any cord," I gasped. "You bring any cord, Raven?"

"No." He just stood there staring at the Limper. The Taken's battered leather mask had slipped sideways. He was trying to straighten it so he could see who we were.

"How the hell am I going to tie her up?"

"Better worry about gagging her first." Raven helped the Limper with his mask, smiling that incredibly cruel smile he gets when he is about to cut a special throat.

I yanked out my knife and hacked at Whisper's clothing. She fought me. I had to keep knocking her down. Finally, I had strips of rag to bind her and to stuff into her mouth. I dragged her over to the pile of stones, propped her up, turned to see what Raven was doing.

He had ripped the Limper's mask away, exposing the desolation of the Taken's face.

"What are you doing?" I asked. He was binding the Limper. I wondered why he was bothering.

"Got to thinking maybe I don't have the talent to handle this." He dropped into a squat and patted the Limper's cheek. The Limper radiated hatred. "You know me, Croaker. I'm an old softee. I'd just kill him and be satisfied. But he deserves a harder death. Catcher has more experience in these things." He chuckled wickedly.

The Limper strained against his bonds. Despite the three arrows, he seemed normally strong. Even vigorous. The shafts certainly did not inconvenience him.

Raven patted his cheek again. "Hey, old buddy. Word of warning, one friend to another. . . . Wasn't that what you told me about an hour before Morningstar and her friends ambushed me in that place you sent me? Word of warning? Yeah. Look out for Soulcatcher. He got ahold of your true name. Character like that, there's no telling what he might do."

I said, "Take it easy on the gloating, Raven. Watch him. He's doing something with his fingers." He was wriggling them rhythmically.

"Aye!" Raven shouted, laughing. He grabbed the sword I had taken from Whisper and chopped fingers off each of the Limper's hands.

Raven rides me for not telling the whole truth in these Annals. Someday maybe he will look at this and be sorry. But, honestly, he was not nice people that day.

I had a similar problem with Whisper. I chose a different solution. I cut off her hair and used it to tangle her fingers together.

Raven tormented the Limper till I could stand no more. "Raven, that's really enough. Why don't you back off and keep them covered?" He had been given no specific instructions about what to do after we captured Whisper, but I figured the Lady would tell Catcher and he would drop in. We just had to keep things under control till he arrived.

Soulcatcher's magic carpet dropped from the sky half an hour after I chased Raven away from the Limper. It settled a few feet from our captives. Catcher stepped off, stretched, looked down at Whisper. He sighed, observed, "Not a pretty sight, Whisper," in that businesslike female voice. "But then you never were. Yes. My friend Croaker found the buried packets."

Whisper's hard, cold eyes sought me. They were informed with a savage impact. Rather than face that, I moved. I did not correct Soulcatcher.

He turned to the Limper, shook his head sadly. "No. It's not personal. You used up your credit. *She* ordered this."

The Limper went rigid.

Soulcatcher asked Raven, "Why didn't you kill him?"

Raven sat on the trunk of the larger fallen tree, bow across his lap, staring at the earth. He did not reply. I said, "He figured you could think of something better."

Catcher laughed. "I thought about it coming over here. Nothing seemed adequate. I'm taking Raven's way out. I told Shifter. He's on his way." He looked down at the Limper. "You're in trouble, aren't you?" To me, "You'd think a man this old would have garnered some wisdom along the way." He turned to Raven. "Raven, he was the Lady's reward to you."

Raven grunted. "I appreciate it."

I had figured that out already. But I was supposed to get something out of this too, and I had not seen anything remotely fulfilling any dream of mine.

Soulcatcher did his mindreading trick. "Yours has changed, I think. It hasn't been delivered yet. Make yourself comfortable, Croaker. We'll be here a long time."

I went and sat beside Raven. We did not talk. There was nothing I wanted to say, and he was lost somewhere inside himself. Like I said, a man cannot live on hatred alone.

Soulcatcher double-checked our captives' bonds, dragged his carpet rack into the shadows, then perched himself on the stone pile.

Shapeshifter arrived twenty minutes later, as huge, ugly, dirty, and stinking as ever. He looked the Limper over, conferred with Catcher, growled at the Limper for half a minute, then remounted his flying carpet and soared away. Catcher explained, "He's passing it on too. Nobody wants the final responsibility."

"Who could he pass it to?" I wondered. The Limper had no heavy enemies left.

Catcher shrugged and returned to the stone pile. He muttered in a dozen voices, drawing into himself, almost shrinking. I think he was as happy to be there as was I.

Time trudged on. The slant of the bars of sunlight grew ever steeper. One after another winked out. I began to wonder if Raven's suspicions had not been correct. We would be easy pickings after dark. The Taken do not need the sun to see.

I looked at Raven. What was happening inside his head? His face was a morose blank. It was the face he wore while playing cards.

I dropped off the log and prowled, following the pattern set by the Limper. There was nothing else to do. I whipped a pine cone at a burl on the log Raven and I had used for cover. . . . And it ducked! I started a headlong charge toward Whisper's bloody sword before I fully realized what I had seen.

"What's wrong?" Soulcatcher asked as I pulled up.

I improvised. "Pulled muscle, I think. I was going to loosen up with some sprints, but something happened in my leg." I massaged my right calf. He seemed satisfied. I glanced toward the log, saw nothing.

But I knew Silent was there. Would be there if he was needed.

Silent. How the hell had he gotten here? Same way as the rest of us? Did he have tricks that nobody suspected?

After the appropriate theatrics, I limped over and joined Raven. By gesturing I tried to make him understand that we would have help if push came to shove, but the message did not penetrate. He was too withdrawn.

It was dark. There was a half moon overhead, poking a few mild silvery bars into the clearing. Catcher remained on the stone pile. Raven and I remained on the log. My behind was aching. My nerves were raw. I was tired and hungry and scared. I had had enough, but did not have the courage to say so.

Raven shed his funk suddenly. He assayed the situation, asked, "What the hell are we doing?"

Soulcatcher woke up. "Waiting. Shouldn't be much longer."

"Waiting for what?" I demanded. I can be brave with Raven backing me. Soulcatcher stared my way. I became aware of an unnatural stir in the grove behind me, of Raven coiling himself for action. "Waiting for what?" I repeated weakly.

"For me, physician." I felt the speaker's breath on the back of my neck.

I jumped halfway to Catcher, and did not stop till I reached Whisper's blade. Catcher laughed. I wondered if he had noticed that my leg had gotten better. I glanced at the smaller log. Nothing.

A glorious light poured over the log I had quitted. I did not see Raven. He had vanished. I gripped Whisper's sword and resolved to lay a good one on Soulcatcher.

The light floated over the fallen giant, settled in front of Catcher. It was too brilliant to look at long. It illuminated the whole clearing.

Soulcatcher dropped to one knee. And then I understood.

The Lady! This fiery glory was the Lady. We had been waiting for the Lady! I stared till my eyes ached. And dropped to one knee myself. I offered Whisper's sword on my palms, like a knight doing homage to his king. The Lady!

Was this my reward? To actually meet Her? That something that called to me from Charm twisted, filled me, and for one foolish instant I was totally in love. But I could not see Her. I wanted to see what She looked like.

She had that capacity I found so disconcerting in Soulcatcher. "Not this time, Croaker," she said. "But soon, I think." She touched my hand. Her fingers burned

me like the first sexual touch of my first lover. Remember
that racing, stunning, raging instant of excitement?

"The reward comes later. This time you'll be permitted
to witness a rite unseen for five hundred years." She
moved. "That has to be uncomfortable. Get up."

I rose, backed away. Soulcatcher stood in his parade
rest stance, watching the light. Its intensity was falling. I
could watch without pain. It drifted around the stone pile
to our prisoners, waning till I could discern a feminine
shape inside.

The Lady looked at the Limper a long time. The Limper
looked back. His face was empty. He was beyond hope or
despair.

The Lady said, "You served me well for a while. And
your treachery helped more than it hurt. I am not without
mercy." She flared on one side. A shadow diminished.
There stood Raven, arrow across bow. "He's yours,
Raven."

I looked at the Limper. He betrayed excitement and a
strange hope. Not that he would survive, of course, but
that he would die quickly, simply, painlessly.

Raven said, "No." Nothing else. Just a flat refusal.

The Lady mused, "Too bad, Limper." She arched back
and screamed something at the sky.

Limper flopped violently. The gag flew out of his mouth.
His ankle bonds parted. He gained his feet, tried to run,
tried to mouth some spell that would protect him. He had
gone thirty feet when a thousand fiery snakes streaked out
of the night and swarmed him.

They covered his body. They slithered into his mouth
and nose, into his eyes and ears. They went in the easy
way and came gnawing out through his back and chest and
belly. And he screamed. And screamed. And screamed.
And the same terrible vitality which had fought off the

lethality of Raven's arrows kept him alive throughout this punishment.

I heaved up the jerky that had been my only meal all day.

The Limper was a long time screaming, and never did die. Eventually, the Lady tired and sent the serpents away. She spun a whispery cocoon around the Limper, shouted another series of syllables. A gigantic luminescent dragonfly dropped from the night, snapped him up, and hummed away toward Charm. The Lady said, "He'll provide years of entertainment." She glanced at Soulcatcher, making sure the lesson had not gone over his head.

Catcher had not moved a muscle. He did not do so now.

The Lady said, "Croaker, what you are about to witness exists only in a few memories. Even most of my champions have forgotten."

What the hell was she talking about?

She looked down. Whisper cringed. The Lady said, "No, not all that. You've been such an outstanding enemy, I'm going to reward you." Strange laughter. "There is a vacancy among the Taken."

So. The blunted arrow, the weird circumstances leading to that moment, came clear. The Lady had decided that Whisper should replace the Limper.

When? Just when had she made that decision? The Limper had been in bad trouble for a year, suffering one humiliation after another. Had she orchestrated those? I think she had. A clue here, a clue there, a strand of gossip and a stray memory. . . . Catcher had been in on part of it, using us. Maybe he had been in on it as far back as when he had enlisted us. Surely our crossing paths with Raven had been no accident. . . . Ah, she was a cruel, wicked, deceitful, calculating bitch.

But everyone knew that. That was her story. She had dispossessed her own husband. She had murdered her sister, if Soulcatcher could be believed. So why was I disappointed and surprised?

I glanced at Catcher. He had not moved, but there was a subtle change in his stance. He was dazed by surprise. "Yes," the Lady told him. "You thought only the Dominator could Take." Soft laughter. "You were wrong. Pass that along to anyone still thinking about resurrecting my husband."

Catcher moved slightly. I could not read the movement's significance, but the Lady seemed satisfied. She faced Whisper again.

The Rebel general was more terrified than the Limper had been. She was about to become the thing she hated most—and she could do nothing.

The Lady knelt and began whispering to her.

I watched, and still I do not know what went on. Nor can I describe the Lady, any more than Goblin could, despite having been near her all night. Or maybe for several nights. Time had a surreal quality. We lost some days somewhere. But see her I did, *and* I witnessed the rite that converted our most dangerous enemy into one of our own.

I recall one thing with a razor-edged clarity. A huge yellow eye. The same eye that so croggled Goblin. It came and looked into me and Raven and Whisper.

It did not shatter me the way it had Goblin. Maybe I am less sensitive. Or just more ignorant. But it was bad. Like I said, some days disappeared.

That eye is not infallible. It does not do well with short term memories. The Lady remained unaware of Silent's proximity.

Of the rest of it there are only flickers of recollection, most filled with Whisper's screams. There was a moment when the clearing filled with dancing devils all glowing

with their inner wickedness. They fought for the privilege
of mounting Whisper. There was a time when Whisper
faced the eye. A time when, I think, Whisper died and was
resurrected, died and was resurrected, till she became
intimate with death. There were times when she was tortured.
And another time with the eye.

The fragments I retain suggest that she was shattered,
slain, revived, and reassembled as a devoted slave. I recall
her pledge of fealty to the Lady. Her voice dripped a
craven eagerness to please.

Long after it was over I wakened confused and lost, and
terrified. It took a while to reason out. The confusion was
part of the Lady's protective coloration. What I could not
remember could not be used against her.

Some reward.

She was gone. Likewise Whisper. But Soulcatcher
remained, pacing the clearing, muttering in a dozen frantic
voices. He fell silent the instant I tried to sit up. He stared,
head thrust forward suspiciously.

I groaned, tried to rise, fell back. I crawled over and
propped myself on one of the stones. Catcher brought me a
canteen. I drank clumsily. He said, "You can eat after you
pull yourself together."

Which remark alerted me to ravenous hunger. How long
had it been? "What happened?"

"What do you remember?"

"Not much. Whisper was Taken?"

"She's replacing Limper. The Lady took her to the
eastern front. Her knowledge of the other side should
shake things loose out there."

I tried to shake the cobwebs. "I thought they were
shifting to a northern strategy."

"They are. And as soon as your friend recovers, we
have to return to Lords." In a soft, female voice, he
admitted, "I didn't know Whisper as well as I thought.

She did pass the word when she learned what happened at her camp. For once the Circle responded quickly. They avoided the usual in-fighting. They smell blood. They accepted their losses, and let us divert ourselves while they started their maneuvers. Kept them damned well hidden. Now Harden's army is headed toward Lords. Our forces are still scattered throughout the forest. She turned the trap around on us."

I did not want to hear it. A year of bad news is enough. Why couldn't one of our coups remain solid? "She sacrificed herself intentionally?"

"No. She wanted to run us around the woods to buy time for the Circle. She didn't know the Lady knew about the Limper. I thought I knew her, but I was wrong. We'll benefit eventually, but there are going to be hard times till Whisper straightens out the east."

I tried to rise, could not.

"Take it easy," he suggested. "First time with the Eye is always rough. Think you could eat something now?"

"Drag one of those horses over here."

"Better go easy at first."

"How bad is it?" I was not quite sure what I was asking. He assumed I meant the strategic situation.

"Harden's army is bigger than any we've yet faced up here. And it's only one of the groups that are on the move. If Nightcrawler doesn't reach Lords first, we'll lose the city and kingdom. Which might give them the momentum to drive us out of the north entirely. Our forces at Wist, Jane, Wine, and so forth, aren't up to a major campaign. The north has been a sideshow till now."

"But. . . . After all we've been through? We're worse off than when we lost Roses? Damn! That isn't fair." I was tired of retreating.

"Not to worry, Croaker. If Lords goes, we'll stop them at the Stair of Tear. We'll hold them there while Whisper runs wild. They can't ignore her forever. If the east collapses, the rebellion will die. The east is their strength.'' He sounded like a man trying to convince himself. He had been through these oscillations before, during the last days of the Domination.

I buried my head in my hands, muttered, ''I thought we had them whipped.'' Why the hell had we left Beryl?

Soulcatcher prodded Raven with a toe. Raven did not stir. ''Come on!'' Catcher grumbled. ''They need me at Lords. Nightcrawler and I may end up trying to hold the city by ourselves.''

''Why didn't you just leave us if the situation is so critical?''

He hemmed and hawed and slid around it, and before he finished I suspected that this one Taken had a sense of honor, a sense of duty toward those who had accepted his protection. He would not admit it, though. Never. That would not fit the image of the Taken.

I thought about another journey through the sky. I thought hard. I am as lazy as the next guy, but I could not take that. Not now. Not feeling the way I did. ''I'd fall off for sure. There's no point you hanging around. We won't be ready for days. Hell, we can walk out.'' I thought about the forest. Walking did not appeal to me either. ''Give us our badges back. So you can locate us again. Then you can pick us up if you get time.''

He grumbled. We batted it back and forth. I kept on about how shaky I was, about how shaky Raven would be.

He was anxious to get moving. He let me convince him. He unloaded his carpet—he had gone somewhere while I was unconscious—and climbed aboard. ''I'll see you in a few days.'' His carpet rose far faster than it had done with Raven and I aboard. And then it was gone. I dragged myself to the things he had left behind.

''You bastard.'' I chuckled. His protest had been a

shuck. He had left food, our own weapons that we had left
in Lords, and odds and ends we might need to survive.
Not a bad boss, for one of the Taken. "Hey! Silent!
Where the hell are you?"

Silent drifted into the clearing. He looked at me, at
Raven, at the supplies, and did not say anything. Of
course not. He is Silent.

He looked ragged around the edges. "Not enough sleep?"
I asked. He nodded. "You see what happened here?" He
nodded again. "I hope you remember it better than I do."
He shook his head. Damn. So it will go into the Annals
unclear.

It is a weird way to hold a conversation, one man
talking and the other head-shaking. Getting information
across can be incredibly difficult. I should study the communicative gestures Raven has learned from Darling. Silent is her second best friend. It would be interesting just
to eavesdrop on their conversations.

"Let's see what we can do for Raven," I suggested.

Raven was sleeping the sleep of the exhausted. He did
not come out of it for hours. I used the interim to interrogate Silent.

The Captain had sent him. He had come on horseback.
He was, in fact, on his way before Raven and I were
summoned for our interview with Soulcatcher. He had
ridden hard, day and night. He had reached the clearing
only a short while before I spotted him.

I asked how he had known where to go, granting that
the Captain would have nursed enough information from
Catcher to get him started—a move which fit the Captain's
style. Silent admitted he had not known where he was
headed, except generally, till we had reached the area.
Then he had tracked us through the amulet Goblin had
given me.

Crafty little Goblin. He had not betrayed a hint. Good thing, too. The eye would have found the knowledge. "You think you could have done something if we'd really needed help?" I asked.

Silent smiled, shrugged, stalked over to the stone pile and seated himself. He was done with the question game. Of all the Company he is the least concerned about the image he will present in the Annals. He does not care whether people like or hate him, does not care where he has been or where he is going. Sometimes I wonder if he cares whether he lives or dies, wonder what makes him stay. He must have some attachment to the Company.

Raven finally came around. We nursed him and fed him and, finally, bedraggled, we rounded up Whisper's and the Limper's horses and headed for Lords. We travelled without enthusiasm, knowing we were headed for another battlefield, another land of standing dead men.

We could not get close. Harden's Rebels had the city besieged, circumvallated and bottled in a double fosse. A grim black cloud concealed the city itself. Cruel lightning rambled its edges, dueling the might of the Eighteen. Harden had not come alone.

The Circle seemed determined to avenge Whisper.

"Catcher and Nightcrawler are playing rough," Raven observed, after one particularly violent exchange. "I suggest we drift south and wait. If they abandon Lords, we'll join back up when they run toward the Windy Country." His face twisted horribly. He did not relish that prospect. He knew the Windy Country.

So south we scooted, and joined up with other stragglers. We spent twelve days in hiding, waiting. Raven organized the stragglers into the semblance of a military unit. I passed the time writing and thinking about Whisper, wondering how much she would influence the eastern situation.

The rare glimpses I got of Lords convinced me that she was our side's last real hope.

Rumor had the Rebel applying just as much pressure elsewhere. The Lady supposedly had to transfer The Hanged Man and Bonegnasher from the east to stiffen resistance. One rumor had Shapeshifter slain in the fighting at Rye.

I worried about the Company. Our brethren had gotten into Lords before Harden's arrival.

Not a man falls without my telling his tale. How can I do that from twenty miles away? How many details will be lost in the oral histories I will have to collect after the fact? How many men will fall without their deaths being observed at all?

But mostly I spend my time thinking about the Limper and the Lady. And agonizing.

I do not think that I will be writing any more cute, romantic fantasies about our employer. I have been too close to her. I am not in love now.

I am a haunted man. I am haunted by the Limper's screams. I am haunted by the Lady's laughter. I am haunted by my suspicion that we are furthering the cause of something that deserves to be scrubbed from the face of the earth. I am haunted by the conviction that those bent upon the Lady's eradication are little better than she.

I am haunted by the clear knowledge that, in the end, evil always triumphs.

Oh, my. Trouble. There is a nasty black cloud crawling over the hills to the northeast. Everybody is running around, grabbing weapons and saddling horses. Raven is yelling at me to get my butt moving. . . .

Chapter Five: HARDEN

The wind howled and flung blasts of dust and sand against our backs. We retreated into it, walking backward, the gritty storm finding every gap in armor and clothing, combining with sweat in a stinking, salty mud. The air was hot and dry. It sucked the moisture away quickly, leaving the mud dried in clots. We all had lips cracked and swollen, tongues like moldy pillows choking on the grit crusting the insides of our mouths.

Stormbringer had gotten carried away. We were suffering almost as much as was the Rebel. Visibility was a scant dozen yards. I could barely see the men to my right and left, and only two guys in the rearguard line, walking backward before me. Knowing our enemies had to come after us facing into the wind did not cheer me much.

The men in the other line suddenly scuttled around, plying their bows. Tall somethings loomed out of the swirling dust, cloakshadows swirling around them, flapping like vast wings. I drew my bow and let fly, sure my shaft would drift astray.

It did not. A horseman threw up his hands. His animal whirled and ran before the wind, pursuing riderless companions.

They were pushing hard, keeping close, trying to pick us off before we escaped the Windy Country to the more defensible Stair of Tear. They wanted every man of us stretched dead and plundered beneath the unforgiving desert sun.

Step back. Step back. So damned slow. But there was no choice. If we turned our backs they would swarm over us. We had to make them pay for every approach, to intimidate their exuberance thoroughly.

Stormbringer's sending was our best armor. The Windy Country is wild and brisk at the best of times, flat, barren, and dry, uninhabited, a place where sandstorms are common. But never had it seen a storm like this, that went on hour after hour and day after day, relenting only in the hours of darkness. It made the Windy Country no fit place for any living thing. And only that kept the Company alive.

There were three thousand of us now, falling back before the inexorable tide that had swamped Lords. Our little brotherhood, by refusing to break, had become the nucleus to which the fugitives from the disaster had attached themselves once the Captain had fought his way through the siege lines. We had become the brains and nerves of this fleeing shadow of an army. The Lady herself had sent orders for all Imperial officers to defer to the Captain. Only the Company had produced any signal successes during the northern campaign.

Someone came out of the dust and howl behind me, tapped my shoulder. I whirled. It was not yet time to leave the line.

Raven faced me. The Captain had figured out where I was.

Raven's whole head was wrapped in rags. I squinted, one hand raised to block the biting sand. He screamed something like, "Ta kata wa ya." I shook my head. He pointed rearward, grabbed me, yelled into my ear. "The Captain wants you."

Of course he did. I nodded, handed over bow and arrows, leaned into the wind and grit. Weapons were in short supply. The arrows I had given him were spent Rebel shafts gleaned after they had come wobbling out of the brownish haze.

Trudge trudge trudge. Sand pattering against the top of my head as I walked with chin against chest, hunched, eyes slitted. I did not want to go back. The Captain was not going to say anything I wanted to hear.

A big bush came spinning and bounding toward me. It nearly bowled me over. I laughed. We had Shapeshifter with us. The Rebel would waste a lot of arrows when that hit their lines. They outnumbered us ten or fifteen to one, but numbers could not soften their fear of the Taken.

I stamped into the fangs of the wind till I was sure I had gone too far, or had lost my bearings. It was always the same. After I decided to give up, there it was, the miraculous isle of peace. I entered it, staggering in the sudden absence of wind. My ears roared, refusing to believe the quiet.

Thirty wagons rolled along in tight formation inside the quiet, wheel to wheel. Most were filled with casualties. A thousand men surrounded the wagons, tramping doggedly southward. They stared at the earth and dreaded the coming of their turns out on the line. There was no conversation, no exchange of witticisms. They had seen too many retreats. They followed the Captain only because he promised a chance to survive.

"Croaker! Over here!" The Lieutenant beckoned me from the formation's extreme right flank.

The Captain looked like a naturally surly bear wakened from hibernation prematurely. The grey at his temples wriggled as he chewed his words before spitting them out. His face sagged. His eyes were dark hollows. His voice was infinitely tired. "Thought I told you to stick around."

"It was my turn. . . ."

"You don't take a turn, Croaker. Let me see if I can put it into words simple enough for you. We have three thousand men. We're in continuous contact with the Rebel. We've got one half-assed witchdoctor and one real doctor to take care of those boys. One-Eye has to spend half his energy helping maintain this dome of peace. Which leaves you to carry the medical load. Which means you don't risk yourself out on the line. Not for any reason."

I stared into the emptiness above his left shoulder, scowling at the sand swirling around the sheltered area.

"Am I getting through, Croaker? Am I making myself clear? I appreciate your devotion to the Annals, your determination to get the feel of the action, but. . . ."

I bobbed my head, glanced at the wagons and their sad burdens. So many wounded, and so little I could do for them. He did not see the helpless feeling that caused. All I could do was sew them up and pray, and make the dying comfortable till they went—whereupon we dumped them to make room for newcomers.

Too many were lost who need not have been, had I had time, trained help, and a decent surgery. Why did I go out to the battle line? Because I could accomplish something there. I could strike back at our tormentors.

"Croaker," the Captain growled. "I get the feeling you're not listening."

"Yes sir. Understood, sir. I'll stay here and tend to my sewing."

"Don't look so bleak." He touched my shoulder. "Catcher says we'll reach the Stair of Tear tomorrow. Then we can do what we all want. Bloody Harden's nose."

Harden had become the senior Rebel general. "Did he say how we're going to manage that, outnumbered a skillion to one?"

The Captain scowled. He did his shuffling little bear dance while he phrased a reassuring answer.

Three thousand exhausted, beaten men turn back Harden's victory-hopped horde? Not bloody likely. Not even with three of the Ten Who Were Taken helping.

"I thought not," I sneered.

"That's not your department, though, is it? Catcher doesn't second-guess your surgical procedures, does he? Then why question the grand strategy?"

I grinned. "The unwritten law of all armies, Captain. The lower ranks have the privilege of questioning the sanity and competence of their commanders. It's the mortar holding an army together."

The Captain eyed me from his shorter stature, wider displacement, and from beneath shaggy brows. "That holds them together, eh? And you know what keeps them moving?"

"What's that?"

"Guys like me ass-kicking guys like you when they start philosophizing. If you get my drift."

"I believe I do, sir." I moved out, recovered my kit from the wagon where I had stashed it, went to work. There were few new casualties.

Rebel ambition was wearing down under Stormbringer's ceaseless assault.

I was loafing along, waiting for a call, when I spotted Elmo loping out of the weather. I hadn't seen him for days. He fell in beside the Captain. I ambled over.

". . . sweep around our right," he was saying. "Maybe trying to reach the Stair first." He glanced at me, lifted a hand in greeting. It shook. He was pallid with weariness. Like the Captain, he had had little rest since we had entered the Windy Country.

"Pull a company out of reserve. Take them in flank," the Captain replied. "Hit them hard, and stand fast. They won't expect that. It'll shake them. Make them wonder what we're up to."

"Yes sir." Elmo turned to go.

"Elmo?"

"Sir?"

"Be careful out there. Save your energy. We're going to keep moving tonight."

Elmo's eyes spoke tortured volumes. But he did not question his orders. He is a good soldier. And, as did I, he knew they came from above the Captain's head. Perhaps from the Tower itself.

Hitherto, night had brought a tacit truce. The rigors of the days had left both armies unwilling to take one needless step after dark. There had been no nighttime contact.

Even those hours of respite, when the storm slept, were not enough to keep the armies from marching with their butts drooping against their heels. Now our high lords wanted an extra effort, hoping to gain some tactical advantage. Get to the Stair by night, get dug in, make the Rebel come at us out of perpetual storm. It made sense. But it was the sort of move ordered by an armchair general three hundred miles behind the fighting.

"You hear that?" the Captain asked me.

"Yeah. Sounds dumb."

"I agree with the Taken, Croaker. The travelling will be easier for us and more difficult for the Rebel. Are you caught up?"

"Yes."

"Then try to stay out of the way. Go hitch a ride. Take a nap."

I wandered away, cursing the ill fortune that had stripped us of most of our mounts. Gods, walking was getting old.

I did not take the Captain's advice, though it was sound. I was too keyed up to rest. The prospect of a night march had shaken me.

I roamed around seeking old friends. The Company had scattered throughout the larger mob, as cadre for the Captain's will. Some men I hadn't seen since Lords. I did not know if they were still alive.

I could find no one but Goblin, One-Eye, and Silent. Today Goblin and One-Eye were no more communicative than Silent. Which said a lot about morale.

They trudged doggedly onward, eyes on the dry earth, only rarely making some gesture or muttering some word to maintain the integrity of our bubble of peace. I trudged with them. Finally, I tried breaking the ice with a "Hi."

Goblin grunted. One-Eye gave me a few seconds of evil stare. Silent did not acknowledge my existence.

"Captain says we're going to march through the night," I told them. I had to make someone else as miserable as I was.

Goblin's look asked me why I wanted to tell that kind of lie. One-Eye muttered something about turning the bastard into a toad.

"The bastard you're going to have to turn is Soulcatcher," I said smugly.

He gave me another evil look. "Maybe I'll practice on you, Croaker."

One-Eye did not like the night march, so Goblin immediately approved the genius of the man who had initiated the idea. But his enthusiasm was so slight One-Eye did not bother taking the bait.

I thought I would give it another try. "You guys look as sour as I feel."

No rise. Not even a turn of the head. "Be that way." I drooped too, put one foot ahead of the other, blanked my mind.

They came and got me to take care of Elmo's wounded. There were a dozen of them, and that was it for the day. The Rebel had run out of do or die.

Darkness came early under the storm. We went about business as usual. We got a little away from the Rebel, waited for the storm to abate, pitched a camp with fires built of whatever brush could be scrounged. Only this time it was just a brief rest, till the stars came out. They stared down with mockery in their twinkles, saying all our sweat and blood really had no meaning in the long eye of time. Nothing we did would be recalled a thousand years from now.

Such thoughts infected us all. No one had any ideals or glory-lust left. We just wanted to get somewhere, lie down, and forget the war.

The war would not forget us. As soon as he believed the Rebel to be satisfied that we were encamped, the Captain resumed the march, now in a ragged column snaking slowly across moonlighted barrens.

Hours passed and we seemed to get nowhere. The land never changed. I glanced back occasionally, checking the renewed storm Stormbringer was hurling against the Rebel camp. Lightning rippled and flickered in this one. It was more furious than anything they had faced so far.

The shadowed Stair of Tear materialized so slowly that it was there for an hour before I realized it was not a bank of cloud low on the horizon. The stars began to fade and the east to lighten before the land started rising.

The Stair of Tear is a rugged, wild range virtually impassable except for the one steep pass from which the

202   GLEN COOK

cordillera takes its name. The land rises gradually till it
reaches sudden, towering red sandstone bluffs and mesas
which stretch either way for hundreds of miles. In the
morning sun they looked like the weathered battlements of
a giant's fortress.

The column wound into a canyon choked with talus,
halted while a path was cleared for the wagons. I dragged
myself to a bluff top and watched the storm. It was
moving our way.

Would we get through before Harden arrived?

The blockage was a fresh fall which covered only a
quarter mile of road. Beyond it lay the route travelled by
caravans before the war interrupted trade.

I faced the storm again. Harden was making good time.
I suppose anger drove him. He was not about to turn
loose. We had killed his brother-in-law, and had engineered the Taking of his cousin. . . .

Movement to the west caught my eye. A whole range of
ferocious thunderheads was moving toward Harden, rum-
bling and brawling among themselves. A funnel cloud
spun off and streaked toward the sandstorm. The Taken
play rough.

Harden was stubborn. He kept coming through everything.

"Yo! Croaker!" someone shouted. "Come on."

I looked down. The wagons were through the worst.
Time to go.

Out on the flats the thunderheads spun off another funnel cloud. I almost felt sorry for Harden's men.

Soon after I rejoined the column the ground shuddered.
The bluff I had climbed quivered, groaned, toppled,
sprawled across the road. Another little gift for Harden.

We reached our stopping place shortly before nightfall.
Decent country at last! Real trees. A gurgling creek. Those
who had any strength left began digging in or cooking.

The rest fell in their tracks. The Captain did not press. The best medicine at the moment was the simple freedom to rest.

I slept like the proverbial log.

One-Eye wakened me at rooster time. "Let's get to work," he said. "The Captain wants a hospital set up." He made a face. His looks like a prune at the best of times. "We're supposed to have some help coming up from Charm."

I groaned and moaned and cursed and got up. Every muscle was stiff. Every bone ached. "Next time we're someplace civilized enough to have taverns remind me to drink a toast to eternal peace," I grumbled. "One-Eye, I'm ready to retire."

"So who isn't? But you're the Annalist, Croaker. You're always rubbing our noses in tradition. You know you only got two ways out while we've got this commission. Dead or feet first. Shove some chow in your ugly face and let's get cracking. I got more important things to do than play nursemaid."

"Cheerful this morning, aren't we?"

"Positively rosy." He grumped around while I got myself into an approximation of order.

The camp was coming to life. Men were eating and washing the desert off their bodies. They were cussing and fussing and bitching. Some were even talking to one another. The recovery had begun.

Sergeants and officers were out surveying the lie of the slope, seeking the most defensible strongpoints. This, then, was the place where the Taken wanted to make a stand.

It was a good spot. It was that part of the pass which gave the Stair its name, a twelve hundred foot rise overlooking a maze of canyons. The old road wound back and forth across the mountainside in countless switchbacks, so that from a distance it looked like a giant's lopsided stairway.

One-Eye and I drafted a dozen men and began moving the wounded to a quiet grove well above the prospective battleground. We spent an hour making them comfortable and getting set for future business.

"What's that?" One-Eye suddenly demanded.

I listened. The din of preparation had died. "Something up," I said.

"Genius," he countered. "Probably the people from Charm."

"Let's take a look." I tramped out of the grove and down toward the Captain's headquarters. The newcomers were obvious the moment I left the trees.

I would guess there were a thousand of them, half soldiers from the Lady's personal Guard in brilliant uniforms, the rest apparently teamsters. The train of wagons and livestock were more exciting than the reinforcements. "Feast time tonight," I called to One-Eye, who was following me. He looked the wagons over and smiled. Pure pleasure smiles from him are only slightly more common than the fabled hen's teeth. They are certainly worth recording in these Annals.

With the Guards battalion was the Taken called The Hanged Man. He was improbably tall and lean. His head was twisted way over to one side. His neck was swollen and purpled from the bite of a noose. His face was frozen into the bloated expression of one who has been strangled. I expect he had considerable difficulty speaking.

He was the fifth of the Taken I had seen, following Soulcatcher, the Limper, Shapeshifter, and Whisper. I missed Nightcrawler in Lords, and had not yet seen Stormbringer, despite proximity. The Hanged Man was different. The others usually wore something to conceal head and face. Excepting Whisper, they had spent ages in the ground. The grave had not treated them kindly.

Soulcatcher and Shapeshifter were there to greet the

Hanged Man. The Captain was nearby, back to them, listening to the commander of the Lady's guardsmen. I eased closer, hoping to eavesdrop.

The guardsman was being surly because he had to place himself at the Captain's disposal. None of the regulars liked taking orders from a come-lately mercenary from overseas.

I sidled nearer the Taken. And found I could not understand a word of their conversation. They were speaking TelleKurre, which had died with the fall of the Domination.

A hand touched mine, lightly. Startled, I looked down into the wide brown eyes of Darling, whom I had not seen for days. She made rapid gestures with her fingers. I have been learning her signs. She wanted to show me something.

She led me to Raven's tent, which was not far from the Captain's. She scrambled inside, returned with a wooden doll. Loving craftsmanship had gone into its creation. I could not imagine the hours Raven must have put into it. I could not imagine where he had found them.

Darling slowed her finger talk so I could follow more easily. I was not yet very facile. She told me Raven made the doll, as I had guessed, and that now he was sewing up a wardrobe. She thought she had a great treasure. Recalling the village where we had found her, I could not doubt that it was the finest toy she had ever possessed.

Revealing object, when you think about Raven, who comes across so bitter, cold, and silent, whose only use for a knife seems so sinister.

Darling and I conversed for several minutes. Her thoughts are delightfully straightforward, a refreshing contrast in a world filled with devious, prevaricating, unpredictable, scheming people.

A hand squeezed my shoulder, halfway between angry and companionable. "The Captain is looking for you, Croaker." Raven's dark eyes glinted like obsidian under a quarter moon. He pretended the doll was invisible. He *likes* to come across hard, I realized.

"Right," I said, making manual good-byes. I enjoyed learning from Darling. She enjoyed teaching me. I think it gave her a feeling of worth. The Captain was considering having everyone learn her sign language. It would make a valuable suppliment to our traditional but inadequate battle signals.

The Captain gave me a black look when I arrived, but spared me a lecture. "Your new help and supplies are over yonder. Show them where to go."

"Yes sir."

The responsibility was getting to him. He hadn't ever commanded so many men, nor faced conditions so adverse, with orders so impossible, staring at a future so uncertain. From where he stood it looked like we would be sacrificed to buy time.

We of the Company are not enthusiastic fighters. But the Stair of Tear could not be held by trickery.

It looked like the end had come.

No one will sing songs in our memory. We are the last of the Free Companies of Khatovar. Our traditions and memories live only in these Annals. We are our only mourners.

It is the Company against the world. Thus it has been and ever will be.

My aid from the Lady consisted of two qualified battle-field surgeons and a dozen trainees of various degrees of skill, along with a brace of wagons brimming with medical supplies. I was grateful. Now I stood a chance of saving a few men.

I took the newcomers to my grove, explained how I worked, turned them loose on my patients. After making sure they were not complete incompetents, I turned the hospital over and left.

I was restless. I did not like what was happening to the Company. It had acquired too many new followers and responsibilities. The old intimacy was gone. Time was, I saw every one of the men every day. Now there were some I had not seen since before the debacle at Lords. I did not know if they were dead, alive, or captive. I was almost neurotically anxious that some men had been lost and would be forgotten.

The Company is our family. The brotherhood makes it go. These days, with all these new northern faces, the prime force holding the Company together is a desperate effort by the brethren to reachieve the old intimacy. The strain of trying marks every face.

I went out to one of the forward watchpoints, which overlooked the fall of the brook into the canyons. Way, way down there, below the mist, lay a small, glimmering pool. A thin trickle left it, running toward the Windy Country. It would not complete its journey. I searched the chaotic ranks of sandstone towers and buttes. Thunderheads with lightning swords aflash on their brows grumbled and pounded the badlands, reminding me that trouble was not far away.

Harden was coming despite Stormbringer's wrath. He would make contact tomorrow, I guessed. I wondered how much the storms had hurt him. Surely not enough.

I spied a brown hulk shambling down the switchback road. Shapeshifter, going out to practice his special terrors. He could enter the Rebel camp as one of them, practice poison magics upon their cookpots or fill their drinking water with disease. He could become the shadow in the darkness that all men fear, taking them one at a time, leaving only mangled remains to fill the living with terror. I envied him even while I loathed him.

*　　　*　　　*

The stars twinkled above the campfire. It had burned low while some of us old hands played Tonk. I was a slight winner. I said, "I'm quitting while I'm ahead. Anybody want my place?" I unwound my aching legs and moved away, settled against a log, stared at the sky. The stars seemed merry and friendly.

The air was cool and fresh and still. The camp was quiet. Crickets and nightbirds sang their soothing songs. The world was at peace. It was hard to believe that this place was soon to become a battlefield. I wriggled till I was comfortable, watched for shooting stars. I was determined to enjoy the moment. It might be the last such I would know.

The fire spit and crackled. Somebody found ambition enough to add a little wood. It blazed up, sent piney smoke drifting my way, launched shadows which danced over the intent faces of the card players. One-Eye's lips were taut because he was losing. Goblin's frog mouth was stretched in an unconscious grin. Silent was a blank, being Silent. Elmo was thinking hard, scowling as he calculated odds. Jolly was more sour than customary. It was good to see Jolly again. I had feared him lost at Lords.

Only one puny meteor rolled across the sky. I gave it up, closed my eyes, listened to my heartbeat. *Harden is coming. Harden is coming,* it said. It pounded out a drumbeat, mimicking the tread of advancing legions.

Raven settled down beside me. "Quiet tonight," he observed.

"Calm before the storm," I replied. "What's cooking with the high and the mighty?"

"Lot of argument. The Captain, Catcher, and the new one are letting them yap. Letting them get it out of their systems. Who's ahead?"

"Goblin."

"One-Eye isn't dealing from the bottom of the deck?"

"We never caught him."

"I heard that," One-Eye growled. "One of these days, Raven. . . ."

"I know. Zap. I'm a frog prince. Croaker, you been up the hill since it got dark?"

"No. Why?"

"Something unusual over in the east. Looks like a comet."

My heart did a small flip. I calculated quickly. "You're probably right. It's due back." I rose. He did too. We walked uphill.

Every major event in the saga of the Lady and her husband has been presaged by a comet. Countless Rebel prophets have predicted that she will fall while a comet is in the sky. But their most dangerous prophecy concerns the child who will be a reincarnation of the White Rose. The Circle is spending a lot of energy trying to locate the kid.

Raven led me to a heighth from which we could see the stars lying low in the east. Sure enough, something like a faraway silver spearhead rode the sky there. I stared a long time before observing, "It seems to be pointed at Charm."

"I thought so too." He was silent for a while. "I'm not much on prophecies, Croaker. They sound too much like superstition. But this makes me nervous."

"You've heard those prophecies all your life. I'd be surprised if they *hadn't* touched you."

He grunted, not satisfied. "The Hanged Man brought news of the east. Whisper has taken Rust."

"Good news, good news," I said, with considerable sarcasm.

"She's taken Rust *and* surrounded Trinket's army. We can have the whole east by next summer."

We faced the canyon. A few of Harden's advance units had reached the foot of the switchbacks. Stormbringer had broken off her long assault in order to prepare for Harden's attempt to break through here.

"So it comes down to us," I whispered. "We have to stop them here or the whole thing goes because of a sneak attack through the back way."

"Maybe. But don't count the Lady out even if we fail. The Rebel hasn't yet faced Her. And they know it to a man. Each mile they move toward the Tower will fill them with greater dread. Terror itself will defeat them unless they find their prophesied child."

"Maybe." We watched the comet. It was far, far away yet, just barely detectable. It would be up there a long time. Great battles would be fought before it departed.

I made a face. "Maybe you shouldn't have shown me. Now I'll dream about the damned thing."

Raven flashed a rare grin. "Dream us a victory," he suggested.

I did some dreaming aloud. "We've got the high ground. Harden has to bring his men up twelve hundred feet of switchback. They'll be easy meat when they get here."

"Whistling in the dark, Croaker. I'm going to turn in. Good luck tomorrow."

"Same to you," I replied. He would be in the thick of it. The Captain had chosen him to command a battalion of veteran regulars. They would be holding one flank, sweeping the road with arrow flights.

I dreamed, but my dreams were not what I expected. A wavering golden thing came, hovered above me, glowing like shoals of faraway stars. I was not sure whether I was asleep or awake, and still have not satisfied myself either way. I will call it dream because it sits more comfortably that way. I do not like to think the Lady had taken that much interest in me.

It was my own fault. All those romances I wrote about her had gone to seed on the fertile stable floor of my

imagination. Such presumption, my dreams. The Lady
Herself send Her spirit to comfort one silly, war-weary,
quietly frightened soldier? In the name of heaven, why?

That glow came and hovered above me, and sent reassurances overtoned by harmonics of amusement. *Fear not,
my faithful. The Stair of Tear is not the Lock of the
Empire. It can be broken without harm. Whatever happens,
my faithful will remain safe. The Stair is but a milemark
along the Rebel's road to destruction.*

There was more, all of a puzzlingly personal nature. My
wildest fantasies were being reflected back upon me. At
the end, for just an instant, a face peeked from the golden
glow. It was the most beautiful female face I have ever
seen, though I cannot now recall it.

Next morning I told One-Eye about the dream as I
hounded my hospital into life. He looked at me and
shrugged. "Too much imagination, Croaker." He was
preoccupied, anxious to complete his medical chores and
get gone. He hated the work.

My work caught up, I meandered toward the main
encampment. My head was stuffy and my mood sour. The
cool, dry mountain air was not as invigorating as it should
have been.

I found the temper of the men as sour as my own.
Below, Harden's forces were moving.

Part of winning is a downdeep certainty that, no matter
how bad things look, a road to victory will open. The
Company carried that conviction through the debacle at
Lords. We'd always found a way to bloody the Rebel's
nose, even while the Lady's armies were in retreat. Now,
though. . . . The conviction has begun to waver.

Forsberg, Roses, Lords, and a dozen lesser defeats. Part
of losing is the converse of winning. We were haunted by
a secret fear that, despite the obvious advantages of

terrain and backing by the Taken, something would go
wrong.

Maybe they cooked it up themselves. Maybe the Captain was behind it, or even Soulcatcher. Possibly it came
about naturally, as these things once did. . . .

One-Eye had trooped downhill behind me, sour, surly,
grumbling to himself, and spoiling for a row. His path
crossed Goblin's.

Slugabed Goblin had just dragged out of his bedroll. He
had a bowl of water and was washing up. He is a fastidi-
ous little wart. One-Eye spotted him and saw a chance to
punish somebody with his foul mood. He muttered a string
of strange words and went into a curious little fling that
looked half ballet and half primitive war dance.

Goblin's water changed.

I smelled it from twenty feet away. It had turned a
malignant brown. Sickening green gobs floated on its surface.
It even *felt* foul.

Goblin rose with magnificent dignity, turned. He looked
an evilly grinning One-Eye in the eye for several seconds.
Then he bowed. When his head came up he wore a huge
frog smile. He opened his mouth and let fly the most
godawful, earthshaking howl I have ever heard.

They were off, and damned be the fool who got in their
way. Shadows scattered round One-Eye, wriggling across
the earth like a thousand hasty serpents. Ghosts danced,
crawling from under rocks, jumping down from trees,
hopping out of bushes. The latter squealed and howled and
giggled and chased One-Eye's shadow snakes.

The ghosts stood two feet tall and very much resembled
half-pint One-Eyes with double-ugly faces and behinds
like those of female baboons in season. What they did
with captured shadow snakes taste forbids me tell.

One-Eye, foiled, leapt into the air. He cursed, shrieked,

foamed at the mouth. To us old hands, who had witnessed these hatter-mad battles before, it was obvious that Goblin had been laying in the weeds, waiting for One-Eye to start something.

This was one time when One-Eye had more than a lone bolt to shoot.

He banished the snakes. The rocks, bushes, and trees that had belched Goblin's critters now disgorged gigantic, glossy-green dung beetles. The big bugs jumped Goblin's elves, rolled them right up, and began tumble-bugging them toward the edge of the cliff.

Needless to say, all the whoop and holler drew an audience. Laughter ripped out of us old hands, long familiar with this endless duel. It spread to the others once they realized this was not sorcery run amok.

Goblin's red-bottomed ghosts sprouted roots and refused to be tumbled. They grew into huge, drooling-mawed carnivorous plants fit to inhabit the cruelest jungle of nightmare. Clickety-clackety-crunch, all across the slope, carapaces broke between closing vegetable jaws. That spine-shaking, tooth-grinding feeling you get when you crunch a big cockroach slithered across the slopes, magnified a thousand times, birthing a plague of shudders. For a moment even One-Eye remained motionless.

I glanced around. The Captain had come to watch. He betrayed a satisfied smile. It was a precious gem, that smile, rarer than roc's eggs. His companions, regular officers and Guards captains, appeared baffled.

Someone took up position beside me, at an intimate, comradely distance. I glanced sideways, found myself shoulder to shoulder with Soulcatcher. Or elbow to shoulder. The Taken does not stand very tall.

"Amusing, yes?" he said in one of his thousand voices.

I nodded nervously.

One-Eye shuddered all over, jumped high in the air

again, wailed and howled, then went down kicking and flopping like a man with the falling sickness.

The surviving beetles rushed together, zip-zap, clickety-clack, into two seething piles, clacking their mandibles angrily, scraping against one another chitinously. Brown smog wriggled from the piles in thick ropes, twisted and joined, became a curtain concealing the frenzied bugs. The smoke contracted into globules which bounced, bounding higher after each contact with the earth. Then they did not come down, but rather drifted on the breeze, sprouting what grew into gnarly digits.

What we had here were replicas of One-Eye's horny paws a hundred times life size. Those hands went weed-plucking through Goblin's monster garden, ripping his plants up by the roots, knotting their stems together in elegant, complicated sailor's knots, forming an ever-elongating braid.

"They do have more talent than one would suspect," Soulcatcher observed. "But so wasted on frivolity."

"I don't know." I gestured. The show was having an invigorating effect on morale. Feeling a breath of that boldness which animates me at odd moments, I suggested, "This is a sorcery they can appreciate, unlike the oppressive, bitter wizardries of the Taken."

Catcher's black morion faced me for a few seconds. I imagined fires burning behind the narrow eyeslits. Then a girlish giggle slipped forth. "You're right. We're so filled with doom and gloom and brooding and terror we infect whole armies. One soon forgets the emotional panorama of life."

How odd, I thought. This was a Taken with a chink in its armor, a Soulcatcher drawing aside one of the veils concealing its secret being. The Annalist in me caught the scent of a tale and began to bay.

Catcher sidestepped me as though reading my thoughts. "You had a visitation last night?"

The Annalist-hound's voice died in midcry. "I had a strange dream. About the Lady."

Catcher chuckled, a deep, bass rumble. That constant changing of voices can rattle the most stolid of men. It put me on the defensive. His very comradeliness, too, disturbed me.

"I think she favors you, Croaker. Some little thing about you has captured her imagination, just as she has caught yours. What did she have to say?"

Something way back told me to be careful. Catcher's query was warm and offhand, yet there was a hidden intensity there which said that the question was not at all casual.

"Just reassurances," I replied. "Something about the Stair of Tear not being all that critical in her scheme. But it was only a dream."

"Of course." He seemed satisfied. "Only a dream." But the voice was the female one he used when he was most serious.

The men were oohing and ahing. I turned to check the progress of the contest.

Goblin's skein of pitcher-plants had transmogrified into a huge airborne man-of-war jellyfish. The brown hands were entangled in its tentacles, trying to tear themselves free. And over the cliff face, observing, floated a giant pink face, bearded, surrounded by tangled orange hair. One eye was half closed, sleepily, by a livid scar. I frowned, baffled. "What's that?" I knew it was not any doing of Goblin's or One-Eye's, and wondered if Silent had joined the game, just to show them up.

Soulcatcher made a sound that was a creditable imitation of a bird's dying squawk. "Harden," he said, and whirled to face the Captain, bellowing, "To arms. They come."

In seconds men were flying toward their positions. The last hints of the struggle between Goblin and One-Eye became misty tatters floating on the wind, drifting toward the leering Harden face, giving it a loathsome case of acne where they touched. A cute fillip, I thought, but don't try to take him heads up, boys. He won't play games.

The answer to our scramble was a lot of horn-blowing from below, and a grumble of drums which echoed in the canyons like distant thunder.

The Rebel poked at us all day, but it was obvious that he was not serious, that he was just prodding the hornets' nest to see what would happen. He was well aware of the difficulty of storming the Stair.

All of which portended Harden having something nasty up his sleeve.

Overall, though, the skirmishes boosted morale. The men began to believe there was a chance they could hold.

Though the comet swam among the stars, and a galaxy of campfires speckled the Stair below, the night gave the lie to my feeling that the Stair was the heart of war. I sat on an outcrop overlooking the enemy, knees up under my chin, musing on the latest news from the east. Whisper was besieging Frost now, after having finished Trinket's army and having defeated Moth and Sidle among the talking menhirs of the Plain of Fear. The east looked a worse disaster for the Rebel than was the north for us.

It could get worse here. Moth and Sidle and Linger had joined Harden. Others of the Eighteen were down there, as yet unidentified. Our enemies did smell blood.

I have never seen the northern auroras, though I am told we would have gotten glimpses had we held Oar and Deal long enough to have wintered there. The tales I have heard about those gentle, gaudy lights make me think they are the only thing to compare with what took shape over the canyons, as the Rebel campfires dwindled. Long, long, thin banners of tenuous light twisted up toward the stars, shimmering, undulating like seaweed in a gentle current. Soft pinks and greens, yellows and blues, beautiful hues. A phrase leapt into my mind. An ancient name. The Pastel Wars.

The Company fought in the Pastel Wars, long, long ago. I tried to recall what the Annals said about those conflicts. It would not all come to the fore, but I remembered enough to become frightened. I hurried toward the officers' compound, seeking Soulcatcher.

I found him, and told him what I remembered, and he thanked me for my concern, but said he was familiar with both the Pastel Wars and the Rebel cabal sending up these lights. We had no worries. This attack had been anticipated and the Hanged Man was here to abort it.

"Take yourself a seat somewhere, Croaker. Goblin and One-Eye put on their show. Now it's the turn of the Ten." He oozed a confidence both strong and malignant, so that I supposed the Rebel had fallen into some Taken trip.

I did as he suggested, venturing back out to my lonely watchpost. Along the way I passed through a camp aroused by the growing spectacle. A murmur of fear ran hither and yon, rising and falling like the mutter of distant surf.

The colored streamers were stronger now, and there was a frenetic jerkiness to their movements which suggested a thwarted will. Maybe Catcher was right. Maybe this would come to nothing but a flashy show for the troops.

I resumed my perch. The canyon bottom no longer twinkled. It was a sea of ink down there, not at all softened by the glow of the writhing streamers. But if nothing could be seen, plenty could be heard. The acoustics of the land were remarkable.

Harden was on the move. Only the advance of his entire army could generate so much metallic rattle and tinkle.

Harden and his henchmen were confident too.

A soft green light banner floated up into the night, fluttering lazily, like a streamer of tissue in an updraft. It faded as it rose, and disintegrated into dying sparks high overhead.

What snipped it loose? I wondered. Harden or the Hanged Man? Did this bode good or ill?

It was a subtle contest, almost impossible to follow. It was like watching superior fencers duel. You could not follow everything unless you were an expert yourself. Goblin and One-Eye had gone at it like a couple of barbarians with broadswords, comparatively speaking.

Little by little, the colorful aurora died. That had to be the doing of the Hanged Man. The unanchored light banners did us no harm.

The racket below got closer.

Where was Stormbringer? We had not heard from her for a while. This seemed an ideal time to gift the Rebel with miserable weather.

Catcher, too, seemed to be laying down on the job. In all the time we have been in service to the Lady we have not seen him do anything really dramatic. Was he less mighty than his reputation, or, perhaps, saving himself for some extremity only he foresaw?

Something new was happening below. The canyon walls had begun to glow in stripes and spots, a deep, deep red that was barely noticeable at first. The red became brighter. Only after patches began to drip and ooze did I notice the hot draft riding up the cliff face.

''Great gods,'' I murmured, stricken. Here was a deed worthy of my expectations of the Taken.

Stone began to grumble and roar as molten rock ran away and left mountainsides undermined. There were cries from below, the cries of the hopeless who see doom coming and can do nothing to stay or evade it. Harden's men were being cooked and crushed.

They were in the witch's cauldron for sure, but something made me uneasy anyway. There seemed to be too little yelling for a force the size of Harden's.

In spots the rock became so hot it caught fire. The canyon expelled a furious updraft. The wind howled over the hammering of falling rocks. The light grew bright enough to betray Rebel units climbing the switchbacks.

Too few, I thought. . . . A lonely figure on another outcrop caught my eye. One of the Taken, though in the shifting, uncertain light I could not be certain which. It was nodding to itself as it observed the enemy's travails.

The redness, the melting, the collapsing and burning spread till the whole panorama was veined with red and poked with bubbling pools.

A drop of moisture hit my cheek. I looked up, startled, and a second fat drop smacked the bridge of my nose.

The stars had vanished. The spongy bellies of fat grey clouds raced overhead, almost low enough to touch, garishly tinted by the hellscape below.

The bellies of the clouds opened over the canyon. Caught on the edge of the downpour, I was nearly beaten to my knees. Out there it was more savage.

Rain hit molten rock. The roar of steam was deafening. Particolored, it stormed toward the sky. The fringe I caught, as I turned to run, was hot enough to redden patches of skin.

Those poor Rebel fools, I thought. Steamed like lobsters. . . .

I had been dissatisfied because I had seen little spectacular from the Taken? Not anymore. I had trouble keeping my supper down as I reflected on the cold, cruel calculation that had gone into the planning of this.

I suffered one of those crises of conscience familiar to

every mercenary, and which few outside the profession
understand. My job is to defeat my employer's enemies.
Usually any way I can. And heaven knows the Company
has served some blackhearted villains. But there was something *wrong* about what was happening below. In retrospect,
I think we all felt it. Perhaps it sprang from a misguided
sense of solidarity with fellow soldiers dying without an
opportunity to defend themselves.

We *do* have a sense of honor in the Company.

The roar of downpour and steam faded. I ventured back
to my vantage point. Except for small patches, the canyon
was dark. I looked for the Taken I had seen earlier. He
was gone.

Above, the comet came out from behind the last clouds,
marring the night like a tiny, mocking smile. It had a
distinct bend in its tail. Over on the saw-toothed horizon, a
moon took a cautious peek at the tortured land.

Horns blared in that direction, their tinny voices distinctly edged with panic. They gave way to a distance
muddled sound of fighting, an uproar which swelled rapidly.
The fighting sounded heavy and confused. I started toward
my makeshift hospital, confident there would be work for
me soon. For some reason I was not particularly startled
or upset.

Messengers dashed past me, zipping around purposefully.
The Captain had done that much with those stragglers. He
had restored their senses of order and discipline.

Something whooshed overhead. A seated man riding a
dark rectangle swooped through the moonlight, banking
toward the uproar. Soulcatcher on his flying carpet.

A bright violet shell flared around him. His carpet rocked
violently, slid sideways for a dozen yards. The light faded,
shrank in upon him and vanished, leaving me with spots
before my eyes. I shrugged, tramped on up the hill.

The early casualties beat me to the hospital. In a way, I was pleased. That indicated efficiency and retention of cool heads under fire. The Captain had worked wonders.

The clatter of companies moving through the darkness confirmed my suspicion that this was more than a nuisance attack by men who seldom dared the dark. (The night belongs to the Lady). Somehow, we had been flanked.

"About damned time you showed your ugly face," One-Eye growled. "Over there. Surgery. I had them start setting up lights."

I washed and got to it. The Lady's people joined me, and pitched in heroically, and for the first time since we had taken the commission I felt like I was doing the wounded some good.

But they just kept pouring in. The clangor continued to rise. Soon it was evident that the Rebel's canyon thrust had been but a feint. All that showy drama had been to little purpose.

Dawn was coloring the sky when I glanced up and found a tattered Soulcatcher facing me. He looked like he had been roasted over a slow fire, and basted in something bluish, greenish, and nasty. He exuded a smoky aroma.

"Start loading your wagons, Croaker," he said in his businesslike female voice. "The Captain is sending you a dozen helpers."

All the transport, including that come up from the south, was parked above my open-air hospital. I glanced that way. A tall, lean, crooked-necked individual was harrassing the teamsters into hitching up. "The battle going sour?" I asked. "Caught you by surprise, didn't they?"

Catcher ignored the latter remark. "We have achieved most of our goals. Only one task remains unfulfilled." The voice he chose was deep, sonorous, slow, a speech-maker's voice. "The fighting may go either way. It's too soon to tell. Your Captain has given this rabble backbone. But lest defeat catch you up, get your charges moving.''

A few wagons were creaking down toward us already. I shrugged, passed the word, found the next man who needed my attention. While I worked, I asked Catcher, ''If the thing is in the balance, shouldn't you be over there pounding on the Rebel?''

''I'm doing the Lady's bidding, Croaker. Our goals are almost met. Linger and Moth are no more. Sidle is grievously injured. Shifter has accomplished his deceit. There is naught left but to deprive the Rebel of their general.''

I was confused. Divergent thoughts found their ways to my tongue and betrayed themselves. ''But shouldn't we try to break them here?'' And, ''This northern campaign has been hard on the Circle. First Raker, then Whisper. Now Linger and Moth.''

''With Sidle and Harden to go. Yes. They beat us again and again, and each time it costs them the heart of their strength.'' He gazed downhill, toward a small company coming our way. Raven was in the lead. Catcher faced the wagon park. The Hanged Man stopped gesturing and struck a pose: man listening.

Suddenly, Soulcatcher resumed talking. ''Whisper has breached the walls of Frost. Nightcrawler has negotiated the treacherous menhirs on the Plain of Fear, and approaches the suburbs of Thud. The Faceless is on the Plain now, moving toward Barns. They say Parcel committed suicide last night at Ade, to avoid capture by Bonegnasher. Things aren't the disaster they seem, Croaker.''

The hell they aren't, I thought. That's the east. This is here. I could not get excited about victories a quarter of the world away. Here we were getting stomped, and if the Rebel broke through to Charm, nothing that happened in the east would matter.

Raven halted his group and approached me alone. "What do you want them to do?"

I assumed the Captain had sent him, so was sure the Captain had ordered the withdrawal. He would not play games for Catcher. "Put the ones we've treated into the wagons." The teamsters were arraying themselves in a nice line. "Send a dozen or so walking wounded with each wagon. Me and One-Eye and the rest will keep cutting and sewing. What?"

He had a look in his eye. I did not like it. He glanced at Soulcatcher. So did I.

"I haven't told him yet," Catcher said.

"Told me what?" I knew I would not like it when I heard it. They had that nervous smell about them. It screamed bad news.

Raven smiled. Not a happy smile, but a sort of gruesome rictus. "You and me, we've been drafted again, Croaker."

"What? Come on! Not again!" I still got the shakes thinking about helping do in the Limper and Whisper

"You have the practical experience," Catcher said.

I kept shaking my head.

Raven growled, "I have to go, so do you, Croaker. Besides, you'll want to get it in the Annals, how you took out more of the Eighteen than any of the Taken."

"Crap. What am I? A bounty hunter? No. I'm a physician. The Annals and fighting are incidental."

Raven told Catcher, "This is the man the Captain had to drag off the line when we were crossing the Windy Country." His eyes were narrow, his cheeks taut. He did not want to go either. He was displacing his resentment by chiding me.

"There is no option, Croaker," Soulcatcher said in a child's voice. "The Lady chose you." He tried to soften my disappointment by adding, "She rewards well those who please her. And you have caught her fancy."

I damned myself for my earlier romanticism. That Croaker who had come north, so thoroughly bemused by the mysterious Lady, was another man. A stripling, filled with the foolish ignorances of youth. Yeah. Sometimes you lie to yourself just to keep going.

Catcher told me, "We're not going it alone this time, Croaker. We'll have help from Crooked Neck, Shifter, and Stormbringer."

Sourly, I remarked, "Takes the whole gang to scrub one bandit, eh?"

Catcher did not take the bait. He never does. "The carpet is over there. Collect your weapons and join me." He stalked away.

I took my ire out on my helpers, completely unfairly. Finally, when One-Eye was ready to blow, Raven remarked, "Don't be an asshole, Croaker. We've got to do it, let's do it."

So I apologized to everyone and marched down to join Soulcatcher.

Soulcatcher said, "Get aboard," indicating places. Raven and I assumed the positions we had used before. Catcher handed us lengths of cord. "Tie yourselves securely. This could get rough. I don't want you falling off. And keep a knife handy so you can cut loose when we go in."

My heart fluttered. To tell the truth, I was excited about flying again. Moments from my previous flight haunted me with their joy and beauty. There is a glorious feeling of freedom up there with the cool wind and the eagles.

Catcher even tied himself. Bad sign. "Ready?" Not awaiting an answer, he started muttering. The carpet rocked gently, floated upward light as down on a breeze.

* * *

We cleared the treetops. Framewood smacked me in the behind. My guts sank. Air whipped around me. My hat blew off. I grabbed and missed. The carpet tilted precariously. I found myself gaping down at an earth receding rapidly. Raven grabbed me. Had we not been tied we both would have gone over the side.

We drifted out over the canyons, which looked like a crazy maze from above. The Rebel mass looked like army ants on the march.

I glanced around the sky, which itself is a marvel from that perspective. There were no eagles on the wing. Just vultures. Catcher made a dash through one flight, scattered them.

Another carpet floated up, passed nearby, drifted away till it became but a distant speck. It carried the Hanged Man and two heavily armed Imperials.

"Where's Stormbringer?" I asked.

Catcher extended an arm. Squinting, I discerned a dot on the blue over the desert.

We drifted till I began to wonder if anything was going to happen. Studying the Rebel's progress palled fast. He was making too much headway.

"Get ready," Catcher called over his shoulder.

I gripped my ropes, anticipating something nervewracking. "Now."

The bottom fell out. And stayed out. Down, down, and down we plunged. The air screamed. The earth rolled and twisted and hurtled upward. The distant specks that were Stormbringer and the Hanged Man also plummeted. They grew more distinct as we slanted in from three directions.

We whipped past the level where our brethren were striving to stem the Rebel flood. Down we continued, into a less steep glide, rolling, twisting, fishtailing to avoid colliding with wildly eroded sandstone towers. Some I could have touched as we hurtled past.

A small meadow appeared ahead. Our velocity dropped dramatically, till we hovered. "He's there," Catcher whispered. We slid forward a few yards, floated just peeping round a pillar of sandstone.

The once green meadow had been churned by the passage of horses and men. A dozen wagons and their teamsters remained there. Catcher cursed under his breath.

A shadow flew from between rock spires to our left. *Flash!* Thunder shook the canyon. Sod hurtled into the air. Men cried out, staggered around, scrambled for their weapons.

Another shadow whipped through from another direction. I do not know what the Hanged Man did, but the Rebels began clawing their throats, gasping.

One big man shook the magic and staggered toward a huge black horse tethered to a picket post at the nether end of the meadow. Catcher took our carpet in fast. The earth slammed against its frame. "Off!" he growled as we bounced. He snatched a sword himself.

Raven and I clambered off and followed Catcher on unsteady legs. The Taken swooped down on the choking teamsters and raged among them, blade throwing gore. Raven and I contributed to the massacre, I hope with less enthusiasm.

"What the hell are you doing here?" Catcher raved at his victims. "He was supposed to be alone."

The other carpets returned and settled nearer the fleeing man. The Taken and their henchmen pursued him on wobbly legs. He vaulted onto the horse's back and parted the picket rope with a vicious swordstroke. I stared. I had not expected Harden to be so intimidating. He was every bit as ugly as the apparition that had appeared during Goblin's bout with One-Eye.

Catcher cut down the last Rebel teamster. "Come!" he

snapped. We dogged him as he loped toward Harden. I wondered why I did not have sense enough to hang back.

The Rebel general stopped fleeing. He felled one of the Imperials, who had outdistanced everybody, let out a great bellow of laughter, then howled something unintelligible. The air crackled with the imminence of sorcery.

Violet light flared around all three Taken, more intense than when it had hit Catcher during the night. It stopped them in their tracks. It was a most puissant sorcery. It occupied them totally. Harden turned his attention to the rest of us.

The second Imperial reached him. His great sword hammered down, pounding through the soldier's guard. The horse ambled forward at Harden's urging, gingerly stepping over the fallen. Harden looked at the Taken and cursed the animal, flailed around with his blade.

The horse moved no faster. Harden smote its neck savagely, then howled. His hand would not come free of its mane. His cry of rage became one of despair. He turned his blade on the beast, could not harm it, instantly hurled the weapon at the Taken. The violet surrounding them had begun to weaken.

Raven was two steps from Harden, I three behind him. Stormbringer's men were as close, approaching from the other side.

Raven slashed, a strong, upward cutting stroke. His swordtip thumped Harden's belly—and rebounded. Chain mail? Harden's big fist lashed out and connected with Raven's temple. He wobbled a step and sagged.

Without thought I shifted aim and slashed at Harden's hand. We both yelled when iron bit bone and scarlet flowed.

I leapt over Raven, stopped, spun. Stormbringer's soldiers were hacking at Harden. His mouth was open. His scarred face was contorted as he concentrated on ignoring pain while he used his powers to save himself. The Taken remained out of it for the moment. He faced three ordinary men. But all that did not register till later.

I could see nothing but Harden's steed. The animal was melting. . . . No. Not melting. Changing.

I giggled. The great Rebel general was astride Shape-shifter's back.

My giggles became crazy laughter.

My little fit cost me my opportunity to participate in the death of a champion. Stormbringer's two soldiers cut Harden to pieces while Shifter held and stifled him. He was dead meat before I regained my self-control.

The Hanged Man, too, missed the denouement. He was busy dying, Harden's great thrown blade buried in his skull. Soulcatcher and Stormbringer moved toward him.

Shifter completed his change into a great, greasy, stinking, fat, naked creature which, despite standing on its hind legs, seemed no more human than the beast he had portrayed. He kicked Harden's remains and quaked with mirth, as though his deadly trick had been the finest jest of the century.

Then he saw the Hanged Man. Shudders ran through his flab. He hastened toward the other Taken, incoherencies frothing his lips.

Crooked Neck worked the sword loose from his skull. He tried to say something, had no luck. Stormbringer and Soulcatcher made no move to help.

I stared at Stormbringer. Such a tiny thing she was. I knelt to test Raven's pulse. She was no bigger than a child. How could such a small package chain such terrible wrath?

Shifter shambled toward the tableau, anger knotting the muscles under the fat across his shaggy shoulders. He halted, faced Catcher and Stormbringer from a tense stance. Nothing was said, but it seemed the Hanged Man's fate was being decided. Shifter wanted to help. The others did not.

Puzzling. Shifter is Catcher's ally. Why this sudden conflict?

Why this daring of the Lady's wrath? She would not be pleased if the Hanged Man died.

Raven's pulse was fluttery when first I touched his throat, but it firmed up. I breathed a little easier.

Stormbringer's soldiers eased up toward the Taken, eying Shifter's gross back.

Catcher exchanged glances with Stormbringer. The woman nodded. Soulcatcher whirled. The slits in his mask blazed a lava red.

Suddenly, there was no Catcher. There was a cloud of darkness ten feet high and a dozen across, black as the inside of a coal sack, thicker than the densest fog. The cloud jumped quicker than an adder's strike. There was one mouselike squeak of surprise, then a sinister, enduring silence. After all the roar and clangor, the quiet was deadly ominous.

I shook Raven violently. He did not respond.

Changer and Stormbringer stood over the Hanged Man, staring at me. I wanted to scream, to run, to crawl into the ground to hide. I was a magic man, able to read their thoughts. I knew too much.

Terror froze me.

The coal dust cloud vanished as quickly as it had appeared. Soulcatcher stood between the soldiers. Both toppled slowly, with the majesty of stately old pines.

I gouged Raven. He groaned. His eyes flickered open and I caught a glimpse of pupil. Dilated. Concussion. Damn it! . . .

Catcher looked at his partners in crime. Then, slowly, he turned on me.

The three Taken closed in. In the background, the Hanged

Man went on dying. He was very noisy about it. I did not hear him, though. I rose, knees watery, and faced my doom.

It's not supposed to end this way, I thought. This isn't right. . . .

All three stood there and stared.

I stared back. Nothing else I could do.

Brave Croaker. Guts enough, at least, to stare Death in the eye.

"You didn't see a thing, did you?" Catcher asked softly. Cold lizards slithered down my spine. That voice was one one of the dead soldiers had used while hacking away at Harden.

I shook my head.

"You were too busy fighting Harden, then you were occupied with Raven."

I nodded weakly. My knee joints were jelly. I would have bolted otherwise. Foolish as that would have been. Catcher said, "Get Raven onto Bringer's carpet." He pointed.

Nudging, whispering, cajoling, I helped Raven walk. He hadn't the least idea where he was or what he was doing. But he let me steer him.

I was worried. I could find no obvious damage, yet he was not acting right. "Take him straight to my hospital," I said. I could not look Stormbringer in the eye, nor did I achieve the inflection I wanted. My words came out sounding like a plea.

Catcher summoned me to his carpet. I went with all the enthusiasm of a hog to the slaughter chute. He could be playing a game. A fall from his carpet would be a permanent cure for any doubts he harbored about my ability to keep quiet.

He followed me, tossed his bloody sword aboard, settled himself. The carpet floated upward, crawled toward the great scrap of the Stair.

I glanced back at the still forms on the meadow, nagged by undirected feelings of shame. That had not been right. . . . And yet, what could I have done?

Something golden, something like a pale nebula in the farthest circle of the midnight sky, moved in the shade cast by one of the sandstone towers.

My heart nearly stopped.

The Captain sucked the headless and increasingly demoralized Rebel army into a trap. A great slaughter ensued. Lack of numbers and sheer exhaustion kept the Company from hurling the Rebel off the mountain. Nor did the complacency of the Taken help. One fresh battalion, one sorcerous assault, might have given us the day.

I treated Raven on the run, after placing him aboard the last wagon to head south. He would remain odd and remote for days. Care of Darling fell my way by default. The child was a fine distraction from the depression of yet another retreat.

Maybe that was the way she had rewarded Raven for his generosity.

"This is our last withdrawal," the Captain promised. *He* would not call it a retreat, but hadn't the gall to call it an advance to the rear, retrograde action, or any of that gobbledegook. He did not mention the fact that any further withdrawal would come after the end. Charm's fall would mark the death-date of the Lady's Empire. In all probability it will terminate these Annals, and scriven the end of Company history.

Rest in peace, you last of the warrior brotherhoods. You were home and family to me. . . .

News came which had not been allowed to reach us at the Stair of Tear. Tidings of other Rebel armies advancing from the north along routes more westerly than our line of retreat. The list of cities lost was long and disheartening, even granting exaggeration by the reporters. Soldiers defeated always overestimate the strength of their foe. That soothes egos suspecting their own inferiority.

Walking with Elmo, down the long, gentle south slope, toward the fertile farmlands north of Charm, I suggested, "Sometime when there aren't any Taken around, how about you hint to the Captain that it might be wise if he started disassociating the Company from Soulcatcher."

He looked at me oddly. My old comrades had been doing that lately. Since Harden's fall I had been moody, dour, and uncommunicative. Not that I was a bonfire at the best of times, mind. The pressure was crushing my spirit. I denied myself my usual outlet, the Annals, for fear Soulcatcher would somehow detect what I had written.

"It might be better if we weren't too closely identified with him," I added.

"What happened out there?" By then everyone knew the basic tale. Harden slain. The Hanged Man fallen. Raven and I the only soldiers who got out alive. Everybody had an insatiable thirst for details.

"I can't tell you. But you tell him. When none of the Taken are around."

Elmo did his sums and came to the conclusion not far off the mark. "All right, Croaker. Will do. Take care."

Take care I would. If Fate let me.

That was the day we received word of new victories in the east. The Rebel redoubts were collapsing as fast as the Lady's armies could march.

It was also the day we heard that all four northern and western Rebel armies had halted to rest, recruit, and refit for an assault on Charm. Nothing stood between them and the Tower. Nothing, that is, but the Black Company and its accumulation of beaten men.

The great comet is in the sky, that evil harbinger of all great shifts of fortune.

The end is near.

We are retreating still, toward our final appointment with Destiny.

I must record one final incident in the tale of the encounter with Harden. It took place three days north of the Tower, and consisted of another dream like the one I suffered at the head of the Stair. The same golden dream, which might have been no dream at all, promised me, ''My faithful need have no fear.'' Once again it allowed me a glimpse of that heart-stopping face. And then it was gone, and the fear returned, not lessened in the least.

The days passed. The miles wore away. The great ugly block of the Tower hove over the horizon. And the comet grew ever more brilliant in the nighttime sky.

Chapter Six: LADY

The land slowly became silvery green. Dawn scattered feathers of crimson upon the walled town. Golden flashes freckled its battlements where the sun touched dew. The mists began to slide into the hollows. Trumpets sounded the morning watch.

The Lieutenant shaded his eyes, squinted. He grunted disgustedly, glanced at One-Eye. The little black man nodded. "Time, Goblin," the Lieutenant said over his shoulder.

Men stirred back in the woods. Goblin knelt beside me, peered out at the farmland. He and four other men were clad as poor townswomen, with their heads wrapped in shawls. They carried pottery jars swinging from wooden yokes, had their weapons hidden inside their clothing.

"Go. The gate is open," the Lieutenant said. They moved out, following the edge of the wood downhill.

"Damn, it's good to be doing this kind of thing again," I said.

The Lieutenant grinned. He had smiled seldom since we had left Beryl.

Below, the five fake women slipped through shadow toward the spring beside the road to town. Already a few townswomen were headed down to draw water.

We expected little trouble getting to the gatekeepers. The town was filled with strangers, refugees and Rebel campfollowers. The garrison was small and lax. The Rebel had no cause to suppose the Lady would strike this far from Charm. The town had no significance in the grand struggle.

Except that two of the Eighteen, privy to Rebel strategies, were quartered there.

We had lurked in those woods three days, watching. Feather and Journey, recently promoted to the Circle, were honeymooning there before moving south to join the assault on Charm.

Three days. Three days of no fires during the chill nights, of dried food at every meal. Three days of misery. And our spirits were their highest in years. "I think we'll pull it off," I opined.

The Lieutenant gestured. Several men stole after the disguised.

One-Eye remarked, "Whoever thought this up knew what he was doing." He was excited.

We all were. It was a chance to do that at which we are best. For fifty days we had done plain physical labor, preparing Charm for the Rebel onslaught, and for fifty nights we had agonized about the coming battle.

Another five men slipped downhill.

"Bunch of women coming out now," One-Eye said. Tension mounted.

Women paraded toward the spring. There would be a flow all day, unless we interrupted. They had no water source inside the wall.

My stomach sank. Our infiltrators had started uphill. "Stand ready," the Lieutenant said.

"Loosen up," I suggested. Exercise helps dissipate nervous energy.

No matter how long you soldier, fear always swells as combat nears. There is always the dread that the numbers will catch up. One-Eye enters every action sure the fates have checked his name off their list.

The infiltrators exchanged falsetto greetings with the townswomen. They arrived at the gate undiscovered. It was guarded by a single militiaman, a cobbler busy hammering brass nails into the heel of a boot. His halberd was ten feet away.

Goblin scampered back outside. He clapped his hands overhead. A *crack* reverberated across the countryside. His arms fell level with his shoulders, palms up. A rainbow arced between his hands.

"Always has to ham it up," One-Eye grumbled. Goblin did a jig.

The patrol swept forward. The women at the spring screamed and scattered. Wolves jumping into a sheepfold, I thought. We ran hard. My pack hammered my kidneys. After two hundred yards I was stumbling over my bow. Younger men began passing me.

I reached the gate unable to whip a grandmother. Lucky for me, the grandmas were goofing off. The men swept through the town. There was no resistance.

We who were to tackle Feather and Journey hastened to the tiny citadel. That was no better defended. The Lieutenant and I followed One-Eye, Silent, and Goblin inside.

We encountered no resistance below the top level. There, incredibly, the newlyweds were still entangled in sleep. One-Eye brushed their guards aside with a terrifying illusion. Goblin and Silent shattered the door to the lovenest.

We stormed inside. Even sleepy, baffled, and frightened,

they were fiesty. They bruised several of us good before we got gags into their mouths and bonds onto their wrists.

The Lieutenant told them, "We're supposed to bring you back alive. That don't mean we can't hurt you some. Come quiet, do what you're told, and you'll be all right." I halfway expected him to sneer, twirl the end of his mustache, and punctuate with evil laughter. He was clowning, assuming the villain's role the Rebel insists we play.

Feather and Journey would give us all the trouble they could. They knew the Lady hadn't sent us to bring them round for tea.

Halfway back to friendly territory. On our bellies on a hilltop, studying an enemy encampment. "Big," I said. "Twenty-five, thirty thousand men." It was one of six such camps on an arc bending north and west of Charm.

"They sit on their hands much longer, they're in trouble," the Lieutenant said.

They should have attacked immediately after the Stair of Tear. But the loss of Harden, Sidle, Moth, and Linger had set lesser captains to squabbling over supreme command. The Rebel offensive had stalled. The Lady had regained her balance.

Her patrols-in-force now harassed Rebel foragers, exterminated collaborators, scouted, destroyed everything the enemy might find useful. Despite vastly superior numbers, the Rebel's stance was becoming defensive. Every day in camp sapped his psychological momentum.

Two months ago our morale was lower than a snake's butt. Now it was on the rebound. If we made it back it would soar. Our coup would stun the Rebel movement.

If we made it back.

* * *

We lay motionless upon steep lichened limestone and dead leaves. The creek below chuckled at our predicament. Shadows of naked trees stippled us. Low-grade spells by One-Eye and his cohorts further camouflaged us. The smell of fear and of sweaty horses taunted my nostrils. From the road above came the voices of Rebel cavalrymen. I could not understand their tongue. They were arguing, though.

Scattered with undisturbed leaves and twigs, the road had looked unpatrolled. Weariness had overcome our caution. We had decided to follow it. Then we had rounded a turn and found ourselves facing a Rebel patrol across the meadowed valley into which the creek below flowed.

They were cursing our disappearance. Several dismounted and urinated down the bank. . . .

Feather started thrashing.

Damn! I screamed inside. Damn! Damn! I knew it!

The Rebels yammered and lined the edge of the road.

I smacked the woman's temple. Goblin clipped her from the other side. Quick-thinking Silent wove nets of spell with tentacle-limber fingers dancing close to his chest.

A ragged bush shivered. A fat old badger waddle-ran down the bank and crossed the creek, vanishing into a dense stand of poplars.

Cursing, the Rebels threw rocks. They clattered like dropped stoneware as they skipped off boulders in the streambed. The soldiers stamped around telling one another we had to be nearby. We could not have gotten much farther on foot. Logic might undo the best efforts of our wizards.

I was scared with a knee-knocking, hand-shaking, gut-emptying kind of fear. It had built steadily, through too many narrow escapes. Superstition told me my odds were getting too long.

So much for that earlier gust of refreshed morale. The unreasoning fear betrayed it for the illusion it was. Beneath its patina I retained the defeatist attitude brought down from the Stair of Tear. My war was over and lost. All I wanted to do was run.

Journey showed signs of getting frisky too. My glare was fierce. He subsided.

A breeze stirred the dead leaves. The sweat on my body chilled. My fear cooled somewhat.

The patrol remounted. Still fussing, they rode on up the road. I watched them come into sight where the way curled eastward with the canyon. They wore scarlet tabards over good link mail. Their helmets and arms were of excellent quality. The Rebel was getting prosperous. They had started out as a rabble armed with tools.

"We could have taken them," someone said.

"Stupid!" the Lieutenant snapped. "Right now they aren't sure who they saw. If we fought, they would know."

We did not need the Rebel getting a line on us this close to home. There was no room for maneuvering.

The man who had spoken was one of the stragglers we had accumulated during the long retreat. "Brother, you better learn one thing if you want to stick with us. You fight when there ain't no other choice. Some of us would have gotten hurt too, you know."

He grunted.

"They're out of sight," the Lieutenant said. "Let's move." He took the point, headed for the rugged hills beyond the meadow. I groaned. More crosscountry.

My every muscle ached already. Exhaustion threatened to betray me. Man was not meant for endless dawn to dusk marching with sixty pounds on his back.

"Damned fast thinking back there," I told Silent.

He accepted praise with a shrug, saying nothing. As always.

A cry from the rear. "They're coming back."

*   *   *

We sprawled on the flank of a grassy hill. The Tower rose above the horizon due south. That basaltic cube was intimidating even from ten miles away-and implausible in its setting. Emotion demanded a surround of fiery waste, or at best a land perpetually locked in winter. Instead, this country was a vast green pasture, gentle hills with small farms dotting their southern hips. Trees lined the deep, slow brooks snaking between.

Nearer the Tower the land became less pastoral, but never reflected the gloom Rebel propagandists placed around the Lady's stronghold. No brimstone and barren, broken plains. No bizarre, evil creatures strutting over scattered human bones. No dark clouds ever rolling and grumbling in the sky.

The Lieutenant said, "No patrols in sight. Croaker, One-Eye, do your stuff."

I strung my bow. Goblin brought three prepared arrows. Each had a maleable blue ball at its head. One-Eye sprinkled one with grey dust, passed it to me. I aimed at the sun, let fly.

Blue fire too bright to view flared and sank into the valley below. Then a second, and a third. The fireballs dropped in a neat column, appearing to drift down more than fall.

"Now we wait," Goblin squeaked, and threw himself down in the tall grass.

"And hope our friends arrive first." Any nearby Rebel surely would investigate the signal. Yet we had to call for help. We could not penetrate the Rebel cordon unnoticed.

"Get down!" the Lieutenant snapped. The grass was tall enough to conceal a supine figure. "Third squad, take the watch."

Men grumbled and claimed it was another squad's turn. But they took sentinel positions with that minimal, obligatory complaint. Their mood was bright. Hadn't we lost those fools back in the hills? What could stop us now?

I made a pillow of my pack and watched cumulus mountains drift over in stately legions. It was a gorgeous, crisp, springlike day.

My gaze dropped to the Tower. My mood darkened. The pace would pick up. The capture of Feather and Journey would spur the Rebel into action. Surrender secrets those two would. There was no way to hide or lie when the Lady asked a question.

I heard a rustle, turned my head, found myself eye to eye with a snake. It wore a human face. I started to yell—then recognized that silly grin.

One-Eye. His ugly mug in miniature, but with both eyes and no floppy hat on top. The snake snickered, winked, slithered across my chest.

"Here they go again," I murmured, and sat up to watch.

There was a sudden, violent thrashing in the grass. Farther on, Goblin popped up wearing a shit-eating grin. The grass rustled. Animals the size of rabbits trooped past me, carrying chunks of snake in bloody needle teeth. Homemade mongooses, I guessed.

Goblin had anticipated One-Eye again.

One-Eye let out a howl and jumped up cursing. His hat spun around. Smoke poured out of his nostrils. When he yelled fire roared in his mouth.

Goblin capered like a cannibal just before they dish up the long pig. He described circles with his forefingers. Rings of pale orange glimmered in the air. He flipped them at One-Eye. They settled around the little black man. Goblin barked like a seal. The hoops tightened.

One-Eye made weird noises and negated the rings. He made throwing notions with both hands. Brown balls streaked toward Goblin. They exploded, yielding clouds of butterflies that went for Goblin's eyes. Goblin did a backflip, scampered through the grass like a mouse fleeing an owl, popped up with a counterspell.

The air sprouted flowers. Each bloom had a mouth. Each mouth boasted walruslike tusks. The flowers skewered butterfly wings with their tusks, then complacently munched butterfly bodies. Goblin fell over giggling.

One-Eye cussed a literal blue streak, a cerulean banner trailing from his lips. Argent lettering proclaimed his opinion of Goblin.

"Knock it off!" the Lieutenant thundered belatedly. "We don't need you attracting attention."

"Too late, Lieutenant," somebody said. "Look down there."

Soldiers were headed our way. Soldiers wearing red, with the White Rose emblazoned on their tabards. We dropped into the grass like ground squirrels into their holes.

Chatter ran across the hillside. Most threatened One-Eye with dire dooms. A minority included Goblin for having shared in the betraying fireworks.

Trumpets sounded. The Rebel dispersed for an assault on our hill.

The air whined in torment. A shadow flashed over the hilltop, rippling across windblown grass. "Taken," I murmured, and popped up for the instant needed to spot a flying carpet banking into the valley. "Soulcatcher?" I couldn't be sure. At that distance it could have been any of several Taken.

The carpet dove into massed arrow fire. Lime fog enveloped it, trailed behind it, for a moment recalled the comet which overhung the world. The lime haze scattered resolved into threadlike snippets. A few filaments caught the breeze and drifted our way.

I glanced up. The comet hung on the horizon like a ghost of a god's scimitar. It had been in the sky so long we scarcely noticed it now. I wondered if the Rebel had become equally indifferent. For him it was one of the great portents of impending victory.

Men screamed. The carpet had passed along the Rebel line and now drifted like down on the wind just beyond bowshot. The lime-colored thread was so scattered it was barely visible. The screams came from men who had suffered its touch. Grisly green wounds opened wherever there was contact.

Some thread seemed determined to come our way.

The Lieutenant saw it. "Let's move out, men. Just in case." He pointed across the wind. The thread would have to drift sideways to catch us.

We hustled maybe three hundred yards. Writhing, the thread crawled on air, coming our way. It *was* after us. The Taken watched intently, ignoring the Rebel.

"That bastard wants to kill us!" I exploded. Terror turned my legs to gelatin. Why would one of the Taken want us to become victims of an accident?

If that *was* Catcher. . . . But Catcher was our mentor. Our boss. We wore his badges. He wouldn't. . . .

The carpet snapped into motion so violently its rider almost tumbled off. It hurtled toward the nearest wood, vanished. The thread lost volition and drifted down, disappearing in the grass.

"What the devil?"

"Holy Hell!"

I whirled. A vast shadow moved toward us, expanding, as a gigantic carpet descended. Faces peeped over its edges. We froze, bristling with ready weapons.

"The Howler," I said, and had my guess confirmed by a cry like that of a wolf challenging the moon.

The carpet grounded. "Get aboard, you idiots. Come on. Move it."

I laughed, tension draining away. That was the Captain. He danced like a nervous bear along the near edge of the carpet. Others of our brethren accompanied him. I threw my pack aboard, accepted a hand up. "Raven. You showed up in the nick this time."

"You'll wish we'd let you take your chances."

"Eh?"

"Captain will tell you."

The last man scrambled aboard. The Captain gave Feather and Journey the hard eye, then marched around getting the men evenly distributed. At the rear of the carpet, unmoving, shunned, sat a child-sized figure concealed in layers of indigo gauze. It howled at random intervals.

I shuddered. "What are you talking about?"

"Captain will tell you," he repeated.

"Sure. How's Darling?"

"Doing all right." Lots of words in our Raven.

The Captain settled beside me. "Bad news, Croaker," he said.

"Yeah?" I reached for my vaunted sarcasm. "Give it to me straight. I can take it."

"Tough guy," Raven observed.

"That's me. Eat nails for breakfast. Whip wildcats with my bare hands."

The Captain shook his head. "Hang on to that sense of humor. The Lady wants to see you. Personally."

My stomach dropped to the ground, which was a couple hundred feet down. "Oh, shit," I whispered. "Oh, damn."

"Yeah."

"What did I do?"

"You'd know better than I do."

My mind hurtled around like a herd of mice fleeing a cat. In seconds I was soaked with sweat.

Raven observed, "Can't be as bad as it sounds. She was almost polite."

The Captain nodded. "It was a request."

"Sure it was."

Raven said, "If she had a grudge you'd just disappear."

I did not feel reassured.

"One too many romances," the Captain chided. "Now she's in love with you too."

They never forget, never let up. It had been months since I had written one of those romances. "What's it about?"

"She didn't say."

Silence reigned the rest of the way. They sat beside me and tried to reassure me with traditional Company solidarity. As we came in on our encampment, though, the Captain did say, "She told us to bring our strength up to the thousand mark. We can enlist volunteers from the lot we brought out of the north."

"Good news, good news." That *was* cause for jubilation. For the first time in two centuries we were going to grow. Plenty of stragglers would be eager to exchange their oaths to the Taken for oaths to the Company. We were in high favor. We had mana. And, being mercenaries, we got more leeway than anyone else in the Lady's service.

I could not get excited, though. Not with the Lady waiting.

The carpet grounded. Brethren crowded around, anxious to see how we had done. Lies and jocular threats flew.

The Captain said, "You stay aboard, Croaker. Goblin, Silent, One-Eye, you too." He indicated the prisoners. "Deliver the merchandise."

As the men slid over the side, Darling came bouncing out of the mob. Raven hollered at her, but of course she could not hear. She scrambled aboard, carrying a doll Raven had carved. It was dressed neatly in clothing of superb miniature detail. She handed it to me and started flashing finger language.

Raven hollered again. I tried to interrupt, but Darling was intent on telling me about the doll's wardrobe. Some might have thought her retarded, to be so excited about such things at her age. She was not. She had a mind like a razor. She knew what she was doing when she boarded the carpet. She was stealing a chance to fly.

"Honey," I said, both aloud and with signs, "You've got to get off. We're going. . . ."

Raven yelled in outrage as the Howler lifted off. One-Eye, Goblin, and Silent all glared at him. He howled. The carpet continued to rise.

"Sit down," I told Darling. She did so, not far from Feather. She forgot the doll, wanted to know about our adventure. I told her. It kept me occupied. She spent more time looking over the side than paying attention to me, yet she missed nothing. When I finished she looked at Feather and Journey with adult pity. She was unconcerned about my appointment with the Lady, though she did give me a reassuring hug good-bye.

The Howler's carpet drifted away from the Tower top. I waved a feeble farewell. Darling blew me a kiss. Goblin patted his breast. I touched the amulet he had given me in Lords. Small comfort, that.

Imperial Guards strapped Journey and Feather onto litters. "What about me?" I asked shakily.

A captain told me, "You're supposed to wait here." He stayed when the others left. He tried to make small talk, but I wasn't in the mood.

I wandered to the Tower's edge, looked out on the vast engineering project being undertaken by the Lady's armies.

At the time of the Tower's construction huge basalt billets had been imported. Shaped on site, they had been stacked and fused into this gigantic cube of stone. The waste, chips, blocks broken during shaping, billets found unsuitable, and overage, had been left scattered around the Tower in a vast wild jumble more effective than any moat. It extended a mile.

In the north, though, a depressed piece-of-pie section remained unlittered. This constituted the only approach to the Tower on the ground. In that arc the Lady's forces prepared for the Rebel onslaught.

No one down there believed his labor would shape the battle's outcome. The comet was in the sky. But every man worked because labor provided surcease from fear.

The pie-slice rose to either side, meeting the rock jumble. A log palisade spanned the slice's wide end. Our camps lay behind that. Behind the camps was a trench thirty feet deep and thirty wide. A hundred yards nearer the Tower there was another trench, and a hundred yards nearer still, a third, still being dug.

The excavated earth had been transported nearer the Tower and dumped behind a twelve foot log retaining wall spanning the slice. From this elevation men would hurl missiles on an enemy attacking our infantry on ground level.

A hundred yards back stood a second retaining wall, providing another two fathom elevation. The Lady meant to array her forces in three distinct armies, one on each level, and force the Rebel to fight three battles in series.

An earthen pyramid was abuilding a dozen rods behind the final retaining wall. It was seventy feet high already, its sides sloping about thirty-five degrees.

Obsessive neatness characterized everything. The plain, in places scraped down several feet, was as level as a tabletop. It had been planted with grass. Our animals kept that cropped like a well-kempt lawn. Stone roadways ran here and there, and woe betide the man who strayed off without orders.

Below, on the middle level, bowmen were ranging fire on the ground between the nearer trenches. While they loosed, their officers adjusted the positions of racks from which they drew their arrows.

On the upper terrace Guards bustled around ballistae, calculating fire lanes and survivability, ranging their engines on targets farther away. Carts laden with ammunition sat near each weapon.

Like the grass and mannered roadways, these preparations betrayed an obsession with order.

On the bottom level workmen had begun demolishing short sections of retaining wall. Baffling.

I spotted a carpet coming in, turned to watch. It settled to the roof. Four stiff, shaky, wind-burned soldiers stepped off. A corporal led them away.

The armies of the east were headed our way, hoping to arrive before the Rebel assault, with little hope of actually making it. The Taken were flying day and night bringing in what manpower they could.

Men shouted below. I turned to look. . . . Threw up an arm. Slam! Impact threw me a dozen feet, spinning. My Guard guide yelled. The Tower roof came up to meet me. Men shouted and ran my way.

I rolled, tried to get up, slipped in a slick of blood. Blood! My blood! It spurted from the inside of my left upper arm. I stared at the wound with dull, amazed eyes. What the hell?

"Lay down," the Guard captain ordered. "Come on." He slapped me a good one. "Quick. Tell me what to do."

"Tourniquet," I croaked. "Tie something around it. Stop the bleeding."

He yanked his belt off. Good, quick thinking. One of

the best tourniquets there is. I tried to sit up, to advise while he worked.

"Hold him down," he told several bystanders. "Foster. What happened?"

"One of the weapons fell off the upper tier. It went off when it fell. They're running around like chickens."

"Wasn't no accident," I gasped. "Somebody wanted to kill me." Getting hazy, I could think of nothing but lime thread crawling against the wind. "Why?"

"Tell me and we'll both know, friend. You men. Get a litter." He snugged the belt tighter. "Going to be all right, fellow. We'll have you to a healer in a minute."

"Severed artery," I said. "That's tricky." My ears hummed. The world began to turn slowly, getting cold. Shock. How much blood did I lose? The captain had moved fast enough. Plenty of time. If the healer was not some butcher. . . ."

The captain grabbed a corporal. "Go find out what happened down there. Don't take any bullshit answers."

The litter came. They lifted me in, hoisted me, and I passed out. I wakened in a small surgery, tended by a man who was as much sorcerer as surgeon. "Better job than I could have done," I told him when he finished.

"Any pain?"

"Nope."

"Going to ache like hell in a while."

"I know." How many times had I said the same?

The Guard captain came. "Going all right?"

"Done," the surgeon replied. To me, "No work. No activity. No sex. You know the drill."

"I do. Sling?"

He nodded. "We'll bind your arm to your side, too, for a few days."

The captain was antsy. "Find out what happened?" I asked.

"Not really. The ballista crew couldn't explain. It just got away from them somehow. Maybe you got lucky." He recalled me saying somebody was trying to kill me.

I touched the amulet Goblin had given me. "Maybe."

"Hate to do it," he said. "But I've got to take you for your interview."

Fear. "What about?"

"You'd know better than I."

"But I don't." I had a remote suspicion, but had forced that out of mind.

There seemed to be two Towers, one sheathing the other. The outer was the seat of Empire, manned by the Lady's functionaries. The inner, as intimidating to them as was the whole to us outside, took up a third of the volume and could be entered at only one point. Few ever did so.

The entrance was open when we reached it. There were no guards. I suppose none were needed. I should have been more scared, but was too dopey. The captain said, "I'll wait here." He had placed me in a wheeled chair, which he rolled through the doorway. I went in with my eyes sealed and heart hammering.

The door chunked shut. The chair rolled a long way, making several turns. I don't know what impelled it. I refused to look. Then it stopped moving. I waited. Nothing happened. Curiosity got the best of me. I blinked.

She stands in the Tower, gazing northward. Her delicate hands are clasped before Her. A breeze steals softly through Her window. It stirs the midnight silk of Her hair. Tear diamonds sparkle on the gentle curve of Her cheek.

My own words, written more than a year before, came back. It was that scene, from that romance, to the least detail. To detail I had imagined but never written. As if that fantasy instant had been ripped from my brain whole and given the breath of life.

I did not believe it for a second, of course. I was in the

bowels of the Tower. There were no windows in that grim structure.

She turned. And I saw what every man sees in dreams. Perfection. She did not have to speak for me to know her voice, her speech rhythms, the breathiness between phrases. She did not have to move for me to know her mannerisms, the way she walked, the odd way she would lift her hand to her throat when she laughed. I had known her since adolescence.

In seconds I understood what the old stories meant about her overwhelming presence. The Dominator himself must have swayed in her hot wind.

She rocked me, but did not sweep me away. Though half of me hungered, the remainder recalled my years around Goblin and One-Eye. Where there is sorcery nothing is what it seems. Nice, yes, but sugar candy.

She studied me as intently as I studied her. Finally, "We meet again." The voice was everything I expected and more. It had humor, too.

"Indeed," I croaked.

"You're frightened."

"Of course I am." Maybe a fool would have denied it. Maybe.

"You were injured." She drifted closer. I nodded, my heartbeat increasing. "I wouldn't subject you to this if it wasn't important."

I nodded again, too shaky to speak, totally baffled. This was the Lady, the villain of the ages, the Shadow animate. This was the black widow at the heart of darkness's web, a demi-goddess of evil. What could be important enough for her to take note of the likes of me?

Again, I did have suspicions I would not admit to myself. My moments of critical congress with anyone important were not numerous.

"Someone tried to kill you. Who?"

"I don't know." Taken on the wind. Lime thread.

"Why?"

"I don't know."

"You know. Even if you think you don't." Flint razored through that perfect voice.

I had come expecting the worst, had been taken in by the dream, had let my defenses fall.

The air hummed. A lemon glow formed above her. She moved closer, becoming hazy—except for that face and that yellow. That face expanded, vast, intense, swooping closer. Yellow filled the universe. I saw nothing but the eye. . . .

The Eye! I remembered the Eye in the Forest of Cloud. I tried to throw my arm across my face. I could not move. I think I screamed. Hell. I know I screamed.

There were questions I did not hear. Answers spooled across my mind, in rainbows of thought, like oil droplets spreading on still, crystal water. I had no more secrets.

No secrets. No thought I'd ever had was hidden.

Terror writhed in me like snakes afraid. I had written those silly romances, true, but I also had my doubts and disgusts. A villain as black as she would destroy me for having seditious thoughts. . . .

Wrong. She was secure in the strength of her wickedness. She did not need to quash the questions and doubts and fears of her minions. She could laugh at our consciences and moralities.

This was no repeat of our encounter in the forest. I did not lose my memories. I just did not hear her questions. Those could be inferred from my answers about my contacts with the Taken.

She was hunting the something I began to suspect at the Stair of Tear. I had stumbled into as deadly a trap as ever snapped shut; Taken as the one jaw, the Lady as the other.

Darkness. And awakening.

She stands in the Tower, gazing northward. . . . Tear diamonds sparkle on Her cheek.

A spark of Croaker remained unintimidated. "This is where I came in."

She faced me, smiled. She stepped over and touched me with the sweetest fingers ever woman possessed.

All fear went away.

All darkness closed in again.

Passageway walls were rolling by when I recovered. The Guard captain was pushing me. "How are you doing?" he asked.

I took stock. "Good enough. Where you taking me now?"

"The front door. She said cut you loose."

Just like that? Hmm. I touched my wound. Healed. I shook my head. Things like this did not happen to me.

I paused at the place where the ballista had had its mishap. There was nothing to see and no one to question. I descended to the middle level and visited one of the crews excavating there. They had orders to install a cubicle twelve feet wide and eighteen deep. They had no idea why.

I scanned the length of the retaining wall. A dozen such sites were under construction.

The men eyed me intently when I limped into camp. They choked on questions they could not ask, on concern they could not express. Only Darling refused to play the traditional game. She squeezed my hand, gave me a big smile. Her little fingers danced.

She asked the questions machismo forbid the men. "Slow down," I told her. I was not yet proficient enough to catch everything she signed. Yet her joy communicated itself. I had a big grin on when I became aware that someone was in my way. I looked up. Raven.

"Captain wants you," he said. He seemed cool.

"Figures." I signed good-bye, strolled toward head-quarters. I felt no urgency. No mere mortal could intimidate me now.

I glanced back. Raven had his arm across Darling's shoulder, proprietary, looking puzzled.

The Captain was off his style. He dispensed with the customary growling. One-Eye was the only third party present, and he, too, was interested in nothing but business.

"We got trouble?" the Captain asked.

"What do you mean?"

"What happened in the hills. No accident, eh? The Lady summons you, and half an hour later one of the Taken goes zuzu. Then there's your accident at the Tower. You're bad hurt and nobody can explain."

One-Eye observed, "Logic insists a connection."

The Captain added, "Yesterday we heard you were dying. Today you're fine. Sorcery?"

"Yesterday?" Time had gotten away again. I pushed the tent flap aside, stared at the Tower. "Another night in elf hill."

"*Was* it an accident?" One-Eye asked.

"It wasn't accidental." The Lady hadn't thought so.

"Captain, that jibes."

The Captain said, "Somebody tried to knife Raven last night. Darling ran him off."

"Raven? Darling?"

"Something woke her up. She whacked the guy in the head with her doll. Whoever it was got away."

"Weird."

"Decidedly," One-Eye said. "Why would Raven sleep through and a deaf kid wake up? Raven can hear the footfall of a gnat. Smells of sorcery. Cockeyed sorcery. The kid shouldn't have awakened."

The Captain jumped in. "Raven. You. Taken. The

Lady. Murder attempts. An interview in the Tower. You have the answer. Spill it.''

My reluctance showed.

"You told Elmo we should disassociate ourselves from Catcher. How come? Catcher treats us good. What happened when you took out Harden? Spread it around and there wouldn't be any point to killing you.''

Good argument. Only I like to be sure before I shoot my mouth off. "I think there's a plot against the Lady. Soulcatcher and Stormbringer might be involved.'' I related details of Harden's fall and Whisper's taking. "Shifter was really upset because they let the Hanged Man die. I don't think the Limper was part of anything. He was set up, and manipulated craftily. The Lady was too. Maybe the Limper and the Hanged Man were her supporters.''

One-Eye looked thoughtful. "You sure Catcher is in on it?''

"I'm not sure of anything. I wouldn't be surprised by anything, either. Ever since Beryl I've thought he was using us.''

The Captain nodded. "Definitely. I told One-Eye to cook up an amulet that'll warn you if one of the Taken gets too close. For what good it'll do. I don't think you'll be bothered again, though. The Rebel is on the move. That'll be everybody's first order of business.''

A chain of logic lightninged to a conclusion. The data was there all the time. It just needed a nudge to drop into place. "I think I know what it's about. The Lady being an usurper.''

One-Eye asked, "One of the boys in the masks wants to do her the way she done her old man?''

"No. They want to bring back the Dominator.''

"Eh?''

"He's still up north, in the ground. The Lady just kept him from returning when the wizard Bomanz opened the

way for her. He could be in touch with Taken who are
faithful to him. Bomanz proved communication with those
buried in the Barrowland was possible. He could even be
guiding some of the Circle. Harden was as big a villain as
any of the Taken.''

One-Eye pondered, then prophesied. ''The battle will be
lost. The Lady will be overthrown. Her loyal Taken will
be laid low and her loyal troops wiped out. But they will
take the most idealistic elements among the Rebel with
them, meaning, essentially, a defeat for the White Rose.''

I nodded. ''The comet is in the sky, but the Rebel hasn't
found his mystic child.''

''Yeah. You're probably right on the mark when you
say maybe the Dominator is influencing the Circle. Yeah.''

''And in the chaos afterward, while they're squabbling
over the spoils, up jumps the devil,'' I said.

''So where do we fit?'' the Captain asked.

''The question,'' I replied, ''is how do we get out from
under.''

Flying carpets buzzed around the Tower like flies around
a corpse. The armies of Whisper, the Howler, the Nameless,
Bonegnasher, and Moonbiter, were eight to twelve days
away, converging. Eastern troops were pouring in by air.

The gate in the palisade was busy with the comings and
goings of parties harassing the Rebel. The Rebel had moved
his camps to within five miles of the Tower. Some company
troops made the occasional night raid, abetted by Goblin,
One-Eye, and Silent, but the effort seemed pointless. The
numbers were too overwhelming for hit and run to have
any substantial effect. I wondered why the Lady wanted
the Rebel kept stirred up.

Construction was complete. The obstacles were prepared.
Boobytraps were in place. There was little to do but wait.

Six days had passed since our return with Feather and

Journey. I'd expected their capture to electrify the Rebel into striking, but still they were stalling. One-Eye believed they had hopes of a last-minute finding of their White Rose.

Only the drawing of lots remained undone. Three of the Taken, with armies assigned them, would defend each level. It was rumored that the Lady herself would command forces stationed on the pyramid.

Nobody wanted to be on the front line. No matter how things went, those troops would be badly hurt. Thus the lottery.

There had been no more attempts on Raven or myself. Our antagonist was covering his tracks some other way. Too late to do unto us, anyway. I'd seen the Lady.

The tenor changed. Returning skirmishers began to look more battered, more desperate. The enemy was moving his camps again.

A messenger reached the Captain. He assembled the officers. "It's begun. The Lady has called the Taken to the lottery." He wore an odd expression. The main ingredient was astonishment. "We have special orders. From the Lady herself."

Whisper-murmur-rustle-grumble, everyone shaken. She was giving us all the rough jobs. I envisioned having to anchor the first line against Rebel elite troops.

"We're to strike camp and assemble on the pyramid." A hundred questions buzzed like hornets. He said, "She wants us for bodyguards."

"The Guard won't like that," I said. They did not like us anyway, having had to submit to the Captain's orders at the Stair of Tear.

"Think they'll give her a hard way to go, Croaker? Gents, the boss says go. So we go. You want to talk about it, do it while you're breaking camp. Without the men hearing."

For the troops this was great news. Not only would we

be behind the worst fighting, we would be in a position to fall back into the Tower.

Was I that sure we were doomed? Did my negativism mirror a general attitude? Was this an army defeated before the first blow?

The comet was in the sky.

Considering that phenomenon while we moved, amidst animals being driven into the Tower, I understood why the Rebel had stalled. They had hoped to find their White Rose at the last minute, of course. And they had been waiting for the comet to attain a more auspicious aspect, its closest approach.

I grumbled to myself.

Raven, trudging beside me burdened with his own gear and a bundle belonging to Darling, grunted, "Huh?"

"They haven't found their magic kid. They won't have everything going their way."

He looked at me oddly, almost suspiciously. Then, "Yet," he said. "Yet."

There was a big clamor as Rebel cavalry hurled javelins at sentinels on the palisade. Raven did not look back. It was just a probe.

We had a hell of a view from the pyramid, though it was crowded up there. "Hope we're not stuck here long, I said. And, "Going to be hell treating casualties."

The Rebel had moved his camps to within a half mile of the stockade. They blended into one. There was constant skirmishing at the palisade. Most of our troops had taken their places on the tiers.

The first level forces consisted of those who had served in the north, fleshed out by garrison troops from cities abandoned to the Rebel. There were nine thousand of them, divided into three divisions. The center had been assigned to Stormbringer. Had I been running things, she would have been on the pyramid hurling cyclones.

The wings were commanded by Moonbiter and Bonegnasher, two Taken I'd never encountered.

Six thousand men occupied the second level, also divided into three divisions. Most were archers from the eastern armies. They were tough, and far less uncertain than the men below them. Their commanders, from left to right, were: The Faceless or Nameless Man, The Howler, and Nightcrawler. Countless racks of arrows had been provided them. I wondered how they would manage if the enemy broke the first line.

The third tier was manned by the Guard at the ballistae, Whisper on the left with fifteen hundred veterans from her own eastern army, and Shifter on the right with a thousand westerners and southerners. In the middle, below the pyramid, Soulcatcher commanded the Guard and allies from the Jewel Cities. His troops numbered twenty-five hundred.

And on the pyramid was the Black Company, one thousand strong, with banners bright and standards bold and weapons ready to hand.

So. Roughly twenty-one thousand men, against more than ten times that number. Numbers aren't always critical. The Annals recall many moments when the Company beat the odds. But not like this. This was too static. There was no room for retreat, for maneuver, and an advance was out of the question.

The Rebel got serious. The palisade's defenders withdrew quickly, dismantling the spans across the three trenches. The Rebel did not pursue. Instead, he began demolishing the stockade.

"They look as methodical as the Lady," I told Elmo.

"Yep. They'll use the timber to bridge the trenches."

He was wrong, but we would not learn that immediately.

"Seven days till the eastern armies get here," I muttered at sunset, glancing back at the huge, dark bulk of the Tower. The Lady had not come forth for the initial scrimmage.

"More like nine or ten," Elmo countered. "They'll want to get here all together."

"Yeah. Should've thought of that."

We ate dried food and slept on the earth. And in the morning we rose to the bray of Rebel trumpets.

The enemy formations stretched as far as the eye could see. A line of mantlets started forward. They had been built from timber scavenged from our palisade. They formed a moving wall stretched across the pie-slice. The heavy ballistae thumped away. Large trebuchets hurled stones and fireballs. The damage they did was inconsequential.

Rebel pioneers began bridging the first trench, using timber brought from their camps. The foundations for these were huge beams, fifty feet long, impervious to missile fire. They had to use cranes to position them. They exposed themselves while assembling and operating the devices. Well-ranged Guard engines made that expensive.

Where the palisade had stood Rebel engineers were assembling wheeled towers from which bowmen could shoot, and wheeled ramps to roll up to the first tier. Carpenters were making ladders. I saw no artillery. I guess they planned to swamp us once they crossed the trenches.

The Lieutenant knew siegework well. I went to him. "How they going to bring up those ramps and towers?"

"They'll fill the ditches."

He was right. As soon as they had bridges across the first, and started moving mantlets over, carts and wagons appeared, carrying earth and stone. Teamsters and animals took a beating. Many a corpse went into the fill.

The pioneers moved up to the second trench, assembled

their cranes. The Circle gave them no armed support. Stormbringer sent archers to the lip of the final trench. The Guard laid down heavy fire with the ballistae. The pioneers suffered heavy casualties. The enemy command simply sent more men.

The Rebel began moving mantlets across the second trench an hour before noon. Wagons and carts crossed the first, carrying fill.

The pioneers encountered withering fire moving up to bridge the final ditch. The archers on the second tier sped their shafts high. They fell nearly straight down. The trebuchets shifted their aim, blasting mantlets into toothpicks and timbers. But the Rebel kept coming. On Moonbiter's flank they got a set of supporting beams across.

Moonbiter attacked, crossing with a picked force. His assault was so ferocious he drove the pioneers back over the second trench. He destroyed their equipment, attacked again. Then the Rebel command brought up a strong heavy infantry column. Moonbiter withdrew, leaving the second trench bridges ruined.

Inexorably, the Rebel bridged again, moved to the final trench with soldiers to protect his workmen. Stormbringer's snipers retreated.

The arrows from the second tier fell like flakes in a heavy winter snow, steadily and evenly. The carnage was spectacular. Rebel troops rolled into the witch's cauldron in a flood. A river of wounded flowed out. At the last trench the pioneers began keeping to the shelter of their mantlets, praying those would not be shattered by the Guard.

Thus it stood as the sun settled, casting long shadows across the field of blood. I'd guess the Rebel lost ten thousand men without bringing us to battle.

Through that day neither the Taken nor the Circle unleashed their powers. The Lady did not venture out of the Tower.

One less day to await the armies of the east.

Hostilities ended at sunset. We ate. The Rebel brought another shift to work the trenches. The newcomers went at it with the gusto their predecessors had lost. The strategy was obvious. They would rotate fresh troops in and wear us down.

The dark was the time of the Taken. Their passivity ended.

I could see little initially, so cannot for certain say who did what. Shifter, I suspect, changed shape and crossed into enemy territory.

The stars began to fade behind onrushing storm clouds. Cold air rushed across the earth. The wind rose, howled. Riding it came a horde of things with leathery wings, flying serpents the length of a man's arm. Their hissing overshadowed the tumult of the storm. Thunder crashed and lightning stalked, jabbing enemy works with its spears. The flashes revealed the ponderous advance of giants from the rock wastes. They hurled boulders like children throw balls. One snatched up a bridge beam and used it as a two-handed club, smashing siege towers and ramps. The look of them, in the treacherous light, was of creatures of stone, basaltic rubble cobbled together in grotesque, gargantuan parody of the human form.

The earth shivered. Patches of plain glowed a bilious green. Radiant ten foot, blood-streaked orange worms slithered amongst the foe. The heavens opened and dumped rain and burning brimstone.

The night coughed up more horrors. Killing fogs. Murderous insects. A beginning glow of magma such as we had seen at the Stair of Tear. And all this in just minutes. Once the Circle responded, the terrors faded, though some it took hours to neutralize. They never took the offensive. The Taken were too strong.

By midnight all was quiet. The Rebel had given up everything but fill work at the far trench. The storm had become a steady rain. It made the Rebel miserable but did him no harm. I wriggled down amongst my companions and fell asleep thinking how nice it was that our part of the world was dry.

Dawn. First view of the Taken's handiwork. Death everywhere. Horribly mutilated corpses. The Rebel labored till noon cleaning up. Then he resumed his assault on the trenches.

The Captain received a message from the Tower. He assembled us. "Word is, we lost Shifter last night." He gave me a look meant to be significant. "The circumstances were questionable. We've been told to stay alert. That means you, One-Eye. And you, Goblin and Silent. You send a yell to the Tower if you see anything suspicious. Understand?" They nodded.

Shapeshifter gone. That must have taken some doing.

"The Rebel lose anybody important?" I asked.

"Whiskers. Roper. Tamarask. But they can be replaced. Shifter can't."

Rumors floated around. The deaths of members of the Circle had been caused by some catlike beast so strong and quick even the powers of its victims were of no consequence. Several score senior Rebel functionaries had fallen victim as well.

The men recalled a similar beast from Beryl. There were whispers. Catcher had brought the forvalaka over on the ship. Was he using it against the Rebel?

I thought not. The attack fit Shifter's style. Shifter loved sneaking into the enemy camp. . . .

One-Eye went around wearing a thoughtful look, so

self-engrossed he bumped into things. Once he stopped and smashed a fist into a ham hanging near the newly erected cook tents.

He had it figured out. How Catcher could send the forvalaka into the Bastion to slaughter the Syndic's entire household, and end up controlling the city through a puppet, through no cost to the Lady's overextended resources. Catcher and Shifter were thick then, weren't they?

He had figured out who killed his brother—too late to extract revenge.

He went around and beat on that ham several times during the course of the day.

I joined Raven and Darling later. They were watching the action. I checked Shapeshifter's force. His standard had been replaced. "Raven. Isn't that Jalena's banner?"

"Yes." He spat.

"Shifter wasn't a bad guy. For one of the Taken."

"None of them are. For Taken. As long as you don't get in their way." He spat again, eyed the Tower. "What's going on here, Croaker?"

"Eh?" He was as civil as he had been since our return from the field.

"What's this show all about? Why is she doing it this way?"

I was not sure what he was asking. "I don't know. She doesn't confide in me."

He scowled. "No?" As though he did not believe me! Then he shrugged. "Be interesting to find out."

"No doubt." I watched Darling. She was inordinately intrigued by the attack. She asked Raven a stream of questions. They were not simple. You might expect their like from an apprentice general, a prince, someone expected to assume eventual command.

"Shouldn't she be somewhere safer?" I asked. "I mean. . . ."

"Where?" Raven demanded. "Where would she be safer than with me?" His voice was hard, his eyes narrow with suspicion. Startled, I dropped the subject.

Was he jealous because I had become Darling's friend? I don't know. Everything about Raven is strange.

Stretches of the farther trench had vanished. In places the middle trench had been filled and tamped. The Rebel had moved his surviving towers and ramps up to the extreme limit of our artillery. New towers were a-building. New mantlets were everywhere. Men huddled behind every one.

Braving merciless fire, Rebel pioneers bridged the final trench. Counterattacks stalled them again and again, yet they kept coming. They completed their eighth bridge about the third hour after noon.

Vast infantry formations moved forward. They swarmed across the bridges, into the teeth of the arrowstorm. They hit our first line randomly, pelting in like sleet, dying against a wall of spears and shields and swords. Bodies piled up. Our bowmen threatened to fill the ditches around the bridges. And still they came.

I recognized a few banners seen at Roses and Lords. The elite units were coming up.

They crossed the bridges and formed up, advanced in fair order, exerted heavy pressure on our center. Behind them a second line formed, stronger, deeper, and broader. When it was solid its officers moved it forward a few yards, had their men crouch behind their shields.

Pioneers moved mantlets across, joined them in a sort of palisade. Our heaviest artillery concentrated on these. Behind the ditch, hordes ran fill to selected points.

Though the men on the bottom level were our least reliable—I suspect the lottery was rigged—they repelled the Rebel elite. Success gave them only a brief respite. The next mass attacked.

Our line creaked. It might have broken had the men had anywhere to run. They had the habit of fleeing. But here they were trapped, with no chance of getting up the retaining wall.

That wave receded. On his end Moonbiter counterattacked and routed the enemy before him. He destroyed most of their mantlets and briefly threatened their bridges. I was impressed by his aggressiveness.

It was late. The Lady had not come forth. I suppose she had not doubted we would hold. The enemy launched a last assault, a human wave attack, that came within a whisper of swamping our men. In places the Rebel reached the retaining wall and tried to scale or dismantle it. But our men did not collapse. The incessant rain of arrows broke the Rebel determination.

They withdrew. Fresh units filled in behind the mantlets. A temporary peace settled in. The field belonged to their pioneers.

"Six days," I said to no one in particular. "I don't think we can hang on."

The first line shouldn't survive tomorrow. The horde would storm the second level. Our archers were deadly as archers, but I doubted they would do well hand-to-hand. Moreover, once forced into close combat they could no longer punish the enemy coming up. Then the Rebel towers would do them as they had been done.

We had cut a narrow trench near the rear of the pyramid top. It served as our latrine. The Captain caught me at my most inelegant. "They need you down on the bottom level, Croaker. Take One-Eye and your crew."

"What?"

"You're a physician, aren't you?"

"Oh," Silly of me. Should have known I could not remain an observer.

The rest of the Company went down too, to perform other tasks.

Getting down was no trouble, though traffic was heavy on the temporary ramps. Men from the upper level and pyramid top hauled munitions down to the bowmen (the Lady must have squirreled arrows for a generation), brought corpses and casualties up.

"Be a good time to jump us," I told One-Eye. "Just scamper up the ramps."

"They're too busy doing the same things we are."

We passed within ten feet of Soulcatcher. I lifted a hand in tentative greeting. He did the same after a pause. I got the feeling he was startled.

Down we went, and down again, into Stormbringer's territory.

It was hell down there. Every battlefield is, after, but never had I seen anything like this. Men were down everywhere. Many were Rebels our men hadn't the energy to finish. Even the troops from up top just booted them aside so they could collect our people. Forty feet away, ignored, Rebel soldiers were gathering their own people and ignoring ours. "It's like something out of the old Annals," I told One-Eye. "Maybe the battle at Torn."

"Torn wasn't this bloody."

"Uhm." He was there. He went back a long way.

I found an officer and asked where we should set up shop. He suggested we'd be the most use to Bonegnasher.

Going, we passed uncomfortably near Stormbringer. One-Eye's amulet burned my wrist.

"Friend of yours?" One-Eye asked sarcastically.

"What?"

"Such a look you got from the old spook."

I shuddered. Lime thread. Taken on the wind. That could have been Stormbringer.

Bonegnasher was a big one, bigger than Shifter, eight

feet tall and six hundred pounds of iron mean muscle. He was so strong it was grotesque. He had a mouth like a crocodile, and supposedly had eaten his enemies in the old days. A few of the old stories also call him Bonecrusher, because of his strength.

While I stared, one of his lieutenants told us to go out to the far right flank, where fighting had been so light no medical team had yet been assigned.

We located the appropriate battalion commander. "Set up right here," he told us. "I'll have the men brought to you." He looked sour.

One of his staff volunteered, "He was a company commander this morning. It was hard on officers today." When you have heavy casualties among your officers they are leading from the front to keep the men from breaking.

One-Eye and I started patching. "Thought you had it easy over here."

"Easy is relative." He looked at us hard, talking about easy when we had spent the day loafing on the pyramid.

Torchlight medicine is a bunch of fun. Between us we treated several hundred men. Whenever I paused to work the pain and stiffness out of my hands and shoulders, I glanced at the sky, perplexed. I had expected the Taken to go crazy again tonight.

Bonegnasher ambled into our makeshift surgery, naked to the waist, maskless, looking like an oversized wrestler. He said nothing. We tried to ignore him. His piggy little eyes remained tight as he watched.

One-Eye and I were working on the same man, from opposite ends. He stopped suddenly, head coming up like that of a startled horse. His eye got big. He looked around wildly. "What is it?" I asked.

"I don't. . . . Odd. It's gone. For a second. . . . Never mind."

I kept an eye on him. He was frightened. More frightened than the presence of the Taken justified. As if some personal danger threatened him. I glanced at Bonegnasher. He was watching One-Eye too.

One-Eye did it again later, while we were working separate patients. I looked up. Beyond him, down at waist level, I caught the glow of eyes. A chill scrambled down my spine.

One-Eye watched the darkness, nervousness increasing. When he finished with his patient he cleansed his hands and drifted toward Bonegnasher.

An animal screamed. A dark shape hurtled into the circle of light, toward me. "Forvalaka!" I gasped, and threw myself aside. The beast passed over me, one claw ripping my jerkin.

Bonegnasher reached the man-leopard's point of impact the moment it did so. One-Eye unleashed a spell that blinded me, the forvalaka, and everyone watching. I heard the beast roar. Anger became agony. My vision returned. Bonegnasher had the monster in a deadly hug, right arm crushing its windpipe, left its ribs. It clawed air futilely. It was supposed to have the strength of a dozen natural leopards. In Bonegnasher's arms it was helpless. The Taken laughed, took a bite from its left shoulder.

One-Eye staggered over to me. "Should have had that guy with us in Beryl," I said. My voice quavered.

One-Eye was so frightened he was gagging. He did not laugh. I did not have much humor in me, either, frankly. Just a reflex sarcasm. Gallows humor.

Trumpets filled the night with their cries. Men ran to their stations. The rattle of arms overrode the strangling of the forvalaka.

One-Eye grabbed my arm. "Got to get out of here," he said. "Come on."

I was mesmerized by the struggle. The leopard was trying to change. It looked vaguely womanish.

"Come on!" One-Eye swore sulphurously. "That thing was after you, you know. Sent. Let's move before it gets away."

It had no end of energy, despite Bonegnasher's immense strength and savagery. The Taken had destroyed its left shoulder with his teeth.

One-Eye was right. Across the way the Rebel was getting excited. Fighting could break out. Time to make tracks, for both reasons. I grabbed my kit and scooted.

We passed both Stormbringer and Soulcatcher getting back. I gave each a mocking salute, driven by I don't know what tomfool bravado. One, I was sure, initiated the attack. Neither responded.

Reaction did not set in till I was safe atop the pyramid, with the Company, with nothing to do but think about what could have happened. Then I started shaking so bad One-Eye gave me one of my own knockout draughts.

Something visited my dreams. Old friend now. Golden glow and beautiful face. As before, "My Faithful need not fear."

There was a hint of light in the east when the drug wore off. I wakened less frightened, but hardly confident. Three times they had tried. Anyone that set on killing me would find a way. No matter what the Lady said.

One-Eye appeared almost immediately. "You all right?"

"Yeah. Fine."

"You missed a hell of a show."

I raised an eyebrow.

"The Circle and the Taken went at it after your lights went out. Only stopped a little while ago. A little hairy around the edges this time. Bonegnasher and Stormbringer got skragged. Looks like they did it to each other. Come here. I want to show you something."

Grumbling, I followed him. "How bad did the Rebel get hurt?"

"You hear different stories. But plenty. At least four of them bought it." He halted at the front edge of the pyramid top, gestured dramatically.

"What?"

"You blind? I got only one eye and I can see better than you?"

"Give me a hint."

"Look for a crucifixion."

"Oh." That told, I had no trouble finding the cross planted near Stormbringer's command post. "Okay. So what?"

"That's your friend. The forvalaka."

"Mine?"

"Ours?" A delightfully wicked expression crossed his face. "End of a long story, Croaker. And a satisfying one. Either way it was, whoever killed Tom-Tom, I lived to see them reach an evil end."

"Yeah." To our left Raven and Darling watched the Rebel move up. Their fingers blurred. They were too far for me to catch much. It was like overhearing a conversation in a language with which you have only a formal acquaintance. Goobledegook. "What's eating Raven lately?"

"What do you mean?"

"He don't have anything to do with anybody but Darling. Don't even hang around the Captain anymore. Hasn't gotten into a card game since we brought in Feather and Journey. Gets all sour whenever you try to be nice to Darling. Something happen while we were away?"

One-Eye shrugged. "I was with you, Croaker. Remember? Nobody ain't said nothing. But now you mention it, yeah, he is acting strange." He chuckled. "For Raven, strange."

I surveyed the Rebel's preparations. They seemed half-hearted and disorganized. Even so, despite the fury of the night, he had finished filling the farther two trenches. His efforts at the nearest had provided a half dozen crossing places.

Our second and third level forces looked thin. I asked why.

"The Lady ordered a bunch down to the first level. Especially off the top."

Mostly from Soulcatcher's division, I realized. His outfit looked puny. "Think they'll break through today?"

One-Eye shrugged. "If they stay as stubborn as they were. But look. They ain't eager no more. They found out we weren't going to be easy. We made them start to wonder. To remember the old spook in the Tower. She hasn't come out yet. Maybe they're getting worried."

I suspected it was more because of casualties among the Circle than because of growing trepidation among the soldiers. The Rebel command structure must be chaotic. Any army falters when nobody knows who is in charge.

Nevertheless, four hours after dawn they began dying for their cause. Our front line braced itself. The Howler and The Faceless Man had replaced Stormbringer and Bonegnasher, leaving the second level to Nightcrawler.

The fighting had become formularized. The horde swept forward, into the teeth of the arrowstorm, crossed the bridges, hid behind the mantlets, streamed around those to hit our first line. They kept coming, a never-ending stream. Thousands fell before reaching their foes. Many who did make it battled only a short while, then wandered off, sometimes helping injured comrades, more often just getting out of harm's way. Their officers had no control.

The reinforced line consequently held together longer and more resolutely than I anticipated. Nevertheless, the weight of numbers and accumulated fatigue eventually told. Gaps appeared. Enemy troops reached the retaining wall. The Taken organized counterattacks, most of which did not attain the momentum to carry through. Here, there, weaker willed troopers tried to flee to the higher level. Nightcrawler distributed squads along the edge. They threw the fugitives back. Resistance stiffened.

Still, the Rebel now scented victory. He became more enthusiastic.

The distant ramps and towers started forward. Their advance was ponderous, a few yards a minute. One tower toppled when it hit fill inadequately tamped in the far trench. It crushed a ramp and several dozen men. The remaining engines came on. The Guard redirected its heaviest weapons, throwing fireballs.

A tower caught. Then another. A ramp came to a halt, in flames. But the other engines rolled steadily forward, reaching the second trench.

The lighter ballistae shifted aim as well, savaging the thousands hauling the engines forward.

At the nearest trench pioneers kept filling and tamping. And falling to our bowmen. I had to admire them. They were the bravest of the foe.

The Rebel star was rising. He overcame his weak start and became as ferocious as before. Our first level units fractured into ever smaller knots, whirling, swirling. The men Nightcrawler had scattered to keep ours from fleeing now battled overbold Rebels who clambered up the retaining wall. In one spot Rebel troops pulled some of the logs free and tried to excavate a pathway up.

It was the middle of the afternoon. The Rebel still had hours of daylight. I began to get the shakes.

One-Eye, whom I hadn't seen since it started, joined me again. "Word from the Tower," he said. "They lost six of the Circle last night. Means there are only maybe eight left out there. Probably none who were in the Circle when we first came north."

"No wonder they started slow."

He eyed the fighting. "Don't look good, does it?"

"Hardly."

"Guess that's why she's coming out." I turned. "Yeah. She's on her way. In person."

Cold. Cold-cold-cold. I do not know why. Then I heard the Captain yelling, the Lieutenant and Candy and Elmo and Raven and who knows all else, all yelling for us to get into formation. Grab-ass time was over. I withdrew to my surgery, which was a clump of tents at the rear, unfortunately on the downwind side of the latrine. "Quick inspection," I told One-Eye. "See that everything is squared away."

The Lady came on horseback, up the ramp climbing from near the Tower entrance. She rode an animal bred for the part. It was huge and spirited, a glossy roan that looked like an artist's conception of equine perfection. She was very stylish, in red and gold brocade, white scarves, gold and silver jewelry, a few black accents. Like a rich lady one might see in the streets of Opal. Her hair was darker than midnight, and hung long from beneath an elegant white and lace tricorner hat trailing white ostrich plumes. A net of pearls kept it constrained. She looked twenty at the oldest. Quiet islanded her as she passed. Men gaped. Nowhere did I see a hint of fear.

The Lady's companions were more in keeping with her image. Of medium heighth, all swathed in black, faces concealed behind black gauze, mounted upon black horses harnessed and saddled in black leather, they resembled the popular picture of the Taken. One bore a long black spear tipped with blackened steel, the other a big silver horn. One rode to either flank, trailing by a rigid yard.

She honored me with one sweet smile as she passed. Her eyes sparkled with humor and invitation. . . .

"She still loves you," One-Eye quipped.

I shuddered. "That's what I'm afraid of."

She rode through the Company, straight to the Captain, spoke to him for half a minute. He showed no emotion, coming face to face with this old evil. Nothing shakes him when he assumes his iron commander mask.

Elmo came hustling up. "How you doing, buddy?" I asked. I had not seen him in days.

"She wants you."

I said something like "Glug." Real intelligent.

"I know what you mean. Enough is enough. But what can you do? Get yourself a horse."

"A horse? Why? Where?"

"Just carrying a message, Croaker. Don't ask me. . . . Speak of the devil."

A young trooper, wearing the Howler's colors, appeared over the edge of the rear of the pyramid. He led a string of horses. Elmo trotted over. After a brief exchange, he beckoned me. Reluctantly, I joined him. "Take your pick, Croaker."

I selected a chestnut mare with good lines and apparent docility, swung aboard. It felt good to be in the saddle. It had been a while. "Wish me luck, Elmo." I wanted to sound flip. It came out squeaky.

"You got it." And as I started away, "Teach you to write those silly stories."

"Let up, eh?" As I went forward I did wonder, for a moment, how much art does effect life. *Could* I have brought this on myself?

The Lady did not look back as I approached. She did make a small gesture. The horseman on her right edged away, leaving me room. I took the hint, halted, concentrated on the panorama instead of looking at her. I sensed her amusement.

The situation had worsened in the minutes I had been

away. Rebel soldiers had attained several footholds on the second tier. On the first our formations had been shattered. The Howler had relented and was letting his men help those below scramble up the retaining wall. Whisper's troops, on the third level, were using bows for the first time.

The assault ramps were almost up to the nearest ditch. The great towers had halted. Over half were out of action. The remainder had been manned, but were so far away the bowmen there were doing no damage. Thank heaven for small favors.

The Taken on the first level were using their powers, but were in so much danger they had little chance to wield them effectively.

The Lady said, "I wanted you to see this, Annalist."

"Eh?" Another sparkling gem from the Company wit.

"What is about to transpire. So that it is properly recorded in at least one place."

I snuck a glance at her. She wore a teasing little smile. I shifted my attention to the fighting. What she did to me, just sitting there, amidst the fury of the end of the world, was more frightening than the prospect of a death in battle. I am too old to boil like a horny fifteen year old.

The Lady snapped her fingers.

The rider on her left raised the silver horn, cleared the gauze from her face so she could bring the instrument to her lips. Feather! My gaze flicked to the Lady. She winked.

Taken. Feather and Journey had been Taken, like Whisper before them. What power and might they possessed was now at the Lady's disposal. . . . My mind scampered around that. Implications, implications. Old Taken fallen, new Taken stepping in to replace them. . . .

The horn called out, a sweet note, like that of an angel summoning the hosts of heaven. It was not loud, yet it rang out everywhere, as if coming from the very firmament. The fighting stopped cold. All eyes turned to the pyramid.

The Lady snapped her fingers. The other rider (Journey, I presumed) lifted his spear high, let its head fall.

The forward retaining wall exploded in a dozen places. Bestial trumpeting filled the silence. Even before I saw them burst forth I knew, and laughed. "Elephants!" I hadn't seen war elephants since my first year with the Company. "Where did you get elephants?"

The Lady's eyes sparkled. She did not respond.

The answer was obvious. From overseas. From her allies among the Jewel cities. How she had gotten them here unnoted, and had kept them concealed, ah, that was the mystery.

It was a delectable surprise to spring on the Rebel at the moment of his apparent triumph. Nobody in these parts had ever seen war elephants, let alone had any notion how to fight them.

The great grey pachyderms smashed into the Rebel horde. The mahouts had great fun, charging their beasts back and forth, trampling Rebels by the hundred, totally shattering their morale. They pulled the mantlets down. They lumbered across the bridges and went after the siege towers, toppling them one by one.

There were twenty-four of the beasts, two for each place of hiding. They had been provided with armor, and their drivers were encased in metal, yet here and there the random spear or arrow found a chink, either felling a mahout or pricking a beast enough to enrage it. Elephants that lost riders lost interest in the fray. The wounded animals went crazy. They did more damage than those still under control.

The Lady gestured again. Again Journey signalled. Troops below lowered the ramps we had used for hauling materiel down and casualties up. The troops off the third level, saving the Guard, marched down, formed up, launched an attack upon chaos. Considering the respective numbers, that seemed mad. But considering the wild swing in fortunes, morale was more important.

Whisper on the left wing, Catcher in the center, fat old Lord Jalena on the right. Drums pounding. They rolled forward, slowed only by the problem of slaughtering the panicked thousands. The Rebel was afraid not to run, yet afraid to flee toward the rampaging elephants between him and his camp. He did little to defend himself.

Clear to the first ditch. Biter, the Howler, and the Faceless whipped their survivors into line, cursed and frightened them into moving forward, to fire all the enemy works.

Attackers to the second ditch, swirling over and around the abandoned towers and ramps, passing on, following the bloody trail of the elephants. Now fires among the engines as the men from the first level arrived. The attackers advancing toward the nether ditch. The whole field carpeted with enemy dead. Dead in numbers unlike anything I had seen anywhere before.

The Circle, what remained of it, finally recovered enough to try its powers against the beasts. They scored a few successes before being neutralized by the Taken. Then it depended on the men in the field.

As always, the Rebel had the numbers. One by one, the elephants fell. The enemy piled up before the attacking line. We had no reserves. Fresh troops streamed from the Rebel camps, without enthusiasm but sufficiently strong to turn our advance. A withdrawal became necessary.

The Lady signalled it through Journey.

"Very good," I muttered. "Very good indeed," as our men returned to their positions, sank down in weariness. Darkness was not far away. We had made it through another day. "But now what? Those fools won't quit while the comet is in the sky. And we've shot our last bolt."

The Lady smiled. "Record it as you saw it, Annalist." She and her companions rode away.

"What am I going to do with this horse?" I grumbled.

There was a battle of powers that night, but I missed it. I do not know for whom it was the greater disaster. We lost Moonbiter, the Faceless Man, and Nightcrawler. Only Nightcrawler fell to enemy action. The others were consumed by the feud among the Taken.

A messenger came not an hour after sundown. I was readying my team to go below, after having fed them. Elmo ran the relay again. "Tower, Croaker. Your girlfriend wants you. Take your bow along."

There is only so much you can fear someone, even someone like the Lady. Resigned, I asked, "Why a bow?"

He shrugged.

"Arrows too?"

"No word on that. Doesn't sound smart."

"You're probably right. One-Eye, it's all yours."

Silver lining time. At least I would not spend my night amputating limbs, sewing cuts, and reassuring youngsters whom I knew would not survive the week. Serving with the Taken gives a soldier a better chance of surviving wounds, but still gangrene and peritonitis take their tolls.

Down the long ramp, to the dark gate. The Tower loomed like something out of myth, awash in the silver light of the comet. Had the Circle blundered? Waited too long? Was the comet no longer a favorable omen once it began to wane?

How close were the eastern armies? Not close enough. But our strategy did not seem predicated on stalling. If that were the plan, we would have marched into the Tower and sealed the door. Wouldn't we?

I dithered. Natural reluctance. I touched the amulet Goblin had given me back when, the amulet One-Eye had presented more recently. Not much assurance there. I glanced at the pyramid, thought I saw a stocky silhouette up top. The Captain? I raised a hand. The silhouette responded. Cheered, I turned.

The gate looked like the mouth of the night, but a step forward took me into a wide, lighted passageway. It reeked of the horses and cattle which had been driven in an age ago.

A soldier awaited me. "Are you Croaker?" I nodded. "Follow me." He was not a Guard, but a young infantry-man from the Howler's army. He seemed bewildered. Here, there, I saw more of his ilk. It hit me. The Howler had spent his nights ferrying troops while the rest of the Taken battled the Circle and one another. None of those men had come to the battlefield.

How many were there? What surprises did the Tower conceal?

I entered the inner Tower through the portal I had used before. The soldier halted where the Guard captain had. He wished me luck in a pale, shaky voice. I thanked him squeakily.

She played no games. At least, nothing flashy. And I did not slip into my role as sex-brained boy. This was business all the way.

She seated me at a dark wood table with my bow lying before me, said, "I have a problem."

I just looked at her.

"Rumors are running wild out there, aren't they? About what's happened among the Taken?"

I nodded. "This isn't like the Limper going bad. They're murdering each other. The men don't want to get caught in the crossfire."

"My husband isn't dead. You know that. He's behind it

all. He's been awakening. Very slowly, but enough to have reached some of the Circle. Enough to have touched the females among the Taken. They'll do anything for him. The bitches. I watch them as close as I can, but I'm not infallible. They get away with things. This battle. . . . It isn't what it seems. The Rebel army was brought here by members of the Circle under my husband's influence. The fools. They thought they could use *him,* to defeat me and grab power for themselves. They're all gone now, slain, but the thing they set in motion goes on. I'm not fighting the White Rose, Annalist—though a victory over that silliness could come from this as well. I'm fighting the old slaver, the Dominator. And if I lose I lose the world.''

Cunning woman. She did not assume the role of maiden in distress. She played it as one equal to another, and that won my sympathy more surely. She knew I knew the Dominator as well as did any mundane now alive. Knew I must fear him far more than her, for who fears a woman more than a man?

"I know you, Annalist. I have opened your soul and peered inside. You fight for me because your company has undertaken a commission it will pursue to the bitter end— because its principal personalities feel its honor was stained in Beryl. And that though most of you think you're serving Evil.

"Evil is relative, Annalist. You can't hang a sign on it. You can't touch it or taste it or cut it with a sword. Evil depends on where you are standing, pointing your indicting finger. Where you stand now, because of your oath, is opposite the Dominator. For you he is where your Evil lies.''

She paced a moment, perhaps anticipating a response. I made none. She had encapsulated my own philosophy.

"That evil tried to kill you three times, physician. Twice
for fear of your knowledge, once for fear of your future."

That woke me up. "My future?"

"The Taken sometimes glimpse the future. Perhaps this
conversation was foreseen."

She had me baffled. I sat there looking stupid.

She left the room momentarily, returned carrying a quiver of arrows, spilled them on the table. They were black
and heavy, silver-headed, inscribed with almost invisible
lettering. While I examined them she took my bow, exchanged it for another of identical weight and pull. It was
a gorgeous match for the arrows. Too gorgeous to be used
as a weapon.

She told me, "Carry these. Always."

"I'll have to use them?"

"It's possible. Tomorrow will see the end of the matter,
one way or the other. The Rebel has been mauled, yet he
retains vast manpower reserves. My strategy may not
succeed. If I fail, my husband wins. Not the Rebel, not the
White Rose, but the Dominator, that hideous beast lying
restless in his grave. . . ."

I avoided her gaze, eyed the weapons, wondered what I
was supposed to say, to not hear, what I was supposed to
do with those death tools, and if I could do it when the
time came.

She knew my mind. "You'll know the moment. And
you'll do what you think is right."

I looked up now, frowning, wishing. . . . Even knowing what she was, wishing. Maybe my idiot brothers were
right.

She smiled, reached with one of those too-perfect hands,
clasped my fingers. . . .

I lost track. I think. I do not recall anything happening.
Yet my mind did fuzz for a second, and when it unfuzzed,

she was holding my hand still, smiling, saying, "Time to go, soldier. Rest well."

I rose zombielike and shambled toward the door. I had a distinct feeling that I had missed something. I did not look back. I couldn't.

I stepped into the night outside the Tower and immediately knew I had lost time again. The stars had moved across the sky. The comet was low. Rest well? The hours for rest were nearly gone.

It was peaceful out, cool, with crickets chirping. Crickets. Who would believe it? I looked down at the weapon she had given me. When had I strung it? Why was I carrying an arrow across it? I could not recall taking them off the table. . . . For one frightened instant I thought my mind was going. Cricket song brought me back.

I looked up the pyramid. Someone was up top, watching. I raised a hand. He responded. Elmo, by the way he moved. Good old Elmo.

Couple hours till dawn. I could get a little shuteye if I didn't dawdle.

A quarter way up the ramp I got a funny feeling. Halfway there I realized what it was. One-Eye's amulet! My wrist was burning. . . . Taken! Danger!

A cloud of darkness reared out of the night, from some imperfection in the side of the pyramid. It spread like the sail of a ship, flat, and moved toward me. I responded the only way I could. With an arrow.

My shaft ripped through that sheet of darkness. And a long wail surrounded me, filled with more surprise than rage, more despair than agony. The sheet of darkness shredded. Something manshaped scuttled across the slope. I watched it go, never thinking of spending another arrow, though I laid another across the bow. Boggled, I resumed my climb.

"What happened?" Elmo asked when I got to the top.

"I don't know," I said. "I honestly don't have the foggiest what the hell happened tonight."

He gave me the once-over. "You look pretty rocky. Get some rest."

"I need it," I admitted. "Pass it to the Captain. She says tomorrow is the day. Win or lose." Much good the news would do him. But I thought he would like to know.

"Yeah. They do something to you in there?"

"I don't know. I don't think so."

He wanted to talk more, despite his admonition about resting. I pushed him away gently, went into one of my hospital tents and curled up in a tight corner like a wounded animal denning up. I had been touched somehow, even if I could not name it. I needed time to recover. Probably more time than I would be given.

They sent Goblin to waken me. I was my usual charming morning self, threatening blood feud with anyone fool enough to disturb my dreams. Not that they didn't deserve disturbing. They were foul. I was doing unspeakable things with a couple of girls who could not have been more than twelve, and making them love it. It's disgusting, the shadows that lurk in the mind.

Revolting as my dreams were, I did not want to get up. My bedroll was toasty warm.

Goblin said, "You want I should play rough? Listen, Croaker. Your girlfriend is coming out. Captain wants you up to meet her."

"Yeah. Sure." I grabbed my boots with one hand, parted the tent flap with the other. I growled, "What the hell time is it? Looks like the sun's been up for hours."

"It has. Elmo figured you needed the rest. Said you had it rough last night."

I grunted, hastily put myself together. I considered washing up, but Goblin headed me off. "Get your war gear on. The Rebel is headed this way."

I heard distant drums. The Rebel had not used drums before. I asked about it.

Goblin shrugged. He was looking pale. I suppose he had heard my message to the Captain. Win or lose. Today. "They've elected themselves a new council." He began to natter, as men will do when frightened, telling me the night's history of the feud among the Taken, and of how the Rebel had suffered. I heard nothing cheering. He helped me don what armor I possessed. I hadn't worn anything but a mail shirt since the fighting around Roses. I collected the weapons the Lady had given me and stepped out into one of the most glorious mornings I'd ever seen.

"Hell of a day for dying," I said.

"Yeah."

"How soon is she going to be here?" The Captain would want us on station when she arrived. He liked to present a portrait of order and efficiency.

"When she gets here. We just had a message saying she would be out."

"Uhm." I surveyed the pyramid top. The men were about their business, preparing for a fight. Nobody seemed in any hurry. "I'm going to wander around."

Goblin did not say anything. He just followed, pallid face pulled into a concerned frown. His eyes moved constantly, watching everything. From the set of his shoulders and careful way he moved, I realized he had a spell ready for instant use. It was not till he had dogged me a while that I realized he was bodyguarding.

I was both pleased and distressed. Pleased because people cared enough to look out for me, distressed because my situation had become so bad. I glanced at my hands. Unconsciously, I had strung the bow and laid an arrow across. Part of me was on maximum alert too.

Everyone eyed the weapons, but no one asked. I suspect stories were making the rounds. Strange that my comrades did not corner me to double-check.

The Rebel arrayed his forces carefully, methodically, beyond the reach of our weapons. Whoever had taken charge had restored discipline. And had constructed a whole armada of new engines during the night.

Our forces had abandoned the lower level. All that remained down there was a crucifix with a figure writhing upon it. . . . Writhing. After all it had suffered, including having been nailed up on that cross, the forvalaka remained alive!

The troops had been shuffled. The archers were upon the third level now, Whisper having taken command of that whole tier. The allies, the survivors from the first level, Catcher's forces, and what not, were on the second level. Catcher had the center, Lord Jalena the right, and the Howler the left. An effort had been made to restore the retaining wall, but it remained in terrible shape. It would be a poor obstacle.

One-Eye joined us. "You guys hear the latest?"

I lifted an inquiring eyebrow.

"They claim they've found their White Rose child."

After reflection I responded, "Dubious."

"For sure. Word from the Tower is, she's a fake. Just something to get the troops fired up."

"I figured. Surprised they didn't think of it before."

"Speak of the devil," Goblin squeaked. He pointed.

I had to search a moment before spotting the soft glow advancing along the aisles between enemy divisions. It surrounded a child on a big white horse, bearing a standard of red emblazoned with a white rose.

"Not even good showmanship," One-Eye complained. "That guy on the bay is making the light."

My insides had knotted in fear that this was the real

thing after all. I looked down at my hands, wondering if this child was the target the Lady had in mind. But no. I had no impulse to speed a shaft in that direction. Not that I could have gotten one halfway there.

I glimpsed Raven and Darling on the far side of the pyramid, hands going zip-zip. I headed that way.

Raven spotted us when we were twenty feet away. He glanced at my weapons. His face tightened. A knife appeared in his hand. He started cleaning his nails.

I stumbled, so startled was I. The knife business was a tick. He did it only under stress. Why with me? I was no enemy.

I tucked my bow and arrow under my left arm, greeted Darling. She gave me a big grin, quick hug. *She* didn't have anything against me. She asked if she could see the bow. I let her look but did not turn loose. I couldn't.

Raven was as restless as a man seated on a griddle.

"What the hell is the matter with you?" I demanded. "You been acting like the rest of us have the plague." His behavior hurt. We had been through some shit together, Raven and I. He had no call to turn on me.

His mouth tightened to a tiny point. He dug under his nails till it seemed he had to be hurting himself.

"Well?"

"Don't push me, Croaker."

With my right hand I scratched Darling's back as she leaned against me. My left tightened on my bow. My knuckles turned the color of old ice. I was ready to thump the man. Take that dagger away and I stood a chance. He is a tough bastard, but I've had a few years to get tough myself.

Darling seemed oblivious to the tension between us.

Goblin stepped in. He faced Raven, his stance as belligerent as mine. "You've got a problem, Raven. I think maybe we better have a sitdown with the Captain."

Raven was startled. He realized, if only for a moment, that he was making enemies. It's damned hard to make Goblin mad. Really mad, not mad like he gets with One-Eye.

Something died behind Raven's eyes. He indicated my bow. "Lady's leman," he accused.

I was more baffled than angry. "Not true," I said. "But so what if it was?"

He moved restlessly. His gaze kept flicking to Darling, leaning against me. He wanted her away, but could not put the demand into acceptable words.

"First sucking up to Soulcatcher all the time. Now to the Lady. What are you doing, Croaker? Who are you selling?"

"What?" Only Darling's presence kept me from going after him.

"That's enough," Goblin said. His voice was hard, without a hint of squeak. "I'm pulling rank. On everybody. Right now. Right here. We're going to the Captain and get this talked out. Or we're unvoting your membership in the Company, Raven. Croaker is right. You've been a pure ass lately. We don't need it. We've got enough trouble out there." He stabbed a finger at the Rebel.

The Rebel answered with trumpets.

There was no confab with the Captain.

It was obvious somebody new was in charge. The enemy divisions came forward in lockstep, slowly, their shields arrayed in proper turtle fashion, turning most of our arrows. Whisper adjusted quickly, concentrating the guard's fire on one formation at a time, having the archers wait till the heavy weapons broke the turtle. Effective, but not effective enough.

The siege towers and ramps rumbled forward as fast as men could drag them. The Guard did their best, but could destroy only a few. Whisper was in a dilemma. She had to choose between targets. She elected to concentrate on breaking turtles.

The towers came closer this time. The Rebel archers were able to reach our men. That meant our archers could reach them, and ours were better marksmen.

The enemy crossed the nearest ditch, encountering massed missile fire from both levels. Only when they reached the retaining wall did they break their formations, streaming to the weak points, where they had little success. They then attacked everywhere at once. Their ramps were slow arriving. Men with ladders rushed forward.

The Taken did not hold back. They threw everything they could. Rebel wizards fought them all the way, and, despite the harm they had suffered, for the most part kept them neutralized. Whisper did not participate. She was too busy.

The Lady and her companions arrived. Again I was summoned. I clambered aboard my horse and joined her, bow across my lap.

They came on and on. Occasionally I glanced at the Lady. She remained an ice queen, utterly without expression.

The Rebel gained foothold after foothold. He tore whole sections of retaining wall away. Men with shovels hurled earth around, building natural ramps. The wooden ramps continued their advance, but would not arrive soon.

There was one island of peace out there, around the crucified forvalaka. The attackers gave it a wide berth.

Lord Jalena's troops began to waver. You could see a collapse threatening even before men turned to eye the retaining wall behind them.

The Lady gestured. Journey spurred his horse forward, down the face of the pyramid. He passed behind Whisper's men, through them, stationed himself at the edge of the level, behind Jalena's division. He raised his spear. It blazed. Why I don't know, but Jalena's troops took heart, solidified, began to push the Rebel back.

The Lady gestured to her left. Feather went down the slope like a daredevil, winding her horn. Its silver call drowned the blare of Rebel trumpets. She passed through the third level troops and leapt her horse off the wall. The drop would have killed any horse I'd ever seen. This one landed heavily, gained its balance, reared, neighed in triumph as Feather winded her horn. As on the right, the troops took heart and began driving the Rebel back.

A small indigo shape clambered up the wall and scuttled to the rear, skirting the base of the pyramid. It ran all the way to the Tower. The Howler. I frowned, puzzled. Had he been relieved?

Our center became the focus of battle, Catcher struggling valiantly to keep his line.

I heard sounds, glanced over, saw that the Captain had come up on the Lady's far side. He was mounted. I looked back. A number of horses had been brought up. I stared down that long steep slope at the narrowness of the third level, and my heart sank. She was not planning a cavalry charge, was she?

Feather and Journey were big medicine, but not medicine big enough. They stiffened resistance only till the Rebel ramps arrived.

The level went. Slower than I expected, but it went. No more than a thousand men escaped. I looked at the Lady. Her face remained ice, yet I felt she was not displeased.

Whisper poured arrows into the mass below. Guards fired ballistae point blank.

A shadow crept over the pyramid. I looked up. The Howler's carpet drifted out over the foe. Men crouched along its edges, dropping balls the size of heads. Those plummeted into the Rebel mass without visible effect. The carpet crawled toward the enemy camp, raining those pointless objects.

It took the Rebel an hour to establish solid bridgeheads

upon the third level, and another hour to bring up enough men to press the attack. Whisper, Feather, Journey, and Catcher mauled them mercilessly. Oncoming troops clambered over drifts of their comrades to reach the top.

The Howler carried his ball-dropping to the Rebel camp. I doubted there was anyone out there. They were all in the pie-slice, awaiting their turns at us.

The false White Rose sat her horse out about the second trench, glowing, surrounded by the new Rebel council. They remained frozen, acting only when one of the Taken used their powers. They had done nothing about the Howler, though. Apparently there was nothing they could do.

I checked the Captain, who had been up to something. . . . He was lining horsemen up across the front of the pyramid. We *were* going to attack down that slope! What idiocy!

A voice inside told me, *My faithful need not fear*. I faced the Lady. She looked at me coolly, regally. I turned back to the battle.

It would not be long. Our troops had put aside their bows and abandoned the heavy weapons. They were bracing themselves. On the plain the whole horde was in motion. But a vaguely slowed, indecisive motion, it seemed. This was the moment when they should have run headlong, swamping us, roaring into the Tower before the gate could be closed. . . .

The Howler came roaring back from the enemy camp, moving a dozen times faster than any horse could run. I watched the big carpet pass over, even now unable to restrain my awe. For an instant it masked the comet, then passed on, toward the Tower. A strange howl wafted down, unlike any Howler cry I had heard before. The carpet dipped slightly, tried to slow, ploughed into the Tower a few feet below its top.

"My god," I murmured, watching the thing crumple,

watching men tumble down the five hundred foot fall.
"My god." Then the Howler died or lost consciousness.
The carpet itself began to fall.

I shifted my gaze to the Lady, who had been watching
too. Her expression did not change the slightest. Softly, in
a voice only I heard, she said, "You *will* use the bow."

I shuddered. And for a second images flashed through
my mind, a hundred of them too quickly for any to be
caught. I seemed to be drawing the bow. . . .

She was angry. Angry with a rage so great I shook just
contemplating it, even knowing it was not directed at
me. Its object was not hard to determine. The Howler's
demise was not caused by enemy action. There was but
one Taken likely to be responsible. Soulcatcher. Our for-
mer mentor. The one who had used us in so many schemes.

The Lady murmured something. I am not sure I heard it
right. Sounded like, "I gave her every chance."

I whispered, "We weren't part of it."

"Come." She kneed her animal. It went over the edge.
I threw one despairing look at the Captain and followed.

She went down that slope with the speed that Feather
had shown. My mount seemed determined to keep pace.

We plunged toward an island of screaming men. It
centered on a fountain of lime thread which boiled up and
spread on the wind, taking Rebel and friend alike. The
Lady did not swerve.

Soulcatcher was in flight already. Friend and enemy
were eager to get out of his way. Death surrounded him.
He ran at Journey, leapt, knocked him off his horse,
bestrode the animal himself, leapt it down to the second
level, ploughed through the enemy there, descended to the
plain, and roared away.

The Lady followed the path he blazed, dark hair streaming.
I stayed in her wake, utterly baffled yet unable to change
what I was doing. We reached the plain three hundred

yards behind Soulcatcher. The Lady spurred her mount.
Mine kept pace. I was sure one or both animals would
stumble over abandoned equipment or bodies. Yet they,
and Catcher's beast too, were as sure-footed as horses on a
track.

Catcher sped directly to the enemy encampment, and
through. We followed. In the open country beyond we
began to gain. Those beasts, all three, were as tireless as
machines. Miles rolled away. We gained fifty yards with
every one. I clutched my bow and clung to the nightmare.
I've never been religious, but that was a time when I was
tempted to pray.

She was as implacable as death, my Lady. I pitied
Soulcatcher when she caught him.

Soulcatcher raced along a road winding through one of
the valleys west of Charm. We were near the place where
we had rested on a hilltop, and encountered lime thread. I
recalled what we had ridden through, back at Charm. A
fountain of the stuff, and it hadn't touched us.

What was happening back there? Was this some scheme
to leave our people at the Rebel's mercy? It had become
clear, toward the end, that the Lady's strategy involved
maximum destruction. That she wanted only a small minority of either side to survive. She was cleaning house. She
had but one enemy left among the Taken. Soulcatcher.
Catcher, who had been almost good to me. Who had saved
my life at least once, at the Stair of Tear, when Stormbringer
would have slain Raven and I. Catcher, who was the only
Taken to speak to me as a man, to tell me a bit about the
old days, to respond to my insatiable curiosities. . . .

What the devil was I doing here, in a hellride with the
Lady, hunting a thing that could gobble me up without
blinking?

Catcher turned the flank of a hill and when, seconds

later, we rounded the same impediment, had disappeared.
The Lady slowed for a moment, head turning slowly, then
yanked her reins, swung toward woods that swept down to
the edge of the road. She halted when she reached the first
trees. My beast stopped beside hers.

The Lady threw herself off her mount. I did the same
without thinking. By the time I gained my feet her animal
was collapsing and mine was dead, standing on stiff legs.
Both had fist-sized black burns upon their throats.

The Lady pointed, started forward. Crouching, arrow
across bow, I joined her. I went carefully, soundlessly,
sliding through the brush like a fox.

She stopped, crouched, pointed. I looked along her arm.
Flicker, flicker, two seconds of rapid images. They stopped.
I saw a figure perhaps fifty feet distant, back to us,
kneeling, doing something swiftly. No time for the moral
questions I had debated riding out. That creature had made
several attempts on my life. My arrow was in the air
before I realized what I was doing.

It smacked into the head of the figure. The figure pitched
forward. I gaped a second, then released a long breath. So
easy. . . .

The Lady took three quick steps forward, frowning.
There was a rapid rustle to our right. Something rattled
brush. She whirled and ran for open country, slapping my
arm as she passed.

In seconds we were on the road. Another arrow lay
across my bow. Her arm rose, pointing. . . . A squarish
shape slid out of the woods fifty yards away. A figure
aboard made a throwing motion our way. I staggered
under the impact of the blow from no visible source.
Spiderwebs seemed drawn across my eyes, blurring my
vision. Vaguely, I sensed the Lady making a gesture. The
webs disappeared. I felt whole. She pointed as the carpet
began to rise and move away.

I drew and loosed, with no hope my arrow would strike a moving target at that range.

It did not, but only because the carpet jerked violently downward and to one side while the arrow was in the air. My shaft ripped past inches behind the carpet rider's head.

The Lady did something. The air hummed. From nowhere came a giant dragonfly like the one I had seen in the Forest of Cloud. It streaked toward the carpet, hit. The carpet spun, flipped, jerked around. Its rider fell free, plummeted with a despairing cry. I loosed another shaft the instant the man hit earth. He twitched a moment, lay still. And we were upon him.

The Lady ripped the black morion off our victim. And cursed. Softly, steadily, she cursed like a senior sergeant.

"What?" I finally asked. The man was dead enough to satisfy me.

"It's not her." She whirled, faced the wood. Her face blanked for several seconds. Then she faced the drifting carpet. She jerked her head at the wood. "Go see if that's a woman. See if the horse is there." She began making come-hither gestures at Catcher's carpet.

I went, mind aboil. Catcher was a woman, eh? Crafty, too. All prepared to be chased here, by the Lady herself.

Fear grew as I slipped through the wood, slow, silent. Catcher had played a game on everyone, and far more shrewdly than even the Lady had anticipated. What next, then? There had been so many attempts on my life. . . . Might this not be the moment to end whatever threat I represented?

Nothing happened, though. Except that I crept up to the corpse in the wood, ripped off a black morion, and found a handsome youth inside. Fear, anger, and frustration overwhelmed me. I kicked him. Some good, abusing dead meat.

The fit did not last. I began looking around the camp where the substitutes had waited. They had been there a

while, and been prepared to stay a while longer. They had
supplies for a month.

A large bundle caught my eye. I cut the cords binding
it, peeped inside. Papers. A bale that must have weighed
eighty pounds. Curiosity grabbed me.

I looked around hastily, saw nothing threatening, probed
a little deeper. And immediately realized what I had.
These were part of the hoard we had unearthed in the
Forest of Cloud.

What were they doing here? I'd thought Catcher had
turned them over to the Lady. Eh! Plot and counterplot.
Maybe he *had* delivered some. And maybe he kept back
others he thought would be useful later. Maybe we had been
so close on his heels he had not had time to collect
them. . . .

Maybe he would be back. I looked around again, frightened once more.

Nothing stirred.

Where was he?

She, I reminded myself. Catcher was one of the shes.

I looked around, hunting evidence of the Taken's
departure, soon discovered hoofprints leading deeper into
the wood. A few paces beyond the camp they reached a
narrow trail. I crouched, looking down an aisle of forest,
through golden motes floating in shafts of sunlight. I tried
to work myself up to go on.

Come, a voice said in my mind. *Come.*

The Lady. Relieved not to have to follow that trail, I
turned back. "It was a man," I said as I approached the
Lady.

"I thought so." She had the carpet under one hand,
floating two feet off the earth. "Get aboard."

I swallowed, did as I was told. It was like climbing
aboard a boat from deep water. I almost fell off twice. As

she followed me aboard, I told her, "He—*she*—stayed on the horse and went on down the trail through the woods."

"What direction?"

"South."

The carpet rose swiftly. The dead horses dwindled beneath us. We began to drift over the wood. My stomach felt like I had drunk several gallons of wine the night before.

The Lady cursed softly under her breath. Finally, in a louder voice, she said, "The bitch. She ran a game on us all. My husband included."

I said nothing. I was debating whether or not to mention the papers. She would be interested. But so was I, and if I mentioned them now I'd never get a chance to poke through them.

"I'll bet that was what she was doing. Getting rid of the other Taken by pretending to be part of their plot. Then it would have been me. Then she would just leave the Dominator in the ground. She would have it all, and be able to keep him restrained. He can't break out without help." She was thinking aloud more than speaking to me. "And I missed the evidence. Or ignored it. It was right there all the time. Cunning bitch. She'll burn for that."

We began to fall. I nearly lost what little my stomach contained. We fell into a valley deeper than most in the area, though the hills to either hand stood no more than two hundred feet high. We slowed.

"Arrow," she said. I had forgotten to ready another.

We drifted down the valley a mile or so, then upslope till we floated beside an outcrop of sedimentary rock. There we hovered, nudging the stone. There was a brisk cold wind. My hands grew numb. We were far from the Tower, into country where winter held full sway. I shivered continuously.

The only warning was a soft, "Hang on."

The carpet shot forward. A quarter mile distant was a figure lying low on the neck of a racing horse. The Lady dropped till we hurtled along just two feet off the ground.

Catcher saw us. She threw up a hand in a warding gesture. We were upon her. I released my shaft.

The carpet slammed up against me as the Lady pulled it upward, trying to clear horse and rider. She did not pull up enough. Impact made the carpet lurch. Frame members cracked, broke. We spun. I hung on desperately while sky and earth wheeled about me. There was another shock as we hit ground, more spinning as we went over and over. I threw myself clear.

I was on my feet in an instant, wobbling, slapping another arrow across my bow. Catcher's horse was down with a broken leg. Catcher was beside her, on hands and knees, stunned. A silver arrowhead protruded from her waist, indicting me.

I loosed my shaft. And another, and another, recalling the terrible vitality the Limper had shown in the Forest of Cloud, after Raven had felled him with an arrow bearing the power of his true name. Still in fear, I drew my sword once my final arrow was gone. I charged. I do not know how I retained the weapon through everything that had happened. I reached Catcher, raised the blade high, swung with a vicious two-handed stroke. It was the most fearful, violent blow I have ever struck. Soulcatcher's head rolled away. The morion's face guard popped open. A woman's face stared at me with accusing eyes. A woman almost identical in appearance to the one with whom I had come.

Catcher's eyes focused upon me. Her lips tried to form words. I stood there frozen, wondering what the hell it all meant. And life faded from Catcher before I caught the message she tried to impart.

I would return to that moment ten thousand times, trying to read those dying lips.

The Lady crept up beside me, dragging one leg. Habit forced me to turn, kneel. . . . "It's broken," she said. "Never mind. It can wait." Her breathing was shallow, rapid. For a moment I thought it was the pain. Then I saw she was looking at the head. She began to giggle.

I looked at that face so like her own, then at her. She rested a hand on my shoulder, allowing me to take some of her weight. I rose carefully, slid an arm around her. "Never did like that bitch," she said. "Even when we were children. . . ." She glanced at me warily, shut up. The life left her face. She became the ice lady once more.

If ever there was some weird love spark within me, as my brothers accused, it flickered its last. I saw plainly what the Rebel wanted to destroy—that part of the movement which was true White Rose, not puppet to the monster who had created this woman and now wanted her destroyed so it could bring its own breed of terror back to the world. At that moment I'd gladly have deposited her head beside her sister's.

Second time, if Catcher could be believed. Second sister. This deserved no allegiance.

There are limits to one's luck, one's power, to how much one dares resist. I hadn't the nerve to follow through on my impulse. Later, maybe. The Captain had made a mistake, taking service with Soulcatcher. Was my unique position adequate to argue him out of that service on grounds that our commission ended with Catcher's death?

I doubted it. It would take a battle, to say the least. Especially if, as I suspected, he had helped the Syndic along in Beryl. The Company's existence did not appear to be in absolute jeopardy, assuming we survived the battle. He would not countenance another betrayal. In the conflict of moralities he would find that the greater evil.

Was there a Company now? The battle of Charm had not ended because the Lady and I had absented ourselves. Who knew what had happened while we were haring after a renegade Taken?

I glanced at the sun, was astonished to discover that only a little over an hour had passed.

The Lady recalled Charm too. "The carpet, physician," she said. "We'd better get back."

I helped her hobble to the remnant of Catcher's carpet. It was half a ruin, but she believed it would function. I deposited her, collected the bow she had given me, sat in front of her. She whispered. Creaking, the carpet rose. It provided a very unstable seat.

I sat with eyes closed, debating myself, as she circled the site of Catcher's fall. I could not get my feelings straight. I did not believe in evil as an active force, only as a matter of viewpoint, yet I had seen enough to make me question my philosophy. If the Lady were not evil incarnate, then she was as close as made no difference.

We began limping toward the Tower. When I opened my eyes I could see that great dark block tilting on the horizon, gradually swelling. I did not want to go back.

We passed over the rocky ground west of Charm, a hundred feet up, barely creeping along. The Lady had to concentrate totally to keep the carpet aloft. I was terrified the thing would go down there, or gasp its last over the Rebel army. I leaned forward, studying the jumble, trying to pick a place to crash.

That was how I saw the girl.

We were three quarters of the way across. I saw something move. "Eh?" Darling looked up at us, shading her eyes. A hand whipped out of shadow, dragged her into hiding.

I glanced at the Lady. She had noticed nothing. She was too busy staying aloft.

What was going on? Had the Rebel driven the Company into the rocks? Why wasn't I seeing anyone else?

Straining, the Lady gradually gained altitude. The slice-of-pie expanded before me.

Land of nightmare. Tens of thousands of dead Rebels carpeted it. Most had fallen in formation. The tiers were inundated in dead of both persuasions. A White Rose banner on a leaning pole fluttered atop the pyramid. Nowhere did I see anyone moving. Silence gripped the land, except for the murmur of a chill northern wind.

The Lady lost it for an instant. We plunged. She caught us a dozen feet short of crashing.

Nothing stirred but wind-rippled banners. The battlefield looked like something from the imagination of a mad artist. The top layer of Rebel dead lay as though they had died in terrible pain. Their numbers were incalculable.

We rose above the pyramid. Death had swept around it, toward the Tower. The gate remained open. Rebel bodies lay in its shadow.

They had gotten inside.

There were but a handful of bodies atop the pyramid, all Rebel. My comrades must have made it inside.

They had to be fighting still, inside those twisted corridors. The place was too vast to overrun quickly. I listened, but heard nothing.

The Tower top was three hundred feet above us. We couldn't get any higher. . . . A figure appeared there, beckoning. It was short and clad in brown. I gaped. I recalled only one Taken who wore brown. It moved to a slightly better vantage, limping, still beckoning. The carpet rose. Two hundred feet to go. One hundred. I looked back on the panorama of death. Quarter of a million men? Mind-boggling. Too vast to have real meaning. Even in the Dominator's heyday battles never approached that scale. . . .

I glanced at the Lady, She had engineered it. She would be total mistress of the world now—if the Tower survived the battle underway inside.· Who could oppose her? The manhood of a continent lay dead. . . .

A half dozen Rebels came out the gate. They launched arrows at us. Only a few wobbled as high as the carpet. The soldiers stopped loosing, waited. They knew we were in trouble.

Fifty feet. Twenty-five. The Lady struggled, even with Limper's help. I shivered in the wind, which threatened to bounce us off the Tower. I recalled the Howler's long plunge. We were as high as he had been.

A glance at the plain showed me the forvalaka. It hung limp upon its cross, but I knew it was alive.

Men joined the Limper. Some carried ropes, some lances or long poles. We rose ever more slowly. It became a ridiculously tense game, safety almost within reaching distance, yet never quite at hand.

A rope dropped into my lap. A Guard sergeant shouted, "Harness her up."

"What about me, asshole?" I moved about as fast as a rock grows, afraid I'd upset the carpet's stability. I was tempted to tie some false knot that would give way under strain. I did not like the Lady much anymore. The world would be better for her absence. Catcher was a murdering schemer whose ambitions sent hundreds to their deaths. She deserved her fate. How much more so this sister who had hurried thousands down the shadowed road?

A second line came down. I tied myself. We were five feet from the top, unable to get higher. The men on the lines took in the slack. The carpet slid in against the Tower. Poles reached down. I grabbed one.

The carpet dropped away.

For a second I thought I was gone. Then they hauled me in.

There was heavy fighting downstairs, they said. The Limper ignored me completely, hurried away to get in on the action. I just sprawled atop the Tower, glad to be safe. I even napped. I wakened alone with the north wind, and an enfeebled comet on the horizon. I went down to audit the endgame of the Lady's grand design.

She won. Not one in a hundred Rebels survived, and most of those deserted early.

The Howler spread disease with the globes he dropped. It reached its critical stage soon after the Lady and I departed, chasing Soulcatcher. The Rebel wizards could not stem it on any significant scale. Thus the windrows of dead.

Even so, many of the enemy proved partially or wholly immune, and not all of ours escaped infection. The Rebel took the top tier.

The plan, at that point, called for the Black Company to counterattack. The Limper, rehabilitated, was to assist them with men from inside the Tower. But the Lady was not there to order the charge. In her absence Whisper ordered a withdrawal into the Tower.

The interior of the Tower was a series of death traps manned not only by the Howler's easterners but by wounded taken inside previous nights and healed by the Lady's powers.

It ended long before I could thread the maze to my comrades. When I did cross their trail, I learned I was hours behind. They had departed the Tower under orders to establish a picket line where the stockade had stood.

I reached ground level well after nightfall. I was tired. I just wanted peace, quiet, maybe a garrison post in a small town. . . . My mind wasn't working well. I had things to

do, arguments to argue, a battle to fight with the Captain.
He would not want to betray another commission. There
are the physically dead and the morally dead. My comrades were among the latter. They would not understand
me. Elmo, Raven, Candy, One-Eye, Goblin, they would
act like I was talking a foreign language. And yet, could I
condemn them? They were my brothers, my friends, my
family, and acted moral within that context. The weight of
it fell on me. I had to convince them there was a larger
obligation.

I crunched through dried blood, stepping over corpses,
leading horses I had liberated from the Lady's stables.
Why I took several is a mystery, except for a vague notion
that they might come in handy. The one that Feather had
ridden I took because I did not feel like walking.

I paused to stare at the comet. It seemed drained. "Not
this time, eh?" I asked it. "Can't say I'm totally dismayed."
Fake chuckle. How could I be? Had this been the Rebel's
hour, as he had believed, I would be dead.

I stopped twice more before reaching camp. The first
time I heard soft cursing as I descended the remnants of
the lower retaining wall. I approached the sound, found
One-Eye seated beneath the crucified forvalaka. He talked
steadily in a soft voice, in a language I did not understand.
So intent was he that he did not hear me come. Neither did
he hear me go a minute later, thoroughly disgusted.

One-Eye was collecting for the death of his brother
Tom-Tom. Knowing him, he would stretch it out for days.

I paused again where the false White Rose had watched
the battle. She was there still, very dead at a very young
age. Her wizard friends had made her death harder by
trying to save her from the Howler's disease.

"So much for that." I looked back at the Tower, at the
comet. She had won. . . .

Or had she? What had she accomplished, really? The

destruction of the Rebel? But he had become the instrument of her husband, an even greater evil. It had been he defeated here, if only he, she, and I knew that. The greater wickedness had been forestalled. Moreover, the Rebel ideal had passed through a cleansing, tempering flame. A generation hence. . . .

I am not religious. I cannot conceive of gods who would give a damn about humanity's frothy carryings-on. I mean, logically, beings of that order just wouldn't. But maybe there is a force for greater good, created by our unconscious minds conjoined, that becomes an independent power greater than the sum of its parts. Maybe, being a mind-thing, it is not time-bound. Maybe it can see everywhere and everywhen and move pawns so that what seems to be today's victory becomes the cornerstone of tomorrow's defeat.

Maybe weariness did things to my mind. For a few seconds I believed I saw the landscape of tomorrow, saw the Lady's triumph turning like a serpent and generating her destruction during the next passage of the comet. I saw a true White Rose carrying her standard to the Tower, saw she and her champions as clearly as if I were there that day myself. . . .

I swayed atop that beast of Feather's, stricken and terrified. For if it were a true vision, I *would* be there. If it were a true vision, I knew the White Rose. Had known her for a year. She was my friend. And I had discounted her because of a handicap. . . .

I urged the horses toward camp. By the time a sentinel challenged me I had regained enough cynicism to have discounted the vision. I'd just been through too much in one day. Characters like me don't become prophets. Especially not from the wrong side.

Elmo's was the first familiar face I saw. "God, you look awful," He said. "You hurt?"

I could do nothing but shake my head. He dragged me off the horse and put me away somewhere and that was the last I knew for hours. Except that my dreams were as disjointed and time-loose as the vision, and I did not like them at all. And I could not escape them.

The mind is resilient, though. I managed to forget the dreams within moments of awakening.

Chapter Seven: ROSE

The argument with the Captain raged for two hours. He was unyielding. He did not accept my arguments, legal or moral. Time brought others into the fray, as they came to the Captain on business. By the time I really lost my temper most of the principals of the Company were present: the Lieutenant, Goblin, Silent, Elmo, Candy, and several new officers recruited here at Charm. What little support I received came from surprising quarters. Silent backed me. So did two of the new officers.

I stamped out. Silent and Goblin followed. I was in a towering rage, though unsurprised by their response. With the Rebel beaten there was little to encourage the Company's defection. They would be hogs knee-deep in slops now. Questions of right and wrong sounded stupid. Basically, who cared?

It was still early, the day after the battle. I had not slept well, and was full of nervous energy. I paced vigorously, trying to walk it off.

Goblin timed me, stepped into my path after I settled down. Silent observed from nearby. Goblin asked, "Can we talk?"

"I've been talking. Nobody listens."

"You're too argumentative. Come over here and sit down." Over here proved to be a pile of gear near a campfire where some men were cooking, others were playing Tonk. The usual crowd. They looked at me from the corners of their eyes and shrugged. They all seemed worried. Like they were concerned for my sanity.

I guess if any of them had done what I had, a year ago, I would have felt the same. It was honest confusion and concern based in care for a comrade.

Their thickheadedness irritated me, yet I could not sustain that irritation because by sending Goblin around, they had proven they wanted to understand.

The game went along, quiet and sullen initially, growing animated as they exchanged gossip about the course of the battle.

Goblin asked, "What happened yesterday, Croaker?"

"I told you."

Gently, he suggested, "How about we go over it again? Get more of the detail." I knew what he was doing. A little mental therapy based on an assumption that prolonged proximity to the Lady had unsettled my mind. He was right. It had. It had opened my eyes, too, and I tried to make that clear as I reiterated my day, calling on such skills as I have developed scribbling these Annals, hoping to convince him that my stance was rational and moral and everyone else's was not.

"You see what he did when those Oar boys tried to get behind the Captain?" one of the cardplayers asked. They were gossiping about Raven. I had forgotten him till then. I pricked up my ears and listened to several stories of his savage heroics. To hear them talk, Raven had saved everybody in the Company at least once.

Somebody asked, "Where is he?"

Lots of headshaking. Someone suggested, "Must have gotten killed. The Captain sent a detail after our dead. Guess we'll see him go in the ground this afternoon."

"What happened to the kid?"

Elmo snorted. "Find him and you'll find her."

"Talking about the kid, you see what happened when they tried to clobber second platoon with some kind of knockout spell? It was weird. The kid acted like nothing ever happened. Everybody else went down like a rock. She just looked kind of puzzled and shook Raven. Up he came, bam, hacking away. She shook them all back awake. Like the magic couldn't touch her, or something."

Somebody else said, "Maybe that's cause she's deaf. Like maybe the magic was sound."

"Ah, who knows? Pity she didn't make it, though. Kind of got used to her hanging around."

"Raven, too. Need him to keep old One-Eye from cheating." Everybody laughed.

I looked at Silent, who was eavesdropping on my conversation with Goblin. I shook my head. He raised an eyebrow. I used Darling's signs to tell him, *They aren't dead*. He liked Darling too.

He rose, walked behind Goblin, jerked his head. He wanted to see me alone. I extricated myself and followed him.

I explained that I had seen Darling while returning from my venture with the Lady, that I suspected Raven was deserting by the one route he thought would not be watched. Silent frowned and wanted to know why.

"You got me. You know how he's been lately." I did not mention my vision or dreams, all of which seemed fantastic now. "Maybe he got fed up with us."

Silent smiled a smile that said he did not believe a word of that. He sighed, *I want to know why. What do you know?* He assumed I knew more about Raven and Darling than anyone else because I was always probing for personal details to put into the Annals.

"I don't know anything you don't. He hung around with the Captain and Pickles more than anybody else."

He thought for about ten seconds, then signed, *You saddle two horses. No, four horses, with some food. We may be a few days. I will go ask questions.* His manner did not brook argument.

That was fine with me. A ride had occurred to me while I was talking to Goblin. I had given up the notion because I could think of no way to pick up Raven's trail.

I went to the picket where Elmo had taken the horses last night. Four of them. For an instant I reflected on the chance a greater force existed, moving us. I conned a couple men into saddling the beasts for me while I went and finagled some food out of Pickles. He was not easy to get around. He wanted the Captain's personal authorization. We worked out a deal where he would get a special mention in the Annals.

Silent joined me at the tail of the negotiations. Once we had strapped the supplies aboard the horses, I asked, "You learn anything?"

He signed, *Only that the Captain has some special knowledge he will not share. I think it had more to do with Darling than with Raven.*

I grunted. Here it was again. . . . The Captain had come up with a notion like mine? And had had it this morning, while we were arguing? Hmm. He had a tricky mind. . . .

I think Raven left without the Captain's permission, but has his blessing. Did you interrogate Pickles?

"Thought you were going to do that."

He shook his head. He hadn't had time.

"Go ahead now. Still a few things I want to get together."
I hustled to the hospital tent, accoutred myself with my
weapons and dug out a present I had been saving for
Darling's birthday. Then I hunted Elmo up and told him I
could use some of my share of the money we had kyped in
Roses.

"How much?"

"Much as I can get."

He looked at me long and hard, decided to ask no
questions. We went to his tent and counted it out quietly.
The men knew nothing about that money. The secret
remained with those of us who had gone to Roses after
Raker. There were those, though, who wondered how
One-Eye managed to keep paying his gambling debts when
he never won and had no time for his usual black
marketeering.

Elmo followed me when I left his tent. We found Silent
already mounted up, the horses ready to go. "Going for a
ride, eh?" he asked.

"Yeah." I secured the bow the Lady had given me to
my saddle, mounted up.

Elmo searched our faces with narrowed eyes, then said,
"Good luck." He turned and walked away. I looked at
Silent.

He signed, *Pickles claims ignorance too. I did trick him
into admitting he had given Raven extra rations before the
fighting started yesterday. He knows something too.*

Well, hell. Everybody seemed to be in on the guesswork.
As Silent led off, I turned my thoughts to the morning's
confrontation, seeking hints of things askew. And I found
a few. Goblin and Elmo had their suspicions too.

There was no avoiding a passage through the Rebel
camp. Pity. I would have preferred to have avoided it. The

flies and stench were thick. When the Lady and I rode
through, it looked empty. Wrong. We'd simply not seen
anyone. The enemy wounded and camp followers were
there. The Howler had dropped his globes on them too.

I'd selected animals well. In addition to having taken
Feather's mount, I had acquired others of the same tireless
breed. Silent set a brisk pace, eschewing communication
till, as we hastened down the outer border of the rocky
country, he reined in and signed for me to study my
surroundings. He wanted to know the line of flight the
Lady had followed approaching the Tower.

I told him I thought we had come in about a mile south
of where we were then. He gave me the extra horses and
edged near the rocks, proceeded slowly, studying the ground
carefully. I paid little attention. He could find sign better
than I.

I could have found this trail, though. Silent threw up a
hand, then indicated the ground. They had departed the
badlands about where the Lady and I had crossed the
boundary going the other way. "Trying to make time, not
cover his trail," I guessed.

Silent nodded, stared westward. He signed questions
about roads.

The main north-south high road passes three miles west
of the Tower. It was the road we followed to Forsberg. We
guessed he would head there first. Even in these times
there would be traffic enough to conceal the passage of a
man and child. From ordinary eyes. Silent believed he
could follow.

"Remember, this is his country," I said. "He knows it
better than we do."

Silent nodded absently, unconcerned. I glanced at the
sun. Maybe two hours of daylight left. I wondered how
big a lead they had.

We reached the high road. Silent studied it a moment,

rode south a few yards, nodded to himself. He beckoned me, spurred his mount.

And so we rode those tireless beasts, hard, hour after hour, after the sun went down, all the night long, into the next day, heading toward the sea, till we were far ahead of our quarry. The breaks were few and far between. I ached everywhere. It was too soon after my venture with the Lady for this.

We halted where the road hugged the foot of a wooded hill. Silent indicated a bald spot that made a good watchpoint. I nodded. We turned off and climbed.

I took care of the horses, then collapsed. "Getting too old for this," I said, and fell asleep immediately.

Silent wakened me at dusk. "They coming?" I asked.

He shook his head, signed that he did not expect them before tomorrow. But I should keep an eye out anyway, in case Raven was travelling by night.

So I sat under the pallid light of the comet, wrapped in a blanket, shivering in the winter wind, for hour upon hour, alone with thoughts I did not want to think. I saw nothing but a brace of roebuck crossing from woods to farmland in hopes of finding better forage.

Silent relieved me a couple hours before dawn. Oh joy, oh joy. Now I could lie down and shiver and think thoughts I did not want to think. But I did fall asleep sometime, because it was light when Silent squeezed my shoulder, . . .

"They coming?"

He nodded.

I rose, rubbed my eyes with the backs of my hands, stared up the road. Sure enough, two figures were coming south, one taller than the other. But at that distance they could have been any adult and child. We packed and readied the horses hurriedly, descended the hill. Silent wanted to wait down the road, around the bend. He told me to get on the road behind them, just in case. You never knew about Raven.

He left. I waited, shivering still, feeling very lonely. The travelers breasted a rise. Yes. Raven and Darling. They walked briskly, but Raven seemed unafraid, certain no one was after him. They passed me. I waited a minute, eased out of the woods, followed them around the toe of the hill.

Silent sat his mount in the middle of the road, leaning forward slightly, looking lean and mean and dark. Raven had stopped fifty feet away, exposed his steel. He held Darling behind him.

She noticed me coming, grinned and waved. I grinned back, despite the tension of the moment.

Raven whirled. A snarl stretched his lips. Anger, possibly even hatred, smouldered in his eyes. I stopped beyond the reach of his knives. He did not look willing to talk.

We all remained motionless for several minutes. Nobody wanted to speak first. I looked at Silent. He shrugged. He had come to the end of his plan.

Curiosity had brought me here. I had satisfied part of it. They were alive, and were running. Only the why remained shadowy.

To my amazement Raven yielded first. "What're you doing here, Croaker?" I'd thought him able to outstubborn a stone.

"Looking for you."

"Why?"

"Curiosity. Me and Silent, we got an interest in Darling. We were worried."

He frowned. He was not hearing what he had expected.

"You can see she's all right."

"Yeah. Looks like. How about you?"·

"I look like I'm not?"

I glanced at Silent. He had nothing to contribute. "One wonders, Raven. One wonders."

He was on the defensive. "What the hell does that mean?"

"Fellow freezes out his buddies. Treats them like shit. Then he deserts. Makes people wonder enough to go find out what's happening."

"The Captain know you're here?"

I glanced at Silent again. He nodded. "Yeah. Want to let us in on it, old buddy? Me, Silent, the Captain, Pickles, Elmo, Goblin, we all maybe got an idea. . . . ."

"Don't try to stop me, Croaker."

"Why are you always looking for a fight? Who said anything about stopping you? They wanted you stopped, you wouldn't be out here now. You'd never have gotten away from the Tower."

He was startled.

"They saw it coming, Pickles and the Old Man. They let you go. Some of the rest of us, we'd like to know why. I mean, like, we think we know, and if it's what we think, then at least you have *my* blessing. And Silent's. And I guess everybodys who didn't hold you back."

Raven frowned. He knew what I was hinting, but couldn't make sense of it. His not being old line Company left a communications gap.

"Put it this way," I said. "Me and Silent figure you're going down as killed in action. Both of you. Nobody needs to know any different. But, you know, it's like you're running away from home. Even if we wish you well, we maybe feel a little hurt on account of the way you do it. You were voted into the Company. You went through hell with us. You. . . . Look what you and me went through together. And you treat us like shit. That don't go down too well."

It sank in. He said, "Sometimes something comes up

that's so important you can't tell your best friends. Could get you all killed.''

"Figured that was it. Hey! Take it easy."

Silent had dismounted and begun an exchange with Darling. She seemed oblivious to the strain between her friends. She was telling Silent what they had done and where they were headed.

"Think that's smart?" I asked. "Opal? Couple things you should know, then. One, the Lady won. Guess you figured that. Saw it coming, or you wouldn't have pulled out. Okay. More important. The Limper is back. She didn't do him in. She shaped him up and he's her number one boy now."

Raven turned pale. It was the first I could recall seeing him truly frightened. But his fear was not for himself. He considered himself a walking dead man, a man with nothing to lose. But now he had Darling, and a cause. He had to stay alive.

"Yeah. The Limper. Me and Silent went over this a lot." Actually, this had occurred to me only a moment earlier. I felt it would go better if he thought some considered deliberation had gone into it. "We figure the Lady will catch on sooner or later. She'll want to make a move. If she connects you, you'll have the Limper on your trail. He knows you. He'd start looking in your old stomping grounds, figuring you'd get in touch with old friends. You got any friends who could hide you from the Limper?"

Raven sighed, seemed to lose stature. He put his steel away. "That was my plan. Thought we'd cross to Beryl and hide out there."

"Beryl is technically only the Lady's ally, but her word is law there. You've got to go somewhere where they've never heard of her."

"Where?"

"This isn't my part of the world." He seemed calm

enough now, so I dismounted. He eyed me warily, then relaxed. I said, "I pretty much know what I came to find out. Silent?"

Silent nodded, continued his conversation with Darling.

I took the money bag from my bedroll, tossed it to Raven. "You left your share of the Roses take." I brought the spare horses up. "You could travel faster if you were riding."

Raven struggled with himself, trying to say thank you, unable to get through the barriers he had built around the man inside. "Guess we could head toward. . . ."

"I don't want to know. I've met the Eye twice already. She's got a thing about getting her side set down for posterity. Not that she wants to look good, just that she wants it down true. She knows how history rewrites itself. She doesn't want that to happen to her. And I'm the boy she's picked to do the writing."

"Get out, Croaker. Come with us. You and Silent. Come with us."

It had been a long, lonely night. I had thought about it a lot. "Can't, Raven. The Captain has to stay where he's at, even if he don't like it. The Company has to stay. I'm Company. I'm too old to run away from home. We'll fight the same fight, you and me, but I'll do my share staying with the family."

"Come on, Croaker. A bunch of mercenary cut-throats. . . ."

"Whoa! Hold it." My voice hardened more than I wanted. He stopped. I said, "Remember that night in Lords, before we went after Whisper? When I read from the Annals? What you said?"

He did not respond for several seconds. "Yes. That you'd made me feel what it meant to be a member of the Black Company. All right. Maybe I don't understand it, but I did feel it."

"Thanks." I took another package from my bedroll. This one was for Darling. "You talk to Silent a while, eh? I got a birthday present here."

He looked at me a moment, then nodded. I turned so my tears would not be so obvious. And after I said my good-byes to the girl, and cherished her delight in my feeble present, I went to the roadside and had myself a brief, quiet cry. Silent and Raven pretended blindness.

I would miss Darling. And I would spend the rest of my days frightened for her. She was precious, perfect, always happy. The thing in that village was behind her. But ahead lay the most terrible enemy imaginable. None of us wanted that for her.

I rose, erased the evidence of tears, took Raven aside. "I don't know your plans. I don't want to know. But just in case. When the Lady and I caught up with Soulcatcher the other day, he had a whole bale of those papers we dug up in Whisper's camp. He never turned them over to her. She doesn't know they exist." I told him where they could be found. "I'll ride out that way in a couple weeks. If they're still there, I'll see what I can find in them myself."

He looked at me with a cool, expressionless face. He was thinking my death warrant was signed if I came under the Eye again. But he did not say it. "Thanks, Croaker. If I'm ever up that way, I'll check into it."

"Yeah. You ready to go, Silent?"

Silent nodded.

"Darling, come here." I squeezed her in a long, tight hug. "You be good for Raven." I unfastened the amulet One-Eye had given me, fixed it on her wrist, told Raven, "That'll let her know if any unfriendly Taken comes around. Don't ask me how, but it works. Luck."

"Yeah." He stood there looking at us as we mounted, still baffled. He raised a hand tentatively, dropped it.

I told Silent, "Let's go home." And we rode away.

Neither of us looked back.

It was an incident that never happened. After all, hadn't Raven and his orphan died at the gates of Charm?

Back to the Company. Back to business. Back to the parade of years. Back to these Annals. Back to fear.

Thirty-seven years before the comet returns. The vision has to be false. I'll never survive that long. Will I?

THE BEST IN FANTASY